Jessica Fellowes is an author, journalist and public speaker. Her bestselling The Mitford Murders series has been nominated for awards in Britain, France, Germany and Italy, and sold into eighteen territories. Jessica is also the author of five official companion books to *Downton Abbey*, various of which hit the New York Times and *Sunday Times* bestseller lists. She has written short stories for *Vogue Italia* and *L'Uomo Vogue*, and made numerous appearances on radio, podcasts and television. She lives in Oxfordshire with her family.

Also by Jessica Fellowes

The Mitford Murders
The Mitford Scandal
The Mitford Trial
The Mitford Vanishing
The Mitford Secret
The Best Friend

JESSICA FELLOWES

THE MITFORD AFFAIR

SPHERE

SPHERE

First published in Great Britain in 2018 by Sphere
This reissue published in 2015

1 3 5 7 9 10 8 6 4 2

Copyright © Little, Brown Book Group 2018
Written by Jessica Fellowes

The moral right of the author has been asserted.

*All characters and events in this publication, other than those
clearly in the public domain, are fictitious and any resemblance
to real persons, living or dead, is purely coincidental.*

A CIP catalogue record for this book
is available from the British Library.

ISBN 978-0-7515-8054-9

Typeset in Electra by M Rules
Printed and bound in Great Britain by
Clays Ltd, Elcograf S.p.A

Papers used by Sphere are from well-managed forests
and other responsible sources.

Sphere
An imprint of
Little, Brown Book Group
Carmelite House
50 Victoria Embankment
London EC4Y 0DZ

The authorised representative
in the EEA is
Hachette Ireland
8 Castlecourt Centre
Dublin 15, D15 XTP3, Ireland
(email: info@hbgi.ie)

An Hachette UK Company
www.hachette.co.uk

www.littlebrown.co.uk

FOR SIMON

CHAPTER ONE

❧

1925

There comes a moment in every child's life that marks definitively their transition to adulthood. That time had not yet come for Pamela Mitford, shivering and peevish on the steps of a narrow house in Mayfair. The night was crisp and cold but it was an attack of nerves that was making her tremble. Beside her was Louisa Cannon, all too aware that fair-haired Pamela was bait for the lions' den within.

'Tell Koko to come and fetch me,' Pam said, her back to the door. 'I don't want you taking me in. It makes me look like a baby.'

'I have to. I promised your mother I would chaperone. And besides, nobody here knows I'm your nursery maid,' replied Louisa, not for the first time. The journey from Asthall Manor in Oxfordshire to London had been a long one, in spite of the familiar train route and a taxi that had appeared at Paddington Station almost the instant they stepped out.

'Please. Go and fetch Koko.'

Koko meant Nancy, the eldest of the six Mitford sisters and

their one brother. Louisa had worked for the family for five years and could tick off the codenames they used for each other like a French vocab test. Reluctantly, she rang the bell, and the door was opened alarmingly quickly by a girl who looked to be almost the mirror of Louisa: of similar height, with the same pale brown hair, though hers was pinned up beneath a mob cap, and a dress that also looked as if it were well made but well worn, most likely a hand-me-down, as Louisa's was from Nancy. Her clean face looked tired but the freckles on her small nose livened her, somehow. She noticed Pamela's back turned to her and the two maids exchanged a look that acknowledged the boat they both were in.

'Good evening,' said Louisa. 'Could you tell me if Miss Nancy Mitford is there, please?'

The maid looked as if she might start laughing. 'I'd better ask who's asking,' she said in an accent that Louisa recognised as coming from south of the river.

'It's her sister, Miss Pamela,' said Louisa. 'Only, she doesn't want to come in with me and I'm not to let her in alone. May I come in and talk to Miss Nancy?'

She gave a nod and held the door open. 'Follow me.'

Along the hall, the girl pointed to a door then disappeared through another. Louisa thought it was odd she hadn't been shown in formally but soon understood why. In a dimly lit sitting room, two large, shabby armchairs faced a fire that crackled and spat. From each, a long thin arm stretched towards the other. The first, a woman's, was clad in a black silk glove to above the elbow; the second was a man's, whose wrist was covered by a stiff white cuff and the sleeve of a dinner jacket, his hand naked bar a heavy gold signet ring. The two were playfully entwining their fingers as if in a sort of Punch and Judy show, the male hand thrusting and parrying, the female lightly poking and withdrawing, allowing itself to be easily caught again.

Louisa had been watching this a beat too long when the head belonging to the gloved hand peered around the side of the chair's wing. The shock prompted by Nancy's bobbed hair had subsided for Louisa some time ago and now she rather admired it. The face was not conventionally pretty but it had its charms, with what moving-picture critics would call 'rosebud lips' painted dark red, a pert nose and big round eyes that were half-closed now, focusing on their erstwhile nursery maid. Louisa registered a typical mix of fondness and exasperation.

'Beg pardon, Miss Nancy,' said Louisa. 'I've come to let you know that Miss Pamela is here.'

At this, the man looked out. His face was all angles and planes, and his hair had been combed so flat and smooth it looked like a sheet of gold beaten onto the skull. Sebastian Atlas. He had been down to Asthall Manor with Nancy a few times, in spite of the fact that Lord Redesdale went puce at the sight of him, much to his daughter's delight and his wife Lady Redesdale's displeasure, though hers was indicated at a lower register. If Lord Redesdale hath fire and fury, Lady Redesdale hath ice and ire.

'Well, why doesn't she come in, then?' drawled Sebastian, flicking Nancy's fingers away and sinking back into the chair. His other hand reached out and picked up a tumbler of whisky.

Nancy gave a dramatic sigh and stood up. She shook out her dress of crumpled silk, weighted at the hem with hundreds of tiny beads in a black and white zigzag pattern. It was her most, perhaps only, fashionable dress and worn with a frequency that drove Nanny Blor to distraction.

'I'm sorry, Miss Nancy,' said Louisa, quickly deciding not to drop the prefix, though that had been their habit not so long ago.

'But Miss Pamela doesn't want me to come up. She thinks it looks childish to have a nursery maid with her.'

Something of Nancy's old look came back then and she gave Louisa a half-smile. 'What a dunce,' she said. 'Chaperones are almost fashionable again, but she wouldn't know that.'

It was Nancy who had proposed to their parents that Pamela come to London, join her for a party or two and make herself known a little, so that they could invite some of them for Pam's birthday dance the next month.

'Otherwise,' Nancy had spelled out, 'you're asking them to come to a stranger's party in the sticks and they'll think it's because we're desperate. It's not like it used to be. It's 1925, Farve.'

'I don't see what difference the year makes,' her father had replied tersely.

'All the difference. You've got to be in the right crowd. You can't show up for any old thing.' Which wasn't, Nancy told Louisa in confidence, exactly accurate. There was nothing 'the crowd' liked more than turning up for any old thing and every old thing, where free-flowing wine and the promise of hot dance was on offer. They knew that they were the beating heart of any gathering and all others were thrown into darkness by their pulsing light. Louisa knew it may have been Pamela's birthday but Nancy planned to make this her own party.

The plan on this particular night was a dinner at the house of Lady Curtis, mother of Adrian and Charlotte. Nancy had met Adrian through Sebastian, in the summer at Eights Week in Oxford, the annual rowing regatta and the only time the female sex were admitted as supper guests within the university's yellow stone walls. She had taken up the ukulele only a few months before and told

4

Louisa it had worked a spell on the men there as if she were a snake charmer in Marrakesh.

Having fetched Pamela from the front steps, the three of them stepped inside the hall. The maid had disappeared but the sound of jazz from a gramophone player could be heard drifting down from up above.

'Must you come too?' Pamela whispered to Louisa as they climbed the narrow staircase carefully, the eldest sister leading the way. 'I'm with Nancy after all.'

'I promised Lady Redesdale,' reminded Louisa. She felt rather sorry for her charge, whom she had heard weeping quietly in the bathroom earlier before finally emerging with a button in her hand that had come off the skirt fastening. Pamela said nothing but passed it to Louisa, who stayed equally silent as she fetched needle and thread and sewed it back on, standing before the gently hiccupping girl.

As the three ascended Louisa braced herself for what was to come. The glimpses she had had of Nancy's friends at Asthall weren't the same as seeing them in their natural habitat, free to indulge in the ways of the New Age. Stepping inside the room felt like disappearing into the society pages of *Tatler*, only with colour. It took a moment for Louisa to adjust her eyes to the blur of young men and women close together, their features both softened and highlighted by the flickering flames of the fire and Tiffany lampshades dotted around. Her eye fell on the detail: a smear of red lipstick on an empty glass; cigarettes in long holders that threatened to singe the hair of anyone standing nearby; headbands with elaborate feathers drooping from them and daring purple socks that showed when a man crossed his legs. Pamela had been swallowed whole by the crowd, like Jonah into the whale, so Louisa found a chair by the wall where she could keep watch on her charge and Nancy's friends.

Standing by a huge fireplace, his fingertips resting on the chimneypiece to steady himself, was Adrian, his glass held out for more whisky, blithely ignoring another young man who poured it. Louisa knew him from his photograph in the papers, usually under a scandalised headline about the antics of the 'Bright Young Things', as well as Nancy's description. His sonorous voice was a shock; it did not seem to belong to his body, as thin as a grass snake. His dark, wavy hair had not been entirely tamed by the cream he'd applied and his light blue eyes, though glassy, paid close attention to Nancy's collarbone as she drew nearer. His bow tie was undone and there was a wet patch on the front of his shirt from a carelessly handled drink. Louisa knew Adrian was considered the catch – if he came to Pamela's party, he was the domino that would make all the others say yes.

'Who have you brought for me, darling?' Adrian asked, talking to Nancy but looking directly at the younger sister. 'She looks like a lamb to the slaughter, the poor dear.' He laughed and drained his glass.

'This is Pamela,' said Nancy. 'She's still only seventeen, so she really is a lamb. Do be gentle, A.' She gave him a look that Louisa knew to be saying the contrary.

Pamela put her hand out and said in as grown-up a voice as she could manage, 'How do you do, Mr Curtis?' which only made him roar with laughter.

'How old-fashioned,' he said, flapping her hand away. 'We don't talk like that, my dear. Call me Adrian. What can we get you to drink?' He turned to tap the man with the whisky bottle on the shoulder but was interrupted by a groan from a woman sitting in a chair nearby. She had rather more unruly curls, hers having been allowed to grow longer and puff out, and though her eyes were brown, not blue, she shared something of the man's sulky

6

lips. She was lean, too, with cheekbones that spoke of centuries of selective breeding.

'Please ignore my brother,' she said, 'he's a bore and far too rude. I'm Charlotte, by the way.'

'I'm Pamela.' She added nothing to this, and stood silently. Apart from a few months in France, Pamela's whole life had been spent in the nursery, in the company of her brother and sisters, or Nanny and Louisa. This was uncharted territory.

'Come, sit down here,' said Charlotte, as she pulled herself out of a chair and picked up two drinks from a tray, handing one to Pamela. Pamela took the glass from Charlotte after thanking her and swigged, only to start spluttering, and when she wiped her mouth with the back of her hand it came away smeared with the lipstick she had daringly put on in the taxi.

'Oh fiddlesticks!' she exclaimed, which made Charlotte titter.

'You're sweet,' said Charlotte. 'Come here, I've got a hanky, let's clean you up a bit. Do admit, it is rather droll.'

Pamela nodded with relief and a giggle of her own.

Before Charlotte had quite finished dabbing at Pam's chin, however, she stopped still and stared at Nancy. Louisa saw she was winding a carriage clock that had been standing upon the mantelpiece. 'Has it stopped?' Charlotte asked.

Nancy paused and gave her an exaggerated wink. 'Party time,' she said. 'I always put the clocks back half an hour to give us a little more.'

'Funny,' said Charlotte, and carried on.

Louisa turned from them and was pleased to see Clara Fischer walking across the room. Clara, referred to as 'The American' by the Mitfords, was closer to Nancy's age at nearly twenty-one but was rather kinder to Pamela. The two of them had spent some time playing with the dogs together at Asthall, chatting easily about their many and varied canine features and how they wished animals could talk, speculating on what they would say. Clara was straightforwardly and enjoyably pretty, with blonde hair tonged into perfect waves and pink, full lips. She always wore light colours in flimsy, delicate materials, which made her look as if she could be unwound like a reel of chiffon ribbon.

She walked towards Pamela. 'Hello . . . I didn't know you'd be here tonight.'

'It was touch and go,' said Pam. 'Farve wasn't too keen.'

'No, I shouldn't think he was.' Clara gave a wry smile. 'Can't say I blame him. Bunch of degenerates.'

Pamela looked around. 'They don't look too bad to me.'

'Don't be deceived. Here, budge up.'

'Clara,' said Charlotte, but there wasn't much warmth to it. 'Have you seen Ted? He's always disappearing to telephone up that wretched Dolly, isn't he?'

'Yes. He's just over there.' Clara looked across to the fireplace, a perfectly plucked eyebrow raised. 'I wonder what those three are in such cahoots about.'

Beside Nancy was Adrian and another smaller, darker man with a long chin and eyes set so deep they could barely be seen. Clara and Charlotte had called him Ted but Louisa recognised him from the newspapers as Lord De Clifford. The trio were looking a tad unsteady on their feet, each one barking with laughter before the other had finished their sentence. Nancy must have sensed the eyes on them because she turned around and waved.

'Come over here,' she said. 'We're plotting the most wonderful thing.'

Charlotte walked over though reluctance showed in her unhurried pace; Clara followed, then turned back to nudge Pamela along. 'She means you, too.'

'Gather round, chums,' said Adrian. His voice was loud and at this instruction, Sebastian appeared out of nowhere and sidled up close to Charlotte, his head in full craning position. He looked bored but Louisa knew this was something of a default posture for Nancy and her friends. She stood to listen as they formed a circle around the fireplace. Adrian's voice lost no volume but had started to slow down and slur, like a record played at the wrong speed.

'Ted's had the most marvellous idea. We're going to do a treasure hunt.'

'What, *now*?' Charlotte's mouth pulled into an even sulkier droop. 'I don't know why you keep going on like those idiots—'

'No, not *now*,' said Adrian. 'These things need planning. At Pamela's dance next month.' He grinned widely and threw his hands up like a circus ringmaster who had just announced that the tigers would be on after the flying acrobats.

Pamela blanched. 'Oh, I don't think that Farve—'

'Do shut up, Woman.' Louisa flinched at Nancy's use of her meanest nickname, devised years before to tease Pamela about her prematurely full figure. 'He doesn't need to know. We'll do it when the 'rents have gone to bed. Then we'll have the run of the house, even the village too if we want.'

'Rather better not to have some ridiculous diary reporter on our trail,' said Sebastian, catching Ted's eye as he did so. The newspapers always had a field day when a young peer was caught up in the wild antics of the London treasure hunts. Not that they didn't love it: Louisa remembered hearing that Lord Rothermere himself had printed a clue in the *Evening Standard*.

Clara clapped her hands. 'Out in the English countryside, you mean? Oh, it'll be pitch black and completely terrifying! How absolutely perfect.'

'Yes,' said Adrian, 'and Nancy tells me there's a graveyard over the garden wall.' He gave a low chuckle and fell slightly backwards before pulling himself upright again. Nancy laughed at this.

'No screeching round in cars, either. We'll do the whole thing on foot. Everyone can write a clue each, with a common object as the answer. Do let's all say yes and then we can work in pairs.' A clever plan to bump up the RSVPs, thought Louisa.

'Who will the winner be?' mused Clara.

'Last man standing, of course,' said Adrian.

And so it was that Adrian Curtis, twenty-two years old, planned his own death three weeks later.

CHAPTER TWO

❧

G uy Sullivan had been at the front desk since eight o'clock that
morning and dealt with precisely three cases so far. An old
lady who had come in wishing to thank the nice young sergeant
who had helped her Tibbles come down from the roof the day
before; a man brought in for being drunk and disorderly who was
now sleeping it off in the cells; and a gold ring that had been found
on the pavement in, strangely enough, Golden Square. Guy had
diligently recorded the message, the statement and the lost property
item, had each one signed and filed and was now standing behind
the desk trying not to slump and yawn for the fifth time. It was half
past ten in the morning and he was at least two hours from his lunch
and seven from going home. He didn't want to be ungrateful for the
position he was in. Hadn't he longed to be a sergeant in London's
Metropolitan Police? He still took pride in polishing the badge on
his helmet and his boots shone like glass, but it was sometimes hard
to tell what use he was or how he might get on. Guy had been a
policeman – that is, a *real* policeman, not working for the railway
police as he had before – for nearly three years now and he wanted
to know when he could start trying for detective.

A conversation he'd attempted along these lines with his superior, Inspector Cornish, had been a damp squib before he'd even started. Cornish had been only too happy to remind the young sergeant that he was in the best police force in the world and if he wanted a promotion he needed to show them a good reason why he had earned one, not stand about waiting for rewards to come to him. But so long as he was kept in the office, as he had been for the previous seven months, Guy couldn't see how he was supposed to show initiative. The policemen who brought 'cases' to the desk didn't want someone like him interfering and anyone who came in of their own accord had to be assigned to another sergeant because Guy wasn't permitted to desert his post.

Guy smoothed his hair down and polished his glasses for the hundredth time that morning. He wondered if it was his eyesight – bad enough that he hadn't been allowed to fight in the war – which put off his boss from assigning him to any significant cases. There had been a bit of teasing around his inability to recognise a familiar face after he'd failed to acknowledge the station's chief inspector when he had entered through the front door out of uniform one morning. Guy had tried to protest that it wasn't that he couldn't see properly, it was simply that he wasn't used to seeing him in plain clothes, but this only added fuel to the fire. How, then, they crowed, would Guy spot a known criminal if he was in disguise? Cornish had overheard the commotion, asked what was going on and ever since that day, Guy hadn't been on the beat. At least, that was how it seemed.

As he was debating whether to organise the outgoing post into alphabetical order or water the plant by the front door, Guy's attention was snapped into focus by a young woman in uniform approaching the desk. The sight was a relatively rare one. There were rumoured to be just fifty of them in the entire force. A couple of years earlier, female uniforms had been given powers of arrest, which had caused quite a stir amongst the men. Even so, the women were generally sent out on the soft jobs, fetching lost children or cats. Guy had hardly even spoken to one. He had seen this one around before once or twice and certainly noticed her pretty smile, but the most noticeable thing about her today was the squirming boy she had gripped by the ear. She marched up to Guy's desk and stood before him, breathing hard, looking both furiously determined and pleased with herself.

'Caught him stealing apples off the wheelbarrow at St James's Market,' she said in the kind of tone Guy knew was meant to suggest she frequently brought hardened criminals to the front desk of the Vine Street police station. He decided to play along.

'Bet it's not the first time he's done it either, is it?'

The policewoman smiled gratefully. 'No. Certainly not.' She slowed her breathing, though she didn't release her hold on his ear. The boy – he looked about fourteen years old – was small for his age and wiry but he could easily have broken away. It was likely he rather fancied a rest in a cell with some soup and bread. 'I think perhaps we'd better get his details down and then we'll talk to the Super about what to do next.'

'Certainly, Constable,' said Guy, which made her smile with pleasure again, something he found he rather liked. Pride lengthened his tall, narrow frame, like a cat showing off. Louisa Cannon had been the last girl to have this effect and he shook his head at the thought. Back to business, Guy took down the boy's name and address, probably false, and summoned another constable to take him away to the cells. The policewoman was dismissed as soon as the uniform arrived and Guy saw her face fall.

'You did well there,' he said. 'One arrest down and it's not even lunchtime yet.'

'Yes, I suppose so,' she said ruefully. Guy took in her neat figure, dressed in a perfectly pressed uniform, slim legs incongruously atop solid black boots with laces. She looked around, checking no one was there to listen. 'It's just that . . .'

'What?'

'I never get to do the proper stuff. You know, real policeman's work. I thought they might let me take him down to the cells but I suppose they'll let him out this afternoon, won't they?'

Guy shrugged and then decided he shouldn't bat her off with patronising flannel. 'Yes,' he admitted, 'they probably will. There's not enough to charge him with. But you still did the right thing. I'm sure he'll think twice next time.'

'Yes, perhaps he will. Thanks.' She straightened up as if to go and then turned to Guy again. 'What's your name, by the way?'

'Sergeant Sullivan,' he said. And then, more softly, 'But you can call me Guy.'

'I will, she said, 'if you call me Mary. I'm Constable Moon.'

'Mary Moon?'

'Yes, but don't you even try. I've had all the jokes you can imagine and some more you can't.'

As they were both laughing at this, another sergeant came up to the desk, on Guy's side this time. 'If you two haven't got anything better to do than stand about giggling, you can come to the briefing room. Cornish is summoning anyone who hasn't been assigned a beat duty today.' He strode off and cornered someone else.

Mary's face brightened even more at this and she started to head off straight away, then stopped and looked back. 'Aren't you coming?'

'I can't,' said Guy, 'I'm not allowed to leave the desk.'

'Just for five minutes?'

Guy shook his head, feeling like a fool.

14

Mary walked back. 'Tell you what – you go, and I'll stand by the desk. I'm sure I can manage for a bit.'

'But what about . . . ?'

'They won't let me do anything proper anyway. You go and tell me about it.'

Guy tried to hesitate a little longer to show her she didn't have to if she didn't want to, but it was no good. He was desperate for this chance.

The briefing room was packed and Inspector Cornish was at the front, already addressing the keen policemen. Guy sneaked in and stood by the wall, ears practically flapping with eagerness to hear. Cornish had a reputation for being a bully but one who brought results, so his coarse turn of phrase was tolerated and plenty found it apt for the business in hand. 'If you can't take it, what are you doing in the Force?' was a phrase Guy had heard a few times, though thankfully never directed at him. Cornish's suit was better tailored than you might expect of an inspector and he was known to drive a beautiful new Chrysler which also seemed somewhat surprising for a man on his wages. There were rumours of back-handers and bribes, but nothing that had stuck, and there was a certain insouciant shrug that Guy had often seen accompany the telling of these rumours, a sort of 'why not?' refrain that had always seemed depressing. But after three years in London's police force, he hadn't seen much to recommend the good nature of men.

'You lot think Christmas means a fat man climbing down your chimney to bring you mittens,' Cornish was barking, 'or an extra large turkey with stuffing for Tiny Tim' – he paused to guffaw at his own joke – 'but for these lowlifes out there, it's all about taking, not giving. And they don't wait for the first door on the advent calendar.' A few policemen tittered politely as if encouraging a music hall act on his opening night. 'Now, we have reason to believe that Miss Alice Diamond is out in full strength and operating her Forty Thieves on Oxford Street, Regent Street and Bond Street. In the last year or two, she's been feeling the heat from our lot and worked the provinces and regional cities instead. But it seems that she's come back home for Christmas and we need to widen our net this time to catch her. So I want as many of you as possible out there, reporting back to me at the end of every shift. Got that?' He leered at the crowd. 'Good. Line up, and Sergeant Cluttock here will give you your assignment. You need to work in pairs and in plain clothes.' With a final squint at the straight-backed men he left the room.

Guy looked around the room helplessly. Everyone was quick to find the other half to their pair, sometimes with as little as a wink or nod to acknowledge firm partnerships. Guy felt a pang for his former comrade, Harry, but although he had carried on working for the London, Brighton and South Coast Railway Police after Guy had been moved to the Met, he had quit even that job a few months ago so that he could work as a musician in the new jazz nightclubs springing up in the city. It wasn't that Guy hadn't friends, or at least friendly acquaintances at the station, but this wasn't about someone amiable to sit next to in the canteen while you ate your pie and mash. This was about who would help you bring in a haul for the attention of Cornish, a partner who would bring you acclaim, praise and promotion. Seven months at the front desk had not advertised Guy as a policeman who would sleuth and stalk with success. He watched, paralysed, as the room emptied two by two, like the animals triumphantly boarding Noah's Ark. When the last had left, rather resembling a pair of laughing hyenas, Sergeant Cluttock started shuffling his papers together and getting ready to go. Guy approached his desk and started to speak, though his mouth was dry and it came out as a croak.

'Excuse me, sir.'

Cluttock looked at him and his moustache glistened. 'What?'

'I wondered if I might have an assignment, sir?'

Cluttock made an exaggerated movement with his head towards the four corners of the room. 'I don't see anyone with you. You heard the boss. You need to work in pairs.'

'Yes, sir. I've got a partner it's just that she ...' He stopped and thought for less than a fraction of a second. 'They're out on another task at present. But back shortly and we could go out on the assignation then.'

'Name?'

'Mine, sir?'

'No, the king of England's shoeshine boy. Yes, *your* name.'

'Sergeant Sullivan, sir. And my partner's is Constable Moon.'

Cluttock looked down his list. 'You can go to Great Marlborough Street. Smaller shops there, not so likely to be targeted but you never know. Report back at six o'clock sharp. Obviously make a note of anything suspicious, talk to the shopgirls and so on. You know the form.' He raised an eyebrow and looked at Guy. 'You *do* know the form?'

'Oh, yes, sir. Thank you very much, sir.' Guy was grinning as if he'd just opened his Christmas stocking and found it contained real gold coins instead of chocolate ones. He stopped and realised Cluttock was staring at him. 'I'm still here, aren't I, sir?'

'Seems you are, Sergeant Sullivan.'

'Not for long, sir.' Guy ran out of the room and back to the front desk.

Mary performed tiny hops of glee when Guy told her the news. 'You gave him my name?' she asked for the third time. 'And he didn't say I couldn't do it?'

17

Guy reassured her once more. 'Yes, I did. And no, he didn't. But there's another problem.'

'What?'

'I'm supposed to be working at the front desk.'

'Well ... why don't you tell whoever organises the rota that you've been assigned on special duties? They'll have to find someone else then.' She deliberately widened her eyes and clasped her hands in prayer. 'Please try. This is my one chance to prove myself. I've *got* to do it.'

If nothing else, Guy knew how she felt. He nodded and walked off, quickly, before his nerve could fail him. To his pleasant surprise, his superior agreed without asking too many questions. Word must have got around that all hands were needed on deck to find Alice Diamond and the Forty Thieves. In what felt like record time, Guy and Mary had each gone home to change out of their uniforms into plain clothes and were heading towards Great Marlborough Street in pursuit of one of the country's most notorious female criminals and her gang.

CHAPTER THREE

~~~~~~

After the party, Nancy, Pamela and Louisa had returned to Iris Mitford's flat in Elvaston Place. Their late hour was betrayed by a long lie-in the next morning and slow responses to Iris's inquisition over a late luncheon. Louisa had helped them pack and accompanied the sisters to Paddington station where they caught the train home in time for supper. Louisa was then free to keep her appointment with the maid from the night before, Dulcie Long.

Louisa had arranged some time before to remain in London for the evening, telling Lady Redesdale that she would like to see a cousin though, truthfully, she had no real family to speak of. Her father had died several years before, her mother had moved from London to Suffolk and her uncle Stephen had joined the army and never been heard from since – and glad of that she was, too. She was an only child and had worked since leaving school at fourteen. When she began working for the Mitfords, far from the Peabody Estate she had grown up in, she'd pretty much lost touch with everyone. Her oldest friend, Jennie, moved in different circles thanks to her cut-glass beauty, though Louisa knew Jennie would always be happy to see her. But the opportunity to combine a trip to London with her monthly Sunday off had been too good to pass up. As much as anything, she wanted to breathe the city air again. After weeks of mud in the country, a stretch of pavement felt almost medicinal. The sour mix of fog and soot might appal Lord Redesdale's bucolic instincts but was as nostalgic a pleasure for Louisa as a slice of her mother's Guinness cake.

At one point she had thought she might meet up with Guy Sullivan but made no fixed plan. Then, at the Curtis house, as Nancy and Pamela were safely sitting down to supper, she had fallen into conversation with the maid who had opened the door.

Perhaps she had been drawn by the girl's London accent, invoking a sisterly feeling. Or it might have been the vanity of liking someone because they were the mirror image of oneself. Louisa's instinct had been close to the mark: Dulcie, like her, worked as both maid and chaperone, to Miss Charlotte. As the two young women assisted the cook with the dinner, they exchanged snippets of gossip and stories of their family's demands and eccentricities. They'd admitted, too, to similar pasts that their employers neither knew nor would understand. It had felt more like coming home than the annual week at her mother's Hadleigh cottage ever had.

Out of this easy chatter, they had arranged to meet by the lions at Trafalgar Square at six o'clock the following night. The meeting point had been Dulcie's idea and Louisa had nearly asked to change it and then told herself not to be so asinine. She shied from the memory of the last time she had been there, with Nancy, right after they had run out of the dance at the Savoy, frightened that there was a man there who might have revealed Louisa's whereabouts to her uncle Stephen. It had caused a row between the two of them when Louisa had tried to tell Nancy that she could not return to the party but then they had bumped into a man who claimed his name was Roland Lucknor. It had marked the start of what had turned out to be a long and tumultuous time between the three of them, involving Guy and the murder of a nurse, Florence Nightingale Shore.

In the years since, while Louisa enjoyed her work for the most part, she missed her friendship with Nancy and felt jealous of her easy move into adulthood. Nancy no longer even slept in the nursery but had moved to the main wing of the house and spent her weekends with friends in Oxford and London, coming home with tales of pranks and parties.

Nor had Louisa seen much of Guy, though they wrote to each other and she enjoyed his funny letters, in which he would write about the mad, bad and dangerous people he came across now he was working for the Met Police. She could see, reading between the lines, that his encounters were rather more fleeting than if he were the arresting officer, but he had never shown any pity for himself in the telling of his stories and she thought that admirable. If not terribly thrilling.

Some ten minutes after six o'clock, Louisa was still standing by the stone lions in her best dress, a navy blue hand-me-down from Nancy that she'd adjusted to fit. Fashionable men and women rushed past on their way to evenings out and Louisa started to fidget, wondering if this had been a good idea after all. Then round the corner came Dulcie, waving to catch her attention.

'Sorry I'm a bit late,' said Dulcie, rushing up with a smile. '*Madame* Charlotte couldn't find her garnet brooch and as that was the only one that would do I had to go on a search with her ...' She stopped to share a knowing look with Louisa and they both giggled. Goodness, it was nice to be able to do this. 'We're getting the number 36 bus,' Dulcie continued. 'Takes us all the way to my old pub. I know we can have a good time in there, have a drink and a knees-up without getting bothered by anyone. Not like round here – it's all hoity-toity types or men asking if they can look up your skirt for a halfpenny, isn't it? Yes, you know I'm right. Come along, girl.'

She started marching off. Louisa took a breath and followed.

CHAPTER FOUR

~~~~~

An hour later they were sitting behind a table in the Elephant and Castle in Southwark, on the corner of a busy junction. This part of London may only have been the other side of the River Thames but it was like a foreign country. The street lamps were fewer and not yet converted from gas to electricity. Everything seemed rougher, darker and slower. There weren't so many motor cars as horses pulling carts; young children streaked along pavements, brushing past – even through – legs, their blurred shapes chased by an irate 'Oi!'. The women hurried along or, if waiting for a bus, talked constantly to each other in an accent that sat vowels at either end of a see-saw. Men walked in long, purposeful strides, heads dipped, cigarettes in the corners of their mouths. Buses rattled past, filled to bursting like canned worms, at least five grubs precariously hanging on the corner pole.

The pub felt no less busy than the street outside but it was brightly lit. Brass fixtures gleamed and the wood on the bar was polished to a high shine. Doubtless the heavily patterned carpet disguised a multitude of past sins but to the naked eye this inn was proudly kept and the punters were dressed in what Louisa's mother would have called their best bib and tucker. There were a few men dotted around, older gents, quietly nursing their pints or playing cards. But most of the customers were women and Louisa noticed with fascination that they were buying their own drinks, sometimes several, and she even saw a pitcher of ale sent over to one of the men, who raised his glass and nodded his whiskery chin in gratitude. The women were young, too, about Louisa's age. You'd know they weren't from Mayfair – their clothes weren't fashionable or sumptuous enough for that – but there was something in the way they carried themselves that gave them an air of confidence to match a millionaire's wife. They weren't downtrodden; they were in charge. She didn't know how that could be when surely they led the same life of drudgery as the women Louisa had grown up around.

Then one of the doors to the pub opened and a woman stepped in, pausing on the threshold, as if waiting while the pub muted its chatter. She remained there a fraction of a minute longer, as the hubbub started up again though more quietly than before. Dulcie elbowed Louisa in the ribs.

'That's Alice Diamond,' she whispered with reverence. 'I hoped she'd show tonight but you can't always be sure.'

Alice Diamond was as tall as a man, wearing a thick brocade coat and on each finger gleamed a large ring set with the obvious stones. Her hair was short and waved, the same shade as the mahogany counter at the bar, but her face lacked colour, the features pushed in like coins in dough, with a dimple in her chin and the silvery line of a scar beneath her left eye. She was followed by three women in formation a few steps behind, chosen courtiers with their monarch.

'Who is she?' Louisa whispered back.

'She's the queen,' said Dulcie, daring to talk more loudly now that the noise had resumed its earlier level. 'She's the one who runs things around here.'

Louisa stared as Alice sat down in a chair by a table in the corner that had remained curiously free as the rest of the pub filled up. Now Louisa knew why: it was Alice's domain. Two of the women sat beside her while the third went to the bar, brandishing a pound note. One woman was stout and plain with an unfriendly look; the other had an undeniably pretty face with long, dark eyelashes and a delicate nose. Dulcie followed Louisa's sightline and leant over again.

'That's Babyface, her lieutenant if you like. Don't be fooled by her looks. She's the most dangerous one of all. Been inside for razoring another woman.'

When the drinks were set down in front of the three women by a young bar waitress, the tray trembling in her hands, they were downed fast, gulped in the gaps between roars of laughter. At this cue, Louisa could almost feel every person in the room unclench their jaws with relief. Today had been a good day for Alice Diamond and she was in the mood for celebrating. That meant everyone could join in.

'What exactly is she queen of?'

'The Forty Thieves,' said Dulcie, and wiped the froth of the beer off her top lip. 'That's the women. Then there's the Elephants, which is all men. Two separate gangs but . . . not, if you see what I mean. Everyone lives within half a mile of here.'

Louisa nodded at this. The names rang a bell but she also wanted Dulcie to think that she was comfortable with this information, familiar even. She didn't want to appear fazed or naive.

'I've heard of the Forty,' said Louisa, giving in to the temptation to make more of her past. An odd kind of bragging. 'When my uncle and I used to work the railway stations, we knew to stay away from the shops on Oxford Street.'

Dulcie grinned. 'That's it, though they've had to move out of London lately. It's been her masterstroke, taking the Forty out to the provinces. Birmingham and Nottingham, Liverpool, that sort of thing. I didn't fancy those places ...' She stopped and gave Louisa a sidelong look.

'You ... ?'

Dulcie nodded. 'Not any more though.' She took a gulp. 'Another?'

Louisa nodded and while Dulcie was at the bar, she took in the room again. It was as if Alice's arrival had put a lens on it – everything seemed sharper, brighter. Louisa saw now that although Alice may have been the ruler of all she surveyed, her subjects – all women – benefited from her status too. Though some of them had coats with worn elbows and boots that needed new soles, most looked fashionable enough to pass for ordinary, well-heeled customers in the big shops. One or two even looked as if they would pass muster in the fur department at Harrods. More than that, there was something in their demeanour that suggested they wore these clothes because they enjoyed them. Hadn't Louisa pressed one or two of Nancy's dresses to her own figure, in a lone moment by the mirror when she was scooping them up from the chair, to take them for mending and cleaning? Once, she'd held a dress at her shoulders, and pinched it by the waist with her arm, twirling her leg out. In a silk dress, no one would ever know she was a servant. But she'd heard Mrs Windsor coming down the hall and hurriedly slung it over her arm, hoping the sweep of red on her cheeks would have faded by the time she made it down the stairs to the laundry room.

Dulcie put their drinks on the table. 'Penny for them?'

'Oh.' Louisa shook her head. 'Nothing. I—'

She was interrupted by a woman coming up to Dulcie and slamming a meaty hand on her shoulder, pushing her down onto the stool. She had thick black hair that looked more like a helmet than a bob, and a shadow around her jawline that could have been stubble. She made a sound that was perhaps meant to be a laugh but came out more like a bark.

'Who's this?' She pointed her chin at Louisa, who flinched. 'We don't allow strangers in here.'

'She's one of us,' said Dulcie. 'Nothing to worry about.'

Louisa wasn't sure how she felt about this answer.

The woman squinted. 'New recruit? I don't remember hearing about that.'

'No,' said Dulcie, 'but she's in the game, too. She won't go squealing.'

'Huh.' The woman seemed appeased, or perhaps she wasn't in the mood for a fight. It was still early. 'See that she doesn't. We're keeping an eye on you.'

'I know.' Dulcie squeezed out a small smile. 'I've come as promised and shown my face, ain't I? I've not run off anywhere.'

The lump on two legs nodded then marched off and resumed her position of watchdog, back to the bar, elbows propping her up, swigging her beer as she watched carefully.

'Sorry,' said Dulcie. 'It's not always as bad as that but I'm under a bit of a cosh, you see.'

'Why?' Louisa was agog.

'I want to leave. My sister's married out and they're worried that if I go too, we'll grass them up. So I've tried to do a deal with them.'

'What sort of a deal?' Louisa sat up straighter.

'I've got to pay them off. It'll be the last thing I'll ever do for

27

them and then I'm out. In fact, I was wondering . . .' She gave a shy look.

Louisa said nothing. She wasn't sure if she wanted to hear what was coming next. Her mind told her no, but her heart was hammering in her chest and the excitement inside was better than anything she'd felt in a very long time.

'I hoped you might be able to help me.'

CHAPTER FIVE

∿

Less than a month later the invitations to Pamela's birthday had been sent out to Nancy's bright young friends and the RSVPs returned. Mrs Windsor, the housekeeper, had hired extra servants for the night and Mrs Stobie, the cook, had spent days ordering ahead and preparing the dinner, as well as the breakfast to be served at the end of the party. Pam had been most interested in this part of the arrangements, sneaking into the kitchen and pleading to be allowed to stir a pot or taught how to roll out pastry.

Louisa and Nanny Blor had had their hands full doing their best to shield the excitement of the party from the younger sisters who would otherwise demand to come down and look at the guests arriving, as they were usually able to do. Not tonight. Lord Redesdale had made an unbidden appearance in the nursery to instruct Nanny that his daughters must not clap eyes on Nancy's 'appalling' friends. 'If an artie appears with a comb in his top pocket, Farve's in danger of a fit,' said Nancy with glee, when Louisa told her what he'd said. The youngest children – Debo at five, Jessica, seven, and Unity, nine – were easily distracted by promises of hot chocolate before bed but Diana, at nearly fifteen, was outraged. Tom, thankfully, was still at Eton and not due home for Christmas hols for another two weeks.

Tonight there was a crackle of anticipation in the air as the logs burned fiercely in the two grates at either end of the hall. The stern oil portraits had been decorated with paper streamers and there were plenty of candles lit, adding to an early festive atmosphere. Advent was not far off, after all. Louisa had been roped in and stood with two other maids holding trays of filled champagne glasses. Lord Redesdale paced impatiently near the front door, while his wife let out tiny exasperated noises as she fiddled with the buttons on Pamela's dress. Nancy had persuaded her parents to hold a costume party for Pamela's coming out dance, and though Pamela had gone along with the idea, now that she was wearing a large, white flouncy dress that made her look – and feel – like a wedding cake, with a wig of ringleted curls, uncomfortably hot and too—

'Enough!' admonished Lady Redesdale. 'You'll have a lovely party if you stop thinking about what you look like.'

Nancy took a glass from Louisa's tray and gave her a wink. She was dressed like a Spanish countess from the eighteenth century, with a tall jewelled mantilla, her bob rather awkwardly splaying out beneath. She had on a sleeveless satin top, an enormous brooch rather daringly set in her décolletage and a skirt that had wide, straight sides coming out of the hips, making her top half rather like the decorated spire on a church roof. Lord Redesdale was fit and lean still, despite his white hair and the lines engraved on his forehead. He wore his shooting tweeds as a costume; Nancy said he would never have been so comfortable at a party. Lady Redesdale looked much older than her husband, not helped by a bright yellow wig that made her complexion seem all the more bare and an ill-fitting medieval dress that Louisa suspected had been pulled out of the bottom of the dressing-up box used for charades at Christmas. It was likely, with so much to organise, that she had forgotten to think about her outfit until that afternoon.

A minute later Nancy seemed to remember whose birthday it actually was and took a second glass from the tray, handing it to Pamela. The younger sister hesitated when Lord Redesdale looked up sharply.

'Stand down, Farve,' said Nancy, 'it will calm her nerves.'

Farve huffed and poked at the fire. Just as Louisa thought her arms might give out and drop the tray, they heard a car draw up outside, then the scrabble of feet on gravel and voices calling out. Mrs Windsor, who acted as butler because Lady Redesdale would employ no male servants, pulled open the door letting in a sharp draught of cold air and the first guest.

On cue, Lady Redesdale and Nancy surged forward and Louisa saw that those arriving were some of those she had seen at the Curtis party. They were most likely early because they were staying as a house party with the Watneys next door, where they had also been hosted for the pre-dance dinner, Lord Redesdale having refused to countenance any of Nancy's friends to their own. Nancy pushed Pamela towards Oliver Watney, the son. There had been plots to pair the two of them off but Louisa couldn't understand why when Pamela was hale and hearty and he so pale and insipid with a permanent cough from childhood tuberculosis. His stern face was not enhanced by his Mad Hatter costume, complete with patchwork tailcoat, and Louisa suppressed a giggle rising in her throat as she walked over with her tray.

'Your friends are perfectly ludicrous,' he said as he took a glass.

'They're not really my friends,' protested Pamela, who was no good at divided loyalties.

'I should hope not,' Oliver continued. 'Especially Adrian Curtis. Ghastly man. Thinks everyone is at his beck and call. I swear to goodness, if he comes near me ...' Louisa didn't hear the end as he walked off with his glass, Pamela nervously trailing behind him.

Sebastian Atlas had arrived as part of the group and now grabbed two glasses from Louisa, his gold head bobbing as he gulped down first one, then the other before putting them back and walking off with a third without so much as a nod to acknowledge her. He appeared to be dressed as a pirate, albeit with no hat or parrot but baggy trousers, a dark waistcoat over a white shirt that gaped loosely revealing a hairless chest, and a red spotted scarf knotted around his neck. Seb approached Clara Fischer, who was hovering a little in the doorway, and put his arm around her waist, but Louisa detected a flinch at his touch.

Briefly, Louisa stepped into the passageway that led to the kitchen and placed more filled glasses on her tray from a table that had been temporarily set up there, before returning to the hall. Another two or three cars must have pulled up in the meantime because the room felt fuller and was noisy with shouts of greetings and exclamations over costumes. Two of Pamela's own friends were beside her, looking rather overawed by the crowd, and Louisa was pleased to see that she appeared determined to show that she was having a good time, though she kept pulling at her dress.

Clara came up, dressed as Tinkerbell, with silvery diaphanous layers that seemed to be almost lit from beneath by her translucent skin. Her big eyes and pretty mouth gave her the look of Mary Pickford and Louisa could believe the rumour that she had travelled to London to get work on the stage. Clara took a champagne glass and hovered beside Louisa for a minute or two.

'Quite the party, isn't it?' she said in a low voice, her New York accent softer than before, and it took Louisa a moment to realise Clara was talking to her.

'Yes. We've been getting it ready for days.'

'I bet. Looks super,' said Clara, sipping slowly. She took a deep breath. 'Oh, there's Ted.' She gave an apologetic smile. 'Well, I suppose I'd better plunge in. Bye!'

'Bye,' said Louisa uncertainly, though Clara had already disappeared as the guests were ushered through to the Cloisters, the outside walkway to the ballroom. Farve hadn't lit oil lamps this time, as he had for Nancy's party three years ago, which made it darker and chillier, but at least no one was choking from the smoky fumes.

Louisa was picking up a few glasses that had been put down on the tables in the hall when the front door was opened and Adrian Curtis rushed in, followed by his sister Charlotte. Louisa started at this reminder of her promise to Dulcie. Not that it had been too far from her mind the entire day. He was brooding, his eyebrows cross-hatched, while his sister was talking to him in a raised voice, her dark eyes fixed on him. Adrian was dressed as a country vicar in half-moon glasses, with a wide white collar and an old-fashioned black straw hat; it made him look serene and, Louisa guessed, infuriatingly supercilious to his sister. Charlotte, a rather half-hearted Queen Victoria, was clearly unamused. They suddenly saw Louisa and Charlotte stopped, mid-sentence.

Adrian flapped his hand towards Louisa without looking at her. 'Well, my dear sister. Do you wish to go on? Pray, do.'

'Shut up,' said Queen Victoria.

33

The three of them stood awkwardly in the room.

'Everyone has gone through to the ballroom,' said Louisa, as if she had neither heard nor seen anything. 'Shall I show you the way?'

She started walking and they followed, a few steps behind. Charlotte did, indeed, *go on* and though she was not shouting, Louisa could hear her. Louisa knew a good servant never listened but sometimes it was impossible not to waggle one's ears. She and Ada used to giggle over snatched bits of conversation that had not been intended for them. She missed those moments, few and far between these days, but she might be able to do the same with Dulcie. Not tonight though.

'You've got to tell Mother the debt you're in,' Charlotte was saying. 'She's got no idea and it's almost Christmas.'

'What's that got to do with anything?' Adrian hissed back.

Louisa couldn't see as the two were behind her but she pictured Charlotte's white shoulders rising with her hackles.

They had reached the ballroom now and Louisa stepped to one side at the door to let them pass by. Neither gave her a second glance.

Inside, the throng was in full sway. While Charlotte and Adrian had come in through the front door by mistake, distracted by their argument, others had been rolling up the drive and disgorging themselves directly to the ballroom, more usually called the library. For the party, the sofa had been temporarily removed and there were a number of chairs along the walls for the chaperones. There were only three or four of these at present, mothers happy to see inside the Mitford house and catch up on gossip with friends. Louisa had discovered that in the upper-class world people acted as if they knew each other and referred to each other as friends or friendly acquaintances even if they had never met. They worked on a system of introductions: like becoming members of a club, you were introduced and seconded by two insiders and then you were in. There may have been no bricks and mortar but there was certainly a membership and club rules to be adhered to if you didn't want to be thrown out and banished from ever re-entering.

Some of these rules were changing, much to the horror of the ''rents', as Nancy's friends referred to the older generation. Divorce had once meant permanent exclusion from society, at least for the women, but since the Duke and Duchess of Marlborough had had their marriage annulled after the war with each invited to as many parties as before, others had been quietly allowed to remain too. 'If Muv and Farve divorced it would spice things up no end,' Nancy had said mock-sadly, 'but I don't suppose they ever will.'

Some rules were etched in steel, however, and given equal ranking: no illegitimate babies, no brown shoes in town, no cut flowers given to a hostess. Nor was knowing these enough. Louisa knew that even if she mimicked the accent perfectly and borrowed the dress and the pearls, she'd be thrown out as a commoner by anyone cut from the upper-class cloth. For all the spoken rules they teased about, there were a million unwritten ones. You only needed to slip up once – to wear the wrongly weighted tweed on a shoot, or ask for a napkin instead of using your handkerchief for cake crumbs on your lip – and the game would be up. At best your so-called friends would giggle behind their hands at your social slips, at worst the door would slam shut and no amount of knocking or money or pleading would get it open again.

Louisa spotted Clara in the crowd, who caught her eye and gave her a small wave. This was almost the sort of thing to close the door but Nancy had explained that Clara would be forgiven almost anything. 'She can't be expected to know and being American she's classless,' said Nancy, who always told these things to Louisa in the same tone that Nanny told Decca why she needed to eat her carrots. The rhythm was one of patient teaching but there was something hectoring in it too. Eating carrots so you could see in the dark and Americans being classless were presented as unarguable facts. Which left Louisa confused as to what to do with the now contradictory information she had been spoonfed by her mother. She still couldn't get used to telling the children to say 'what' instead of 'pardon'. There was a gap in between the two worlds and sometimes she got vertigo at the thought of it opening wide enough to fall into.

A few of the guests had flushed faces already, though whether they were too hot in their costumes or had drunk too much wine – a glass or two with their dinner before arriving for the party would have given them a head start on the champagne – Louisa couldn't tell. Pamela, she was relieved to see, did not have a glass in her hand. She was nervous enough without wine adding to it. Nancy was dancing with Oliver Watney, who looked pained by the event, but she wasn't looking at him anyway, apparently carrying on several other conversations as they wheeled around the floor. Louisa recognised two or three others who had been down for the weekend at other times: Brian Howard, a sickly-looking man with sunken eyes but he made Nancy roar with laughter; Patrick Cameron who was regularly wheeled out as a dance partner for Nancy and now for Pamela too. Excitingly, there were two girls who had been in the papers frequently, the Jungman sisters, who were older than Nancy and daringly captivating with their beautiful faces and zest for mischief. They had come tonight as a pair of milkmaids, complete with buckets that threatened to slosh onto the floor. Lord Redesdale had already been spotted watching them with his eyes popping out of his head, his wife's restraining hand on his elbow.

Louisa felt a nudge at her back and a dry whisper in her ear. 'Louisa, you're wanted in the kitchens.'

'Yes, Mrs Windsor. Right away.'

She ducked down, out of the party, back to where she belonged.

CHAPTER SIX

❧

A few hours later, after Mrs Stobie had gone stiffly to bed, grumbling that she was getting too old for this sort of thing, Louisa and Ada were standing by the kitchen sink. The borrowed maids had done most of the clearing from the ballroom as well as the washing up, so there wasn't too much left to do. The kedgeree and bacon had been cooked and left in the oven, which would be sent up with coffee and toast for the breakfast at about two o'clock. Aside from this, Louisa knew her main task of the night had yet to be completed.

Louisa hoped Dulcie would arrive soon, as they had privately arranged. This was to be some time earlier than the official half past two that had been agreed between Lady Curtis and Lady Redesdale. Charlotte's mother had requested that her maid collect Charlotte and take her back to the Watneys', in order to ensure that her daughter did not remain in mixed company at a late hour. Dulcie was to walk from the Watneys', only half a mile next door, but Hooper would be on hand to drive them back. This was the compromise reached as Charlotte did not want the embarrassment of a chaperone at the party, when none of her friends would have one there. It also meant that Dulcie and Louisa had only a short measure of time to complete their task.

Only a few minutes before, Mrs Windsor told Louisa that Lady Redesdale had rung for two mugs of cocoa to be sent up to her room. This meant that the party for her mistress, and the other guests of her generation, was over. The savouries had been served and the housekeeper had already set out the tray of glasses with bottles of whisky and port in the drawing room for the younger ones to help themselves. After taking the cocoa up, Mrs Windsor would not go to bed – she would be the last to do so – but would read alone in her sitting room.

By this hour, there weren't too many people left. While Nancy had been successful in bringing down her friends from London, as well as a few more from Oxford, the greater number had come from Lord and Lady Redesdale's own address book and were, accordingly, of a disposition where a delayed bedtime was a disruption akin to snowfall in the month of May. Besides, they knew that after midnight was for the young and had no desire to impede. Disappointingly, the most dazzling elements had departed too: Brian Howard had promised to deliver the Jungman sisters back to London that night as their cousin was marrying the next day and they had to attend the wedding. Louisa and Ada, with a couple of the other maids, had stood on the drive when they left, unable to resist having a final peep at the star-dusted figures, shrouded in long coats with fur collars. The milk buckets had been slopped out thoughtlessly on the drive before they got into the car, the white liquid pooling in the gravel. Hooper wouldn't be happy to see that in the morning.

There had been one minor drama earlier, when Clara's friend Phoebe Morgan, a raven-haired beauty dressed as Cleopatra, had tripped over one of Lord Redesdale's dogs in the passageway and sprained her ankle badly. Not wanting to miss out by returning to the Watneys' early, where she was staying, she was now propped up on the sofa by the fire, a cold press on her leg, a hot toddy in her hand.

'Perhaps I ought to see if she needs anything,' said Louisa. She hoped the treasure hunt would have started before Dulcie arrived.

'What you mean is, perhaps you could go and have a snoop at the party,' teased Ada.

'Back in a tick.' Louisa playfully whipped the drying-up cloth on Ada's arm.

As she crossed the hall, she could hear that somebody had set up the gramophone player in the drawing room and the scratchy crackle of the latest music could be heard. Louisa pushed open the door and was greeted by a fug of heat and cigarette smoke. Sebastian and Charlotte were dancing, rather more languidly than the beat from the song playing, Charlotte's head leaning on his chest, her eyes closed. On one sofa by the fire, watching them closely, was Phoebe, her leg up but the colour back in her cheeks, with two others squeezed beside her. On the opposite sofa was a jumble of bodies that Louisa mentally untangled into a further four people. Wigs had been discarded and the women had shaken their hair out, though Nancy still had on her mantilla and Adrian his vicar's glasses and hat. He appeared to be in the middle of explaining something, puffing intermittently on the stub of a fat cigar, his posture giving him the look of addressing the entire group, even though only Nancy was listening with any great attention.

Clara, as pretty as a Toulouse-Lautrec portrait even at the end of the party, was talking quietly to Ted. He was in costume, as Dracula Louisa supposed, but it was impeccably made, a thick velvet cape tied around his shoulders over a dress suit. Nancy had been beside herself at his acceptance of the invitation, written on almost card-thick writing paper with the ancient De Clifford crest on the top.

Louisa hesitated, wondering if she should make her presence known with a cough or go in and quietly collect some empty glasses, when Nancy saw her and called out, 'Lou-Lou!'

Louisa smiled. It had been a while since Nancy had called her by her old pet name.

'Just the person, come here. We're going to do a game and we're down one because of poor old Phoebe. Will you make up the numbers for us?'

Louisa looked to see if there was someone standing beside her. 'Me, Miss Nancy?'

'Yes, you,' Nancy said, waving her over. Louisa's stomach turned over. She felt suddenly dowdy in her plain dress and thick woollen stockings. She had never worn a scrap of make-up in her life. The faces and bodies around her seemed to blur into a rainbow of sequins, feathers and red nails. Nancy stood up, clapping her hands and calling everyone to attention. Sebastian and Charlotte broke apart and each took a perch on the opposite arms of a sofa. Pamela, whose birthday it was, after all, gave a wide yawn and looked across at her sister apprehensively. Her own friends had left – most of them still seventeen and chaperoned by their mothers – and Louisa guessed that Pamela had been on the verge of trying to go to bed herself, only she wouldn't have wanted to miss out on anything happening at her own party. Nancy would crow about it for weeks.

'We're going to do the treasure hunt now,' said Nancy.

At this, Charlotte gave a big sigh. 'Really, *must* we?'

'Yes! *All* of us.' Nancy addressed the room, the pleasure of being the star of the show written on her face. At least, Louisa hoped it was that and not champagne. Nancy suffering the effects of a late night was rare but it was not a pleasant thing for the house the following morning. 'There are eight of us to play now Lou-Lou is here, so we can work in pairs. You all know how it works. When you've found your answer, bring it back here and Seb or Phoebe will give you the next clue. We've got eight clues and everyone gets the same ones, but in a relay so that no one is looking for the same thing at the same time. Winner is the first to do all nine.'

'A proper treasure hunt!' exclaimed Clara. 'The ones in London have become so loathsome lately, with all the boys gatecrashing them with their fast cars.'

'Thank you, Miss Fischer,' said Adrian drily. 'We do our best, you know.'

'Oh, you silly,' said Clara, slightly pink. 'You know what I mean.'

'I'm going to pair up with Clara,' bossed Nancy. 'Pamela, you've got Louisa.'

Phew, thought Louisa.

'Ted, you go with Togo – Oliver, I mean. Sorry, Oliver.' Oliver's thin face was even more pinched at Nancy's use of the Mitford nickname for him. 'That means Adrian and Charlotte together, but you're brother and sister so that's all right.'

'If we must,' said Adrian, blowing smoke rings above his sister's head, who regarded him with a stony face. 'I thought I was pairing with Seb.'

Sebastian gave a sly look at Phoebe on the sofa. 'There's been a change of plan,' he said. Phoebe gave a brief smug smile but Charlotte turned her head away when he said this, showing a sudden interest in a button on her shirt.

'In that case,' said Adrian, 'as we're such a small number, I think we should work alone. We don't need two brains when each of us has got a perfectly good one.' He paused. 'Some of us have at any rate.'

Was this a way of getting rid of Louisa? She tried not to feel offended and succeeded slightly; he wouldn't have meant her particularly because he probably hadn't noticed she was in the room. Even so, she was left with a dry feeling of disappointment, though perhaps she should have been relieved that it wouldn't get in the way of the commission that still lay before her. Nancy didn't so much as look at Louisa as she said, 'Fine. We can all work alone then.'

Louisa knew this was her cue to leave but she wanted to see how it played out. Pamela started fidgeting beside her.

'Everything all right, Miss Pamela?' whispered Louisa.

Pamela gave a tight nod and the hint of a smile. 'Yes,' she whispered back, her eyes checking that Nancy was facing away. 'I was rather pleased when you were going to be with me. The rest of them make me a bit nervous.'

Louisa sympathised entirely. 'Don't worry,' she mouthed but didn't dare say any more as she saw that Nancy had walked across the room to her desk by the window – partly obscured by a screen because Lord Redesdale did not like the sight of her typewriter when he was having a drink after dinner – and picked up a book, *Alice in Wonderland*. Louisa had read it to Decca and Unity often, each of them enthralled by the idea of sliding down a hole into a world where everything could be the exact opposite of the familiar and logical. It gave her a giddy feeling to think that things didn't have to follow the rules.

Nancy opened the book and took out a sheaf of papers, on which it was clear to see typed words, if not what the words were. Nancy had bought herself the typewriter only a few months earlier and it was her most precious possession. The other sisters were firmly denied any access, though, as it had turned out, she was rarely heard on it herself. Louisa suspected Nancy liked the machine to be partly on view because she had taunted her family for some time about the novel she was writing, but if she was ever seen at it, she was always writing by hand in an old exercise book. The habit must have been too stuck.

'As you all know, everyone was asked to contribute a riddle each, which means there will be eight clues you don't know the answer to and one that you do, though you'll still have to hunt the house for the answer. Everyone was supposed to use a commonly found object as their clue's answer though I don't trust that one or two of you won't have made that difficult.' Nancy did a comical eye roll in the direction of Adrian, who grinned in return. 'I shall now hand them to Sebastian. Darling, would you do the honours and read out the first? I thought we could all race the first, just for fun, and then you can hand out the rest as people come back.'

'Certainly, m'lady,' said Seb facetiously. His hair was as burnished gold as ever with not a strand out of place but his eyes were glazed. Was he drunk, or something else? Something about the way Seb stood up and took the clues from Nancy's hand made Louisa flinch.

He stood, legs apart and firmly planted on the Persian rug. 'You'll see me when there are six legs if not hanging on a peg. I can make a beast go faster and a human need a plaster. What am I?'

There was a moment's silence then Seb picked up his glass, sloshing with whisky, and raised it in the air. 'Good luck, everyone, and may you all return the heroes you are.'

There was a cheer and each guest stood up, whispering and talking excitedly. Louisa exited the room with Pamela. 'Do you know what it meant?' she said.

Pamela's response was quick. 'I think I do!' she said happily. 'Thanks, Lou-Lou.'

Louisa smiled with more confidence than she felt. The task was yet to be completed and she was deeply uncertain now that she had done the right thing in committing to it.

CHAPTER SEVEN

※

With the treasure hunt under way, there was the sound of footsteps and giggles echoing around the ground floor of the house as each of the players ran off looking for the answer to the first clue. Louisa took her chance to head upstairs and check which of the female guests' bedrooms were still empty. All Dulcie had asked for was a room to meet Adrian Curtis in. 'It has to be single woman's room because that way he'll accept an invitation to go up,' Dulcie had explained. Louisa had her hopes pinned on Iris Mitford, Lord Redesdale's sister. She was generally put in a bedroom that was in the same passage as her brother's dressing room but with a large bathroom between the two. Known as 'the buttercup bedroom' for its yellow walls, it was one of the smallest but the only one Iris would sleep in, having once claimed it to be the only room she believed wasn't haunted. Louisa knew that Lady Redesdale and her sister-in-law habitually had a long chat together at the end of the night in her ladyship's bedroom and Louisa felt sure that after a party they'd have even more to gossip about than usual. The passage was empty and Lord Redesdale's light was on, so he must have been changing. Once he had gone to bed in his own room he'd be asleep shortly after. Iris's room was dark but there was no sound within. It was empty.

Good. The hot chocolate must have been taken up by Mrs Windsor ten minutes ago and Louisa estimated that they had under an hour to make this plan work. She had hesitated to go along with it at first, but when they'd worked it out over their drinks at the Elephant and Castle, the request had seemed, if not quite innocent, then certainly nothing too awful. Dulcie had explained that she only needed a chance to talk to Adrian, who was refusing to see her alone. 'At home he protects himself with company at all hours,' she'd said, 'and I don't know when we'll get to Oxford again. Besides, you'll know the geography of the place.' Why Dulcie needed to talk to Adrian Louisa hadn't liked to ask: some things shouldn't be spelled out but were easily guessed at. He was an arrogant young man and she a pretty maid. They wouldn't be the first or the last.

Louisa quickly walked down the back stairs to the kitchen, now empty and with the swabbed-down look of a ship's galley. Ada had left, mopping the floor as she walked backwards to the garden door before going home. The mop had been left leaning just inside and Louisa retrieved it, picking up the bucket of grey water. As Louisa crossed back to the sink, she heard a soft knock and although she had been expecting it, such were her nerves that she jolted, sloshing water onto her dress.

'Bugger,' she said. Another Mitfordism, one of Lord Redesdale's, that she had picked up. Her mother would have boxed her ears at the shock of it.

Carefully, she put the bucket down and went to open the door. Dulcie pushed in quickly, as if someone outside might have been watching her. She looked around, checking to see who was in the kitchen.

'Is anyone else here?' she whispered. Her skin looked translucent; even the freckles seemed to have disappeared and she was sweating slightly, though the half-mile walk from the Watneys' house would have done that, even on a cold night like this one.

'No,' said Louisa, feeling strangely calm and in control now that it was actually happening. The bald fact was that she was about to let a girl who had once run with a gang of thieves into a guest's bedroom without anyone else's knowledge. It was not exactly the kind of thing Mrs Windsor would do. 'Lady Redesdale has gone to bed and her sister-in-law has joined her. They've had hot chocolate sent up to them. You should have a clear three-quarters of an hour.'

Dulcie looked at her watch, which hung loosely on her narrow wrist. It looked too big for her and rather smart, a man's watch perhaps. 'In that case, you'd better show me to the room now, and I'll wait for him there. Where are the other servants?'

'Gone home or to bed. There's only Mrs Windsor but she's in her sitting room,' said Louisa. 'So long as we don't bump into either Mr Curtis or his sister, no one will realise you weren't one of the maids working at the party. You'd better take your coat off though.'

'Oh, yes, good thinking,' said Dulcie. She unbuttoned her brown wool coat, another piece in her wardrobe that could have come from Louisa's, and left it draped over a kitchen chair. All their life was uniform, it seemed, whether as maids or the lower class. They both knew that even if Clara or Sebastian saw her, they wouldn't connect her as the maid at the Curtises' party in London. It was rare for a servant in another household to be recognised: who took a drink and looked at the face of the person holding the tray?

'Follow me, we'll go up the back stairs.' The pair of them went up two floors, sticking close to the edge of the staircase, where it was less likely to creak. Just before the landing, Louisa held a hand out behind her to stop Dulcie. She looked up and down the passageway – there was nobody there. In the faint distance, they heard squeals of laughter and muffled footsteps running on rugs.

Along the passageway to the right were the bedrooms she had already checked. Louisa pointed out the door to Dulcie. Lord Redesdale's door was closed and no light appeared beneath.

'Be quiet,' she whispered, 'Lord Redesdale has only just gone to sleep. I'll keep an eye out, make sure no one comes in and surprises you.'

'Where?'

'There,' said Louisa, pointing to thickly swagged curtains opposite the bathroom, the window behind them overlooking the churchyard.

'Right,' said Dulcie. She swallowed hard, then turned right and Louisa turned back.

After a quick sweep of the hall, which was empty, and the morning room – only Oliver was in there, examining a letter opener on Lady Redesdale's desk – Louisa stopped outside the dining room. She could hear Nancy and another female voice – Charlotte's? – in the smoking room. She guessed that Adrian, with his reputation for being brilliant, according to Nancy, would have moved on to his second clue already and she hoped his answer lay close by; she didn't want to hunt all over the house. Louisa approached the door, her heart beating fast, going over and over the lines in her head that she had promised to say. Her hand on the glass handle, she stopped when she heard two voices inside. Adrian's, yes, she was sure but also . . . Pamela's. She had a talent for clue-solving, clearly. Louisa thought quickly and stepped inside.

The dining room was only half lit. The table had been cleared away from the family's pre-dance dinner, and no candles had been left burning but there were two electric lamps in the wall that had been switched on. Their pools of light were bright but did not circle far and the rest of the room was in shadow. Pamela was rummaging through a drawer in the sideboard, Adrian standing on the other side in the semi-dark, smoking a cigarette. He was talking in his deep monotone, and Pamela was making girlish noises, half-protestations.

' . . . Ted knows you're much more suitable,' he was saying, 'I've told him so. He can't keep on with that tart, Dolly.'

'I'm sure she's very nice,' Pamela said into the drawer where the napkin rings were held. Not that they were ever used, Lady Redesdale not agreeing with the fuss and cost of laundering napkins.

Louisa stepped inside and closed the door behind her. At this, Adrian spoke tersely.

'What is it?'

'Beg pardon, Mr Curtis. I didn't mean to interrupt. I've got a message for Miss Pamela.'

Pamela had already stopped her rummaging and was looking at Louisa bashfully, as if she'd been caught doing something she shouldn't have been doing.

'Lady Redesdale wants you in her bedroom,' Louisa said. It was all she could think of. At least by the time Pamela and her mother had had a confused conversation establishing that she wasn't wanted after all, Louisa's part in this would be over.

'Oh bother,' said Pamela. 'Now I'll be all out of order with everyone else and get behind. I was so sure I was doing well.' But she didn't question Louisa's message, nor consider that her mother could be disobeyed, as Nancy would have. Pamela left the room but Louisa didn't follow her. Adrian stepped towards the sideboard and pocketed a fork but when he saw Louisa was still standing there he gave her a quizzical look.

'I've a message for you, sir,' she said.

'Who from?'

'Miss Iris Mitford.' She paused, allowing the inference to sink in. 'I can show you the way.'

Adrian looked taken aback but recovered quickly. 'I didn't see that one coming,' he muttered. 'Right, on you go. Be quick about it.'

Louisa walked out into the hall, Adrian behind her. Clara was there, on her hands and knees, her head and shoulders hidden by the marble-topped console table.

'That's quite some sight,' laughed Adrian as he walked past. There was a thud, then an 'ow!' and Clara slid her head out. She didn't stand up but remained on all fours, her hair fluffed up and a huge grin on her face. But when she saw Adrian, she blanched, before going back under the table.

'Not sure she'll find what she's looking for under there,' said Adrian, half to himself. 'Though it's not the first time Clara's tried to get what she wanted on her knees.'

Louisa halted slightly when he said this, and Adrian coughed but said no more and the two of them continued up the stairs. On the second floor, Louisa could see the light on behind the guest bedroom door, with a pair of slippers placed outside it. This was their pre-agreed sign that the way was clear. Now she thought about it, it was a piece of good luck that Pamela had been in the room with Adrian; hopefully she would delay Iris's return. Wordlessly, Louisa stopped by the door and indicated to Adrian that they had arrived. He didn't even look at her as he went inside.

After another quick check that there was no one in the passageway to see her, Louisa slipped behind the curtains. From here she should be able to hear if Iris came back and forewarn Dulcie. The slippers outside were not just a signal; if the aunt saw them there, the noise she would make picking them up would give Dulcie time to position herself as a maid in the room turning down the bedcovers. Adrian they would leave to splutter and try to explain himself, if it came to that. Hopefully, it wouldn't.

Behind the curtains was a low bay window, and Louisa was able to perch on the sill, drawing her feet up, so that there would be no sign of her toecaps. She tried to relax but her heart was pounding and the blood was rushing through her ears like the waves on the beach at St Leonards. She had a sudden memory of sitting by the sea, eating hot salty chips with Guy Sullivan and had a pang of missing him. For all the complications that had followed that moment, Guy himself was a man of straightforward goodness. She wasn't sure that, right this second, she could say the same for herself.

Louisa's ears pricked suddenly. There was shouting coming from the guest room. Adrian's voice was the loudest, with Dulcie's quieter but insistent. She tried desperately to make out what they were saying but with the thick curtains and a door between her and them, all she could hear were the occasional words: *No right*, *outrageous* and *liar*.

Only a minute later did Louisa realise she had been listening so intently to the shouting that she missed the sound of someone else coming along the hall and stopping by the buttercup bedroom. Louisa pulled the curtains apart, less than an inch, enough to see Pamela standing by the door, her head in the Madame Pompadour wig bent towards it. Louisa couldn't see her face, only her rigid shoulders, but there was no mistaking her fear and seriousness. Like Marie Antoinette facing the guillotine.

What should she do? She knew Pamela mustn't hear any more and mustn't see Dulcie coming out of the room. Dulcie had been adamant that no one knew about her and Adrian, and she wanted to keep it that way. 'People only interfere and make trouble,' she'd said.

Then, before she could make a decision, there was the sound of a loud crack from behind the door. Sudden, quick and grisly. A stick? Bone? Like a starting gun, it sent Pamela running off down the passage, flying down the stairs to the hall. Louisa panicked and fled, too, down the back stairs to the kitchen, but not before she heard the door open and close behind her and heavy footsteps that could only have been Adrian's.

CHAPTER EIGHT

~~~~~

Flushed, Louisa had only just made it into the kitchen when Pamela came in, calling her name in distress.

'Louisa,' she said, her skirts bunched up around her waist where she held them up, so that she didn't trip over them as she ran. Her wig was askew, her face ashen with alarm. 'Louisa, I think something ghastly has happened.'

Louisa steadied herself, grateful that, in her distress, Pamela hadn't noticed Louisa catching her own breath.

'What is it? I'm sure it can't be that bad,' she said, using the standard grown-up's response to a child's anguish. She had learned it from Nanny Blor, who could take the sting out of the worst of her charges' fears, whether a teddy bear's head had come off or there was a snarling stray dog on the village road. Louisa wished Nanny's stalwart person was here now but she was tucked up in bed.

Pamela stopped, let her skirt fall back down and with both hands took Louisa's in hers. 'It's so strange. When I went to Muv's room she said she hadn't sent a message.'

54

Louisa could only bluff this out. 'Perhaps I misheard?'

Pamela shook her head. 'It's not important now. When I got there, Aunt Iris asked me to fetch a book from her room, something she wanted to show Muv. But when I got to the door I could hear voices in there. The door was shut and I didn't dare open it but I swear I overheard Mr Curtis arguing with someone. He has that distinctive voice, doesn't he?' She looked to Louisa for approval, who nodded. 'Then he said, "No one will believe you, no one will care," and there was this terrible sound . . .' Her words faded.

'What sort of sound?' asked Louisa, though she knew perfectly well. It was still echoing in her head.

'A sort of bang, or crack. Like something being broken. Someone being hit. I've just seen Mr Curtis in the hall, so it wasn't him. I think he hit someone and they might be hurt. We need to go and check.'

'No!' Louisa spoke too soon and Pamela looked at her, shocked.

'Why not?'

'Because you don't know that's what happened. You might have misheard.'

Fear turned Pamela's mood quickly and she became indignant. 'I know what I heard.'

'But supposing Mr Curtis didn't hit anybody? What if it was something breaking by accident? Or what if the person he was arguing with was someone here? One of Miss Nancy's friends?' pressed Louisa, more soothingly this time. 'Let's wait and see. Perhaps it's part of the game everyone is playing.'

Pamela was mollified by this. 'Yes, perhaps. Thank you, Louisa.' She looked about her, slightly shamefully. Louisa could see she wanted to get back to the treasure hunt but didn't want to look as if she was dismissing this event too quickly. Louisa did it for her. 'Go back to the others. Go on, have a good time. I'll take a look upstairs, check there's nothing to worry about, and I'm sure there isn't.'

Pamela nodded and ran out of the room.

That was close. Louisa needed to find Dulcie, and fast.

CHAPTER NINE

~~~~~

Louisa raced back up the stairs but before she had reached the top, she almost slammed into Dulcie who reared back in fright. There was a raised weal by one eye, which was only half open and bloodshot; the other was pink from tears and exhaustion.

'He hit you.' It wasn't a question.

'I'm fine.'

'Stop,' said Louisa. They stood still on the stairs, where there was no light except from the passageway at the top and from the kitchen below. Like rats in a pipe. 'What happened?'

'What does it look like?' said Dulcie coldly.

'Is he going to tell on you? Or on me?' Louisa could feel her job slipping away from her grasp.

'No, there's more in it for him if he doesn't,' Dulcie said. 'Let me get past. I know you're trying to look out for me but you're only going to make things worse.'

'He might not but Miss Pamela might.'

This halted Dulcie in her tracks. 'What? What are you saying?'

'She came up to the room. I didn't see her because I was behind the curtains and I didn't hear her because you and Mr Curtis were shouting. She overheard. She might have heard what you were arguing about. Pamela doesn't know you but she might guess something if she sees that black eye. What if she tells his sister?'

Dulcie stared out into the darkness below. 'I'll hide until it's time to take Miss Charlotte back, then. I've got to go. It's always us lot they suspect first.'

'*Dulcie*,' said Louisa, frightened, though for whom she couldn't say. She leant back slightly, and the maid pushed past her and ran off, leaping down the stairs two at a time, into the kitchen and out through the back door. Louisa's legs shook like Mrs Stobie's prized trifle and she walked slowly down and into the kitchen. What did she mean, they were suspected first? Suspected of what?

Standing there, adrenalin and fear coursing through her, she couldn't think straight as to what to do next. She didn't trust Adrian Curtis's next move. Louisa did not like the man, whether for his superciliousness or the pinpricks of deep black that passed for pupils in his pale blue eyes. Nancy found him charming and funny but she was swayed by his sneering jokes, his connections and his Oxford education.

This wasn't helping. For all Louisa knew he was back at the party, telling the others about Dulcie and revealing that she, Louisa, had sent him upstairs with a message that had turned out to be a lie. Pamela would be horrified. Louisa wasn't sure quite what to do with herself. The original plan had seemed so simple, as if nothing could go wrong. The only difficulty had been her conscience, which now she could feel pricking at her like a thousand needles.

Dulcie's coat, which had been left on the back of a chair, had gone, and so had she. Louisa glanced at the clock that hung above the range and assisted Mrs Stobie with her perfectly timed cakes. It had just gone half past one. The kitchen was completely empty

58

and still, though she could hear the occasional thump and running footsteps of the guests as they hunted for their clues. She knew nobody would come in here – servants' quarters were respectfully out of bounds on the whole – but she needed to know if Adrian was causing any trouble. She would go out on the pretence of clearing up after the party, though she knew this was a risk. Mrs Windsor wouldn't approve: after a certain hour, the family and guests were expected to see to themselves and have some privacy from the servants.

But when Louisa went into the hall, it was empty and she couldn't hear much of anything going on. There were signs of party detritus, though nothing too awful – a few glasses, some discarded pieces of costume on a chair by the front door. Where were they all? She felt as if she were intruding and walked on tiptoe so as not to click on the wooden floors. Just as Louisa was wondering whether to go into the drawing room, Nancy appeared. She looked at Louisa a little curiously but not at all crossly. It was easy to see that she was having the time of her life. In her hand she held a matchbox in a silver case that Louisa recognised as one usually in Lord Redesdale's study.

'I came out to see if anything needed clearing away,' said Louisa, but her voice trailed off. She knew Nancy would see through it for the excuse it was. But she was clearly in a forgiving mood.

'Oh, well, do carry on. I'm going to fetch my next clue now. I think I'm doing frightfully well. By the way, have you seen Woman anywhere?'

Louisa was caught off-guard by this. 'Um, not for a while. Why?'

'Sebastian was looking to give her a birthday present after midnight, that's all. I wanted to know what it was.' She gave an arch look. 'Poor baby, I'm sure it's only a tease. He wouldn't really want anything to do with her.'

Louisa chose not to dignify this statement and made her excuses. It would be safer to wait in the kitchen until Dulcie returned to fetch Miss Charlotte.

A scream.

Was it?

Another.

It was. It wasn't inside the house, definitely outside. The sound was faint but definite. Louisa had been in the kitchen reading but alert, like a dog sleeping with one eye closed, waiting for Dulcie. Hastily, she closed her book and ran down the passageway to the hall. Clara came out of the dining room, her silky Tinkerbell costume dulled and flattened now, her hair mussed. Her lipstick had rubbed off, leaving a purplish line around the edges, and her neck was flushed with red marks.

'What was that?' she said to Louisa, 'is it part of the game?'

Louisa felt the blood drain from her face. 'I don't think it was.'

They went out through the front door and onto the path, quickly joined by Ted, who was smoothing back his Dracula hair, looking a little shamed. Sebastian came out soon after, shivering in the night air, still wearing his pirate costume, with most of his shirt's buttons undone. Another cry, of anguish more than fear this time, came from the other side of the church wall. They all rushed through the gateway and as they did Louisa heard Charlotte coming out of the house asking what was going on, her voice shrill. Nancy was close behind her.

Where were Pamela and Oliver? They came last, though separately, Pamela as white as a sheet. Oliver came out blinking, as if he'd been asleep.

By this time, the group had gone through the archway into the graveyard, which lay on the other side of the path that ran alongside the front of the house. The ground was sodden with night-time damp and the moon's light was filtered by clouds, barely pushing through. A faint wind blew and in the stillness could be heard the gentle rustling of leaves in the trees. The gravestones of men, women and children who had lived and died under queens and kings from Elizabeth I to George V were black shapes rising from the earth. Everything was cast in shadow but there was one clear sight, cruelly revealed in a shaft of moonshine.

On the wet ground at the base of the church tower, an arm across his neck and his legs twisted beneath him, mouth open and eyes staring without sight, was the broken, dead body of Adrian Curtis. Standing beside him, with a purpling black eye and hands over her silenced mouth, stood the stricken figure of Dulcie Long.

CHAPTER TEN

G uy and Mary met outside Oxford Circus Tube, as had become their habit in the last few weeks. The first time they almost hadn't recognised each other out of their uniforms and buttoned up in long, heavy coats, partly to keep out the cold and partly to look as incognito as possible. The wretched boredom and frustration of no success had been trying on their tempers but on this morning Guy was hopping on his feet like a six-year-old boy on his birthday, feeling the promise of catching a thief as certain as that of a surprise wrapped up in paper and a ribbon. They'd been instructed to stick to the smaller shops of Great Marlborough Street, which ran parallel to Oxford Street, one or two side streets away – alleys that provided nifty escapes for the shoplifters if they weren't operating with a getaway car.

'*Cars?*' said Mary. 'Do girl thieves have cars?'

Guy nodded. The night before he had picked up some extra information from one of the other sergeants before he left the station and thought it could change their luck. 'Nice cars, too,' he said. 'Alice Diamond, the ringleader, drives a black Chrysler.'

Mary gave an impressive low whistle. 'And they say crime doesn't pay . . .'

'Oi,' said Guy, laughing. 'We'd better hop to it.'

'To do what exactly?' The two of them had slipped through to Little Argyll Street and were walking slowly, eyes squinting against the sun.

'I've had a think,' said Guy. 'What Sergeant Bingham said to me was that although the Forty Thieves have got a reputation for being tall and well dressed they never wear the things they steal. Too risky or too obvious, I suppose. So what they do is pass the goods on to a fence. He sells it all on for them.'

'A fence?' asked Mary.

'That's the name for someone who sells on stolen goods.'

'Who does he sell them to?'

Guy shrugged. 'Black market, I suppose. Some individuals. There's always someone willing to pay cheap for something worth more. But here's my idea.' He paused while they dodged around an old man who was walking slowly in front of them on the pavement. 'Seeing as Soho and these little shops are so close to Oxford Street, it makes sense to me that they'd get rid of the dresses or fur coats they'd stolen as quickly as possible. I think we should look out for things being sold *to* the shops, rather than being sold out of them.'

Mary looked at him and – yes, he was sure – it was with admiration. Well, why not? Guy felt as if all things were possible today.

But Mary said: 'I'm not too sure about that. They're not exactly going to waltz straight from Debenham and Freebody and just sell it over another counter round the corner, are they? It'll be done somewhere out of sight.'

The balloon had been deftly pricked by a sharp pin. 'They might,' Guy blustered.

'They might,' said Mary diplomatically. 'Still, there's no reason we shouldn't look out for the fences. They're men, I suppose?'

Eager to cover up his ignorance, for Sergeant Bingham had only told him the little he knew, Guy nodded sagely. 'Not good men, either. Alice Diamond's band, the Forty Thieves, is closely associated with the Elephant and Castle gang. They all come from the same corner of London.'

'Oh, I've heard of them. Guns and fast cars. There was that chase last year, from Piccadilly and all around London,' said Mary. 'The cars were supposed to be going at fifty miles per hour. I hardly knew you could go that fast.'

Guy looked into the distance as if recalling the very moment the chase had begun. 'Yep, they can. Come on, let's try these shops first.' Guy turned to her with a smile. 'Good luck,' he whispered and took Mary's arm.

Four hours and several shops later, they were feeling tired and disillusioned. It was clear that there were going to be no quick results on this with this new tactic. Avoiding other plain-clothes policemen seemed to be harder than finding one of the Forty or their fences.

'We're not being clever enough,' sighed Guy as they tramped along the street, avoiding the eyes of another pair of station colleagues walking in the opposite direction.

'Is there someone we could talk to, to find out more?' said Mary.

'More about what?'

'I don't know, about the Forty, about the men that sell their stolen goods ... Something that could give us a lead. At the moment we have absolutely nothing.'

Guy was gratified to hear this ambition from Mary. He knew that quite a few of the constables saw this operation as an excuse to do less work, wandering about the streets and stopping off in cafés for tea. But she knew there was a chance here for them to show what they were really made of.

'There is one place we could try,' he said hesitantly. 'It's a risk, I'm not sure anyone there will talk to us. But I've got a secret weapon ...'

'Socks?' said Mary. She was crouched down with a black and white dog nuzzling her hands.

'I inherited the name,' said Guy. 'It's a long story but he was given to me by ...' He wasn't sure how much to go into his acquisition of the dog, a scruffy but cheerful mutt that had belonged to Louisa's uncle, who did not share the pet's character. 'Let's just say the two of us took to each other.'

'I can see that,' laughed Mary. Socks was jumping up at Guy now, keen to earn his favourite rub behind the ears.

'He used to belong to a nasty sort and I have a feeling that some of his old cohorts might talk to us if they see Socks. It's likely they'll know about fences and how to track them down.'

'It's worth a try.'

'Are you sure you want to? It's after six o'clock now, you could just go home.'

'And stare at the walls while I eat my soup? No thanks. I'd much rather do whatever it is we're about to do,' said Mary.

They had gone to collect Socks from Guy's house in Hammersmith, where he still lived with his mum and dad. From there, it was only two short bus rides to Chelsea and the pub that stood at the edge of the Peabody Estate where Louisa Cannon had grown up.

'We're just two people stopping for a drink on the way home, remember?' said Guy to Mary as they approached the Cross Keys.

'Yes, don't worry. Even I have been to a pub before.'

Guy pushed the door open and Socks ran in ahead of them, his nose twitching at the rich smells that lay within. Thankfully, it was a Friday night and the pub was already packed with men primed to spend the contents of the brown envelopes they'd earned that week. Or money they'd pilfered, Guy thought, but he kept it to himself. The air was thick with smoke, covering the pungent sweat of the hardworking and unwashed. Full pints and half-empty glasses lined the bar where the men leaned over, squeezed together like toes in a tight boot. There were a few booths, too, and side tables, with almost every stool taken, but Guy spotted a table vacant in the corner and nodded to Mary to sit there. There were no other women except for the barmaids but Guy could see she was determined not to be intimidated.

'Ginger beer?' he mouthed at her and she nodded.

Guy pushed his way in politely at the bar, the men either side grunting mildly but not stopping him either. He saw a few glances in his direction and knew he looked out of place. Not only was he a stranger, his glasses and squeaky-clean short hair marked him out as a white-collar man. Bravely, he returned one or two of the looks and ordered his drinks. Socks was nowhere to be seen.

Back at the table, Guy sat down and handed Mary her glass. 'What's Socks up to?' he asked.

'Over there,' she said. 'He's found a friend, I'd say.'

Guy looked over and saw an old man patting Socks, who was sitting up, his eyes fixed on the man's pockets. Before too long, the man had reached in and given the dog a titbit of something, with a laugh. The man saw Guy watching and pointed at Socks.

'He yours?' he asked.

Guy nodded and, to his surprise, the old man came over to them, Socks trotting behind. He looked to be about eighty years old with a generous sweep of snow-white hair brushed off his forehead, and though his trousers and jacket were frayed, they looked clean. His eyes reminded Guy of a monkey's, deep set and shining. He found a stool from nearby and put it down by their table, raising his glass to them both as he sat down.

'I take it you're a friend of Stephen's,' he said.

Mary covered up her surprise fast when Guy said, 'From a while back.'

'I always loved his old dog. I'm Jim, by the way.'

'Bertie,' said Guy quickly, 'and this is Mae.'

'Nice to meet you, Mae,' Jim doffed an imaginary cap. 'What happened to Stephen then? He disappeared from here all of a sudden and we none of us heard from him again.'

'Joined the army,' said Guy, taking a long draught to cover up his nerves. 'Probably posted abroad.'

'Probably dodging someone he owes money to,' chuckled Jim.

Guy took a breath and looked around, as if making sure no one could hear them. Jim leaned in.

'That's the official story anyway.'

'What's the unofficial one?'

'Went South. Joined the Elephants.'

Jim sucked his teeth. 'Nasty lot. He'd have a job if he got mixed up with them.'

Guy motioned towards Mary. 'Mae here, she's thinking of join-ing the Forty Thieves.'

'The girls? Clever lot they are. Not sure you can just sign up though. Think you have to be born into it, like.'

'I was,' said Mary, surprising Guy with a bang-on south London accent.

'Oh, going back to your roots are you?'

'Something like that,' Mary answered, still pitch-perfect.

'I thought they didn't work in London no more,' said Jim. 'Got too hot, what with all the police all over their case.'

'Where else could they work?' Guy asked, too quickly. Jim gave him a sharp look.

'Anywhere there's big shops. Manchester, Birmingham. Tell you what.' Jim turned behind him and motioned for another old man to come and join them. He hobbled over slowly, his beer sloshing against the edge of his glass with each heavy step.

'What?' he said when he arrived, though his tone wasn't unfriendly.

'Would you like my stool?' said Guy, getting up.

'Ahh, no,' chuckled the old man. 'Do me good to stand, been sittin' all day. What can I do you for, then?'

'What do you know about the Forty Thieves?' said Jim before turning back to Guy and Mary. 'Pete here – isn't nothing he doesn't know about what goes on in this city.'

Pete gave a low laugh again. 'I don't know about that but the Forty, that's the women. Said to have been around for a couple of hundred years in one form or another. I don't know who the leader is now. We used to have a cousin who got mixed up in it before the war.' He raised an eyebrow. 'You asking?'

Mary pushed her chin out, as if defiant. 'Might be,' she said.

Pete took a drink. 'Well, I don't know how they're going on now. I heard they was moving out of London.'

'That's what I told them,' said Jim.

'The latest wheeze is getting themselves work as maids in big country houses,' continued Pete. 'Easy way to nab stuff.'

'How do they get rid of it?' said Guy.

'Tell you what, my glass is looking a bit empty,' said Jim, waggling it. There was a good third left.

Guy turned to Mary. 'Do us a favour?' he said, and handed her some coins. He felt guilty, knowing she'd have to deal with an unwelcome comment or two from the other drinkers but he didn't want to risk missing anything. She grimaced slightly but got up and went to the bar. Harry leaned over with a leer.

'She your girl?'

'Something like that,' said Guy.

'You want to watch out, if she goes in with the Forty. They don't like their girls to look outside, if you catch my meaning.'

Guy felt his throat constrict, making it hard to swallow. 'What happens?'

'They call in favours from the Elephant lot,' interjected Pete. 'They arrange things. Selling on what they've nicked and, when necessary . . .' He drew a finger across this throat.

Guy was grateful that Mary put two full glasses down on the table before them at that moment. 'Where do they sell it on?'

But he'd pushed his luck. 'You're asking a lot of questions,' said Jim and his voice had turned like cream left out in the sun. 'What's it all for?'

Guy wasn't sure but it seemed as if either Pete or Jim had made some sort of signal without his realising. Three or four men at the bar had turned around and were staring at them. He stood up quickly, Socks scrabbling out from under the table where he'd been dozing at his feet. 'We're grateful to you but we'd best be on our way home now. Come on, Mary.'

'I thought you said her name was Mae,' said Jim, putting his drink down.

'Slip of the tongue,' said Guy and started to push past Jim, with Mary close behind. Several of the men had turned their backs to the bar, watching the scene. Guy had just reached the front door of the pub and closed his grip around the handle when he felt Mary jerk herself back around. The men had advanced towards her but Mary stood her ground, Socks at her side.

'I wouldn't if I was you,' she said in a threatening voice. 'Remember what I told you about what I was born into.'

The men held back, puzzled, and Jim put an arm out to stop them. He looked at Mary and grinned.

'Stand back, lads,' he said. 'No need to fight tonight.'

With relief, Guy opened the door and he, Mary and Socks stepped outside into the black night. They had got what they wanted, after all, and they knew where they needed to go to next.

CHAPTER ELEVEN

﹏﹏

Sebastian broke the silence, stepping forward and gently taking Dulcie by the shoulders. 'You'd better come inside,' he said, his voice thick with whisky and shock.

Louisa tried to catch her eye but Dulcie stared at the ground, her hands still over her mouth, her feet stumbling as Sebastian guided her along. What had happened? A second fight between Dulcie and Adrian? She'd not seen Dulcie since she'd run down the stairs and out of the back door. Anything might have happened. It had.

And Pamela, oh God. What would Pamela say about what she had heard earlier in her aunt's room? Would she tell the police that Louisa had sent her upstairs and that there had been no message? Would she be a suspect? Maybe she *should* feel guilty. She'd let Dulcie into the house and shown her to an empty bedroom in which to have a meeting with a man who, an hour later, was dead. Louisa's throat started to close and she wished everyone would go, quickly, before she started screaming in fear and confusion herself. She had a sudden and complete longing for Guy to be at her side, calm and steady, with his arms around her giving her comfort. She had never felt so alone.

The others were reacting to the terrible sight before them, too. Charlotte had nearly dropped to the ground herself but Ted caught her and walked her back to the house, Nancy on the other side, shielding her and preventing her from looking over her shoulder. Louisa asked Clara to take Miss Pamela, who was not crying but gulped huge hiccups. When the rest of them had walked back out through the archway, Louisa stepped nearer to the body. That he was dead there was no doubt. Already there was a white sheen over his face, the death mask. Rigor mortis had not yet set in and she wondered if she should straighten him out so that there weren't difficulties later, then decided that might be classed as interfering with the scene of the crime. If it was a crime. Perhaps he fell. Might he not have jumped? A sick joke on the treasure hunt. Anger rose fast for a selfish suicide from a nasty man who must have thought life not only short but brutish, too. Then she calmed herself; she must wait for the inevitable arrival of the police. Nothing lay on the ground beside his lifeless body but the black straw hat he had been wearing as his vicar's costume, which had landed some way away. She left that, too, and made her way back to the house.

Lady Redesdale and her sister-in-law were down in the hall in their dressing gowns by the time Louisa came in, as well as a few of the other guests, friends of Lord and Lady Redesdale who had gone to bed early too. Three or four were not there, presumably having managed to sleep through the commotion. Louisa had not followed the others through the front door – whether through habit or a desire not to upset the protocol when everything else was upside down she wasn't sure – but had gone around the back in her usual way and entered into the hall through the green baize door that separated the family's quarters from the servants. Everybody seemed to be standing about as if in a queue at the post office, shuffling their feet quietly and not speaking to each other. The only sound was of Charlotte's crying, an arrhythmic series of sobs and hiccups. The candles had gone out but lights had been switched on, which made everything unnaturally bright, as if it was suddenly morning. Lord Redesdale came out of the telephone cupboard off the hall, also in his dressing gown, tightly belted.

'Right. I've called the police and they're on their way. There's no use in us standing about here in the cold, let's go into the drawing room.'

Sebastian, still holding Dulcie, who was moving slowly and with tiny, unsure movements, like a terrified child, led the way from the hall. Phoebe had come out to see what had gone on but soon returned to her position on the yellow sofa, limping. Pamela was being comforted by her mother, who had upon her face an accustomed look, set not to reveal anything of what she was really thinking. In the drawing room, Louisa poked the fire and added a couple of logs, then fetched blankets from a window seat and gave them to the women. Her movements were professional and mechanical. Nancy had removed her mantilla and Pamela her wig, leaving their heads bare and flattened, their faces sickly white.

'I'll fetch Mrs Windsor and make some hot milk, my lady,' Louisa said, and exited quickly, both thankful to get out of there and desperately anxious that she could not talk to Dulcie. Louisa was sure she couldn't have committed the murder but was there some other part she had played in it? Did she trick Adrian into going to the church tower somehow, knowing he'd meet his death? But if she had, why would she have arranged to meet him earlier in the house? Nothing made sense.

In her sitting room, Mrs Windsor had fallen asleep in an under-sized and overstuffed armchair, her mouth wide open, her book dropped to the floor, a light snore trembling her top lip. Louisa shook her awake by the shoulder and explained what had happened, so far as she could tell.

'Mr Curtis? Dead?' exclaimed the housekeeper.

Louisa nodded. 'They're all in the drawing room, waiting for the police. I'm going to make some hot milk for them. There's breakfast all ready but I don't think anyone will much fancy eating.' Her voice trailed off.

'Yes, yes,' said Mrs Windsor, as she stood, brushing stray hairs off her face, the other hand groping for her cap. She looked as if she was trying to summon from memory the page of a book that explained how to look after one's lord and lady immediately after the sudden death of a guest. It wasn't obvious that any answer came to her.

By the time Louisa and Mrs Windsor returned to the drawing room with the steaming mugs, together with some biscuits and a fruitcake they had found in the larder, there was a policeman in the room. Another policeman, they overheard, was in the churchyard, inspecting the body.

Clara was sitting on the window seat, her knees under her chin and a blanket wrapped around her shoulders. She took the mug from Louisa gratefully. Louisa dared to talk to her. The American had always been friendlier to her than the others. 'What's happened?' she whispered.

Clara looked at the group by the fire. Lady Redesdale had an arm around Pamela's shoulders, who had stopped hiccupping and now looked merely frightened and exhausted. Sebastian was staring into the fire, his hands in his pockets, and Charlotte was next to Nancy, who seemed very much out of her depth as the young woman cried and cried beside her. Ted, divested of his Dracula cloak, was talking quietly to a serious-looking Lord Redesdale. Although the fire had been well stoked, there was a chill in the room. Louisa could feel the cold creep into her fingertips. She realised Dulcie wasn't there.

'They've taken the maid off for questioning,' said Clara. 'Looks as if she did it. Can you *imagine*?' She stopped to take a gulp of milk. 'I mean, she was Charlotte's chaperone, her mother's *maid*. They've had a murderer living under their roof.' Her big eyes grew wider. 'They fed her. They paid her.' She shuddered and squeezed her eyes shut, as if hardly able to believe what had gone on right before her. Though of course, she hadn't seen it. Nobody had.

Louisa nearly dropped the tray.

'She didn't do it!'

It was out before she could stop herself.

Clara looked up at her in surprise and there was movement by the fire as one or two heads turned in their direction.

'Beg pardon,' gasped Louisa. She put the tray down on a side table and fled, without a thought as to where she was running or even exactly what she was running from.

Only a few steps into the hallway she felt a heavy hand on her shoulder.

'Come with me, miss,' said the policeman. 'Our detective inspector would like a word with you.'

Louisa turned around, rolling her shoulder so that he would take his hand off. Old habits died hard. He was a young policeman, his hair cut so short behind his ears there was a pink line around the edges. He looked both a little afraid of her and equally determined she would not slip away from him. Something of her old insouciance came back, a memory of an instinct that had never been far from the surface all those years ago.

'Keep your hair on,' she snapped. 'I was only going to the kitchen.'

'Follow me,' he said, and turned. It was infuriating that he knew she would obey.

'You don't know the way,' she said. 'I presume we're going to Lord Redesdale's study?' If there was a detective inspector carrying out interviews, she knew that's where he'd have been sent. She pushed past him and marched quickly, ignoring his protests before he fell into a sullen silence as they walked down the passage, across the hall and along further corridors before reaching the sturdy door of the Child-Proof Room. Here, she stood to one side. She had no wish to orchestrate the next step.

Dulcie's words from their last conversation rang in her head: 'It's always us lot they suspect first.'

CHAPTER TWELVE

Inside the room, a man Louisa assumed was the local detective inspector was sitting behind Lord Redesdale's desk, which as usual was covered in the detritus of his household accounting, newspaper clips and fishing paraphernalia. The winter months were when Lord Redesdale spent his time untangling lines and re-tying feathers onto hooks. There was a small desk lamp with a green glass shade that had been switched on, its definite arc throwing his eyes and forehead into shadow. All she could see was a magenta bulbous nose, pocked like the moon, overhanging a neat moustache and fleshy lips. He sat with his arms folded, leaning back as far as he was able on the wooden chair. Lord Redesdale was not a believer in comfort while work was being done.

In front of the desk was a spindly chair that usually had nothing heavier than a few copies of *Country Life* resting on it but now bore the weight of Dulcie Long. Louisa could see her shoulders tensed, her back straight. Every hair on her head seemed to be alive to the atmosphere but she did not turn when the policeman and Louisa came in. Dulcie seemed unable to take her eyes off the moustache opposite her, like a rabbit caught in headlights.

'This is Miss Louisa Cannon, sir,' said the policeman. 'She's the live-in maid, the one who was with the party when the body was discovered.'

'Thank you, Peters,' said the lips in the spotlight. 'You'd better return to the group in the drawing room. Make sure nobody leaves.'

'Yes, sir,' said Peters, and left.

Louisa stood behind Dulcie. She could almost feel the body heat coming off her and longed to be able to put a reassuring hand on her shoulder. But if she did that, she couldn't save her own skin. One of them had to get out of here.

The detective inspector leaned forward and Louisa saw his red-rimmed eyes. He'd been called out late, most probably had had to get out of bed for it, and he wasn't looking too thrilled. Still, the effort had been made for a death. It deserved his proper attention. His eyes narrowed and focused on Louisa.

'Do you know this woman?'

Louisa thought back to that night in the Elephant and Castle. 'Yes,' she said.

He made an impatient click and spoke again. 'How *well* do you know her?'

'Not very, sir. We met when I accompanied Miss Pamela to a supper in Mayfair last month, at Lady Curtis's house.' Each formal word was another brick in her fort.

'And did you meet again?'

'Tonight, sir. She came in through the back door, which I was expecting. It had been previously arranged with Lady Redesdale that she would accompany Miss Charlotte back to the Watney house. Hooper was to drive them back.'

The inspector made another attempt to lean back, failed and cracked his knuckles instead. He looked first at Dulcie and then at Louisa, each stare a shade too long for comfort. No movement came from Dulcie, though there was a faint creak from the chair.

'What time did Miss Long arrive?'

'I couldn't be sure, sir. It was late, the party had almost finished and there were just a few of them left.'

'You were alone in the kitchen when she arrived?'

'Yes, sir. Mrs Stobie, that is, the cook, had gone to bed. The maids had gone home and Mrs Windsor was in her sitting room.'

'Did you show her to a bedroom upstairs?'

Louisa wasn't sure where this was leading – did he know that Dulcie and Adrian had had a meeting? That she had helped this happen? Surely not. Dulcie had given her word that nobody would discover that Louisa was a part of it, or they would both lose their jobs. She took the risk that Dulcie had not given her away.

'No, sir. I left the kitchen when she arrived, to go and clear away any empty glasses from the party. I assumed she would remain there to wait until it was time to take Miss Charlotte back to the Watneys.'

'Where were you when Miss Long was heard screaming outside?'

'I'd gone back to the kitchen and was getting the breakfast ready,' said Louisa.

'And was Miss Long there?'

Louisa hesitated for the briefest second. 'No, sir. I assumed she had already gone to fetch Miss Charlotte.' She hoped this wasn't giving Dulcie away but what else could she do?

The inspector leaned forward onto the desk. He lifted a cloth like a waiter revealing *steak au poivre* beneath a silver dome but what Louisa saw was a glinting collection of jewellery: a long string of pearls, a sapphire and diamond bracelet, a few rings, pairs of earrings. Louisa almost jumped with the shock. Had Dulcie stolen these things? She felt betrayed and yet ... She knew Dulcie had been one of the Forty Thieves, didn't she? And she, Louisa, had let her into the house. She had knowingly let a thief into the house and shown her to an empty bedroom, with the assurance that she would have at least half an hour undisturbed in there. What else might that make her guilty of? Louisa's heart hammered and she could feel her breath getting shorter. She needed to concentrate on staying calm, and innocent. Whatever happened, she was innocent of murder.

'You see, what I can't understand is how Miss Long came to have these in her pocket when she was due to collect Miss Charlotte,' began the inspector. 'Not only did she have time to go to Miss Iris Mitford's bedroom, but she apparently chanced upon a room that was safely empty. Yet Miss Long has never been to this house before.' His voice was calm. He spoke with all the assurance of a professor who has concluded a mathematical equation in minutes that had bewildered the students for days. He knew, beyond the shadow of a doubt, that he was absolutely right.

Louisa knew that Pamela would tell the inspector about the argument she had overheard between Mr Curtis and a woman, who could only have been Dulcie. Dulcie's eye had been blackened by Mr Curtis, she had been found with a pocketful of stolen jewels and was standing by the body when seen for the first time by the rest of the party. She made a decision quickly and could only pray that she wouldn't come to regret it.

'I can't explain that to you, sir,' she said. 'After I left the kitchen I didn't see her again until I heard the screams from outside and . . . well, you know the rest.'

'Seems I do,' said the inspector, and Dulcie's shoulders began to shake. 'You can go now, Miss Cannon, but I don't want you going anywhere, you understand? Nobody is to leave this house.'

CHAPTER THIRTEEN

~~~~~

S hortly after breakfast was over, served at eight o'clock sharp as usual – wild horses and murder unable to drag Lord Redesdale from his daily routine – everybody who had gone out to the churchyard the night before was gathered in the library at the request of Detective Inspector Monroe, as he had now introduced himself. Louisa, as one of the witnesses to have seen Dulcie by the body of Adrian Curtis, was included. The few guests that had slept through everything had either left early, in horror probably, or were taking coffee in the morning room.

The blue-tinted winter sun shone through the wide bay window. Remains of the party had been cleared from the night before but for an ashtray that had been left carelessly on a high shelf and not spotted by Ada who had been in at dawn to sweep and dust. The sofa had been pushed back into the centre of the room and the wooden chairs for the chaperones had been stacked and moved. With borrowed jerseys worn over their costumes, wigs and props discarded long ago, the guests were pale imitations of their borrowed personas. Pamela's eyes were red but she was hardly alone: nobody bore the effects of a refreshing night's sleep. Aside from the inspector's interviews that carried on through the night, there hadn't been enough beds made up and any empty room would have been too cold, so most of them had kipped on armchairs or sofas in the drawing room with scratchy woollen blankets.

Louisa scanned the library and saw Lord Redesdale standing by the chimneypiece, tapping out his pipe into a saucer. Nancy, Clara and Charlotte sat together on the sofa, slightly apart, with the bereaved sister smoking a cigarette, no longer bothering with the long silver holder she had had the night before. Phoebe had her leg propped up on a low stool, while Sebastian sat on a small armchair, legs crossed, also smoking. Ted was standing by the piano and Oliver Watney sat on the stool, ashen, his hands shaking as he pretended to flick through sheets of music. He could hardly be planning to give a recital.

Lady Redesdale, her sister-in-law Iris and Pamela sat on the window seat, not touching and not looking at each other. Dulcie was not in the room.

'Thank you all for gathering this morning,' Monroe started, ignoring a huff from Lord Redesdale. 'I understand some of you are keen to get away back to London but it was important that I talk to you all together first. I'm sure I don't need to explain why. You'll be relieved to hear that I think we have already found our culprit.'

He gave a small cough, as if suppressing a look of pleasure. Louisa's heart started thumping like a rabbit's back foot.

'All of this will of course have to be submitted to the coroner's office for their report, but I have arrested Dulcie Long for both the theft of a significant amount of jewellery and the murder of Mr Adrian Curtis.'

Louisa reeled at this but had to contain herself and not let anyone see her shock. The knowledge – and the guilt – that Dulcie had stolen from the bedroom had been more than enough to bear last night. Hearing the detective say he had arrested Dulcie for *murder* felt like a kick to her stomach. She had been as naive as Pamela, and she had had the vanity to call herself worldly. Oh God.

Charlotte started to weep again and Clara took her hand. Louisa noticed Charlotte snatch it away without interrupting the rhythm of her tears.

'It seems that there was an argument between Mr Curtis and Miss Long shortly before his death, when he followed her into the bedroom of Miss Iris Mitford. We can surmise that he saw her stealing the jewels and confronted her over it.' He glanced around the room, as if to be sure he held his audience, before carrying on. 'Miss Pamela overheard their argument, as well as the sound of what we believe was Mr Curtis hitting Miss Long, from which she sustained a severe black eye.

'Miss Curtis has discreetly informed me that there had been, shall we say, a relationship of a certain kind between Mr Curtis and Miss Long in the recent past and it is my contention that she lured him to the bell tower of the church with the promise of a further liaison.' He coughed, this time to cover up embarrassment, and Lord Redesdale went almost puce with repressed fury. Lady Redesdale simply looked away.

'There, using the element of surprise, she succeeded in her ultimate aim and pushed Mr Curtis out of the high gap, from where he fell to what we believe would have been an almost instant death. Miss Long then ran out and in the realisation of what she had done began the screams which alerted the rest of the party, and that is when most of you came out to the churchyard to discover both the victim and the culprit.'

Monroe looked around again and took out a large handkerchief to give his nose – no less brutally purple in the cold light of day – a long, slow wipe. There was complete silence.

Louisa felt dazed. She hadn't suspected Dulcie of coming to the house to steal but she had been completely wrong. She'd told herself that they shared something similar, understood each other in a way that made them sympathetic. But she realised now that that didn't mean she really knew who Dulcie was. In short, she had to face the probability that Dulcie had done it and betrayed her, too.

CHAPTER FOURTEEN

⁓

Guy had taken the conversation at the Cross Keys pub as a warning not to try and go near the dangerous-sounding fences, if, as he suspected, they were drawn from the Elephant and Castle lot. So they were back to trying to find the women, the Forty Thieves. To this end, he and Mary Moon (he couldn't help but call her by her full name, even in his head), had devised a system which he found rather pleasing at first. He would walk alone into a shop, perhaps a furrier's or a jeweller's, the sort of place they imagined would appeal to a Forty thief, and engage the most senior member of staff in a detailed conversation about their wares. Thus, any passing Forty member would be tempted into theft because they would believe that the very person who might otherwise notice their tricks – Guy knew he'd be suspicious as a plain-clothes policeman, being a man in a woman's shop – was distracted. Mary was to come into the shop five or so minutes after Guy had entered and would be able to observe easily any sign of a fellow customer helping themselves to goods with no intention to pay.

Well, that was the plan. But in two days of loitering around the small shops of Great Marlborough Street Guy had suffered lengthy monologues of information on the manufacturing history, design points and price value of a number of items, including – but not limited to – ladies' dress watches, fox-fur stoles, a dog collar studded with paste jewellery and a set of crystal glasses. So far the closest they had got to danger was the moment when Guy had almost bought the dog collar for Socks. There had been absolutely no sight of any thieving while he and Mary were on the lookout. In fact, he had the distinct sensation that it was the two of them that were beginning to be eyed suspiciously by the shopgirls.

At the end of the previous shift, news had reached Guy that a third arrest had been made. There was no confirmation as yet of any connection with the Forty but there had nonetheless been several pints drunk in the pub around the corner from Vine Street station in the evening. Even Cornish had dropped in for a glass of whisky and a congratulatory slam on the back of the arresting officer. Guy had left after two pints and walked most of the way home, grateful for the cold night air on his face as if it could blow away the storm clouds that gathered somewhere behind his forehead.

The following morning, as he and Mary walked down Oxford Street, stepping around four-day-old puddles, sleek with oil, the large department stores reared into view and he made a decision.

'We'll do Debenham and Freebody today, Constable Moon,' said Guy, careful not to break the rhythm of their walk.

'Aren't some of the men posted there already?' Mary had asked, pulling at her left earlobe as she spoke. It was a tic that Guy had begun to find rather endearing.

'Maybe, but we've got the advantage with you. We know the bigger shops are reporting thefts. But two men standing in a dress department look wrong, the Forty won't go anywhere near them. They might as well be carrying signs to say they're police. But with you, no one would suspect a thing.'

'You say that, but we haven't had any joy yet.' Conscious, perhaps, of her lobe-pulling, Mary crossed her arms. She didn't pout, it wasn't her style, but Guy knew she was raring to score an arrest. He knew this because he felt exactly the same way.

'Think about it. Stands to reason they're more likely to target a bigger place. Easier to hide and plenty of genuine customers about. They know there aren't enough staff to watch them even if they act suspiciously. The last arrest was made there.'

'But what if we're on someone else's territory?' That earlobe again.

'We'll cross that bridge if we have to. I think Cornish will be less worried about that if we've nabbed a Forty, don't you?'

'Hmmm, yes, I suppose so.' They had stopped at the corner of the road and while they waited for a gap in the traffic, Mary took a cigarette out of a thin silver case. She offered Guy one, who shook his head but smiled as he did so.

'I know,' she said, 'but it feels rude somehow not to ask you anyway.' She handed him the lighter and he lit the cigarette for her. Another ritual. They had been quick to create these patterns with each other and he felt a stirring of something in the pit of his belly. Whether it was pleasure or unease he couldn't quite say.

They weren't in uniform, which blurred the lines too. Without the clean, sharp cut of their navy jackets and polished boots, there had been a gradual but definite slip into civilian behaviour even when on duty. Guy was dressed a shade more elegantly than his usual Saturday civvies, with a tiepin and the folded triangle of a starched white handkerchief peeping out of his breast pocket. It was designed to give the illusion of a man used to spending time in discreetly expensive shops, as he asked intricate questions about the silk lining of a mink stole.

Guy wondered if Mary had adopted a different character with

her outfit, as surprising as the accent she had adopted in the pub, but he thought probably not. Her dark grey suit with its pleated skirt and narrow jacket were fashionable but not vogueish. Was that what he meant? He'd heard his sister-in-law describe someone with this bastardised word and he could hear that it was a compliment, so he assumed that it meant someone who looked as if they could be photographed by *Vogue*. At any rate, Mary Moon certainly looked that way when she turned slightly sideways, twisting her narrow waist so that it looked even tinier and arching her spine as she leant her head back to blow out a plume of smoke. It was a funny thing because usually when someone was seen out of uniform for the first time, it took a puff out of their sails; they looked less authoritative. With Mary it was different. In her uniform she looked like a small girl who'd been fishing in a dressing-up box but her own clothes gave her back her courage. It was easier to see the spunk it must have taken for her to join the police in the first place.

'Let's go to Debenham and Freebody,' Guy persisted, 'and at least try. If we don't strike gold, or diamonds . . .' He grinned. 'Well, no one will be any the wiser.'

Mary stamped the cigarette beneath her foot and adjusted her hat. It was her sister's and a touch too large for her, slipping down over her forehead when she looked down, but it was expensive-looking with navy netting that pulled down to the tip of her nose.

'Yes,' she said, 'let's go.'

CHAPTER FIFTEEN

Two hours later they had walked over almost every inch of the department store Debenham and Freebody. Guy had picked up and inspected several glass vases, silk ties and a full cutlery set in polished silver. Mary had resisted trying on a number of adorable frocks in the name of research. Their stomachs were starting to rumble now, more from boredom than actual hunger, but the promise of a bowl of soup and a warm roll in a nearby café would soon be too difficult to resist. At least they hadn't seen any of their fellow policemen and Guy wondered if the ones who had been sent there had decided to try pastures new as well. As the lunch hour approached, the shop began to fill up with secretaries and telephone operators, lingering over the cosmetics and perfumes on the ground floor. Mary was idling, trying out a cherry-coloured Revlon lipstick on the back of her hand and Guy was impatient to get out of there. He wasn't comfortable standing about with so many women peering at themselves closely in minuscule mirrors.

'I'm going up to the haberdashery department,' he said.

Mary blushed and rubbed out the deep purple smudge. 'I'm coming with you.'

Guy was comforted by the bolts of material that lined the walls up on the third floor, with a smell of cotton that reminded him of home. At one end, standing by a long table, a saleswoman pulled out long reams of a vivid green linen from a thick roll before slicing it off expertly with her pinking shears. She looked the same age as his mother and shared the same no-nonsense style of all those women who had grown middle-aged before the war: grey hair pulled back into a bun, half-moon glasses balancing above her eyebrows, ready to slide down when needed. Even though he had seen her just that morning, Guy felt a pang of missing his mother. He needed her reassuring smile and for her to tell him that everything would work out just fine.

The assistant and the woman who was buying the cloth were apparently sharing a joke, both stifling giggles as the cloth was folded and put in a brown paper bag. What did women always find to laugh about together? Even when they hardly knew each other, just a nod and a wink was enough to set them off. It was like all of the female sex were in on a secret joke that men would never – could never – understand. Mary was standing by the sewing machines, picking up different packets of needles and reading the backs, as if searching for a very specific size, though Guy could see that her eyes were constantly looking around the department. It was busy now, with several people looking through the spools of cotton thread, quilting squares and yards of ribbon.

Guy's eye was caught by one woman who was rather taller than the rest and elegantly dressed. She didn't strike him as a telephonist somehow, with her long brocade coat and a smart black hat. She carried herself with confidence and moved slowly around the department, fingering the edges of various bolts of fabric but not apparently requesting assistance from anyone. It was then Guy realised that there was a cluster of three plump shopgirls standing by the tills, their heads bobbing up and down as they whispered to each other, their hands fluttering. With their tucked-in white shirts they looked like a trio of finches pecking for seeds. Slowly – too slowly – Guy realised the beady eyes of the shopgirls were following the tall woman around the room and she was clearly getting them into something of a flutter. Who was she? Perhaps a music hall star – she had a slightly old-fashioned look about her, though she couldn't have been much more than twenty-five years old. She might be one of those Hollywood actresses from the pictures that Mary liked to read about in magazines; she'd tried to interest him in one or two of the articles but they weren't for him. He couldn't really understand why anyone would want to know what an actor ate for lunch or what their house looked like. Wasn't the point to believe in their character on the screen, not know what they were like in real life? And who they were in real life could hardly be as interesting as their persona in the film, where they might be a princess or a dragon-slayer, or even—

A hand clutched his arm and Guy turned round to see Mary, her hat slipped so far forwards he could only just see her eyes behind the net. Her breathing was shallow and quick.

'What is it?' he said, but not loudly.

'Over there,' said Mary, nodding her head in the direction of the long table where the green material had been laid out only a few minutes earlier. The shop assistant had her glasses on her nose now as she stood by her table, quite still with the shears in her hand, watching the tall woman too. But that wasn't who Mary was looking at. Mary had her grey eyes fixed on a girl standing in front of a stack of silk rolls wearing a cheap-looking buttoned up long coat with an unusually wide skirt beneath it. If her face wasn't so pinched, Guy would think she had indulged in a few too many suet puddings.

'Have you seen anything?' he whispered.

Mary shook her head. 'Not quite but ... there's something off. Look at her skirt, it's too big.'

The birds by the shop till had stopped their pecking and although one of them was ringing up a customer's cloth on the till, the others were rooted to the spot. Then the tall woman, who had been moving slowly, picked up her pace, turned right and disappeared around the corner. When she was out of sight, the shopgirls visibly exhaled and when Guy looked at the one with the glasses, she, too, had a look of relief pass over her face before she busied herself with tidying her station again. Mary's hand, however, clutched his arm as tightly as before. She jerked him and nodded again at the pinched-face woman, who had moved away from the stack of silks and was edging towards the doorway, her hands in her pockets, almost as if she was holding herself in.

Guy shook his arm and Mary let go, then he walked towards the doorway, his steps small and fast. Before he could get there, a large woman with a straw shopping basket on one arm stood in his way, her bulk almost the width of the narrow aisle between the cutting table and a wall of material. She was holding a pince-nez with her other hand and leaning down to peer at the pattern.

'Excuse me,' said Guy, not wanting to touch her but needing, urgently, for her to stand up straight and give him enough room to squeeze past. Out of the corner of his eye, he could see the wide back of the cheap coat heading fast towards the exit. The woman straightened up but turned to face him, her bulk and the basket blocking the way, the pince-nez still held up, through which she narrowed her eyes at Guy.

'I beg your pardon, sir,' she said in an unapologetic tone that indicated an impatience with the serving class. 'I was merely—'

'My apologies, madam,' said Guy, not willing to hear what she was doing. He really didn't care. 'I must get past.'

The woman raised her shoulders, lowered her pince-nez and took a deep breath. She was preparing to deliver a lecture on manners and the behaviour of men in what was clearly a department for women who needed to take their time over domestic requirements. At least, Guy assumed she was preparing to say this but he wasn't going to stick around to find out if he was right or wrong.

Then, as the wide skirt disappeared around the corner from his view, Guy saw Mary streak after her, the hat bumping up and down as she almost ran. If he was Theseus, he'd slay this Minotaur with its opera glasses but he was no Greek hero. Guy turned his back on the beast and followed another way out of the maze, making his way towards the exit in time to hear Mary proclaim, delight in her voice, 'I think you'd better come with me, miss.'

As if a jolt of electricity had passed through all the persons there, the atmosphere was changed in a second. Guy ran around to Mary, trembling as she held on to her hostage, who was jerking her arm and shouting that this was an outrage. Guy took her other arm and – he couldn't help himself – turned to Mary with a wide grin on his face; he wiped it off when the young woman started yelling even more loudly.

'Keep quiet,' said Guy. 'Anything you need to say to us can be said at the station.'

The thought flashed through his mind that he hadn't actually seen the woman steal anything; he hoped to God that Mary had. As if reading his mind, she stopped pulling and resorted to sullen mutterings about the fact that she hadn't done anything, the assault on her person and character and so on. Guy was intensely aware of the eyes of the customers as they escorted her through the store, including an uncomfortable ride in the lift down to the ground floor. As they were about to exit into the street, Guy and Mary holding an elbow each, a red-faced man in a morning suit came puffing up. He gave Mary a quizzical look and addressed Guy.

'Can you tell me what's going on here?'

Guy pulled up short, aware that he and Mary weren't in uniform. The scenario must have looked rather peculiar.

'I'm Mr Northcutts,' continued the man, his face settled down to peony pink, his white hair sticking out in tufts. 'The general manager,' he explained, seeing his name elicited no reaction.

'Beg pardon, sir,' said Guy. 'I'm Sergeant Sullivan of Vine Street police station, and this is Constable Moon.' The manager didn't even bother to look around at Mary but kept his eyes on Guy. 'We've made an arrest – we have reason to believe this young lady has been stealing items from your store, in the haberdashery department.'

'Yes, yes,' said Mr Northcutts, batting this aside, 'but what about ...' He lowered his voice and leant in towards Guy. The hostage went completely quiet and leant in too.

'What about ...?'

'Alice Diamond.'

Guy felt the woman respond and he clutched her arm a little tighter.

'She was in here, too,' said Mr Northcutts. 'The shopgirls know what she looks like. It's an old trick – she comes in, distracts them and while they're all watching her, the likes of this one –' he jerked a thumb '– get away with it. Well, almost.'

Alice Diamond had been in there too? The pride Guy had felt in nabbing a shoplifter was immediately obliterated by the fear that Cornish would discover he'd let the prize slip away. Not for the first time, Guy cursed his short-sightedness. It was as if he thought he'd caught a ten-pound cod only to find nothing more than a mackerel and weeds on the end of his hook. He was almost tempted to let the woman go. But not quite.

Mr Northcutts was still talking, expressing his sorrow that the police time and again missed the biggest trick of all, the cost to his store ... Guy cut him off.

'Mr Northcutts, I think you'd better come and give a statement if there's anything you've witnessed that could be important to this charge. But if you would please excuse us now, we had better proceed to the station.'

There was silence as several pairs of eyes watched the scene unfold before them. The anecdote would enliven many a dinner and pint in the pub that evening. People bustled through the doors from the street, only to be pulled up short by an arrangement of still figures dotted on the shop floor, some mid-poise, like casts of Pompeii.

'I ain't done nothing,' the captive shouted as Guy and Mary walked her through the door and out into the cold air of the street. They could only hope that she *had*.

CHAPTER SIXTEEN

❦

Louisa had always been enchanted when winter wrapped its icy arms around the Cotswold stone of Asthall Manor, perhaps because it had been in this cold season that she had first seen the house and its spell had been cast upon her. Awaking on that very first morning, she had seen the carpet of frost rolled out on the fields beyond the garden wall; close up were cobwebs laced with tiny, frozen drops of dew. It had seemed to her like another world and, in a way, it was. Growing up in London, she had had to look up to the sky to see a distance as great as the one she could cast across the land owned by Lord Redesdale.

The girls would complain about the cold, stamping their feet dramatically in the nursery and threatening to close the windows their mother insisted were kept open by six inches all the year round (though of course they never would dare). Nanny Blor chafed them gently, fetching woollen jumpers that smelled of lavender from the dried bundles kept in the drawers to deter hungry moths. Louisa almost enjoyed the tingle at the end of her nose, while her hands warmed on the range in the kitchen. Each morning, before the sun was up, Ada would silently lay and light a fire in Lady Redesdale's bedroom before going down to the kitchen to help Mrs Stobie prepare breakfast. Even now she was married and lived out in the village she still came in for this task and Louisa wondered who might have to do it when she left: Ada had confided she was pregnant. 'An early Christmas present,' she'd laughed, and though Louisa was happy for her, at the same time she saw only years of further domestic drudgery ahead for her friend.

Winter lost its allure in the days after the death of Adrian Curtis. Unbroken, indistinguishable chilly hours followed one after the other as if they would never end. Even sunrise and sunset showed no difference in their grey light. Nobody had the desire to engage in their usual pastimes, all of which seemed either too frivolous or tiring. Nancy whined of exhaustion, which was most unlike her, and even Lady Redesdale had taken to her bed for three days, complaining of a heavy cold, asking for soup to be brought to her on a tray twice a day. Lady Redesdale was never ill. Lord Redesdale went on long walks with his dogs, coming home as dusk fell and retiring immediately to the child-proof room, where the fire now had to be laid each evening. The dining room was left dark and Mrs Stobie was querulous, uncertain each mealtime as to who was about and if anybody would eat anything she cooked.

Up in the nursery, Nanny Blor and Louisa tried to maintain normality for the younger ones who at least remained unaware of what had gone on, though they certainly knew something had happened. Debo sucked her thumb rather more ferociously than usual – 'you'll have no thumb left,' Nanny Blor would say three times a day – but otherwise played quietly with her doll's house, a battered thing now that five sisters had already been through it. Decca and Unity, when not in the schoolroom with the governess, sat together on a window seat, talking in low whispers. They didn't appear to be playing a game but whatever they were doing with words was giving them great amusement. It was something of a relief to hear giggles spiralling out of their bedroom.

Diana, who had already been in a white fury for not being allowed to attend the party even before she realised she had missed probably the greatest sensation that Asthall had ever seen, withdrew into herself entirely except for when either Pamela or Nancy were around, when she would pester them with questions and berate them for not sticking up for her to be at the party in the first place. This had resulted in either slammed doors or tears, if not both. Either way, it was wearying behaviour.

Louisa was dazed. Though Ada had tried to press her for details, she had found that she was unwilling to discuss any of it. She felt a vague sense of guilt, as if she had made this happen, though she knew rationally she had not. Had she encouraged Dulcie in some way? Had she denied to herself the truth of who she was and what she was capable of, blinded by the dazzling glamour of the Forty? Or had it been an overwhelming desire to help Dulcie, to enable her to escape her past as she herself had done? She didn't know. Everything she had been sure of now seemed alien. She tried to choose a book from the library to read and stood before the shelves, unable to remember which authors she liked. Her appetite deserted her, too, as if she could no longer judge what tasted well and what did not. She realised after three days that she had not once glanced at a looking glass. There was an absence of physical self so strong that when she walked down the path to the village one afternoon she had started at the sight of her shadow stretching out long before her.

On the morning after, the rest of the party had left quickly, although they had been forced to wait for DI Monroe's permission. When he had told them his enquiries for the moment were over, they had stirred stiffly in symphony, like a chain of paper dolls. Hot tea and toast had revived them enough to set off. Clara left with Ted, who pulled his car out of the drive slowly; Sebastian alarmed them as his car spun on the wet gravel and looked for a fraction of a second as if it were heading straight for the giant oak that grew in the middle of the drive. Charlotte, however, had stayed, too hysterical to go anywhere. Lady Redesdale, against her belief in 'the good body' healing itself, had called in the local doctor and he had sedated the grieving sister, allowing her to sleep straight through for nearly two days. Louisa divided her duties between Nanny Blor in the nursery and Charlotte in the blue bedroom, which necessitated much running up and down the stairs. At one point she found herself holding on to the banister rails as if climbing a steep ladder that threatened to fall in a high wind.

If the inquest did not demand an autopsy, Adrian's funeral would be held ten days later. Louisa had been in Charlotte's room, stoking the fire, when she had heard her wake from her long deep sleep. Charlotte was lying sideways, knees pulled up high, staring wide-eyed at her. It was possible that she couldn't remember where she was.

Louisa rushed over and poured out a glass of water, then helped Charlotte sit up and drink it. When Charlotte had finished the last drop, she sank back, exhausted from the effort. Then her eyes blinked open and she sat up again, springing forward like a cuckoo in a clock.

'Adrian,' she said.

'Try not to get upset,' coaxed Louisa, knowing she was talking in meaningless platitudes.

'He's dead.' Charlotte spoke as if she hoped she were asking a question when she knew it was a statement of fact.

Louisa nodded. 'Let me get Miss Nancy for you.'

'No!' said Charlotte, but then she seemed to take in her surroundings, and Louisa, and realised she needed to know what was going on.

In the end, it was Pamela that Louisa found first. She had come in from riding and was walking shoeless across the hall in her jodhpurs and jacket, her hair mussed because she could never be bothered with a net under the hat. Pamela had shown another side to herself in the last few days, a resilience and refusal to panic that had been impressive. Her refuge, as ever, was horses and food, and so long as she was indulging in either of those, she seemed to be almost her normal self. Louisa judged that, on balance, Pamela might be better than Nancy for Charlotte in this present state.

'Miss Pamela,' called out Louisa.

Pamela stopped and turned. 'Yes?'

'Miss Charlotte has woken. Might you go up and see her? I think she needs the company.'

Pamela took this in, then pushed her shoulders back. 'Yes, absolutely. Send up some tea and toast, won't you? Or better still, bring it yourself.'

Louisa was taken aback; Pamela had never issued an order before. 'Yes, Miss Pamela, right away.'

They went their separate ways.

CHAPTER SEVENTEEN

～～～

The inquest into the death of Adrian Curtis took place at Banbury Crown Court just five days after the event. Lord Redesdale wanted nothing to do with it but all those who had discovered Dulcie beside the body were requested to be at the inquest in case any of the statements taken down on the night needed to be corroborated by a second interview. This announcement had caused a certain amount of shouting, which culminated in an unhappy encounter between Lord Redesdale and his favourite dog. In the end, Lord Redesdale drove one car with his wife, Nancy and Charlotte, while Louisa and Pamela were driven in by Oliver Watney's mother, with her son, who looked throughout the entire journey as if he was about to be sick out of the window. He didn't manage a word beyond 'Good morning,' but the mother spoke enough for the two of them, making her feelings of outrage and disappointment very clear. Pamela stared out of the window and Louisa wanted to squeeze her hand but was stopped by the realisation that Pamela was too old for that to be comforting any more. Yet, she could have done with someone squeezing *her* hand. (Debo seemed instinctively to understand this and would tightly grip Louisa's palm with her chubby, soft fingers when they walked around the garden.)

The courtroom was disappointingly unimpressive, with slate-grey walls, a large desk for the coroner and rows of benches for those attending. The jury with two women and ten men sat off to the side, each one studiously avoiding the glances of anyone but the coroner. Louisa was shocked by Dulcie's appearance. In only a few days she seemed to have grown thinner and her pretty face was pale. The black eye she had sustained that fateful evening had faded, with shades of yellow and purple only hinted at around the edges. She caught Louisa's glance but looked away again quickly; a policeman stood beside her but she wore no handcuffs.

The coroner, Mr Hicks, began by introducing himself and expressing regret for the events of the early hours of November the twenty-first and asked the jury to listen attentively to the evidence placed before them. Mr Hicks emphasised that the inquest was to establish the cause of death and was not a trial but statements had been taken on the night, though further questions may be asked if necessary on this day. Louisa looked across at Charlotte, who sat between Lord and Lady Redesdale, her skin so white that Louisa could see the thin blue veins on her eyelids. In that moment, she must surely have missed her long-dead father and a mother who seemed unable to bear anyone's grief but her own – the rumour was that Lady Curtis had not left her bedroom since news of her son's death had reached her. Beside Charlotte, Lord Redesdale looked as if a night back at Ypres in 1917 would be preferable to this room and a crying young woman at his elbow. The others had arrived from London just before proceedings began – Sebastian, Ted, Clara and Phoebe – and slipped into the row behind the Mitfords, their faces as grave as statues in a museum.

'The court calls The Honourable Miss Pamela Mitford to the stand.'

Pamela walked over to the witness box, in reality a low plat-form with a sort of balcony around it. Her face still bore the milky plumpness of childhood but she had borrowed one of her mother's dark brown coats and skirts with a cream, high-necked shirt. It was a touch old-fashioned and beyond her years, a lamb dressed as mutton.

'Could you please confirm your name and where you live.'

'Pamela Mitford, Asthall Manor.'

'The party on the evening in question, the twentieth of November, was to celebrate your eighteenth birthday, was it not?'

Pamela confirmed that it was.

'Could you please tell the jury what you told Inspector Monroe of your encounter with the deceased shortly before his death?'

Pamela hesitated and looked down at her feet briefly. 'It wasn't really an encounter, m'lud.'

'I'm Mr Hicks, not a judge,' he corrected her, though not unkindly. 'Just tell the jury please.'

Pamela nodded and turned to face the jury. Louisa could see that her eyes were not fixed on any of their faces but on a blank spot on the wall behind them. 'The party was nearly over, there were just a few of us left, and we were doing a treasure hunt. Only a small one, around the house. We'd started the game when I got a message from my mother to go and see her in her room.'

'How did you receive this message?'

'From my nursery maid; she came and told me.'

'And where were you?'

'In the dining room, with Adrian Curtis.'

There was a ripple through the room, a small intake of breath and movement as people shifted slightly on the hard, wooden seats.

Mr Hicks leaned forward. 'How did Mr Curtis seem at that time?'

Pamela twisted around, unsure whether to address the coroner or the jury. 'He seemed fine. I mean, I didn't notice anything different about him. I'd only met him once before. We were in the same room because we'd both guessed our second clues and we were looking for them in there.' She turned to the jury. 'You see, you get a clue and then the answer is an object of some kind—'

'I'm sure the ladies and gentlemen of the jury know how a treasure hunt works,' interrupted Mr Hicks, 'even if they aren't the Bright Young Things of London.' He raised his eyebrows and there was a titter in the room.

A red flush crept up Pamela's throat. 'Yes, of course.'

'Please, carry on. You had the message . . . ?'

'I went to my mother's room and she was there with my aunt, Miss Iris Mitford. It seemed that she hadn't sent a message but as I was there—'

'Did you say Lady Redesdale *hadn't* sent a message?'

'No, sir. My maid later explained that she was concerned that I was in a room alone with a gentleman and that my parents might not approve.' Pamela's chin wobbled very slightly. It was true that Louisa had said this to her in the days after the murder, in case it was questioned later. Thank goodness she had.

Mr Hicks wrote something down. 'I see. Carry on.'

The windows of the coroner's court were blackened with soot and there were bars across the outside, so little light could get through but Louisa could see the white sky had turned dark grey.

'Seeing as I was there, my aunt asked if I could fetch a book for her from her room. She wanted to show a passage from it to my mother.' She hesitated, perhaps worried that she was including unnecessary detail or maybe only to take in some air. 'So I hurried along to the yellow room, my aunt's room. It's no more than a few minutes' walk away, close to my father's dressing room.'

'Was your father in there?'

'I believe so. The light was off so I assumed he was asleep.' She paused, and Mr Hicks motioned for her to continue. 'The door was shut but I could hear an argument ...'

'Did you know who was in the room?'

'No. But I recognised Mr Curtis's voice. He was arguing with a girl but I didn't know who it was at the time.'

'Did you realise later who it was?'

There was a pause. Louisa held her breath.

'Yes,' said Pamela. 'She had a very distinctive accent, from south London. I heard it later, when ... well, when we had discovered Mr Curtis.'

'Had you ever met her before?'

'Not quite.' Pamela's tone indicated she was emboldened by her certainty. 'I had seen her working as a maid when I attended a supper at Mr Curtis's house in London the month before.'

'Had you noticed her at the party earlier that evening?'

'Not so far as I was aware.'

'Is the maid in this room now?'

Pamela nodded.

'Could you identify her, please?'

Pamela pointed to Dulcie, who returned her gaze, forcing Pamela to be the first to look away. Mr Hicks indicated she should continue her account.

'I only stood there for a few seconds and was about to leave when I heard a loud noise, a crack of some sort. It gave me a shock, and I ran off.'

'What did you do after that?'

'I went to the kitchen to tell Louisa, that is – Louisa Cannon, my nursery maid.'

'Why did you tell Miss Cannon?'

Louisa had the distinctly uncomfortable sensation of eyes on her, though the jury couldn't have known who she was.

Pamela paused. 'I didn't know who else to tell. Everybody else was on the treasure hunt and in different places around the house. I was disturbed by the row I'd heard.'

'What did Miss Cannon say to you?'

Pamela's eyes flickered over Louisa then back to the jury. 'She said that we couldn't know for sure what it was about, that it might have been part of the game. She told me to rejoin the party.'

'I see. You can stand down now, Miss Mitford. You have been extremely helpful.'

Pamela returned to her seat beside her mother, who did not touch her but gave her a tight smile that vanished from her face almost as soon as it had arrived.

Next was Dulcie. She was escorted to the box by the policeman, who stood behind her throughout. He was shaped like a snowman and whether he could have sprinted after an escaping witness was highly doubtful. But Dulcie wasn't going to be running anywhere.

After the usual introduction and confirmation of her name and address – which she gave as the home of Lady Curtis in Mayfair, though the likelihood of her returning there was vanishingly small – the coroner began his line of questioning.

'Please tell the jury how you came to be at Asthall Manor.'

'It had been arranged that I would collect Miss Charlotte, to take her back to Mrs Watney's house where we were staying.'

'Mrs Watney's house was close by?'

Louisa saw Mrs Watney sit up straighter at this mention of her in court and look around as if she might be catching admiring glances. She wasn't.

'About half a mile down the road.'

'What did you do when you arrived at the house? Were you met by anyone?'

'Yes, sir. The maid, Louisa, let me into the back entrance to the kitchen.' Dulcie looked defiant in spite of the plain sacking uniform of a remand prisoner, a straight grey dress with a dirty white shirt beneath, too large for her narrow frame.

There was a pause. 'Did Louisa Cannon show you the bedroom upstairs?'

'No, sir.' Had Dulcie answered too quickly? Louisa felt the heat in her face burning. 'She said she needed to go and clear away from the party and she left me alone in the kitchen.'

'But you didn't stay in there, did you?'

Dulcie spoke quietly. 'No, sir. I saw the back stairs and I took them.'

'What was your intention at that moment?'

'I thought I might see an empty bedroom and . . .' She paused. It was shocking to hear it said out loud like this and when Louisa remembered her part in it, it was all she could do to prevent herself from hiding under the seat. Dulcie continued, more definite than before. 'I thought I might see something as would be worth taking.'

'Was this common practice for you, Miss Long? To enter into an unknown house and search for something to steal?'

'No,' said Dulcie. 'I ain't never done it before while working for Lady Curtis.'

'So you had done it *before* working for your present employer?'

Dulcie was silent.

'For the sake of the court record, the witness neither confirms nor denies this,' said Mr Hicks. 'Carry on.'

'I went upstairs and didn't see no one. I saw a bedroom door that was open and when I looked inside it was empty. I knew they was all at the party, so I took my chance.'

'Shortly after this, Mr Curtis came into the room?'

'Yes.'

'Had you previously arranged to meet him in there?'

Dulcie shook her head.

'The witness has indicated no,' said Mr Hicks.

Louisa's mouth was completely dry.

'What happened when he came into the room?'

Beads of sweat like dew on a cobweb were forming on Dulcie's hairline, and her knuckles, gripping the witness balcony, had turned white, but she kept a steady gaze. For a reason she could not identify Louisa turned to look behind her, where a few scattered people sat, members of the press mostly, she assumed. In the far corner, looking no less like a paean to the contours of the Maris Piper, sat the woman who had threatened Dulcie in the Elephant and Castle. She was watching Dulcie very closely and Louisa knew that Dulcie was alive to this. There could be no misstep here.

'He caught me stealing jewellery from the dressing table in there.'

'And what was his reaction?' Mr Hicks had his pen poised.

'He was angry. He told me to put the things back, and when I refused, he hit me.'

'Where did he hit you?'

'On my eye, here.' Dulcie put a hand to her left eye.

Mr Hicks folded his arms on his desk. 'Was it then you determined to exact your revenge?'

'What, sir? No, sir. No, I did not!' Dulcie's voice rose but her hands held on tightly to the balcony before her, and Louisa knew she would fall otherwise.

'You arranged to meet him at the church bell tower then?'

'No. Nothing more was said. He left the room and shortly after, I left too.'

'So the fact of your meeting at the church later that night was pure coincidence?'

Dulcie's face registered the hopelessness of her situation but she said nothing more that would redeem her before the jury. 'I didn't meet him, sir. I only saw . . .' She didn't manage to finish the sentence.

'Tell us, Miss Long, what happened after you left the room.'

Dulcie paused but not for too long – not long enough to be registered as recalling a story of invention. Her eyelids flickered and she looked like a child by the school railings, wondering where her mother was.

'I went downstairs, to the kitchen, and collected my coat. There was nobody else there.'

'Yes? Then what?' Impatience had crept in to Mr Hicks's measured tones.

'It wasn't time yet to collect Miss Charlotte and I didn't want anyone to see my eye. I decided to wait outside.' She stopped talking for a moment and Mr Hicks looked down at his notes.

'According to the inspector's report, the night was cold but dry. The moon was hidden by cloud.' He regarded the witness. 'Did you have a torch on you?'

'No sir, but there was some light coming from the windows of the house. I walked around the garden then sat in an old summerhouse for I don't know how long but I got cold. Then I thought I'd go to the churchyard, I'd seen it on my way up earlier.'

'An unusual choice for a stroll in the middle of the night. Most people would be too frightened if they thought they were going to be alone. But you knew you'd be meeting Mr Curtis, didn't you?'

'No, sir, I didn't!' Dulcie almost raised her voice but brought herself back again. 'It's just, well, I ain't frightened of no ghosts, I don't believe in them. I thought, if I couldn't get inside, I could wait on a bench in the church or something for a bit.'

There was a shuffle beside Louisa. She'd almost forgotten she was sitting with the others. Lord Redesdale and Pamela were exchanging glances: they believed in ghosts, though it was some-thing they had to keep to themselves as Lady Redesdale firmly decried it as tosh. The two of them insisted there had been water dripping in the path for several nights by the window of Lord Redesdale's child-proof room, yet no tap was there nor puddle collected.

'I walked into the graveyard,' Dulcie continued, and heads turned towards her. It was a circus and the maid on the stand was the freak show. 'It was dark but I suppose the church was easy to see. It's got white bricks, it glowed almost.' She withdrew slightly into herself at that. 'I started to walk towards the back where I thought the door might be and then I saw . . .'

Everyone knew what Dulcie saw, and everyone held their breath.

'Tell the jury, Miss Long.'

'Mr Curtis, dead, sir.' Dulcie's head hung low and her knuck-les loosened their grip; she swayed slightly but did not faint. The thought came into Louisa's mind of a cold slice of apple pie she had put on a plate for herself in the pantry; she had planned to eat it when they returned, as a bolstering treat after what she had anticipated would be a long and difficult day. She pictured a spoonful of the soft fruit and pastry going into her mouth, but it turned to ashes.

CHAPTER EIGHTEEN

~~~~~

The walk from Debenham and Freebody to the Vine Street station was only ten minutes. Usually. With a young woman kicking and shouting for most of it as Guy and Mary almost carried her along Oxford Street, it took closer to half an hour. By the time they staggered in through the open door of the station, Guy was sweating and Mary had taken her hat off and was clutching it instead.

One of the old hands was at the front desk, his handlebar moustache so luxuriant it looked as if a small badger had settled in for a nap beneath his nose. He grinned at Guy and Mary, neither of whom were exhibiting the disciplined poise required of police officers but who had clearly brought in a catch worth bragging about.

'What have we here, then?' he said. It was a joke amongst policemen to talk like the cartoons in the *Daily Express*.

Guy, still holding an elbow, marched up to the desk, panting. 'A young woman, caught shoplifting in Debenham and Freebody, sir,' he said. 'We need an interview room straight away.'

At this the policeman's eyebrow was raised. '*We* do?'

'Me and Constable Moon, sir.'

'Constable Moon can go and tidy herself up. I'll take you into an interview room and fetch Inspector Cornish, I know he's about.' He started to look down a list on his desk, checking which room was free.

Mary stepped back, fury clouding her face, but she said nothing. She didn't let go of the hostage's arm, though she was no longer trying to get away but stood there, sulky and silent. Guy leaned forward, his voice lowered but firm. 'Excuse me, sir, but Constable Moon was a vital part of this arrest. She needs to be in the interview room too.'

The policeman shrugged and the badger turned over in its sleep. 'As you wish. Cornish will deal with it. Go to the third door on the left down there.'

In the interview room, Guy asked Mary to pat down the young woman's skirts. She kicked and wriggled, shouting that she didn't have nothing but eventually gave up when Guy said, 'Give it up, miss. You're in *here*,' and gestured to the dirty brown and buff painted walls, the closed metal door with its peek-a-boo square slot.

Mary scrabbled her fingers around the sides of the skirt, looking for an opening like she was drawing curtains, and found beneath the upper layer two bolts of lavender silk. She pulled them out and laid them on the table. 'What's that, then?'

The woman shrugged.

'Your name?' said Guy, his notebook and pencil at the ready.

'Elsie White.'

'Age and place of residence?'

'Nineteen. Thirty-six Dobson Road.'

'South of the river, I suppose?' said Guy.

'If you like,' she said, smiling at her own insolence. It probably wasn't even her real name.

Just as Guy was about to threaten her with a charge for obstruction of the law, the door clanged open and Cornish strode in, all big checks and shoulders, blocking out the light from the hall. He clocked Elsie and Mary and grinned at Guy. 'Landed two fish, have you?'

'No, sir,' said Guy, 'just the one.' He inclined his head at Elsie, still standing in the middle of the room. None of them had thought to use the chairs.

'Who are you then?' barked Cornish at Mary.

'Constable Moon, sir,' she said. 'I was on duty with Sergeant Sullivan, in plain clothes. Undercover, you see—'

Cornish waved her away with a hand that looked recently manicured, plump flesh peeking from beneath clean, short nails. 'Fine.' He turned back to Guy. 'What happened, and am I interested?'

Guy felt the blood rush in his ears. 'We were in Debenham and Freebody's haberdashery department at about eleven o'clock this morning when we noticed that the shopgirls had their eyes on a tall lady who was walking around not buying anything.'

Cornish dragged a chair out, squealing its back legs and sat down heavily. Guy stopped talking while the inspector pulled out a cigar, clipped off the end and lit it. He did not hurry and all the while the rest of them stood motionless, as if cursed in a fairy tale. He nodded at Guy, and the spell was broken.

'While everyone's attention was elsewhere, Constable Moon spotted this woman here acting suspiciously and as she was exiting the department, Constable Moon ran after her—'

'Forget about that for a minute,' said Cornish, exhaling a grey wreath of smoke that floated to the ceiling and hovered there. 'This tall woman, that's what I'm interested in. What did she look like?'

Guy was thrown by this. 'She wore a dark coat and hat, expensive I'd say.' He faltered. 'I'm not sure I saw much else, sir.' Damn his eyesight. Damn it, damn it. What the hell *had* she looked like? What had he missed?

'It was my fault, sir,' said Mary quickly, and Cornish pulled himself up a little straighter. 'I distracted Sergeant Sullivan, I mean. I told him to come in my direction, to apprehend this woman.'

'Your foolishness allowed Alice Diamond to get away,' said Cornish, plucking each word like bits between his teeth.

Guy looked at Mary in alarm. So the shop manager was right. Had he said something? Had he telephoned to the station? It was possible.

Cornish puffed again. 'She's clever though, I'll grant her that. Even if you had apprehended her, it's unlikely she'd have had anything about her person. She leaves that to her lowly subjects.' He exhaled on the last word, blowing smoke directly onto Elsie's face; she grimaced but did not cough. 'Find out who she was going to pass it on to.'

'Sir?'

'The fence, Sullivan.'

With one hand on his thigh, Cornish heaved himself up. 'Take the statement, make the notes and lock her up. You've done well.'

The roar in Guy's ears subsided.

'But you could have done better. A lot better. Get your spectacles checked, Sullivan.' The door banged shut.

CHAPTER NINETEEN

After Dulcie's interview, court was adjourned until after lunch, which was spent by their desultory group in a café around the corner. It gave Louisa a chill to think of the many bereaved and criminal persons that had passed an hour there, awaiting a verdict. Charlotte was still fragile, and walked between Lord and Lady Redesdale, who bore her with stoicism. Pamela looked exhausted after the ordeal of her interview but refused any comments of sympathy. 'It's nothing compared to what Charlotte is going through.'

Unable to bear the stifling fug of kitchen heat and bacon fat in the café, Louisa stepped outside and saw Ted and Clara whispering on the pavement. Instinctively, she withdrew and stood slightly hidden in the doorway. They were smoking cigarettes, huddled by a lamp-post. Louisa strained to hear although the street was relatively quiet. Impossibly, it seemed everyone else was blithely continuing with a normal day in town.

'What if they ask you again where you were that night?' said Ted.

Clara, her pink coat chalky from the street dust, pulled a face. 'They won't, but you don't need to worry. I'm not going to spill any beans.'

'*The* beans,' Ted muttered.

'For Chrissakes!' said Clara. 'Whatever it is you English say.'

Ted looked up and seemed to catch sight of Louisa's coat in the doorway. 'We'd better go back in.' He ground his cigarette out on the pavement and stalked back into the café but Louisa had already gone before him and was sitting back in her seat before he had closed the door behind Clara.

What beans? Lord De Clifford and The American were colluding in some kind of secret from that night but whether it was connected to the murder, Louisa couldn't guess at. Whatever it was, it was serious enough that they needed to keep it from the police. All she could conclude was that neither Ted nor Clara were where they said they had been when Adrian's murder was committed.

The more Louisa thought about it, looking across at Nancy and her friends, the more she thought how odd it was that, apart from Charlotte of course, none of them seemed terribly sad about Adrian Curtis's death. There was shock at the murder and how sudden it had been but Louisa had yet to hear anyone say they missed him or wished it hadn't happened. From what she had seen, Adrian had been boorish and unattractive, but surely that wasn't a reason to kill him?

There was something else puzzling too: why would Dulcie admit to the theft but not to the murder? Obviously, one crime was less serious than the other but if she had killed Adrian, would she not deny everything and try to wash the stain of accusation clean away? Whatever the answer, the mysterious conversation between Ted and Clara made Dulcie's arrest questionable. Louisa had to hold on to her original instinct: that Dulcie was sincere when she'd said she was going straight. The theft had to have been the final job she did for the Forty. The murder was done by someone else. But who?

CHAPTER TWENTY

❦

Back in the court, the ladies and gentlemen of the jury were as immobile as wooden soldiers propped up in the same places, their blank expressions unchanged. A pathologist, Mr Stuart-Jones, was brought to the stand, a cool-mannered man with shoes that shone like a colonel's. In a curt, dry series of responses to the coroner, he confirmed the death of the victim, the broken bones sustained in the fall, the cause of death – a cervical fracture – and the appearance of bruises on his neck and upper arms that were concurrent with a struggle having occurred moments before. Broken glasses, confirmed to have been worn by the victim as part of his costume, were found on the floor of the bell tower, which further indicated a struggle.

Immediately afterwards, Detective Inspector Monroe was called, his purple nose as swollen as ever. Mr Hicks had asked him to summarise the whereabouts of the guests in the house at the deduced time of murder.

'There were a number of guests in the house,' began Monroe portentously. 'Of those playing the treasure hunt, I will state the rooms they were in at the moment the alarm was first raised.

Lord De Clifford was in the boot room, Miss Clara Fischer in the dining room, Mr Sebastian Atlas and Miss Phoebe Morgan in the drawing room—'

The coroner had given a cough. 'Sorry, do go on.'

'Miss Charlotte Curtis and Miss Nancy Mitford were in the morning room, Mr Oliver Watney in the telephone cupboard, Miss Pamela Mitford in the smoking room. The maid, Miss Louisa Cannon, was in the kitchen. The remaining guests, Lord and Lady Redesdale, the children and the servants were all in their respective bedrooms except for Mrs Windsor who was in her sitting room and the groom, Hooper, in his room above the stables. They were not asleep but they did not hear the commotion.'

'Could you also confirm for the court what was found upon Miss Long's person when interviewed?'

'A platinum ring with sapphire and diamond stones, a pair of gold and ruby earrings, a pearl necklace, a sapphire and diamond bracelet and a gold necklace inset with rubies and diamonds. These were all items that Miss Iris Mitford confirmed belonged to her.'

'Thank you, Detective Inspector, you have been most concise.'

Monroe stood down and, it seemed to Louisa, forced himself to resist the instinct to take a bow.

There were further closing remarks but Louisa did not listen. She could only focus on the pathetic figure of Dulcie, slumped on the bench. As the jury filed out to consider their verdict, Dulcie's words ran around her mind as they had for days, like a Hornby train set: 'It's always us lot that gets suspected first.' Surely Dulcie was innocent? She couldn't have had the strength to push a man out of a window and it didn't make sense that she would meet him in the church after they had had the row in the bedroom. Nor did Louisa like what she had overheard Ted and Clara saying, though she couldn't say what it meant.

Only that this case was not as black and white as DI Monroe claimed it to be.

In less than twenty minutes the jury returned. One woman, who looked to be not much older than Dulcie, had pink eyes that betrayed tears but the rest remained as impenetrable as ever. The foreman stood at Mr Hicks' request and when asked, replied they were returning a verdict of unlawful killing.

'A young man's life has been tragically and senselessly cut short,' Mr Hicks orated to the room, which was absent of sound. He may have looked like a man who had worn nothing in his life more daring than a pink carnation in his buttonhole but he delivered his final remarks like a Roman emperor in a toga with a crown of golden leaves around his head.

'Mr Adrian Curtis was a man who had much to look forward to in life and who might have made a significant contribution to society. Miss Dulcie Long, I hereby officially charge you with theft and murder in the first degree. You will be remanded in prison to await trial without bail.' There was no gavel to be banged, only a sheaf of papers shuffled as the policeman led Dulcie away. This time, she wore handcuffs.

CHAPTER TWENTY-ONE

*n the interview room, Cornish had slammed the door shut behind him. Elsie White, still standing in the middle of the room from when Mary had searched her skirts, started to snicker but closed up when Guy turned on her. Anger boiled inside him and he wanted to throw the chair at her, to see it splinter into matchsticks on the floor. Mary put a hand out to him, palm up.

'Don't,' she said, as if she knew. 'We'll go out again, and again, and again. We'll get her.'

Elsie laughed then, a rumble that rose from her belly and escaped through a wide-open mouth, grey teeth showing. 'You'll never get her,' she gasped as the last sniggers rolled out and finished with a hiss. 'You can't get none of us.'

Mary walked up behind Elsie then and with a strength Guy had not suspected was there, used her hands to propel Elsie by the shoulders, forcing her to sit down on a chair by one side of the table. Mary indicated to Guy that the two of them should sit on the chairs opposite. Elsie's mouth hung slack as she watched them take their positions. Guy laid out his notebook and pencil before him.

'I think you'll find, Miss White,' he began, 'that we have got you here, in possession of stolen goods and with Constable Moon and myself able to testify to your theft.'

Elsie tried a defiant smile but failed.

'If the judge is in a good mood, you might get away with . . . Oh, what do you think, Constable Moon?'

Mary crossed her arms and put a mock-thoughtful expression on her face. 'If he's feeling very reasonable, I suppose Miss White would only be looking at a few months.'

Still, Elsie was silent.

'I have a funny feeling,' said Guy, 'that Miss White here will show a bit of previous. I think we could be looking at eighteen months' hard labour.'

Mary nodded. 'I think that's our most likely scenario.'

'Unless, Miss White, you could be persuaded to give us a little bit of help as to the whereabouts of some of your esteemed colleagues?' Guy wanted to put his hands under the table so he could cross his fingers.

'I ain't no grass,' she said stoutly.

'You don't have to give us names,' said Guy. He was thinking quickly. He needed to be sure of getting a result and he had to go for whatever she would give him. There wasn't a lot to bargain with here. A woman like Elsie wouldn't be too afraid of prison. 'What I want to know is where I can find some of those men who are the go-betweens for you and your like.'

Elsie shook her head. 'I don't know what you're talking about. If you're going to charge me, get on with it. I could do with getting my head down in a cell for a bit.'

'We'll stay here as long as it takes,' said Mary. Guy was struck by her cool.

'You know what I mean,' said Guy. 'Fences. Men who take your stolen goods and sell it on. Where do they sell it?'

121

Elsie pursed her lips together in a thin, pale line and shook her head.

'If you give me a name,' said Guy, 'we can bring that nasty eighteen-month sentence down to six. If you give me several names, we can make it disappear altogether.'

Elsie's lips remained a slash but her eyes moved uncertainly. It was the tiniest wobble but it was all that Guy needed.

'One name, Elsie.'

'I ain't giving you no names, not for nothing,' she said, less sure of herself than before.

'Then give us a place, somewhere to find them. Perhaps somewhere that all kinds of people go, that we could easily stumble across. Then no one would know you'd told,' Guy persisted. 'A pub, or working men's club. Something like that.'

Mary leaned forward. 'Elsie, have you got a child?'

Elsie started at this and screamed, 'You ain't touching my Charlie!'

Mary smiled reassuringly. 'We're not going to do anything to Charlie. But don't you think eighteen months would be a long time to be apart from him?'

'One name,' repeated Guy.

'The 43 Club,' said Elsie. 'That's all you're getting from me. Now let me go.'

CHAPTER TWENTY-TWO

﹏﹏

B ack at the house, Louisa curled up on the armchair by the fire in the nursery. Nanny Blor had fetched her a cup of tea and two crumpets, and Unity and Decca brought her a blanket. The young girls did not know why Louisa was in need of comfort but they seemed to be enjoying the turned tables. Even Debo had pattered down to her bedroom to fetch a favourite toy rabbit, one ear long gone, and when she brought it back Louisa heaved Debo on to her lap. The baby of the six children had blonde curls as plump and round as her tummy and a nature as sweet as honey – unless you tried to stop her sucking her thumb and then the dam would burst, said Nanny Blor. Louisa wasn't sure why she needed the children close by her except that somewhere between the house and the courtroom she had lost any feeling of her feet hitting the hard ground, as if it were something spongy instead, like moss. Coupled with this was an overwhelming desire to crawl into a small, dark box and stay there for hours. Of course, she wouldn't, there was work to do and soon the unerring routine of bathing the children and putting them to bed provided its own soothing oil on her troubled waters.

Pamela had not come up to the nursery when they had returned but stayed below, in the drawing room with her parents. Charlotte had returned to London with Sebastian, Ted, Phoebe and Clara, as planned, and was expected to go and see her mother. There was the funeral to prepare for. Nancy was also downstairs, or so Louisa thought. Sometime after she and Nanny Blor had had their supper, sitting opposite each other in the nursery rather more quietly than usual, Nancy had appeared at the doorway. She was in jodhpurs and an old blue jumper with a hole in one elbow, her hair looked unbrushed, pushed back with her fingers, and though she had the white skin of the classic English rose, she had flushed cheeks for the first time in days and glittering eyes.

'I thought I'd come up and see you both,' she said. 'It's been an age and everyone is in a filthy mood downstairs. Have you had pudding yet? I could fancy a bit of something sweet.'

Semolina with a generous pouring of cream and a dollop of raspberry jam had just been put in front of Louisa but she hadn't had a mouthful yet. She'd been wondering how she could eat it, and gratefully pushed it across the table.

'Here,' she said, 'have mine. I'm not hungry for any more supper.'

'Thanks, Lou-Lou,' said Nancy, tucking herself into the table, as if she was still six.

Nanny Blor had been leaning forward a touch anxiously, her spoon hovering halfway between bowl and mouth, but when Nancy took Louisa's semolina her shoulders relaxed. They ate in a comfortable silence until the last mouthful had been chased around the bowl. Nancy sat back and looked as if she was about to say something, then thought better of it.

'Cat got your tongue?' said Nanny.

'Something like that.'

'I'm off to sit by the fire then.' Nanny heaved herself up and looked fondly at Louisa and Nancy. 'I've got a rather good mystery on the boil and I wouldn't mind getting back to it.'

Louisa stood and started to clear the plates to put on the tray for the maid but Nancy wanted to talk. 'Poor Charlotte. Her own maid. What do you think made her do it?'

Louisa lifted the tray and held it against her, resting slightly on a hip. 'I don't think she did do it.'

'What do you mean? There was no one else there. She was found by his body, Pam heard them arguing beforehand. What more do you need?'

The tray felt heavy. 'What if there was someone else there?'

Nancy stood. She took the tray from Louisa and put it on the table. 'What are you talking about? Who?'

'I don't know ...' Louisa put her hand across her eyes, like a child, pretending that no one was there to hear what she was about to say out loud. All day she had been thinking about the woman who sat in the court throughout the inquest, as if reminding Dulcie to stay silent about her connections with the Forty. Why was she doing that if not to protect Alice Diamond? Did this mean Dulcie was protecting someone by admitting to the theft? And what of that conversation between Ted and Clara? But Louisa could not voice any of this without revealing her own betrayal of the very house she was in. She realised that she resented Nancy and the freedoms she had, that she, Louisa, could not have. What was there between them except the sheer luck of the families they were born into? That resentment had been building – for years? – and it fused now in a white hot fury that throbbed behind her eyes.

'It just none of it makes sense,' she burst out. 'Why would they row and then meet again? And how could she have the strength to do it? It must have been someone else.'

'What are you going to do about it?' Nancy's face was flushed.

Louisa hadn't known this before but she knew it now. 'I'm going to prove it. I'll find whoever it was and prove she didn't do it.'

'Be careful, Lou-Lou,' said Nancy. 'You may have to decide whose side you're on. Dulcie's – or ours.'

CHAPTER TWENTY-THREE

Lady Redesdale had, unusually, chosen to spend the morning in the library, sitting in the bay window where the sun streamed in. She kept having to shift a little along the window seat as the rays moved to keep the warmth on her back while she leaned over a stack of Christmas cards. Louisa was sitting by her sewing basket on a wooden chair close to the fire – despite the sunshine it was a cold December day – as Decca and Unity played with the doll's house and Debo tried to join in, her clumsy attempts to move miniature furniture always interrupted by a bossy order to do it differently. The cumbersome toy had been carried down from the nursery by Lord Redesdale and Tom, home for the holidays, much to everyone's delight and certainly the reason they had all gathered together, though they were presently waiting for father and son to come back from a walk. Diana was in the schoolroom with the governess but only after she had raged during breakfast that she saw no need to learn 'stupid French' and Nanny Blor had agreed that the people on the Continent couldn't make as nice a cup of tea but their language *did* sound so nice, which had made Louisa smile.

Pamela and Nancy sat on either side of their mother, helping with the Christmas cards – Nancy choosing names out of the address book, Pamela licking envelopes and stamps. Everyone had been in a companionable silence for almost an hour and Louisa was just beginning to think that boredom would settle in soon when she heard Nancy start to talk in a pleading tone that threatened to turn quickly into a whine.

' ... more than a month since I've been to London. I've been invited to the theatre on Thursday night and then there's a dance on Friday, a fundraiser for widowed mothers and simply *everyone* will be there. Even Lord De Clifford has a ticket and he might be a match for our old Pam.'

Nancy leaned over and winked at her sister who yelped and cried that she cared nothing for Ted, but it was too late – her cheeks were already aflame.

Lady Redesdale stayed bent over a card until it was signed and handed over to Pamela. Then she sat up and turned to her eldest daughter.

'Koko, after everything that has happened here, you cannot go out dancing. It wouldn't be seemly.' She picked up another card, indicating that the conversation was closed.

'It was three weeks ago. What are we supposed to do, wear mourning for a year? We're not Victorians.'

Lady Redesdale raised an eyebrow at this. 'Maybe you are not but I was born under the good queen, you know.'

'Well, things have changed, Muv.' She lowered her voice, 'I'm not going to get married at this rate. It's going to be my third season next year ...'

This, Louisa knew, was an embarrassment and the Mitfords' Achilles heel. Diana's presentation at court would be in less than three years' time and she was already beautiful enough for it to be a concern that she would be 'caught' before Nancy. As difficult as Nancy could be, and as frequently as she declared that there was too much fun to be had to be in want of a husband (did she mean it? Louisa wasn't sure), none of them wished that humiliation upon her: to be bridesmaid to her younger sister's bride. 'You might as well join the convent,' Ada had snickered when they were gossiping in the kitchen.

Lady Redesdale's pen halted and hovered above the card, a wasp in the flower bed.

'And look at Woman,' continued Nancy, her voice back to its normal level. 'She's being presented at Court next year and thanks to what's happened she's going to be terrified, thinking every party ends in murder.'

'That's enough!' Lady Redesdale slammed down her pen and Pamela stood up, dropping the stamped envelopes onto the floor, and exclaiming at the same time: 'I am not *frightened*! I'm not a baby!'

A slow smile spread across Nancy's face, one Louisa knew well – it meant she had unsettled the object of her teasing and there was little she seemed to enjoy more. Even Decca, Unity and Debo had stopped mid-play to hear how this would end, Decca holding a tiny bed in the air.

Nancy neither moved nor altered her tone of voice. 'Louisa can chaperone us. I think we could do with the change of scene, don't you?'

As she finished speaking, there was a rush of cold air into the room and Lord Redesdale stepped inside with Tom close behind, bringing with them the scent of mulched leaves and woodsmoke. Lady Redesdale glanced their way, then sat down again smoothly.

'I'll discuss it with your father,' she said, and that was the end of the conversation.

*

Of course, Nancy got her way and the following Wednesday she, Pamela and Louisa boarded the train from Shipton-under-Wychwood to Paddington, and then went on to stay with Iris Mitford at her flat in Elvaston Place. The first night was spent decorously, as if to prove their good intentions, with an early supper and bed. The morning was given to errands and a long walk through Hyde Park, with Nancy and Pamela in sympathy with one another for once, arm in arm on the path. Louisa walked beside them, unable to stop herself from catching their high spirits.

'Oh, it's such heaven to be away from the beasts,' exclaimed Nancy.

Pamela squealed, 'Don't be so disloyal, Koko!'

'I mean the hairy dogs, of course,' Nancy said, eyes wide, and the two of them dissolved into giggles.

At six o'clock the sisters had changed into cocktail dresses, with low heels and long gloves. Their blonde and dark curls respectively made them an attractive pair alongside one another. Louisa, naturally, wore the same frock she had put on that morning: it had been explained that theatre tickets had been bought for them, 'But not for you, darling – you'll have to wait for us in the foyer until the show's over.' Louisa had tried to brush aside the humiliation and disappointment she felt. What? Had she really imagined she would be invited too?

'Of course,' she said, and Iris had nodded in approval.

The show was *Hay Fever* at the Criterion Theatre in Piccadilly and when they arrived all the glamour and lights of London were in their full blazing glory, casting a haze of white light on a sky that would be deep black above Asthall. They had got there early and stood by the programme stand admiring the painted tiles and vast stained glass windows while they waited. 'I suppose the theatre is the new church,' said Nancy and was given a reproving look by Pamela. Soon Clara came up to them, breathless with excitement and decked out in what Louisa privately thought was rather too much make-up and a golden dress that was cut dangerously low at the front and back, long pearls emphasising the depth. Instead of gloves, she wore a mass of thin metal bangles that covered each arm from wrist to elbow, a rather daring look. Perhaps she had got the idea from the pictures in the newspaper of Josephine Baker, the sensational dancer in Paris. Clara kissed Nancy and Pamela, then beckoned them in to her.

'There's a rumour that Noël Coward himself is going to be here tonight,' she said gleefully. 'It's my big chance!'

'What do you mean?' said Pamela.

'To be in his next play, of course. I'm an actress,' said Clara with pride.

'Are you?' Nancy couldn't keep the scorn out of her voice. 'What have you been in?'

Clara tried to look casual. 'Nothing, yet. But I've done several casting calls. Back in the States, you know.'

As Clara said this, Sebastian sidled up. No one had noticed him come in but he was suddenly at Clara's shoulder, slickly suited, a sneer on his lips. 'I'll bet you have, Miss Fischer.'

Clara jumped and, rather than greet him, walked off to buy herself a programme. Nancy moved forward and gave him a light kiss on his cheekbone.

'Hello, darling,' she said, 'you really mustn't tease.'

'That's rich coming from you. Anyone else here yet?'

Pamela looked towards the door. 'Here's Ted, and someone I don't know.'

'Dolly,' said Sebastian drily. 'Is she your love rival?'

'She's nothing of the sort,' said Pamela, and Louisa liked her

131

mature defiance. She was learning how to handle Nancy's friends and it would hold her in good stead.

Ted had his arm draped casually around Dolly's shoulders. She was rather shorter than him and expensively decked out. She wore a long mink coat that must have cost more than all of Nancy and Pamela's wardrobes put together but smiled nervously as they approached. Louisa saw Ted allow himself the briefest of glances to flicker in Clara's direction before sweeping his dark eyes on to the Mitford sisters.

'Kind of you all to show up,' he said.

'Oh, no, it's really kind of you,' said Pamela. 'I'm awfully bucked to be here.' Nancy gave her a withering look but held her tongue.

Finally, Charlotte came in, looking even more fashionably thin than before but without the haunting sadness that had clouded her during the inquest. She greeted everyone with cordiality, if not enthusiasm. 'Am I late?' she asked.

'No,' said Nancy. 'They haven't rung the bell yet but seeing as we're all here, shall we take our seats?'

They headed towards the stalls, quickly lost in the throng of chattering theatregoers, none of them giving Louisa so much as a backward glance.

Twenty minutes later, the last of the audience had left the foyer, taking with them the buzz of anticipation for a show that had been the talking point of London's theatreland for weeks. Louisa decided she'd rather not sit in the bar alone – it wasn't as if she could order a drink without looking like a woman of the night – so she found a chair that presumably belonged to an usher, close to the programme stand. She had a book with her, a newish Agatha Christie she'd borrowed from the library in Burford, *The Man in the Brown Suit*, but her attention kept wandering – the noise of the

London traffic outside and people walking past were too distracting. And her mind was on Dulcie: how was she coping? Here they all were, gallivanting at the theatre, not a worry between them, or so it seemed, while she languished in Holloway Prison. She knew Dulcie wasn't a complete innocent, of course. But neither was she. Louisa knew how it felt to be driven by desperation and even if Dulcie had been a thief, she still earned the right to some protection. She had none from her former mistress, who had been as quick as the rest of them to believe that her maid was capable of such a violent and ugly act.

There was a creak behind her and Louisa saw Sebastian coming out of the side door, in that slightly catlike way he had. He didn't appear to notice her but stepped outside. Louisa was intrigued, by his stealthy manner if nothing else, and slid to the theatre's large front doors with its glass panes. She peered through and saw Sebastian standing close to a man, slightly shorter than him, in a dark hat and coat. Louisa thought she caught a flash of red at the collar. Their conversation was brief: Sebastian handed something over – money? – and received something in turn. She couldn't see what it was but it was small because he slid it immediately into his jacket pocket. Quickly, she went back to her seat and picked up her book again, making sure that if he should notice her this time, she would look completely absorbed by the narrative.

CHAPTER TWENTY-FOUR

～～～

Half-dozing, Louisa started when she heard the roar of applause that signalled the end of the play. The doors were opened by ushers and the audience came out like a big sigh after a secret had finally been told. There was a general rush of people to the loos and cloakrooms, as well as back out into the street and the surge of cold air from the open doors woke Louisa up properly. She scanned the crowd but Pamela found her first, eyes bright.

'Oh, Lou, it was such fun! Honestly I don't think I've laughed so much in for ever.'

Louisa could hardly mind such harmless enjoyment. 'I'm glad,' she said.

'But look, Clara says we're to go backstage. She knows one of the actors in the show. We're all going. Follow me.'

Outside, Pamela and Louisa almost ran to catch up with the others, who had turned left out of the front door and into Jermyn Street, where a small black and white sign discreetly announced the stage door. They got there just in time to catch the tails of Ted, the last of the group to be admitted by the doorman who was clearly making as much of a song and dance out of their admission as anything that had happened on the stage earlier. 'No more than eight people in the dressing room,' he called after them. 'Fire regulations. I'll have to come in and count—'.

He was cut off by Ted who turned around and thrust a pound note into his hand as he shook it. 'It's a great pleasure, sir,' said Ted smoothly, 'we're all so thrilled to see our good friend Miss Blanche. I'm sure you understand.'

The doorman halted and doffed his cap, slipping the note into his pocket. 'Yes, sir. Have a good evening, all.' He took his seat up behind the cramped desk by the door and looked perfectly satisfied.

When they got to dressing room number six, however, they realised the doorman was right. Even if one disregarded fire regulations, the room was tiny and they could barely squeeze in as five or six people had already got there before them. Blanche was clearly a popular actress, loudly declaring her delight at the attention as she poured out champagne for her guests. She was still in her stage make-up but wore a silk Japanese kimono tightly belted around her narrow waist. The room was brightly lit and on the huge mirror she had stuck several cards and photographs from well-wishers. On the dressing table with her wigs there was a vase of dying flowers and another of freshly cut white roses. Clara was up close to her friend, drinking in her every word, as well as the champagne in great gulps, and Sebastian was talking nineteen to the dozen to another young man in there, who didn't appear to be getting much of a word in edgeways. Dolly was standing alone, sipping her drink and saying nothing, while Ted stood beside her eyeing the other men in the room like a bulldog guarding a steak from a pack of strays.

While Louisa and Pamela were standing awkwardly in the corridor, wondering what to do, Charlotte pushed her way out of the room, followed closely by Nancy. Charlotte looked as if she was going to leave entirely but Nancy tugged on her coat.

'Don't go,' she pleaded. 'Let's stay here a bit longer. We might all go on somewhere?'

'I'm not in the mood,' snapped Charlotte.

Louisa shrank back into the shadows. Not that Charlotte would have noticed her but she felt somehow that she was intruding on a private conversation.

'Didn't you enjoy the play?' asked Pamela, rather bravely.

'Dolly can't buy our favour even if she bought all the tickets.' Charlotte pulled her elegant velvet coat even more tightly. 'Adrian was dead set against Ted marrying her, you know.'

'What was it to do with him?' Nancy could never stop herself where anyone else would understand certain topics were off limits.

Charlotte lit a cigarette and gave a sigh. 'Ted's father was killed in a motoring accident when he was nine so his mother used to send him to come and stay with us in the holidays. He was Pa's godson and he needed some sort of man in his life, I suppose. When Pa died three years ago, Ted took it even more badly than Adrian and so Adrian took on the role of father. Suited his pomposity.' She gave a bitter laugh. 'Not that Ted was grateful. Actually, I think he was a little bit in love with me. He used to defend me against Ade when we had our fights.' She took a final puff and stamped it out with her heel. 'Now Adrian's gone and that bitch has taken over Ted. No, I *didn't* enjoy the play. Can we go now?'

Nancy absorbed this. Louisa could practically see her taking the notes down in her mind but before she could reply they heard a strident man's voice behind them.

'How simply ghastly, my dear. Perhaps I could do better for you next time?' followed by a thunderclap of laughter. Nancy, Pamela, Charlotte and Louisa swung around to see a modishly dressed man with soft eyes framed by eyebrows as thin as a woman's. It was unmistakably the author of the play, Mr Noël Coward. There was a crowd of three or four men and women behind him, tittering. Nancy blanched and Pamela cast about as if trying to find somewhere to disappear to but Charlotte looked as if she had been insulted and wasn't going to take it. She pushed past them and stalked off down the corridor.

Nancy chose her move. 'Mr Coward,' she said, 'some of us cut our tongues when we speak too sharply.' He had stopped and was standing before her, hips very slightly bent to one side, amusement on his lips. 'You, as we heard tonight, polish the blade.'

Mr Coward laughed like jelly. 'I say,' he said, draping an arm around Nancy's waist. 'You are a scream. Do tell me all about *you* ... ' He led her inside the packed room, which miraculously made space for him. Louisa and Pamela, gripped by this turn of events, couldn't help but watch from the doorway. Clara turned and saw Nancy enter more or less on Noël Coward's arm. She tried to cover her anger, fixing a smile on her face, but it was clear she felt she had lost her chance. Dolly and Ted exited then, squeezed out by the new intake. Dolly looked at Clara, then the playwright and leaned into Ted's ear.

'She won't be able to sleep her way to the top with *that* one at any rate,' she sneered, and marched off, Ted fast behind her, muttering soothing things Louisa couldn't quite hear.

Pamela and Louisa looked at each other. 'What shall we do?' said Pamela.

'We had better wait for Nancy,' said Louisa. She felt out of her depth.

Pamela pulled Louisa out of the doorway. 'I feel like an absolute lemon standing here. And I'm starving.'

Louisa looked up and down the corridor; other dressing rooms had their doors open, light and noise spilling out of each one. 'Perhaps we could leave a note for her with the doorman, and find something to eat in a café nearby?'

Pamela nodded. 'Yes, please.'

They crept away and walked back to the entrance, left a message and stepped out into Jermyn Street. The doorman, rather more friendly now, had told them they could get supper at the new Kit-Cat Club on Haymarket and that he would let the friends of Miss Blanche know they could be found in there. Pamela had started to say that she couldn't go to a *club* but he explained that it had a grill restaurant, an American notion, which meant you could order quite late at night. 'In fact,' he said, as if proffering a piece of life's wisdom, 'they don't even start serving supper until ten o'clock. And then all the crowd turns up, quite a gay lot, as I understand it. There's a cabaret at midnight.' He winked at this and Pamela hurriedly said goodbye and stepped out.

Louisa's stomach felt as empty as a balloon, unused to missing out on the clockwork routine of meals in the nursery. Nancy and her friends apparently used cigarettes and alcohol to stave off any real appetite – certainly nobody ever seemed to mention the need for food. 'I don't think we'd better go there,' said Pamela.

'No, perhaps not.' Now Louisa felt both hungry and disappointed. She'd have liked to catch sight of the dressed-up men and women, not to mention the show. As they stood, wondering what to do, a little fazed by the cacophony of lights, people and traffic making it feel like eleven o'clock in the morning rather than at night, Clara appeared in front of them. She'd been crying, and some of her make-up was running down her face in black streaks.

'Clara!' said Pamela. 'What's happened?'

Clara sniffled and looked at them both. Even with stained cheeks and huge, wet eyes, she was still undeniably pretty. Everyone else looks like a red-faced baby when they cry, thought Louisa, and only just stopped herself from saying *it wasn't fair* out loud. Nursery phrases could be contagious.

'Nothing that hasn't happened before,' she said, and outrage flashed in her face. 'I don't think there's a decent man out there. They're all b—' She seemed to remember Pamela's youthful innocence suddenly and stopped herself. 'I just wish someone would give me a chance without asking me to . . .' Again, she didn't go on. Clara gave a small hiccup and put her hand on her mouth. 'Oh, God,' she said. 'I'm drunk.'

'Is Nancy coming out now?' asked Pamela, doing her best to politely ignore Clara's last statement.

Clara nodded. 'With *Sebastian*.' She practically spat his name out and Pamela recoiled in shock.

'Has he done something, Clara?'

Clara looked about her, at the people rushing past. No one was watching. She put a finger on her lips and stumbled slightly as she pulled on her evening bag, hanging from a long, thin chain. She opened the clasp and showed it to Pamela and Louisa.

'He won't do it again though. None of them will.' They looked inside and caught the glint of a knife, nestled against the pink silk lining and a jewelled powder compact.

'*Clara*—' began Pamela but the American starlet hopeful had staggered off and the next thing they heard was violent retching as she was sick into the gutter of Jermyn Street.

CHAPTER TWENTY-FIVE

❧

A few days after Elsie White's arrest, Guy and Mary were still on undercover duty, walking along Oxford Street, though not hopeful of lightning striking twice. It was that desultory part of the day when boredom causes hunger but it was too early to stop for luncheon. The sky was a heavy grey and rain threatened. Traffic rumbled past and people hurried but the shops looked mostly empty. It wasn't close enough to Christmas yet for panic-buying. The two of them stopped by a newsstand, and Mary picked up the new *Tatler* magazine, flicking through the party pictures at the back. 'Who are all these people?' she laughed. 'Look at their funny names. Ponsonby, Fitzsimmons, La-Dee-Dah.'

'La-Dee-Dah?' Guy pretended to look at her sternly over the top of his glasses. 'Is that your official report of the attendees?'

'Yes,' said Mary in the tones of a news announcer. 'Miss La-Dee-Dah was seen out dancing at the Ritz with Mr Tiddlydum at a fundraiser for the fallen soldiers.'

They were laughing at this when Guy saw a headline on page three of *The Times* that made him stop. He handed over a few coins to the paperboy before he could get shirty with him for reading it for nothing. 'Joynson-Hicks's War on Vice,' he said.

'What's that?'

Guy read for a bit. 'He's a politician, out to shut down the nightclubs. Not the ones the toffs go to but the ones in Soho. The 43 gets a mention. Look, see, this is the problem we've talked about, it outlines it here.' He pointed to the paragraph and handed it to Mary, who read it, slightly battling with a sharp breeze as she did so.

'The police need to go in to the clubs to spot the vices but if they go in then they're indulging in the very thing they're supposed to be shutting down,' she summed up. 'How will they do it, then?'

'Beats me. Here's a picture of George Goddard. He's running the Vice Squad from Savile Row station. Not far from us.'

'We need to go there,' said Mary, handing it back to him.

'I know we do but we've been over this, haven't we? Cornish can't give us permission to go and we can't go without permission.' Guy pinched the bridge of his nose where his glasses sat, feeling the beginnings of an ache there.

'Then we go off-duty.'

Guy sighed and rolled the paper up. 'But we're never off-duty, are we?'

'You told me your friend Harry is in a band there,' said Mary.

'Yes but ...'

'Well, that's it, then. If for some reason we are caught going there we only need to say we went in to watch Harry. You don't have to do anything illegal while you're there, you know.' Mary was imploring him and she was quite hard to resist when she did that.

'All we have to do is pop in and see what it looks like. We can ask around and we might pick something up. It's better than nothing, which is all we've got at the moment.'

'Not tonight,' said Guy.

'Not tonight then,' agreed Mary, 'but soon.'

Guy could see she had already begun to count down the hours.

CHAPTER TWENTY-SIX

~~~~~

Before they had left Asthall Manor, Louisa had requested that she be excused for three hours while they were in London, to visit a relative in lieu of time off the following week. Having studied a copy of Lord Redesdale's map of London, with its Tube map printed on the back, Louisa estimated that if she left at eight o'clock in the morning, she could be back by eleven, in good time to accompany the sisters shopping. Lady Redesdale had been grudging but she did accede. In the meantime, Louisa had written a letter to Holloway Prison, requesting that she visit their prisoner, Dulcie Long. As Dulcie was still on remand, the process was fairly quick and she received permission in time. All of this had been relatively smooth, and Louisa was lulled into a sense of ease until she found herself walking towards the prison that Friday morning.

As she turned into Camden Road, she saw through the trees what could only be a prison looming into her line of sight like a castle in a fairy tale. Coming up closer made the experience no more comfortable, with giant griffins of stone arched over the entrance, itself dominated by the grey bricks laid to a height that were a match for Jack's beanstalk. There were turrets and crosses carved into the towers, the windows mere slits, too mean to allow anything in so pleasant as a view or a ray of sunshine. Louisa pulled her coat a little tighter and pushed her shoulders back because she knew she had to do this.

In some ways, she was comforted by the sight of others who looked like her and her sort. A line of prison visitors began to queue up by the wooden door, which had started to take on an almost comical effect, as if a wizard and his dragon would be waiting for them on the other side. There were mostly women, in cheap hats and thin coats, sometimes a smear of rouge on their grey faces, but there were a few men, too, in caps and Homburg hats, dark jackets with the collars turned up, almost every one with a cigarette pinched between forefinger and thumb. One woman stood out for being young and pretty. She clutched the hand of a small child in a coat with a velvet collar, holding on to her teddy bear like a lifebelt.

As a bell chimed in the distance, the door swung open and they all filed in, each ready to hand over their name and be patted down by the warden, whose manner revealed nothing but a poisonous combination of boredom and suspicion. Louisa steadied her feet and reminded herself that she had nothing to feel guilty about. The question was: did the person she was visiting?

Signed in, the visitors were instructed to follow a prison officer down a series of corridors. Each door needed to be unlocked, clanged shut and locked again before they went through the next one, herding them in between the gaps like sheep. At last, they reached the visitors' room, divided by a long line of what looked like open cupboards, as if in a pawnshop. Guards stood around the edge, ears twitching; to a man their arms were folded and resting on large stomachs. Louisa was told the number of her corresponding hatch and took her seat before the wooden screen with an open square, covered by iron grating. She waited a few minutes until Dulcie arrived on the other side, her face drawn, her collarbone almost slicing through the grey uniform. Louisa was struck again by their similarities, though this time it was like looking in a mirror that reflected how her life could have looked, a harsh reminder of the path she did not take. She tried not to flinch at the defeat that showed in Dulcie's face, though the young woman smiled at her arrival.

'I didn't believe it when they said you would be coming to see me,' she said. 'I thought you'd want nothing more to do with me.'

Louisa hesitated. Despite having come all this way and her sympathy for Dulcie, she still wasn't entirely sure what she thought of her. 'Those jewels,' she began, and Dulcie looked down when she said it. 'Why did you take them? Was that the deal with ... you know ...' She didn't dare say 'the Forty' in here. 'That you told me about?'

Dulcie gave a small nod but said nothing.

Louisa looked about her but no one seemed to be listening. She kept her voice low, even so. 'You know that I understand something of it but I wouldn't have let you into the house if I'd known ...'

Dulcie looked up then and her eyes had filled. 'I know,' she said. 'I had to lie to you about that. But I promise I wouldn't have done it if I'd had any choice. And I haven't lied to you about anything else, I promise.'

'I saw that woman, from the pub. She was there during the inquest,' said Louisa. 'Was she making sure you didn't say anything about them?'

'Yes,' said Dulcie, barely managing to form the word.

'Are you protecting them, Dulcie? Because I don't think you should. I think they can look after themselves.' Louisa felt bolder now.

A shadow passed across Dulcie's face. 'They know I'm in here; they've sent me a none-too-gentle reminder that I'm not to say anything. Suits them to have me stuck.'

Louisa looked down at her lap and gathered her courage, then faced Dulcie again through the narrow window. 'Did you do it?' she whispered.

Dulcie almost cried out but stopped herself. 'No, it wasn't me. I don't know what happened but it wasn't me.'

'Then there has to be a way of proving it.'

'There isn't,' said Dulcie. 'I'm done for in here, and I'm done for outside. And if they don't get me they'll get my—'

She broke off abruptly. 'Your what?' asked Louisa.

'My sister, Marie. It would be better if you just forgot about me altogether.'

Louisa turned her head slightly but the nearest guard's attention was on a woman two tables down who looked to be in danger of kissing the prisoner she was visiting.

'But you could hang for this,' said Louisa.

'Please, drop it.'

Louisa tried to smile. As if either of them could talk about the weather or the latest Mary Pickford picture. 'Of course.'

'What are you doing in London anyway?'

'Acting as chaperone. Miss Nancy and Miss Pamela have a dance tonight, somewhere in Chelsea.'

'Do you think Miss Charlotte will be there?'

'I don't know,' said Louisa truthfully. 'Maybe. She was at the theatre last night.'

Dulcie grimaced. 'All that lot do is go to parties. If she's there, will you give her a message from me?'

'I don't know, Dulcie.'

Dulcie's shoulders sagged. 'No, you're right. You can't do

that. It was only a small thing – I don't even know why I thought of it.'

'What was it?' Louisa tried to give Dulcie an encouraging look. 'In case the right moment does come up, I might as well know.'

'It's just that her dressmaker will be waiting for Miss Charlotte to collect her dress and be paid and she's one of us, you know. She needs the money. Mrs Brewster, at 92 Pendon Road in Earl's Court.'

Louisa hesitated, far from certain that she'd do this favour. 'Fine. Dulcie, who do you think did it? It has to be someone who was at the party, doesn't it?'

Dulcie's face closed. 'I know you mean to help but leave it alone. I tell you, it's hopeless. The trial's after Christmas and then that'll be me done for. There's nothing anyone can do. Forget it.'

Louisa was flooded with the memory of her uncle Stephen, of everything she had done and got away with. Dulcie was no better and no worse than her, and she'd been trying to get herself on the right track. It was sheer bloody bad luck. The kind of luck their sort always got doled out because no one else could understand how impossible it was to change it. If you lived amongst thieves, you were treated like one, and in the end, desperate, hungry, you thought you might as well become one, too. That's bad enough but then try and change your spots and see how no one lets you. Almost no one, that is. Louisa had been given another chance – it was hard but it wasn't impossible. She couldn't give up on Dulcie, not yet.

CHAPTER TWENTY-SEVEN

⁓

When Louisa arrived back at Iris Mitford's flat, she felt ready for bed again but it wasn't yet even noon. She found Pamela and Nancy in the drawing room with their aunt, a lean woman in her mid-forties, handsome and wild for her generation, with red lipstick. (Her sister-in-law would sooner be dead than be seen with cosmetics on her skin.) Mischief and steel shone in her grey eyes. Iris adored the young, by which she did not mean children, and was apt to emphasise the need to be beautifully dressed and entertaining in life. When Iris had heard about Pamela's fancy dress party for her eighteenth, she had warned the sisters to 'win the man, not the prize'. ('Yet Iris never has,' Nancy said, earning her a slap on the arm from Pamela.)

Pamela leapt up when Louisa came in, and the nursery maid guessed that she had interrupted one of Iris's spicier stories about Edwardian life, one that Lady Redesdale might not have approved of. It was Iris who had told Nancy of the well-known trick of 'corridor creepers', to walk on the edge of staircases so as to avoid making a giveaway creaking noise. 'Even so,' Nancy had explained on the train down, 'it's rather funny, because Iris was always known for being a bit of a do-gooder. I suppose now she's in a flat with some money, she can do what she likes.' The envy in Nancy's voice was ill disguised.

'But she loves animals, like I do,' chimed in Pamela. 'Once, she wrote a letter to *The Times* agreeing with the Duchess of Hamilton's claim that goat's milk was "highly palatable" and that people should be encouraged to drink it. And she looked after all the chickens at Batsford, Grandpa's place, collecting the eggs and so on.' When Louisa had met Iris Mitford, she had found this bit the hardest to believe, but Pamela swore upon its truth.

'Hello, Louisa,' said Pamela, 'I was just telling Iris about the supper we had last night.' A lie, but a good one. Pamela's ability to recount the detail of every morsel she'd eaten was renowned. Iris didn't stir at Louisa's entrance; her legs were crossed and she was smoking a cigarette in a long holder.

'Good morning,' said Louisa, careful to avoid saying 'Iris', which would have been quite wrong, or 'Miss Mitford', which would have displeased her. Although her formal address was, strictly speaking, 'Miss Mitford', she preferred to be known by her first and last names with no prefix. 'I just wanted to let you know I was back and ready to take Miss Nancy and Miss Pamela on their errands.'

Iris gave her a lazy look. 'Very well, off you go, girls. Come down and see me before you go out tonight. I want to check on what you're wearing.' The sisters giggled and gave their aunt a kiss on the cheek goodbye.

At six o'clock, after a day agreeably spent shopping and successfully completing their small jobs, as well as sneaking in a pot of hot chocolate in the café at Peter Jones, the girls were back at the house, changed and in the drawing room ready for inspection. Iris, too, was dressed for dinner, in a black crêpe de Chine dress that fell only a few inches below her knees, with an Egyptian-style pendant on a gold chain that looped well below her waist. Standing by the chimneypiece like a soldier on parade was Pamela, straight-backed in sufferance against the curves that prevented her dress from hanging fashionably but at least the marmalade colour suited her well. Nancy was wearing her beaded dress again, only this time she had a new pair of rather dashing long gloves with tiny purple buttons all along the side, from wrist to elbow.

'I shall be out with Colonel Maltravers tonight,' Iris was saying, 'and I don't know what time I shall return. Don't disturb me in the morning, girls. Gracie will see to everything.' There was a pause and a wolfish flash of teeth as she smiled. 'You look ravishing. Don't let the side down, will you?' The spell between them was broken, and in a flurry of kisses and goodbyes the girls ran out to pull Louisa with them and into a waiting taxi outside.

There was a dinner first, a small one that a friend of Lady Redesdale's had arranged, which Louisa sat out, awkwardly waiting alone in the hall while the clink of cutlery and polite murmur of conversation could be heard from the dining room. When that was finally over, they took a second taxi although the dance was not far away, in Lower Sloane Street. Nancy and Pamela had chattered excitedly on the way but almost before they had walked in, Louisa could sense it was going to be a disappointment. Though there was a sprinkling of men, these were outnumbered by women of Nancy's age, though they were none of them good-looking, and most appeared to be squired by elderly aunts. Louisa stifled her laugh when she saw an elderly gentleman in a top hat leaning on a walking stick, who screwed his face up in displeasure each time he went to sip his drink and the sprig of mint tickled his nose.

Pamela spotted two girlfriends and went over to them, while

Nancy swiped a glass from a passing waiter and pouted. A band played a desultory waltz, though it was too early for anybody to be dancing, and the aunts began to sit down in clusters along the edges of the room like territorial ravens. Louisa stood beside Nancy for the moment, not yet quite able to face the stark fact that she belonged with the dusty chaperones.

'This is going to be deathly,' said Nancy, and Louisa pulled a sympathetic face. Nanny Blor had taught her that their duty was to remind the girls how lucky they were in even the most desperate of circumstances but even Nanny couldn't have pretended that Nancy was going to have fun tonight. A stout woman with a broad neck and an equine profile bore down upon them and Louisa stepped back quickly.

'Nancy, my dear,' she boomed, 'so delightful you came, especially after all that *ghastly business* with the Curtis death.' This last was said in a stage whisper which only someone standing outside the room could have failed to hear.

'Mrs Bright,' said Nancy in icy tones, 'my mother sends her regards to you and your husband. We were *so* sorry to hear about Paul's expulsion from Oxford.'

Mrs Bright reared back. 'It was a voluntary departure after a misunderstanding,' she muttered, but the knife had gone in. 'Do send my regards in return.' She cantered off.

Pamela rejoined them and her face looked drained. 'It's all anyone's talking about,' she whispered to Nancy. Neither of them needed to ask what she meant.

Nancy drained her drink. 'Look, we have to stay for a bit because Muv's got her spies here, reporting on our movements. She's worse than the bloody Reds. Don't look so surprised, Woman. You know how she is. But we can sneak out and go to a nightclub.'

'We can't!' gasped Pamela. 'Muv will find out.'

'There's no reason why she should,' said Nancy. 'We can come back here, before the end, so that we're seen saying goodbye to Mrs Bright and the rest of them.'

Louisa started to speak but Nancy shushed her. 'You don't have to be a part of it, Lou. You stay here, and if any of it comes out later then I'll just say you didn't know.'

'That's all very well but I do know,' said Louisa. More than that, she wanted to go to a nightclub too, *much* more than she wanted to stay and join the ravens, but she knew better than to give herself away. She had long since learned that any sign of eagerness before the upper classes was as bad as dousing yourself in cold soup; they would do their best to hold you at arm's length. Affected nonchalance was the only way to get ahead. Unless you were American, of course, the exception that proved the rule as in so many other things. Clara Fischer was as eager as a Labrador puppy and her circle of friends were just as charmed. The knife in Clara's bag appeared in Louisa's mind again: had she used it before? Why on earth would she need to keep one with her? She pulled herself back: there wasn't anything she could do about it now.

The three of them stood and looked out at the room. Things hadn't improved. If anything, even the waiters were beginning to take on a pall of despair.

'There is nothing so depressing as a party that fails,' said Nancy. 'I'd rather be at a wake. At least then you're allowed to sob all the way through it.' Pamela laughed at this and Nancy looked gratified.

'Then let's talk to as many people as we can, so they'll all report back favourably, if asked,' said Pamela affably.

The two sisters looked at Louisa expectantly. 'Fine,' she said, pretending to have been swayed. 'But I'm coming with you because I need to know you're safe, and that you come back here in good time.'

'I knew it,' said Nancy, as a hush fell and an announcer called for the lords, ladies and gentlemen to come through to the ballroom. 'Meet me back here in twenty minutes,' she whispered. 'No one will notice if we slip away then.'

Soon enough, Nancy was leading them out of a French window at the back of the ballroom. Without their coats they were freezing cold but walked quickly around the side of the building and on to the street, where Nancy hailed a taxi as if she'd been doing it all her life. She saw Louisa looking at her.

'Sometimes I tell Muv I'm going to visit Tom at Eton and get the train to Oxford instead to spend the day. Don't look so shocked, Lou, I'm twenty-one. It's silly not to get out now and then.' They clambered into the cab and Nancy directed the driver to 43 Gerrard Street, Soho.

'Soho, Nancy? Is that wise?' Louisa had never been there but, like everyone else, she'd read the articles in the *Daily Sketch* of prostitutes, pimps and hard drinking. Since the arrival of flappers, jazz musicians and the Black Bottom dance, not to mention the stories of cocaine overdoses and illegally sold alcohol, the picture painted was of an unusually sordid place.

'They'll all be there,' Nancy replied confidently. Pamela stayed silent but strangely didn't look too nervous.

The taxi was speeding along now, approaching the harum-scarum roundabout at Hyde Park, where cars zoomed in from four different points to join the spinning wheel and you could only hope to fly off at the right junction.

'How do you know?' asked Louisa.

'Because Ted is engaged to Dolly Meyrick, and she's running the place now her mother's in Paris lying low for a few months. So all the gang go there.' Nancy pulled a mock-sad face at Pamela. 'Sorry to mention her again, darling.' Pamela ignored this.

'Dolly is Mrs Meyrick's daughter?' Louisa was amazed at this piece of news. The fact that she was engaged to Lord De Clifford was pretty extraordinary, too. Mrs Meyrick, as anyone who enjoyed a bit of society gossip knew well, was a cause célèbre for her infamous nightclubs and her frequent arrests.

'Yes,' said Nancy, eyebrow raised. 'Mind you, it might not happen. Ted's not yet twenty and he won't get his mother's permission. Mind you, *she* was an actress when she married his father and some might say – they certainly will say – Ted's only marrying his mother like all men do.'

'Naunce, you mustn't be so naughty,' chided Pamela, but they all exploded into a firework of giggles and nose snorts, a welcome relief that seemed to release weeks of anxiety, let alone that evening's tension. As Piccadilly came into view, with Eros before a backdrop of vast signs of coloured bulbs advertising Army Club Cigarettes and 'Cannes – the sea-side of flowers and sports', resplendent with cascading lights for a pink and orange sunset on a blue sea, adrenalin surged through Louisa as if she, too, had been plugged into the generator.

The doorway to the 43 Club gave nothing away of what lay behind it. It may have been late at night on the long narrow street but it felt as busy as market day at Burford, with men and women crowding the pavement, as well as one or two drunks stumbling. Louisa thought she could see a fight starting out of the corner of her eye. When they got out, the taxi sped off, not wanting to pick up business there, and Nancy knocked on the closed door. It was opened by a huge man in black tie who gave them a quick appraising glance, if a slightly questioning one in Louisa's direction, and waved them in.

Just inside the hall was a window, behind which sat a pretty young girl with hair as bright as a new copper coin. She gave them a toothy smile and asked for ten shillings each – 'membership fees' – which Nancy handed over.

'I raided the piggy bank before we came down,' she explained.

'Not Unity's?' said Pamela, but Nancy merely gave a wicked grin in reply. They could hear clearly the fast beat of a jazz band, with the high-pitched strains of a trumpet lilting across the top as they walked down the steep short staircase, the walls on either side painted nail-varnish red. At the bottom they came out into a semi-lit room and Louisa was hit by a wall of smoke, heat and noise that was as intoxicating as wine. Nancy gave a cry and stuck a hand up to wave to someone before she pushed into the moving crowd, the bodies forced apart and coming back together like water. Pamela put her arm through Louisa's and shouted into her ear, 'I don't know anyone here, Lou.'

'Follow Nancy,' Louisa shouted back. And they dived into the sea together, Louisa almost hoping she'd never come back up for air again.

CHAPTER TWENTY-EIGHT

～

As Nancy had predicted, the circle of friends were at the club –
Sebastian, Clara, Ted and Charlotte. Phoebe was there, too.
They were spread across two tables, awash with half-empty and
full glasses of champagne, at the edge of the dance floor. Others
were with them, none of whom Louisa recognised but who bore
the marks of their kind: kohl-lined eyes, lips the colour of bruised
plums and sharply bobbed hair for the women; sallow faces and
evening dress for the men, with the occasional dandy. The whites
of their eyes flashed through the cigarette smoke as they drank in
Louisa and Pamela, and she felt as if she were walking towards a
sacrificial altar. Clara came up to them and embraced Pamela in
a hug, then pulled a face of secret apology. Their last sight of her
hadn't been picturesque.

'Life goes on, doesn't it, darlings?' she said, then appraised
Pamela. 'You look simply marvellous. Yes, you will definitely *do*.'
Pamela's pleasure was easy to see. Clara looked at Louisa then, and
said quite seriously: 'You know, you really are pretty. You should get
your hair shingled. Then nobody will be able tell you're a maid.'
Louisa wasn't sure how to react to this but Clara wasn't waiting

for a reply – she had spun on her heels to face the band on their small raised stage with her hands thrown wide, like a music hall announcer.

'You're so lucky you came tonight, it's Joe Katz's spot.' Her voice was unable to disguise the admiration, but Louisa couldn't take it in at that moment – there was too much crowding in on her senses, the pounding music and the moving bodies, the smoke and the thrill of danger that was running a finger up and down her spine.

'Here.' A glass was thrust into Louisa's hand, she didn't see by whom. Her throat was parched and she drank it in one gulp, immediately feeling the lightness in her head. She hoped Pamela hadn't seen her. Nancy was buried deep in the crowd, talking fast to Sebastian and Ted, who had his arm around Dolly's waist. Dolly was less shy here it seemed for she would turn now and then to issue an order to a waitress, but otherwise she hung on to her beau's every word. Charlotte sat by a table, alone and sullen, smoking with frequent, staccato inhalations. She looked as if she'd just had a row or was brewing to start one. Or perhaps she was just sad. Nancy had gossiped in the taxi that Charlotte's mother had yet to emerge from her room, appearing no longer to care what happened to her daughter now that her son was gone. Clara had taken Pamela by the hand and led her to the dance floor, where they had both been taken up immediately by two young bucks with slicked-back hair and impish grins. Louisa could see Pamela's head bobbing down to the young man's – he was, unfortunately, an inch or two shorter – as she tried to ask polite questions over the music and invariably had to ask him to repeat the answer, which she couldn't hear. Louisa ducked behind Clara and refilled her glass, then took a good long look at Joe Katz and his band.

At that moment, Joe's back was turned to the club as he conducted his band of musicians. There must have been twelve of them or so, seated and dressed in sharp suits, each one with an instrument – saxophone, trumpet, trombone. Abruptly, the beat changed and Joe swung around, grasped the tall microphone that stood on the stage before him and began to sing. It was only then Louisa saw that Joe was black-skinned, with high cheekbones, even white teeth and an expression in his eyes that seemed to look directly at her and ask her to jump right in. He sang a song of – what else? – starry nights and love, each note like molten gold.

Louisa felt the rhythm take her body over and before she knew it, she was moving into the dancers who pulsed as one, shimmying and sliding to the hot jazz. Every hair on Louisa's body seemed to stand on end and she felt as if her skin could light touch paper. She had been wearing a jacket over her simple tunic dress, but she shrugged it off and threw it onto a chair. If she never saw it again, what did she care? Joe's voice wove its way through the bodies like a silk scarf wrapping around them. Louisa felt herself reined in tighter and tighter. As she got closer to the centre, she exchanged brief glances and smiles with the others there, men and women alike, both friendly and seductive. A line of sweat ran down her front and still she kept moving. Her shoulders shook and her hips swayed until she had the startling revelation that they were all in motion as a single, amorphous living thing. Her mind was filled with nothing but the music and Joe's voice of romance and darlings. Everything, everything, fell away and the only thing that mattered was to keep on dancing. A man would come close and start to move in symmetry with her and she would smile, allow him and then, when she had had enough, she would sidle away and carry on alone. She was happy like that. Once, a woman who wore a dress of lilac feathers, came closer than any man, slid up and down her side and breathed into her ear, 'Keep going *just* like that.' So she did.

No one knew she was a servant. No one knew she grew up on a Peabody Estate. No one knew the things she was frightened of in the night when she lay alone, before dawn stroked her with its rosy fingers. No one knew that she was exultant in happiness in this moment, in a way that she had never known before and was suddenly terrified she would never know again. They knew nothing of her, she knew nothing of them and nobody cared. It was perfect.

Of course, it had to end.

The band stopped, Joe announced a break and the dancers fell away. Louisa's legs burned, the sweat on her back cooled and her mouth was dry. She spotted Clara and Pamela, still together, and walked over to them. Pamela grabbed Louisa: 'Isn't he wonderful?' she exclaimed.

'Who?' said Louisa, though she knew she didn't need to ask.

'Joe Katz!' said Pamela, her voice breathless. She, too, had been dancing and her hair was delightfully loose, the curls shaken out. So everyone was in love with Joe, and Louisa saw several women crowding around him as he walked to the bar.

'Where's Nancy?' asked Louisa, conscious of her duties now the music had stopped. She had no idea what time it was. Pamela pointed to a table close by and Louisa saw Nancy there, smoking a cigarette and in conversation with Charlotte. She was wondering whether she dared interrupt, when she felt a tap on her shoulder. She turned around and at first couldn't see anyone, but when she dipped her head slightly she saw Harry standing there, a wide grin on his face. Harry was a friend of Guy Sullivan's and they had been in the railway police force together. He was diminutive but with the good looks of a Hollywood film star, all deep-blue eyes and a dimple in his chin. 'Harry!' she exclaimed. Knowing somebody in here had elevated the experience by several notches – now she really felt a part of it.

'Miss Louisa Cannon,' he said silkily and took her hand to kiss it, one eyebrow lifted as he did so. 'It's a pleasure to see you here.'

'How are you?' she said, happily. 'What are you doing here?'

'I'm in the band,' he said, jerking his thumb to the stage. 'Good, isn't it? That Joe is quite something.'

'You're in the band! I didn't see you. What instrument?'

'Ha, well, God left a few inches off when he made me, I can't be seen when I'm sitting in a chair,' he laughed. 'I'm on the trumpet. I quit the police, do the music full time now. Couldn't be better.'

Louisa felt a wave of nostalgic pleasure wash over her. 'It's so lovely to see you, Harry. How's Guy?'

'Haven't seen too much of him lately. It's not really his kind of thing this club, but we should try to get him along now you're turning up here. He's always pleased to see you, you know.'

Louisa blushed. 'I know. I like seeing him, too.'

Harry gestured to her empty glass, 'Let's get you a drink.' He summoned a waiter and asked for a bottle of champagne. 'Why not?' he said, seeing her face. 'We should celebrate seeing each other.' When they had their drinks and found a spot to sit down, Harry lit a cigarette and turned to her again. 'Now, tell me, what's a nice girl like you doing in a place like this?'

'What do you mean?'

'Well, this place. It's full of disreputable types. Musicians, gangsters, women of the night ... Mind you, it's safe here. We never seem to get a police raid.'

'I had no idea,' said Louisa, pulling a shocked face which quickly gave way to a chuckle. 'Those are my people,' she joked. There was a pause and she stopped smiling. 'What do you mean, gangsters?'

'Oh, nothing like the hoodlums you read about in New York, though some of them like to pretend they're the same, for the glamour. But we get a few, drug runners mostly. And –' he bent in close, whispering in Louisa's ear '– Alice Diamond. She's a regular.' He sat back up and tapped the side of his nose with a finger.

Louisa's blood ran cold. Alice Diamond came in here?

'She's not here tonight, usually comes in on a Saturday. After a good day's haul on Bond Street, I should imagine. She's known as an underground queen, running a gang of forty girl thieves, or so the story goes. You wouldn't know it to look at her though, all chichi dresses and diamonds on every finger.' He grinned, pleased with himself for providing such good gossip.

'When did you last see her?' said Louisa, completely sober now.

'Just last weekend. She's pretty regular. Think she likes old Joe, but then – who doesn't?'

Louisa gave a weak smile and knocked back her glass. If Alice Diamond came here, this could be her chance to meet her, and find out what she could that would help free Dulcie.

All she knew was that she would do whatever it took. If she couldn't beat Alice Diamond and her gang, then maybe she'd have to join them.

CHAPTER TWENTY-NINE

～～～

The following morning, Louisa woke relieved to remember that the three of them had made it back to the party in Lower Sloane Street in time – at least according to the clock in the hall – sneaking in to say goodbye to their host. It hadn't looked as if anything had turned for the better in their absence and when Louisa considered the night she'd almost missed, she sent a prayer of thanks into the air. She didn't believe in God, despite all those Our Fathers she'd recited at school and the weekly Mitford trip to church where Lord Redesdale timed the vicar's sermon ('not a second over ten minutes') but after hearing Joe Katz's music, she suspected some other kind of spiritual magic had been at work.

Harry's mention of Guy Sullivan had unsettled her too. Louisa realised it had been some months since she had last seen him. In so many ways, to fall in love and marry Guy would be a nice, simple and probably happy ending. At twenty-three she knew her mother thought her time was running out. But so far as Louisa could see, marriage for a man might mean the beginning of a new chapter, with a wife to look after him and children to watch grow up, but for a woman it meant years of domestic toil. When she read in the newspapers about the women who were working as scientists or politicians, even flying planes in America, she never failed to notice that these women were rarely married.

She shook her head: What did all this matter? There was work to get on with.

Louisa left the kitchen where she had lent a hand to Gracie, and knocked on Pamela's door.

'Good morning, Lou,' said Pamela, hitching up her tweed skirt and grunting slightly as she did up the buttons. 'I think I'd better have half a grapefruit for breakfast. There was an article about it in *The Lady*. Apparently the juices in the grapefruit burn away anything bad you eat afterwards.'

Louisa took the Nanny Blor line of ignoring this sort of comment but in any case Pamela was anxious to discuss the night before. 'You don't think Muv will find out what we did, do you?' she continued.

'There's no reason she should, unless you say something.' Louisa tried to sound a warning note in her voice, hoping it would keep Pamela quiet.

'No, I won't. She wouldn't understand anyway. It was like another world there, wasn't it? That music, and the dancing ... So many gorgeous dresses and, oh. Cocktails.' She put a hand to the side of her head and grimaced.

Pamela carried on poring over the details of the clothes worn, the drinks served and, of course, the canapés that had occasionally appeared. 'Such a sweet idea, tiny little squares of toast with pâté, and spoonfuls of caviar on biscuits. Do you think Mrs Stobie would do something like that? Farve would have an absolute fit.'

Louisa smiled with her but felt suddenly fatigued at the thought of their return to Asthall Manor. Were her ties to the Mitfords coming loose? She wasn't conscious of having pulled the string but nor was she in any rush to stop it coming undone.

'Do you know what Miss Nancy's plans are for the rest of the day?'

'Not much, I shouldn't think,' said Pamela. 'She said something about meeting up with Clara for tea.'

'Would you like to come out with me?' asked Louisa. 'I've got an idea.' Something had just occurred to her and now she couldn't let go of it.

Pamela sat up on the edge of the bed. 'Yes, do let's. I need the fresh air.'

Not ten minutes later the two of them stood before a hair salon, the December wind buffeting their coats, their hands firmly holding onto their hats. Inside, through the plate-glass shop front, they could see elegant women sitting at chairs, men standing behind them, wielding scissors like Greek gods wreaking revenge.

'Are you sure about this?' said Pamela.

'Yes, quite sure.' Louisa felt a curlicue of excitement and giggles wind up through her chest.

Inside, a young woman sitting at a desk looked up; her hair was perfectly coiffured in waves that shone like a newly fallen conker. 'Can I help you, madam?'

'Yes, I'd like a shingle cut, please.'

The walls were painted in lilac and there was a miniature poodle lying on a basket by the receptionist, its fur dyed the same shade. Pamela shook Louisa by the shoulder and pointed to it, alarm on her face.

'It's like Antoine de Paul's,' said the receptionist pointedly, and when she saw the name provoked no reaction, she sighed and went on, 'You know, the famous hairdresser Monsieur Antoine?' Louisa wasn't sure that imitating a hairdresser's poodle-dying techniques was a recommendation but she wasn't going to back out now.

Pamela took a seat on a low white sofa by the window and

picked up a *Tatler*, while Louisa was led to a chair before a mirror. Unpinned, her hair hung down to below her shoulders, neither curly nor straight, an unremarkable colour. After it had been washed, she watched as long chunks of it fell to the floor, before the hairdryer and hot tongs that sizzled and made her ears twitch nervously. When it was finished Louisa looked at herself in amazed admiration. She had shining waves which brought her hair out into a richer shade of brown and the short, blunt edges of the bob made her chin sharper, her eyes bigger.

Pamela looked up from her magazine. 'Oh my goodness. Farve's going to have convulsions.'

Louisa felt so good, almost powerful, that she whispered to Pamela as if she was sharing a secret. 'Don't you want to do it, too?'

Pamela gave a little gasp. 'Oh!' She blushed, and then she looked down at herself despairingly. 'I *do*. I think. But I don't dare.' She paused. 'Nanny *would* be cross to hear me talking like this. You know she always says nobody's looking anyway.' They both laughed at this, knowing Nanny's nuggets of wisdom well.

Back out on the bright streets of Chelsea, they walked along enjoying the Christmas decorations in the shops. Louisa felt buoyant and it helped that she attracted one or two glances from young men as they walked past.

Pamela said, 'You know, I can't change my hair too drastically but perhaps I could order a new dress?' A rueful smile. 'I've got some birthday money to spend and Sebastian made a comment about the one I was wearing last night that wasn't rude exactly but . . .'

Something came back to Louisa in a flash. She'd completely forgotten about it but now she scrabbled in her pocket for a scrap of paper – she'd written it down in pencil when she'd left the prison then dismissed it from her mind. She brought the note out, *Mrs*

Brewster, 92 Pendon Road, Earl's Court. 'Yes,' she said to Pamela, 'Dulcie mentioned a seamstress to me before. Maids share useful information like that, you know.'

'Dulcie? The maid that . . . ?' Pam trailed off uncertainly.

'Yes, but don't worry about that. This is the name of Miss Charlotte's dressmaker. I expect there will be a dress that Miss Charlotte needs picked up. We could do her a favour and ask about something for you at the same time. There's no harm in that, is there?'

'No.' Pamela smiled warmly. 'Not at all. Thank you, Lou-Lou.'

'Right, then,' said Louisa, feeling full of gladness and hope, that magic that only a new frock can bring. 'Let's go – there's no time like the present.'

And arm in arm, with extra springs in their feet, the two women fairly bounced to South Kensington station.

CHAPTER THIRTY

⁓

Pamela and Louisa caught the London Underground to Earl's Court and, following directions from a ticket officer, made their way down a couple of shabby side streets before arriving at Mrs Brewster's building. The front door had been left on a latch – there were several flats and clearly one or two of them had custom that came and went with some regularity – and they climbed the threadbare carpet to the third floor, where there was a small brass sign with a card that announced BREWSTER. They knocked and soon heard a shuffle on the other side and two bolts being drawn. An old woman pushed her head between the door and the frame. She looked more belligerent than nervous but Louisa decided to give her the benefit of the doubt.

'Hello, I'm Louisa Cannon and this is Miss Mitford. Beg pardon for not telephoning to you first but we have been recommended to you by Miss Charlotte Curtis.'

The door swung open and the tiny but unbent figure walked off down the hall without waiting to see if they followed her. She turned into a room on the left that was little bigger than the boot room at Asthall Manor and scarcely more furnished. A long wooden table stood in the centre, a pile of materials folded at one end, with various sewing tools beside it. A black and gold Singer machine occupied the head of the table, as solidly as any man of the house. The walls had evidently been papered some years ago, the seams buckling and edged with accumulated London grime. Draped over the backs of chairs, or hanging off randomly banged-in nails in the wall, were a variety of dresses, none of which would have looked out of place in a smart shop in Knightsbridge. The dressmaker herself wore a white apron tied around her frail figure. There were pins stuck in her apron straps and ribbons trailed out of the pocket. When she reached the table, she touched it, as if winning a race, and then walked around to the other side, standing behind it. Louisa had the distinct feeling that she did that to protect herself. Yet, Mrs Brewster gave them a smile and Louisa noticed now that though her skin was lined, it was olive-dark, too, and while her hair was flecked with grey around her temples the rest was jet black and pulled into a full bun high on her head. When she spoke, they were surprised – though perhaps they shouldn't have been – to hear a strong Italian accent.

'*Signorina* Curtis sent you?' she enquired, her eyes lively.

'Yes,' said Pamela. She and Louisa had agreed on this small white lie beforehand. 'I'd like a new dress, something more fashionable. Well.' She gestured to her suit, which was dark green and woollen, perfectly serviceable for Sunday church in Asthall but not for an afternoon in town. Louisa had felt a pang when she'd done that, perhaps for the end of Pam's childhood. The Pamela of even a few months ago couldn't have cared less what she was wearing, so long as she was outside riding her beloved horse or chatting with Mrs Stobie about the plans for Sunday luncheon.

'I understand perfectly, *signorina*,' said Mrs Brewster. She put her hands together and looked around the room, her narrowed eyes alighting on a simply cut but ravishing dress of silvery devoré velvet with a scoop neckline, not too low, and a drop waist. 'Something like this?' She walked around the table and held it up against Pamela.

'Yes,' said Pamela, delight infusing her voice. 'Just like this!'

'You cannot 'ave this one. This one is meant for Miss Peake but we can do it like this for you, a little bit different, no?' She went over to her pile of materials and pulled out a long length of velvet the colour of honey, almost a match for Pamela's hair. 'This, I think,' she said, holding it against Pamela's collarbone. 'With perhaps this . . .' From her pocket she brought out a deep-pink satin ribbon. 'Something like this for the belt?'

The last time Louisa had seen Pamela this happy was when she was appraising the gloss on a chocolate eclair shortly before eating it.

'May I use the bathroom?' asked Louisa. She didn't really need it but she felt Pamela needed this moment on her own with the seamstress, to be a grown-up and make her own decision about her dress.

'Down the hall on the left,' said Mrs Brewster busy with the velvet, pins already between her lips.

Louisa took her time, lingering over her reflection in the mirror as she admired her new haircut, trying it out at different angles and even using a hand mirror she found by the sink to look closely at the shingled cut and the sharp 'v' that it formed on the back of her neck. She was practically middle-aged according to Diana, but she thought that perhaps she didn't look it. Would *she* ask Mrs Brewster for a new frock? It probably wasn't the done thing for a girl and her maid to share the same dressmaker. Eventually, she went out but was stopped in her tracks when she saw the door opposite was slightly open and a young boy, perhaps three years old, was standing there shyly watching her. Louisa bent down.

'Hello,' she said warmly. 'What's your name?'

The boy said nothing but continued to look at her with enormous blue eyes. His dark hair had been closely cut, no babyish curls left, but he had dimples where his knuckles would be in a few years, and eyelashes that were as thick as curtains. He wore a pair of sky-blue shorts that matched the colour of his eyes, but Louisa could see they had been patched more than once and his white shirt was butter-soft from constant rewashing.

'I'm Louisa,' she continued, but he suddenly withdrew and closed the door.

Mrs Brewster was noting down the last of Pamela's measurements when Louisa returned.

'Who is that little boy?' she enquired, wondering as she did if she should have asked, but curiosity had got the better of her.

'The *bambino* is not mine,' said the dressmaker. 'I look after him for a little extra money, though I spend nearly all of it on his food. It is hard work for an old lady like me but since *mio caro signore* Brewster has passed to the other side, I must earn what I can …'

She trailed off and when she started speaking again it was to agree a price with Pamela for the dress, which would be finished and ready for collection in a week's time. Louisa asked if there was a dress or bill to be collected for Miss Charlotte Curtis and Mrs Brewster was only too delighted to have been reminded; she pressed a note into Louisa's hands. The task completed, the two of them were ushered out of the dressmaker's door and back out into the street.

Pamela took Louisa by the arm. 'Come on, let's get back to my aunt's and get ready for tonight. I want to go back to the 43.'

Louisa knew it was her place to refuse this, but how could she? She felt as giddy at the idea as her charge.

CHAPTER THIRTY-ONE

⌒

This time, the three young women were prepared. Louisa had money in her pocket, Pamela had bought a new pair of silk stockings and Nancy had rung up Clara, to be sure she and the others would be there. Of course, Louisa had no new dress so made do with her Sunday best, which had the merit of contrasting white lace collar and cuffs, fortunately packed because Nanny Blor had once forewarned her always to take something smart when going up to London 'just in case'. She did, of course, have her freshly bobbed hair, which made her feel as dashing as any young thing. Perhaps she'd catch Joe Katz's eye tonight.

The two sisters had supper with their aunt, who had returned, then bid them goodnight. As previously arranged, they both apparently went to bed but once in their room, changed into their frocks.

'We lay down with just the bedspreads over us, hoping that Iris wouldn't put her head round the door to say goodnight,' Pamela had told Louisa breathlessly in the taxi later. 'If she had, she might have noticed that Nancy had gone to bed with earrings!' The daring had thrilled her.

Louisa was waiting for them on the corner of Elvaston Place

at the arranged hour, having sneaked out of the flat separately. It wasn't too cold but there was something of the festive promise to come that made the night feel more wintry, and she pulled her hat further down over her ears. She could see one or two houses had put Christmas wreaths on their front doors, and the street lamps shone their brilliant white light. They greeted each other with nervous smiles without saying anything, as if their aunt might hear them from fifty yards away and two floors up. Quickly, they walked away, their eyes peeled for a taxi.

Pulling up outside the 43, the tall man standing guard gave them a brief look of recognition, allowing them to slip past him and hand over their shillings to the woman behind the desk before making their way down the narrow stairs as if they were regulars. As before, the smoke and the music hit them first and Louisa breathed it in like the fresh air of a spring morning in the country. She was a city girl, after all. Perhaps it was petrol fumes and brick dust that powered her lungs.

The room was even more crowded than it had been the night before, the wooden chairs and tables around the sides of the dance floor pushed even further from the edge. The band appeared to be in full swing and Louisa was pleased to spot Harry this time, on his trumpet, eyes squeezed shut in concentration, sweat pouring down the sides of his face. Joe Katz stood on the platform, both hands on his mic, his body swaying like a reed in the breeze, his voice mellifluous, his eyes watching the room. For a brief second, Louisa thought he locked on her, registering her new haircut, but she quickly told herself she must have imagined it. There were so many dancers on the floor this evening there was hardly space to move, let alone shimmy or foxtrot. Almost as a single body they rippled to the music, Joe Katz's voice a stone that he threw in their water.

And then, Louisa saw her. Alice Diamond. In the middle of the crowd, she might not have been easily spotted but she was the tallest woman there. Nevertheless, she danced well and Louisa could see that she was light on her feet in spite of her height. Her hair was fashionably done, her face made up with rouge and false eyelashes and though she was still irredeemably plain the look of pure bliss that smoothed her features gave her a look that showed her somehow more at ease in her own skin than before. Louisa noticed that there were three women, stylish too, close by her, neither quite dancing nor standing still, as if keeping lookout. Could it really be her? But if it was, how was it that nobody else seemed to register this astonishing fact?

Then Louisa almost laughed out loud at her own idiocy. It was, of course, for that reason precisely that Alice Diamond came to the 43: because she would be left completely alone, just as everybody else was. The dark walls, the dim lights, the beat of the dancing bodies to the intoxicating music: it levelled all comers, wherever they came from.

Nancy and Pamela had started to move through the crowd, weaving in and out of the moving parts as waiters held trays aloft and people went to and from the dance floor. Louisa counted them all as if on a school trip. Sebastian, Charlotte, Clara, Phoebe and Ted were in the same spot as the previous night. Clara greeted Nancy and Pamela warmly before taking in Louisa's haircut and giving her a thumbs up. Louisa couldn't help it – it was pleasing to be noticed.

Pamela was about to walk off when she stopped. 'Have you got that bill from the dressmaker? I can give it to Charlotte now.' Louisa fished it out of her pocket and handed it over, and watched Pamela walk across to Charlotte, who was sitting at a table rather glumly, her made-up eyes fixed on Sebastian. He looked glassy-eyed, with one arm around a woman who was heavily made-up and wearing a dress that dipped dangerously low at the front. She was trying to attract the attention of a waiter though Louisa could see the table in front of them was already laden with drinks, a jug of coffee and a box of chocolates, opened but with none eaten. Louisa was about to turn away when her eyeline snagged on the woman suddenly jerking away from Sebastian before delivering a sharp slap to his cheek and walking off. There was a stillness in the people immediately nearby but Sebastian merely shrugged a shoulder and, with a slight swaying motion, pulled out a chair and sank into it. Charlotte went and sat next to him; she looked as if she might be trying to show him the bill Pamela had given her but Sebastian waved his hand, batting her away. At the same time, Louisa saw his other hand in his pocket, checking something was there.

Louisa was conscious of staring so turned back to Alice in the centre of the room, but her head was dipped, talking to someone, and Louisa couldn't be sure now that it was her. Louisa felt a tap on her shoulder and was surprised to see Phoebe there. She was sweating slightly, tendrils of her hair stuck to her forehead, and held open a palm, giving Louisa a knowing look. In her hand was a small silver tin, the lid hinged open with what looked like white talcum powder heaped inside.

'Want some?' she slurred. 'Bit of the real stuff. Seb gave it to me.'

Louisa couldn't help it; she was rather shocked. 'No, thank you.' She knew she sounded prim but hopefully Phoebe was too drunk to notice.

Phoebe closed the box and started swaying to the music, her eyes half-closed and glassy. 'I used to be one of the Merry Maids here, you know.'

'Oh, did you?' Louisa was doing her best to appear politely interested.

'Yeah, that's why I thought ... you and me, we're almost the same.' She gave a hollow laugh and gestured at the crowd. 'They call me their friend but they're not, they never forget where I've come from. They just use me for my *good looks*.' She leant nearer, giving Louisa a wink and Louisa was quite afraid she might fall over. 'That's why I wasn't asked to the theatre.'

'I see.' Louisa was trying to sound as non-committal as possible because a conversation with a drunk never felt as if it was going to end well. But then Louisa worried that she might seem unfriendly, and perhaps Phoebe felt as she did. Despite wearing the right clothes, her good looks and even the invitations to be with Nancy and her set, she could never be truly 'one of them'.

'It's good to see your ankle is better.'

Phoebe laughed at this, guffawing into the back of her hand. 'That wasn't even true.'

'What?'

'I mean, I tripped on the dog but my ankle was fine. I just wanted to be alone with Sebastian. But that stupid cow can't ever leave him be.' She grimaced and looked over to where Charlotte was talking to Sebastian, though he still looked indifferent. 'Think I'll go over there now, actually.'

Phoebe had *lied* about her sprained ankle?

Abruptly, the music stopped and Phoebe went scuttling off, leaving Louisa feeling exposed in the absence of sound as everyone rushed to their tables or up the stairs to the bar. She couldn't go and sit with Pamela and Nancy but she did not want to let them out of her sight either. They were in this together but she didn't trust Nancy not to give her the slip.

Instead, Louisa walked across to where the band was and this time it was she who tapped Harry on the shoulder. He was mopping his brow with a large handkerchief and when he saw her he laughed. 'We have to stop meeting like this. What are you doing here again?'

Louisa put her hands up, palms out, a mock-apology. 'The girls wanted to come and I have to look after them.'

He gave her a knowing look and then did a comical about turn. 'I say,' he said with a low whistle, 'you've had your hair cut. It looks good, Miss Cannon. It really does.'

Louisa was pleased and gave a half-shimmy. 'Why thank you kindly, sir.'

'You know, Guy might be here tonight,' he said. 'After you came, I dropped him a line, suggesting that he should and he said he'd come this weekend. I must say, I've been trying all this time to get him here, then I only need to drop your name . . .'

'All right, Harry,' said Louisa, 'stop your teasing. But I would like to see him.'

'Let's go and find him. I've got ten minutes and, besides, if he is in here, I need to make sure he's safe from the Merry Maids.'

'Who are they?'

'Officially they're dancers employed by the club,' said Harry. 'Unofficially . . .' He winked and Louisa got his meaning.

'Fine but I can't leave this room, I need to keep an eye on the girls,' said Louisa. 'If Guy is here, please tell him to come and find me.'

'Gotcha,' said Harry and nipped off, his nimble frame easily finding the gaps between the men and women.

Louisa leaned against the wall, feeling safe in the shadows, content to watch the people as they smoked and drank. She was lost in her thoughts when she heard a gentle voice ask, 'Hey, lady, got a light?'

Nobody appeared to be there and then she realised the voice came from behind her, low down, from someone sitting down in even deeper shadows. White teeth flashed a handsome smile. Joe Katz.

'Oh, I'm so sorry, I don't,' she blustered. Damn. Why didn't she keep matches in her purse?

'Don't give it another thought, doll. I probably shouldn't anyway, the doc's told me it's no good for my voice.'

'Yes,' said Louisa, kicking herself for not coming up with some sort of funny quip like a proper flapper would.

'Ain't I seen you here before?' Joe asked, still sitting down, holding his unlit cigarette.

'Last night,' she said, and dared herself to carry on talking. 'I think your music is wonderful, Mr Katz.'

'Call me Joe.'

'Joe.'

'That sounds sweet on you.' He gave a low chuckle and stood up. 'It's been a pleasure, Miss . . . ?'

'Cannon. Louisa Cannon. I mean, call me Louisa.' Damn, she couldn't think straight.

'Louisa.' He seemed to roll her name like a body turning in the night. 'Forgive me but I'd better get back to the music.' She thought for a second he was going to kiss her but then he took her hand and kissed that instead, and his lips were soft and warm. Just as they might feel upon her own.

CHAPTER THIRTY-TWO

~~~~~

Seconds later, Louisa felt the atmosphere change, as if everyone had received a secret signal, and the room was packed again, everyone at the ready with either drink or dance partner in hand, waiting for the music to cue their next move.

When Louisa looked up she jumped: Guy was standing only a few yards away, a look of bewilderment on his face. Taller than most of the people in the room, his round glasses glinted in the light that was thrown by the lamps on the tables and the glass beads of the women's dresses and jewellery. She stepped out and went towards him and tried to dismiss thoughts of Joe Katz, as if Guy would be able to read upon her face the picture of his kiss.

'Guy,' she called, 'it's me, Louisa.'

'You've cut your hair,' he said, too stupefied to say hello.

'Yes,' she said, having to raise her voice over the insistent stretches of trumpet that looped around the tinny keys of the piano. A real conversation was pointless. 'I'm with Miss Nancy and Miss Pamela.' She jerked her head in their direction, though she wasn't entirely sure they were still sitting there.

'I see. I did wonder ...' He leaned in closer, his eyebrows

wrinkled in concern. 'I read in the newspaper about what happened. It must have been terrible. How is everyone?'

Louisa started to reply but was interrupted by a pretty young woman coming up and thrusting a hand out to her. 'Hello, I'm Mary Moon,' she said, 'I work with Guy.'

'Hello,' said Louisa, uncertain as to what this meant. She looked at Guy but his face gave no answer. Mary Moon – what a farcical name – was wearing a dress that was perhaps supposed to be fashionable but looked fussy to Louisa, with too many things going on, patterns and sequins and things.

Mary clasped her hands in front of her and looked around the room, eyes wide. Guy beckoned Louisa a little closer and whispered in her ear. 'Harry says there's a rumour Alice Diamond is here tonight,' he said.

It was her, then.

'Have you seen her?' asked Louisa.

He shook his head. 'No, but we're going to look. It's a bit strange doing undercover work in this get-up but … needs must.' Louisa noticed now that he was holding a top hat.

'I thought you came here because Harry asked you to come along.' She felt mean for pointing this out when Guy had obviously wanted to impress her with his police work.

'Yes, but now we're here … Never off duty and all that.' He looked uncomfortable.

'Perhaps we should get something to drink?' said Louisa.

Guy agreed and asked a waiter for fruit cup for the three of them. When the waiter had gone, Mary said to Guy that if they were going to be undercover, he should have asked for gin or champagne like the regular customers. 'But that would mean drinking illegally,' he protested. 'It's after ten o'clock.'

'You're not on duty,' Louisa pointed out.

'Never off,' he repeated but gave up arguing the point. The waiter returned with a tray, a glass jug of dark red liquid and three glasses, plus the bill. Guy squinted at it and gasped. 'Two pounds?' he said, 'are you having me on?'

The waiter shrugged. 'I don't set the price,' he said, in what Louisa recognised as an Italian accent. Why was she coming across so many Italians all of a sudden?

Guy dug into his pocket and paid, then took a sip from his glass and almost spluttered it out again. 'It's gin!' he said, furious to see Mary and Louisa laughing.

'That's how they do it, then,' said Mary, who mimicked the waiter's exaggerated shrug and took a sip herself. It almost made Louisa like her.

A heartbeat later, Guy straightened up and pushed his glasses up his nose. 'Will you excuse me?' he said, 'I'm going to take a quick look-see.'

'I'll come with you,' said both Louisa and Mary at the same time. Guy looked at them, his eyebrows crinkled together.

'No, thank you,' he said, 'it's something I need to check alone. Back in a minute.'

They both watched him move off. The music was still playing, though Louisa thought her ears had adjusted to it, filtering it out and dampening the harsher, higher notes somehow.

'Isn't he marvellous?' said Mary to Louisa, peeking at her over the rim of her glass.

Louisa was taken aback. 'Yes, I suppose so.'

'There aren't many of them like that, in the police I mean,' she carried on, as if reciting a short speech. Had she practised it? Surely not. 'He's kind and gentle. But fun, too.' She held Louisa's eye. 'I know you're a good friend of his. Do you know if he's ... well, walking out with any kind of girl?'

Louisa felt cross. 'No, I don't know. Why should I know?'

'Oh, I just wondered,' said Mary, her pink lips sipping at the sweet drink.

'I'm going to dance,' said Louisa. 'You can wait here for Guy.' She abandoned Miss Moon, irritated at having been riled by her.

Louisa found she wasn't able to dance as she had before, feeling too self-conscious to lose herself in the music, so decided to check on Nancy and Pamela. She'd kept them in sight, in the corner of her eye, but she could see now that Nancy was dancing with a gentleman of some sort, quite close to the tables, while Pamela and Charlotte were sitting together, talking. Or rather, Pamela was looking flustered and Charlotte was talking. Before she could get there, Clara came up and moved her slightly to the side.

'Hey, Louisa,' she said gently, 'I wouldn't go over there just now.'

'What do you mean?'

Clara indicated Charlotte with her head. 'She's a little wary of you. You see, she thinks you were friendly with Dulcie and it's worrying her. That bill Pamela passed along from the dressmaker?'

Louisa felt irritation rise up in her again. 'Why?'

'Oh, don't be offended, toots. It's a difficult time. You know how it is.'

'No,' said Louisa, 'I don't know.'

Clara regarded her coldly and when she next spoke her voice was clipped, her accent taut if still American. 'Don't forget who you are. If you must know, Miss Charlotte thinks that it's strange Dulcie knew where to go to steal the jewels. I'm sure there's a perfectly reasonable explanation, but you can understand ...'

As if a blanket had been thrown over her head, Louisa felt suffocated and trapped. This place, which had felt like a refuge only twenty-four hours before – a safe, warm retreat from the world with nothing but music and people who judged by nothing except dance – had become one of cold accusations, putting her *in her place*.

'Tell Miss Pamela and Miss Nancy that I will be waiting for them in the ladies' cloakroom upstairs,' she said. 'We will need to leave within the hour.'

As Louisa walked away, the music tempo increased and the dancers around her picked up the faster beat. Mary was still standing by the edge of the dance floor looking rather lost, and Louisa spotted Guy walking back towards her. He didn't look comfortable in his suit and she could see his glasses steaming up but she picked up the pace so that she could intercept him before he reached Mary.

'Louisa,' he said. He hadn't expected to see her there.

'What's the matter?'

Guy paused and checked behind him. 'It's just – I thought I saw another undercover policeman in here.'

'Someone you know?'

'Not really, he's very senior – in charge of the Vice Squad, operating out of the Savile Row station.'

'Does it matter that he's here?'

'I suppose not but he might not like to see me here, too, on his patch. I think I'd better go.' There was a pause, while they heard Harry on his trumpet execute a flourishing solo. 'Sorry, Louisa. I was so pleased to see you.'

'Me too. Perhaps another time. Goodbye, Guy.' Without even turning to see if Mary Moon was watching them, Louisa left, moving as fast as she could through the crowd, up two flights of stairs and into the ladies' cloakroom. Why was she feeling so upset? She couldn't say.

This room was almost as packed as the dance floor, with women jostling for space in front of the mirror to apply more lipstick and comb their hair; others sat on the two pink velvet sofas and chatted animatedly in groups of three and four. There was a short queue for the loos, and one woman standing in the middle of the room who appeared to be re-hitching her stockings clip by clip, her skirt bunched up almost to her waist. There was no music, though the noise from below could be heard, and several of the women were smoking, giving the darkly painted room a clubbish air. When the woman finished doing her stockings and stood up, Louisa was shocked to realise it was 'Babyface', whom Dulcie had pointed out in the Elephant and Castle. The tattoos on both her arms might have given her away but tonight she had concealed them beneath long evening gloves. The Forty knew how to put on the posh. It made sense, of course, that if Alice Diamond was here, so would her closest cohort be, but it was still something of a heart-stopping moment to be this near to her, both frightening and thrilling at once. Louisa had read about roller coasters in America, where people would sit in a train of tiny, open carriages and travel along tracks that looped around and upside down. Those who had tried it described the feelings of nauseous terror along the way before giddy joy on landing safely at the bottom. She knew what they meant.

It was possible that Babyface would know about Dulcie, and the fence she had arranged to meet to hand over the money and jewellery. But how could she possibly ask her? She couldn't. The frustration she felt strangled her throat.

A woman rushed in and went up to Babyface, and Louisa was close enough to be able to hear what they were saying. 'The bloody little blighters have got in,' said the woman, young too and in an expensive-looking dress of red velvet, but she spoke with a thick south London accent.

'Who let them in?' said Babyface, practically growling.

'I don't know, but with Mrs M. away whoever's on the door didn't recognise them. They're down there now causing a scene. What if they see Alice?'

'Nothing she can't deal with but we'd better go down. They're only meant to shift the stuff, not come in, not after that row. She'll go mad and I don't want her brawling tonight.'

The two of them left, Babyface clicking her fingers and summoning several others who put away their lipsticks and quickly followed her. Louisa was only a few steps behind, her mind racing as quickly as her feet. What did she mean 'they're only meant to shift the stuff'?

As the women reached the basement, it didn't take long for them to register the change in atmosphere. The music was still loud and fast but the dancers were huddled closer together, keeping themselves as far away as they could from a rowdy group of young men who had taken over a number of the tables. Though dressed in dark suits, with slicked-back hair, they had a rough look about them and were clearly drunk. Louisa could see one man arguing fiercely with a waiter about an order and several of them had grabbed women by the waists and were either attempting to kiss them or clamping them close to their bodies while they moved and laughed, not caring that their dance partners were grimacing and trying to push them off. A large man that Louisa had seen before with thick black eyebrows and salted hair started marching towards them, several waiters flanking him and then, all at once, a fight broke out.

The music didn't seem to stop but beat more insistently than ever, providing a rhythm to the punches that were now flying, as tables and chairs were knocked over. A few women were shrieking but they were soon bundled out of the club. Louisa edged around and grabbed Nancy and Pamela.

'We've got to get out of here,' she said and pulled them out.

Pamela looked worried, Nancy annoyed, but Louisa couldn't worry about that. Once they got to the stairs people were pushing and shoving, making them slip, but Louisa felt safer for having got out.

Louisa spotted Babyface just ahead of them, with an arm around the waist of the woman who could only be Alice Diamond, whom she'd seen earlier. Then, as everyone came up into the hall on the ground floor, making a grab for their coats, the two women were nowhere to be seen. They couldn't have got out to the front door, nor gone up the stairs to the cloakroom because Louisa would have seen them, she was sure. Then she spotted Dolly Meyrick emerging from a dark corner at the back of the hall, smoothing down her hair and looking as if she was trying to steady her breathing. Ted's girl. There was a connection, Louisa knew it.

CHAPTER THIRTY-THREE

～～

The next morning, Louisa had to pack Nancy and Pamela's bags for their return to Asthall Manor. They had got up early – force of habit made it none too difficult – and gone down for breakfast with their aunt. Neither of them particularly wished to prolong the occasion so Louisa knew she didn't have long to get them ready. They would catch the ten o'clock train from Paddington and once home Louisa would be thrown back full pelt into the usual nursery routine. Nanny Blor understandably would be eager to earn some rest after her helper had had her days away in London. There was just one thing Louisa needed to do before they left. Buckling up the brown leather suitcase and setting it on the floor, Louisa stepped quietly down to the hallway. There was only one telephone and it wasn't possible to have a private call but with Iris and the girls at breakfast, perhaps she could risk it.

'Vine Street station, please,' said Louisa to the operator.

'Right away, miss,' came the high-pitched voice back. There was a click and a connection and then a policeman asking how he could help.

'May I talk to Sergeant Sullivan?'

There was a hesitation at the other end of the line; the police-man presumably had expected to take down the details of a lost item or a crime that had been committed.

'Is it something I could help you with, miss?' he asked. Why did they all assume she was a miss and not a madam?

'No, I'm sorry, it's not,' she said, as unapologetic as she could make herself sound.

'Right then. Hold on, please.'

She heard the clunk of the receiver as it was laid upon the desk and then the heavy tread of the policeman as he went in search of Guy. Finally, more footsteps and a rustle as the phone was picked up again.

'Hello? Sergeant Sullivan speaking. Who is this?'

'Guy, it's Louisa.'

'Is everything all right?'

'Yes, yes, it's just I thought you should know what happened last night.'

'What happened?'

'Not long after you'd left, some sort of mob arrived and started causing trouble. A fight broke out and we ran out.'

'I'm sorry to hear that.' He really did sound relieved. 'But you're fine?'

'Yes, we're fine. It's just that I'm pretty sure Alice Diamond *was* there last night.'

'What? How do you know?'

'Someone pointed her out.' She could hardly say she already knew what she looked like, could she? 'When I was in the ladies' cloakroom, I overheard someone warn one of the women in there that a fight was about to happen and they said, "They're only meant to shift the stuff, not come in." Then they all ran off.'

'That would make sense,' said Guy, excitement in his voice.

'The Forty have fences, men who sell on their stolen goods so the women don't handle that end of the business. I've had a tip-off that they go to the 43.'

Louisa absorbed this fact, trying to think how it fitted in. Right now, she couldn't but she knew she'd need to keep it stored away. 'The thing is, Alice Diamond was just ahead of us on the stairs and I know she didn't leave through the front door, or go up the stairs to the ladies' cloakroom. I'd have been able to see it.'

'What are you saying?'

'I think Dolly Meyrick smuggled her out of the club, through a secret back exit.'

There was a short silence, while Guy processed this information. 'Did you witness this?'

'Not exactly. She was there, and then she wasn't, and then I saw Miss Meyrick. She's the owner's daughter, you know, running the club while her mother's in Paris.'

'Supposedly,' said Guy.

'Oh, maybe, yes. Anyway, I saw the daughter come out of a dark corner, looking a bit flustered. I can't think of any other way they could have got out.'

It seemed a bit pathetic now. But at least it was more than that silly girl, Miss Moon, would have seen last night. Not to mention that Pamela would be pleased. Perhaps Lord De Clifford would call off the engagement once he knew what his fiancée had done.

'Thank you, Miss Cannon, we'll look into it.' He'd called her that because there would be others overhearing the conversation, she knew.

She heard a noise from the dining room, cutlery chinking on the plates as it was laid down.

'I'd better go. I hope it helps.' Louisa rang off before he could reply and only just in time before the maid, Gracie, stepped out into the hall and looked at her sternly.

'Just waiting for Miss Nancy and Miss Pamela,' said Louisa with as much authority as she could muster, 'we'll be setting off for the station shortly.'

Whichever way she turned, it seemed, there was a close-run thing.

While Louisa was gathering Nancy and Pamela together with their things, getting ready to return to Asthall Manor, Guy put down the telephone in the police station and wondered what he should do next.

Harry would know about the fight, so Guy sent him a note asking him to telephone the station as soon as he could. He hadn't heard anything that morning about whether the police had been called to the club, though it was hardly likely Miss Meyrick would have wanted them alerted, with alcohol clearly being served illegally.

Harry slept long hours after a night at the club, so it was almost four o'clock when Guy was called again to the telephone.

'Hello, Guy. What's this about then? What am I ringing you for?' said Harry in his usual good-natured way. 'Are you going to ask me about Miss Cannon again?'

'No,' said Guy shortly. 'That's over.'

'I wasn't sure it had even begun,' said Harry, joshing.

But Guy was in no mood for it. 'I heard there was a fight at the club last night. Do you know anything about it?'

'You're not going to make me regret asking you down, are you?' said Harry. 'I asked you as a chum, not a policeman.'

Guy decided to keep his usual refrain about being 'never off duty' to himself for the time being. 'No, of course not. I won't do anything about it but I'm interested.'

'It was the Elephant and Castle mob, the lads that is,' said Harry.

'They don't often come down and if Mrs Meyrick's on the door she recognises them and won't let them in. But she's away at the moment, officially at least, and whatever girl was there obviously didn't realise. They kicked off all right. Left everything in a state. They always do.'

'What about Alice Diamond? Louisa said you told her she was in the club, too.'

There was a short pause, and then Harry said, 'Yes, she does come in. She's not very hard to spot and everyone knows who she is. But her girls behave unless someone starts a fight. Then they brawl like men. Not seen them do that for a while though. There must be some sort of disagreement going on between them this week.'

'OK, thank you, Harry.'

'You're not going to start asking awkward questions, are you?'

Guy crossed his fingers. 'No, don't worry. I'm not going to spoil your gig.'

'That's it, then?'

'That's it, pal. You're free to go.' Guy put down the telephone. Now he had something to tell Cornish.

Having checked his boots and belt buckle were polished to a high shine, Guy knocked on the door of Cornish's office, his heart, if not quite in his mouth, then somewhere halfway up his throat and doing battle with his Adam's apple. He knew Cornish was in there but couldn't hear any response, so knocked again and this time elicited an impatient 'Come in!' from the other side.

The inspector's office was not much bigger than the large desk he sat behind and was barely furnished. A picture of the king hung on the wall and there was a window that looked out onto the back of another wing, beside which a police van was parked. Cornish was shuffling through some papers, a look of weariness on his face.

When Guy came in he barely looked up and when he did it was to say, 'Oh, it's you, is it?' and return to his papers.

'Good afternoon, sir,' said Guy, standing as ramrod straight as he could manage.

Cornish mumbled something in reply but didn't look up.

'I've had some information about Alice Diamond that I think may be of use to you, sir.'

At this Cornish stopped his shuffling and raised his head expectantly.

'It seems she frequents the nightclub at 43 Gerrard Street, and was seen there last night.'

Cornish sighed and put his papers down. 'Oh really? And what was she seen doing there?'

Guy realised he hadn't asked this. 'Nothing, sir. That is, I don't know, sir. I just received information, confirmed by two witnesses, that she was at the nightclub, and left shortly after a fight broke out.'

'Was she seen stealing anything? Heard boasting about her successful thefts?'

'No, sir. Not so far as I'm aware, sir.' The room hadn't felt warm when Guy first went in but he was sweating under his arms now.

'I'd like to say it's useful to have confirmation that she's in London but we knew that already. It's of absolutely no consequence to know that Alice Diamond was seen in a nightclub. Unless she was seen drinking?' A hopeful note in his voice.

'I can't confirm that, sir.'

'Then it's absolutely bloody useless,' Cornish roared. 'Get out and don't come back until you've got something worth my time to hear.'

CHAPTER THIRTY-FOUR

In the daytime, 43 Gerrard Street looked like just another scruffy townhouse in Soho. The pavements were black with grime and there were fewer people about. It would be another two or three hours before the punters started showing up for their illicit pleasures. Ignoring the bell that advertised Mr Gold the tailor on the top floor, Guy knocked firmly and was immediately faced by a man who appeared to fill the entire doorframe as if he'd been made to measure for it.

'Ja?' This must be German Albert, the notorious doorman of the 43.

Guy was in full uniform, so it was unlikely that German Albert couldn't guess at his business. He certainly wouldn't be trying to get an early drink. 'I'd like to see Miss Meyrick.'

The door was slammed in his face and Guy stood there wondering what to do, when a minute later it was opened again and the hulking figure beckoned him to follow. They walked past the desk where the entry fees were collected, past the staircase which curved down to the dance floor in the basement and up to the cloakrooms on the first floor, and turned into what appeared to be a small sitting room, wallpapered with a busy flowery pattern and two sofas with cushions of all sizes scattered across them. There was a fireplace and a tiger-skin rug before it, which brought to Guy's mind the ditty of the saucy novelist ('would you like to sin/with Elinor Glyn/on a tiger skin/or would you prefer/to err with her/on some other fur?'). His brothers had been fond of chanting it until their mother caught them and gave them a clip on the backs of their heads. Sitting, thankfully, on a sofa and not lying on the rug, was a young woman with dark, skilfully waved hair and a smart woollen suit of olive green. She couldn't have looked further from the Merry Maids of her mother's nightclub, but rather more as if she had prepared for a board meeting. A ridiculous thought. No woman had ever been in a board meeting. Guy reminded himself sharply to focus on the matter in hand, and ignore the seduction of the fire and the heady scent from the vase of lilies set upon a nearby table.

The woman stood and put out her hand. 'Good afternoon, officer. How may I help you?'

Guy felt wrong-footed. 'Good afternoon. You are Miss Dorothy Meyrick?'

'Yes but everyone calls me Dolly. Please, take a seat.' She gestured to the sofa opposite. Guy sat down and immediately sank into the cushions. It was impossible to sit up straight unless he perched on the very edge, but pulling himself up to that position took an embarrassing struggle with his long arms and legs. It was like fighting with a cloud.

Dolly laughed. 'I'm so sorry. They're rather more for comfort than practicality. Can I get you a drink? We have a very good single-malt whisky here.'

'No thank you, ma'am.' Guy recovered his equilibrium – he hoped – and pulled out his notebook and pencil.

'Oh, officer,' she purred, 'please put that away. I'm sure that whatever we have to talk about can be sensibly discussed before you need to go writing anything down?' She made it sound so unreasonable of him to disagree that he reluctantly put them back in his pocket.

'I believe someone called Alice Diamond was here last night?'

Dolly's face looked blank. 'Really, officer, you can't expect me to remember all of my valued clients. There must have been almost a hundred people here.'

'But you welcome them on the door, do you not? You see each one as they come in?'

'You're right, officer ... Do *you* have a name? It would be so much more friendly.'

'Sergeant Sullivan.' Guy was doing his best not to be won over easily but the heat of the fire was getting to him.

'Sergeant Sullivan, you are absolutely right. I *should* have been doing that last night but I was busy with one or two other things. I'm sure you can appreciate how it is for me, having to run this place without my mother. Some of the staff are not so used to taking orders from a girl like me and occasionally I need to take them to one side to make sure they are doing as I ask.' She paused. 'Are you sure you wouldn't like a drop of whisky? Or a glass of wine?'

'No thank you.'

'Well, last night there was Susie collecting the members' fees, you see. And unfortunately, she let in a rabble of boys who did cause a bit of a fuss. She won't be on the door again.'

'Do you know these boys?' asked Guy, beginning to understand now how skilful some could be at avoiding answering a question they didn't like.

'They come sometimes, not often. Nothing we can't handle,' she said in tones of pure caramel. She turned her body sideways, as if to warm herself from the fire, and looked at him, her head tilted. 'Sergeant Sullivan, we have protectors. Men like you, who are so kind as to look out for us in return for the merest favour. It's so pleasant to spend time in our little club. Perhaps you might like to do the same?'

Guy was flummoxed. 'I beg your pardon, madam?'

She laughed as if he'd just told the funniest joke. 'Oh, I'm only a "miss" – though not for long, I'm engaged to Lord De Clifford, you know.'

Guy knew this titbit of information was supposed to put him in his place. *This is not the face of a nightclub hostess*, she was saying, *this is the future wife of a peer of the realm. And you are a lowly uniform police officer.*

She narrowed her eyes. 'You find this surprising?'

'Oh, no, of course not.' Wrong-footed again. 'Congratulations are in order, ma'am. I mean, Miss Meyrick.'

'Thank you,' she said, politely. 'There have been one or two who have demurred, shall we say? But they were easily dealt with.'

'I see.' Guy wasn't quite sure what the message was here. This woman spoke in code but he didn't know how to break it.

'If you come back here, we'd look after you. And I'm sure, you being the *sympathique* man that you are, so strong you seem too . . . I'm sure you'd look after us.'

Guy didn't know how to reply to this but he was given no chance in any case.

'And now, my dear Sergeant, you must excuse me. It's another busy night at the coalface for me, so I must go and get things ready. Albert is waiting for you just outside this door.' She stood and he saw he must stand too, which took another humiliating altercation with three small cushions, then he shook her hand and left. Absolutely none the bloody wiser.

CHAPTER THIRTY-FIVE

Back home at Asthall, the atmosphere had started to lighten at last since the grim death of Adrian Curtis and everyone had started to look forward to Christmas. Mrs Stobie would mutter crossly about the extra work needed, yet there was an almost constant flurry of stirring and delicious smells of baking from the oven. Pamela snuck into the kitchen as often as she could and though the cook would complain that she had enough to do without teaching her, Louisa caught a look of pleased approval on her face when Pamela brought out a tray of perfectly golden mince pies, the pastry crimped at the edges as neatly as the hem of a dress.

One morning, not long after they had returned from London, Nancy came into the kitchen after breakfast, where Louisa had returned the tray from the nursery and Pamela was rooting about in the larder, searching for another bag of currants. When she emerged, triumphant, Nancy gave her a withering look. 'Honestly, you *are* an old woman. Anyone would think you were a kitchen maid.'

Louisa saw Ada bristle slightly at this but it was Pamela who retorted, 'What would be so wrong if I were?'

Nancy ignored her and waved a letter she had in her hand. 'Lou-Lou, it was you I came to see. Jennie's coming down for tea tomorrow – she and Richard are on their way to stay with his parents and asked if they could come by. I thought I'd let you know. You're old friends, aren't you?'

'Yes, thank you,' said Louisa, though it had been a long time since she had seen Jennie and she couldn't help but feel a little hurt that Jennie hadn't written to her. They had been friends at school and grown up together in the same pocket of Chelsea but Jennie had been elevated out of their world when she met her husband Richard Roper, an architect and a bohemian. She had married up and although she was still the same, sweet Jennie, she moved in completely different circles now, particularly since they had moved to New York three years before. If there was a chance for the two of them to talk, Louisa would be glad to take it. After all, it was with Jennie that Louisa had first met Nancy, which had led to her job as nursery maid at Asthall; she had everything to be grateful to Jennie for, didn't she?

In the end, it wasn't as hard as she'd feared. After Jennie and Richard had had tea with Lord and Lady Redesdale in the library, the bell had been rung and Louisa came down. Usually, at this time, it was to fetch the youngest girls after their daily hour with their parents, but today Lady Redesdale said that she would take them up, while Lord Redesdale and Richard retired to his study for a cigar. Jennie and Louisa were to be left to themselves, which was kind of her employer, though she had probably been encouraged by Nancy. Louisa felt nervous of sitting down in the library, which she knew was inane as there was no one else in there and Jennie was hardly her mistress. Yet they weren't quite equals any more, highlighted by Louisa's apron to Jennie's chic brown cashmere dress and matching coat trimmed with mink, and perhaps, she thought sadly, the force of servile habit had subsumed even Louisa's manners of friendship. To avoid the decision of whether to sit or stand one way or another, Louisa pretended to busy herself with tidying a sewing basket on the floor as they talked. Her heart ached as she wondered whether to talk to Jennie about what was really on her mind. Before she could, Jennie had a confession of her own.

'There's something I've got to tell you darling,' she whispered. 'I'm pregnant. Not far gone yet, so it's not showing and Richard doesn't want to tell anybody until we've told his parents. That's why we're on our way to them now.'

Louisa stood and embraced her friend. 'That's lovely news. When are you due?'

'Late July. A summer baby – everyone says they're happy creatures.' Jennie radiated with the good news, her porcelain skin lit from within.

'Any baby will be happy with you for a mother,' said Louisa. She was genuinely pleased for her friend.

'I hope so.' A shadow crossed Jennie's face. 'I'm just a bit worried that ... well, it's going to be different to how we were brought up, isn't it? Supposing I get things wrong.'

'Every mother thinks that, and you have Richard by your side. You'll do it perfectly, I know you will. And besides, you've got me – you can ask me. I know everything there is to know about how to bathe a baby.'

Jennie laughed. 'Yes, and anyway, we'll have a nanny so I probably won't be doing any of that.'

Louisa knew that Jennie hadn't meant to offend by pointing out to her that while she was paid to bathe another woman's babies, Jennie wouldn't even be looking after her own, but it still stung.

But who else could Louisa turn to? She needed to confide in the one person who understood both the world she had grown up in and the one she worked in now. Not to mention that something had been bothering her lately about Dulcie and she had to thrash it out with somebody.

'There's something I wanted to talk to you about,' Louisa began, wondering as she did if she would – should – go on.

'What, darling?'

As briefly as she could, and in something of a tumble, Louisa told her the long story of the last few weeks, from meeting Dulcie and going to the Elephant and Castle, to the death of Adrian Curtis, the 43 nightclub, the strange behaviour of Nancy's friends, Alice Diamond and the Forty Thieves. Even Joe Katz got a mention. Jennie barely interrupted except to ask her to repeat an astonishing claim here and there. At the end, Louisa was close to tears.

'What shall I do, Jennie?' she pleaded.

'I can't quite think. Which bit do you mean? There's such a lot to take in.'

'It's just that, as you said, we're not where we used to be any more, but we don't always fit in to this new life. I know I have a better life than Ma did, my work is easier and the Mitfords look after me well. But I see those women—'

'Which women?'

'The Forty and even the dancers at the nightclub. They look so independent. They wear lovely clothes, they do what they want to do. They're not beholden to anyone.'

Jennie flashed angrily. 'They're thieves and prostitutes, Louisa. It's no life. You know it! You and I have worked to escape that.' She looked around, as if afraid someone might hear her. Was her husband not truly aware of how she had lived before she met him? 'Don't you *dare* even think about it.'

'Don't be like that. I just feel as if I don't fit in anywhere. I don't know what to do.'

'*This* is what you're going to do,' said Jennie, nearly spitting the words out. 'You're to tell the police about Dulcie and her connection to the Forty. What were you thinking, keeping it secret? Supposing she's lying to you?'

'I can't do that, she'll be killed.' Louisa had never felt so pathetic.

'Louisa. Dulcie ran with the Forty; you don't know if she's to be trusted. How do you know that she wasn't a key to the murder? It's too much of a coincidence, isn't it? She steals jewels and the next thing is, she's found next to the body.'

'Yes, but there has to be more to it than that. Things aren't adding up. I noticed she wore a watch that night. Why would she have done that if not because she needed to know the time?'

Jennie looked confused by this change of direction. 'What do you mean?'

'I think she must have arranged to meet someone at the bell tower and that's why she needed to be sure of the time. Not Adrian. It doesn't make sense that she would meet him in the house and then again in the church. I mean someone who was going to take the stolen jewellery from her. That's how the Forty get rid of their stuff – they have fences who pass it on for them. It means the Forty don't have to hold onto it. I think whoever she was meeting must have killed Adrian Curtis.'

'Then why doesn't she say so?'

'Because it means grassing up the Forty or one of their fences, whoever it was who did it. Then they'd kill her *and* her sister.'

Jennie thought this over. 'She's a dead woman walking either way then. But to choose this route must mean there's someone she's protecting.' A beat passed. 'She's protecting herself, of course. Hasn't she set you up to be the one to tell the police about the Forty?'

'What do you mean?'

'She took you to the pub, didn't she? She told you about the Forty, and then she asked you to find a room to meet Adrian Curtis in.'

Louisa worked this over. 'You think she meant for me to tell the police, so that she wouldn't be the one who let the cat out of the bag? You think Dulcie knew the murder was planned and she's set them up, so long as I play my part?'

'Precisely.'

'But then I'd have to admit to the Mitfords that I knowingly let a thief into the house. Not that I knew she was going to steal anything.'

Jennie's look was not a forgiving one. 'But you did, didn't you? And I feel the blame of that. I brought you to them. They have looked after you and this was how you repaid them. You owe them more than that. You owe *me* more than that.'

Without saying goodbye, Jennie strode out of the room and Louisa was left alone, staring at the fire.

CHAPTER THIRTY-SIX

~~~~~

Guy and Mary Moon were at Vine Street police station, eating sandwiches over a desk piled high with brown foolscap files that had gathered the crumbs of several lunches. Guy was keen to get back out on the streets but felt badly for Mary who had been told in no uncertain terms to stay in the station in case any women officers were needed to deal with lost children or female victims of crime. In spite of their successful arrest of Elsie White, the chief inspector had said he couldn't have all his officers out looking for the Forty Thieves and Mary had been held back.

'It's so frustrating,' she was saying, mouth full of white bread and ham. 'I *know* there must have been women selling packets of cocaine in the 43 but unless CID send me in there undercover, I can't do anything about it.'

'I don't know, Mary,' said Guy. 'It's dangerous work. I wouldn't be too keen if I was you.'

Mary sighed and looked out of the window, chewing. 'I just want to get out of here sometimes.'

A constable came over to the desk. 'Sorry to interrupt the party,' he smirked, 'but there's a telephone call for you.'

Guy went pink and stood up, brushing the crumbs off his lap. 'Sorry. Back in a minute.'

At the front desk, Guy picked up the telephone that had the flashing light. 'Sergeant Sullivan here,' he said, formally. Perhaps it was Miss Meyrick, having remembered that Alice Diamond had been at the club and seen doing something he could arrest her for.

'Guy? It's me. Louisa.'

'Oh, hello.' The image of Joe Katz kissing Louisa's hand came to his mind.

'Look, there's something important I need to tell you. It's a police matter but I don't want this to be an official thing.'

'I'm not sure I understand.' The complications of Louisa came flooding back to Guy.

'Nor do I, really.' There was a sound that could have been either a sob or a swallowed laugh. 'Just hear me out and then help me decide what to do. Please.'

It was lunchtime, the station was quiet. 'Yes. What is it?' The phone was silent. 'Louisa? You still there?'

'Yes, I'm here. It's about Adrian Curtis, the murder, I mean. I know something about Dulcie Long, the maid that's been arrested for it. She was also arrested for stealing from one of the guests staying that night, which she has admitted to.'

'I remember.'

'There's something that I should have mentioned to the police then and I didn't. She's one of the Forty Thieves, and I knew it before she came to Asthall. In fact, she took me to their pub.'

'What do you mean, their pub?'

'It's a pub they all go to. The Elephant and Castle. If you want to find Alice Diamond and the rest of them, that's where they'll be, most nights.'

'What's the connection with Adrian Curtis?'

Louisa swallowed hard. This was the even bigger admission. 'Before the party, Dulcie asked me to find an empty bedroom for the two of them to meet privately that night. I had to help trick him into meeting her there.'

'What?' Guy sounded incredulous.

'She told me she needed to talk to him and he was refusing. She worked for his mother and sister but he lived in Oxford, so it was hard for her to get to him. They'd had a . . . you know.'

'I can guess.'

Louisa was grateful that they were talking on the telephone and Guy couldn't see how deeply the shame coloured her. 'That was when he caught her stealing, and hit her. That's why the police think she's guilty – because they'd already had a row.'

'Go on.' Guy's tone was less friendly each time he spoke.

'What if Dulcie had arranged to meet a fence that worked for the Forty to hand over the stolen jewels later that night? She hinted to me that if a theft ever got reported, it was the maids that always got suspected first.'

'With good reason, it would seem,' interjected Guy.

'Yes, all right. The point is, if she knew she was going to steal she also would have had to make sure that she didn't have the jewels on her when they were reported missing. Meeting a fence would have solved that.'

'I know the Forty have been working as maids in big country houses,' said Guy. 'An easy way for them to get their hands on valuable items.'

'Then the other day, I remembered that Dulcie was wearing a watch that night, when she'd not had one on before. I noticed at the time that it was too big for her, as if it was borrowed. I think she must have needed it because she had arranged to meet someone at a particular time.'

'She was supposed to collect Miss Charlotte, wasn't she?'

'Yes, but she could have relied on a clock in the house for that. I think she was going to hand over the jewels to someone from the Forty or one of their go-betweens.'

'But I'm still not making the connection with Adrian Curtis's death.'

'I don't know exactly, but I think Dulcie arranged to meet the fence at the bell tower. Where Adrian Curtis was pushed off.'

'Why would they have asked Mr Curtis to be there?'

'Perhaps Dulcie didn't but the fence did. I think that Dulcie had arranged to meet a man but the murder happened first. I didn't know she was going to steal from one of the guests, I swear. I thought she needed to talk privately to Adrian Curtis, no more than that. She told me she was trying to get out to go straight, she liked her work as a maid. But her sister has married outside and when Dulcie wanted out too the Forty got jumpy, threatening her unless she proved she'd be loyal. Now she's been accused of the murder and she can't tell the police it was the Forty because they'll kill her *and* her sister. And it's just lately I've realised that she meant for me to tell you. Well, the police. I think that's why she took me to the pub.'

'I think I see that. She is setting up the Forty and using you to do it,' said Guy, slowly, trying to piece it all together in his mind. 'I still don't understand why Mr Curtis got caught up in it though.'

'I don't want to think this,' said Louisa slowly, carefully. 'But she'd had a row with him. I think maybe she did mean for him to be hurt. I still can't believe she'd have planned to murder him but it's not impossible.'

'Either way, Dulcie Long *is* an accessory,' said Guy, 'even if she didn't actually push him off the bell tower but the fence did.'

Louisa's voice sounded very small at the other end of the telephone. 'Yes, I suppose she is.'

'And you knew she was a thief, and you showed her to an empty room in the house,' said Guy. 'Which means you are involved, too.'

There was no sound from the other end, just shallow breathing.

Guy forced himself not to care; he had to get everything that was needed now.

'What about the man? Did anyone see him, or could Dulcie have made him up?'

'No one saw him.' Louisa's voice was faint.

'There's no alibi for Dulcie Long and you're telling me she was involved with the Forty – and you knew that.' He stopped – he thought he might stop breathing. 'You let her into the house. You betrayed everybody, Louisa. How could you do it?'

But he was talking into an empty line. Louisa had hung up.

Guy's palms were sweating, his heart racing. He had to think carefully about what to do next. This wasn't his case, so he couldn't be seen interfering. Yet, he had been ordered by Cornish to find a fence who worked for the Forty, and if Dulcie's connection could be proved, then Dulcie Long would be as good as convicted and hanged. And he wanted to be the police officer who got that conviction.

CHAPTER THIRTY-SEVEN

Pamela's dress was ready for collection from Mrs Brewster and she was determined to get it in time for Christmas and the hunt ball – even if Nancy did declare them the dullest of all parties, 'stuffed nose to tail with men who want to marry their mothers, obligingly surrounded by girls who look just like them'. If Nancy could have had her way, she'd have yo-yoed to London each week, so Pamela knew it would be the work of a moment for the two of them to gang up on their mother and persuade her to let them return once more before they were trapped at Asthall by the festivities. Louisa, naturally, was to accompany them.

'Isn't it rather too much to ask of Iris to put you up again?' Lady Redesdale queried, though Louisa could hear that Nancy had already found the chink in her armour and knew she was weakening.

'No, Muv,' said Pamela, interjecting supportively. 'She says it's awfully helpful to have us there because we run errands for her and things.'

'If you're quite sure,' said Muv, 'then, fine. But not for too long. You can take the morning train tomorrow and be back in time for tea the following day. I have a meeting for the local Conservatives and I'd like you both there.'

Delight at going to London overlaid the usual groans made at this request and Pamela kissed her mother in gratitude, who waved her off. 'Go on, then. Don't forget to ask your father if there's anything he needs picking up from the Army and Navy.'

On the train down, the three of them had a carriage to themselves in first class. The conversation turned, as it frequently did, to the murder of Adrian Curtis and what had happened on that night.

'I still don't understand why Adrian went to the bell tower,' said Nancy.

'Dulcie must have asked to meet him there,' said Pamela, 'when they were talking in Aunt Iris's bedroom.'

'Yes, but they weren't talking, they were arguing. Why would he agree to meet her there when they had just had a row? It doesn't make sense.' Nancy's brow was furrowed appealingly; it made her look rather young again. Nancy turned to Louisa. 'Don't you know more, Lou? You met Dulcie when we came to the party in London, didn't you? Did she say anything to you then?'

Louisa hoped her shirt was buttoned high enough not to reveal the inevitable red blotches that would be forming on her neck. She knew she wasn't guilty – she hadn't known anything of a murder, and she was still certain of Dulcie's innocence, at least of the act itself. But she'd done wrong, she knew that, too. 'No, of course not,' she said.

Pamela stared out of the window, watching the flat fields and hedgerows speed past. Soon they would turn to neatly laid out allotments and rows of suburban houses, before the last tunnel had the train emerge tightly between narrow terraces like blackened piano keys and their arrival at Paddington Station.

'The treasure hunt was his idea,' Pamela murmured. 'What if Adrian orchestrated his own death?'

'Oh, you really are perfectly absurd. I think it was Ted who said it first anyway,' expostulated Nancy. She snatched up a magazine and turned the pages without looking at them.

But Louisa thought the sisters might be on to something. If Lord De Clifford had suggested the treasure hunt and Dulcie did meet a fence from the Forty that night, then he would be the obvious link because the gang showed up at his fiancée's nightclub. And there had been that mysterious conversation she'd overheard between Lord De Clifford and Clara, the beans that she'd promised not to spill. Not to mention the knife in Clara's bag. Phoebe, who used to work for the 43, could be caught up in it too somehow – she'd admitted to faking her ankle sprain. It was too much to pull together but there had to be a thread between them. Whether this was a plot with Dulcie or against her, Louisa couldn't guess at.

Once their cases had been dispatched to their rooms and they had said a friendly hello to Iris, the three of them went on their way to Mrs Brewster. Nancy had invited herself along too, to check that Pamela hadn't made a ghastly mistake, as she so charmingly put it. When they knocked on the door, Mrs Brewster took a few minutes to open it and when she greeted them, she looked thinner than before, if not simply more tired. The deep grooves on her face almost threw shadows and her olive skin had taken on a grey pallor. Nonetheless, she clapped her hands and led them through to her workroom with its tottering piles of materials undiminished. Nancy began to exclaim over dresses that were hanging up, fingering their soft velvets and smooth silks. Mrs Brewster brought out Pamela's dress and the girl gasped happily at the way the honey-coloured material hung heavily, the pink sash a touch of genius.

'You must try it, *signorina*,' said Mrs Brewster. 'If I need adjust anything, I do it today. Needle and thread, I have plenty here.' She laughed again but it sounded hollow.

Louisa, standing in the doorway, edged out of the room and looked down the hall, wondering if the little boy was there. This time she had brought a few clothes for him, old cast-offs from the nursery that she knew wouldn't be missed. Something about his blue eyes hadn't left her since she'd seen him. She stole down the hallway, knowing she wouldn't be missed in that moment. Outside the door he had peeked out of the previous time, she hesitated for a moment, then knocked gently and pushed it open. Inside was a tiny kitchen, with a window that looked out onto the backs of surrounding flats, the wintry light flooding onto the boy, seated at a table, his hand clutching a crayon, eyes as big as moons. He started at her appearance.

'Hello,' said Louisa, 'Don't worry, I'm a friend.' She crouched down so her gaze was level with his. He watched her every move and his fingers tightened on the crayon but he was mute. 'I'm Louisa, but you can call me Lou. What's your name?'

The boy's bottom lip started to tremble but he said nothing. Suddenly the door was pushed open wider and Mrs Brewster came in.

'What is this?' she asked. 'Did he make a noise? I tol' you, *bambino*, you must stay quiet.'

Louisa straightened up. 'He didn't do anything, Mrs Brewster. I wanted to come and say hello. I brought some clothes for him, things we don't need any more.' She held out the small package, wrapped in brown paper. The old woman took it and put it on the table.

'*Grazie*,' she said. 'Clothes are kind but food is what we need.'

Louisa felt admonished, as if she had failed in her responsibility to the boy. 'But, why?' she asked. 'Haven't you got enough work?'

'Oh, work! Yes, I have plenty. But too much. And still not enough – the rent is up, up, up, all the time. Mr Brewster, he leave me with nothing, *niente*. Only his gambling debts. And the mother of this *bambino*, she in prison, she send me no money.'

A thought came into Louisa's mind and she immediately dismissed it as ridiculous.

'What are you going to do?' she asked.

Mrs Brewster looked at the boy sadly. 'I like him, poor child, he knows not why he came into this world. But I cannot feed him, he will have to go to the workhouse. It's him or me.'

'What about his father?'

'Oh, I dunno about him. Dead or gone away, who knows.' She shrugged.

'You can't send him to the workhouse.' Alarmed, Louisa whispered this, though the boy could hardly have understood what it meant. *She* knew well enough. The workhouse was the great fear, the bogeyman of Louisa's childhood; if you lost your job, if you became sick, you went to the workhouse. It was the place where poor people went to die.

The thought of a moment ago pushed itself back. That Dulcie had deliberately sent Louisa to Mrs Brewster and it wasn't to do a favour for Miss Charlotte.

'Is his mother Dulcie Long?' she suddenly asked, the words out before she could stop herself. Mrs Brewster's eyebrows shot up into her hairline.

'*Si*,' she said, 'but how could you know?'

So this was the real reason Dulcie had sent Louisa to Mrs Brewster's. The funny thing was, it wasn't that the boy looked like his mother that had planted the seed of curiosity in Louisa's mind. It was that he looked like the late Adrian Curtis.

CHAPTER THIRTY-EIGHT

Louisa put two more lumps of sugar in her already very sweet tea. She was sitting alone in the kitchen of Iris Mitford's flat, while Nancy and Pamela had luncheon with their aunt. The cook was in the room but they hadn't spoken much; she was a taciturn Scot, more concerned with the crackling on her pork than a fretful fellow servant. As Louisa stirred, her mind went round in similar circles. There was no proof, of course, that this boy was the son of Dulcie Long and Adrian Curtis. It was no more than a hunch, a connection between one pair of blue eyes and another. Did Charlotte Curtis know? If Louisa was right about this then surely she must have done – Dulcie would have to have been in the Curtis household when she got pregnant, been sent away to have the baby and then returned to their employment. And now that Louisa set it out like that in her mind, it sounded outlandish. Would Lady Curtis re-employ a maid who had been made pregnant by her son?

Perhaps, if that maid needed to be kept quiet.

And did this information mean they now had a motive for

Dulcie to kill Adrian? If the Forty had discovered that she had had an affair with him, outside their closed ranks, she might have been afraid for her life. If Adrian was threatening to let people know he was the father of the child, that would be a strong reason. But would Adrian have told anybody? So far as Louisa had ever heard about this sort of thing happening, the baby would be put up for adoption and everything would be hushed up. Which could be why Dulcie had been secretive about her son. She may have told Lady Curtis that he had been adopted and not confessed to still seeing him, even paying for him to be looked after. Had Dulcie been asking Adrian for money for their boy, and was that the cause of their row?

What she needed to do was talk to somebody who could give answers. But who? She would talk to Dulcie if only she could be certain that Dulcie would tell no more lies. She felt she'd made a great mistake in thinking that because she and Dulcie came from similar backgrounds they were the same or somehow complicit. They were not.

Yet, whatever Dulcie was doing, she was not protecting herself. She was walking towards her trial knowing she was going to be found guilty of the murder and unable to say anything about it. Guy might be looking into the Forty connection but it was going to be nigh on impossible for him to find anything and harder still to prove they had anything to do with the murder. They needed something more concrete and this was possibly their only hope. If Louisa could help Dulcie prove that Adrian was the father of her child, if she even let the court know she had a child, perhaps it would save her from hanging.

When luncheon was over, Louisa was summoned by the bell to the drawing room. Even a flat such as this, neither large nor small, had clearly demarcated areas that served much as the grander state rooms of a palace. Pamela stood as Louisa came in and a voice spoke harshly: 'Don't stand up when a *servant* comes into the room!'

Both Pamela and Louisa stopped still as though playing a game of musical statues until the man who had spoken disappeared behind a rustle of the newspaper. Nancy and Iris were drinking coffee, mildly embarrassed at this outburst. Pamela nudged Louisa to turn around and go out into the hall. 'Sorry,' she mouthed. Louisa shook her head to say it didn't matter. Nor did it really; it was only another one of those tiny knocks to her confidence that she was quite used to. Only she did wonder sometimes if the hammer might chip her at such an angle one day that she completely crumbled.

'Let's go out for a walk,' said Pamela. 'I don't much like my aunt's visitor and I could do with getting away.' They gathered their coats and hats and went out, shutting the door gently behind them.

Outside it was still light, a watery kind of day, cold but brisk, with women in full-length fur coats and men with mufflers wrapped around their necks. Almost automatically they headed for Peter Jones in Sloane Square, with its pretty Christmas trees in the windows. Both Louisa and Pamela liked the café on the top floor, where you could look out across the tops of the red brick houses of Chelsea.

'What was going on this morning, then?' said Pamela, when they were sitting down with a pot of tea between them, the milk in a blue and white jug.

'What do you mean?' Though she knew perfectly well.

'There was some sort of commotion going on between you and Mrs Brewster when I was trying on the dress.'

Louisa paused, then decided that she needed to talk to somebody and Pamela was a good bet. Pam wasn't like the rest of her sisters and all the more attractive for it. Nanny Blor called her a rock and she was – the ballast of the family. Where Nancy and Diana could be flighty and moody, Pamela was steady and kind. And she had proved herself to be someone reliable and calm in a crisis in the last few weeks. Though she was nervous about anything on her own behalf, when it came to others a formidable coping streak came to the fore. Louisa admired her.

'She's looking after a small boy of about three. I saw him last time and there was something about him that meant I couldn't quite forget him, so when we returned today, I took some of Tom's old baby clothes for him.'

Pamela gave an approving nod. 'That was kind of you.'

'But that's not it,' said Louisa. 'Mrs Brewster had told me that she wasn't related to the boy, only looking after him to earn some extra money. This morning, she said that the boy's mother was in prison, unable to send any money and she can't afford to feed him. She may have to send him to the workhouse.'

'Oh dear, that is terribly sad.' Pamela poured the milk into their cups, already full of stewed tea. Louisa could never quite get used to putting the milk in second.

'The thing is . . .' Louisa took a moment, hoping she was doing the right thing. 'The boy is Dulcie Long's son.'

Pamela put the jug down and stared at her. 'Are you sure?'

'That's what Mrs Brewster said and I can't see that she's got any reason to lie.'

'How extraordinary. The poor boy. I don't suppose he'll ever see his mother again.'

'No, nor his father.' In saying this, Louisa hoped her tactic would work.

'How do you know? Who is he?'

'I can't be absolutely certain but he very strongly reminds

me of Adrian Curtis.' Louisa kept Pamela in her sights, reading her reaction.

'Oh, really,' said Pamela, 'that's too far-fetched.'

'Why?'

'Because . . . well, it can't be proved. And you're just saying that because what? The boy has dark hair?'

'It's more about the eyes, I think. But it would make sense, wouldn't it?'

'Make sense of what? You've lost me now.' Pamela drank some tea and sat up straighter, like a headmistress putting a pupil in her place.

'Miss Charlotte told the police that her brother and their maid had had . . . '

'What the newspapers call "an understanding",' helped Pamela.

'Yes. And perhaps the boy was something to do with the row they had that night. Even perhaps of her motive.'

'I thought you thought she was innocent?'

Louisa sighed and put her hands in her lap. 'I did. I don't know what to think now.'

'I don't know that it's really for you to think anything. Shouldn't all this go to the police? Although I can't see what good it could do.' Pamela looked stern, as if she was annoyed that Louisa had put this burden upon her, and perhaps she was right to be.

But Louisa couldn't drop the matter. 'There are other things that aren't making sense,' she began.

'What do you mean?'

'I don't think everyone is telling the truth about what happened that night.'

'And by everyone . . . ?'

'The players of the treasure hunt,' said Louisa, hardly daring to look Pamela in the eye.

'Be careful, Lou-Lou.'

It came out in a rush, then. 'I overheard Lord De Clifford talking to Miss Clara at the inquest, asking her not to spill the beans about where she was that night. And Miss Phoebe admitted to me that she hadn't sprained her ankle.'

'What?' Pamela was shocked.

'She said that she had pretended, so that she could be left alone with Mr Atlas.' Right or wrong, Louisa felt relieved to have got it out in the open.

'There you are, then. I admit it's not good but it's a reason.' Pamela pushed her cup away. 'I think you had better trust in the police. They did take statements that night, I'm sure they've investigated properly. If you are concerned, perhaps you had better go through the proper channels.'

'You're right, I'll talk to Guy Sullivan. He'll know what to do.'

'Good,' said Pamela, 'I can't help feeling this would all be best left in the hands of the professionals.' Louisa had been reprimanded, she knew. Whatever happened next, she mustn't involve the Mitfords any further. The only problem was, she didn't think this was possible.

CHAPTER THIRTY-NINE

After a telephone message had been left for him, Guy came to meet Louisa that evening at the corner of Elvaston Place. She had stolen out while the girls had supper with their aunt, and he had clocked off work for the day. She stood, waiting under a lamp post, hoping she didn't look like a working girl, her coat buttoned up, her hat pulled down and her hands jammed into her pockets. Her breath steamed in front of her and she stamped her feet but it was only a few minutes after she got there that she saw him coming down the road. Out of uniform, he still struck a fine figure, tall and lean, with a long overcoat and a brown felt Homburg hat. He had what looked like a home-made knitted scarf wrapped around his neck and chin, and something about that was rather touching. His glasses glinted and, as always, he came quite near before he realised she was standing there waiting for him, with a grin that showed the gap between his teeth. Oh, the relief of his smile – she had been sure he would have nothing more do with her after her revelation last time that she had allowed Dulcie into Asthall Manor, despite knowing of her history.

'You're like the buses,' he said. 'I never see you and then you show up twice.'

'Very funny,' she said. 'Shall we walk around the block? It's too cold to stand still but I haven't got enough time to get a cup of coffee.'

They set off down the London pavements, clean slates of grey alongside the tall houses with their cream pillars lined along the street. Round the corner was the Natural History Museum, Louisa's favourite building in her home city, with its red, blue and white bricks, gargoyles grinning down on the passers-by. As a child her annual treat had been a visit to see the dinosaurs, though what she had really loved were the vast glass cases of seashells with their delicate colours that her mother had told her held the sounds of the sea.

They walked in silence for a minute or two, Louisa not knowing how to begin but Guy started first.

'I can't pretend I wasn't shocked by what you said last time,' he said. 'To be honest, I'm not entirely sure what I'm doing here except that when you ask to see me, somehow I can't refuse.' He gave a rueful smile.

'Thank you. I know it must be difficult. But you must believe me that it was the lesser of two evils. I did it because I believed her life would be in danger otherwise.'

'I do know that,' said Guy. 'In fact, I thought about it – I haven't been able to think of much else – and I wondered if it wasn't Dulcie who was supposed to be pushed off the bell tower.'

'That wouldn't explain why Mr Curtis was there though.'

'It could just have been a terrible coincidence.'

'No.' Louisa shook her head. 'Anyway, there's something else. The reason I wanted to speak to you. It's nothing definite, it's just a hunch, but I can't do anything about it so I had to tell you.' She told Guy of her visits to the dressmaker, the discovery of the boy and who his mother was and her suspicion that Adrian Curtis was the father.

At the end of her tale, they had reached the Cromwell Road and were heading towards Knightsbridge, past the Victoria and Albert Museum. Guy was deep in thought.

'We'd better turn round,' she said, and pulled on his elbow. After a few minutes she couldn't stand it any longer. 'Well? What do you think?'

'There are so many things to think and none of them certain,' said Guy, 'that's the difficulty. Will Dulcie admit to the child?'

'I don't know. She didn't tell me about him but Mrs Brewster knew her name, so that must count for something.'

'If the child is hers, surely she wouldn't commit murder and risk imprisonment?'

'That's what I think,' said Louisa. 'She hasn't abandoned the boy, she's made sure he's looked after. But he must be a secret from her family as no one is sending Mrs Brewster any money.'

'If Adrian Curtis was the father, I wonder if he knew.'

'I think he must have.' Louisa was animated now, almost walking sideways in a bid to look at Guy as they spoke, his face coming in and out of the shadows as they walked under the yellow light of the street lamps. 'If it happened when Dulcie was working there as a maid, then he must have been complicit in her having the baby and then coming back to work. She could hardly have hidden her condition.'

'That's true,' said Guy. 'He wasn't sympathetic enough to marry her though.'

'No,' said Louisa, 'but he'd hardly be the first.'

'Are you saying you think she's innocent?' asked Guy. 'What of the fence you thought she was meeting that night?'

'We don't know that for certain. And there are other things I've found out that make me question it.'

'Such as?'

'Dulcie isn't the only one with a connection to the Forty who was there that night. Lord De Clifford was at the party – in fact, the treasure hunt was his idea, Nancy said – and his fiancée—'

'Is Dolly Meyrick, who runs the 43, where the Forty go,' finished Guy.

'I also heard Lord De Clifford and Clara have a strange conversation where he was asking her not to reveal where she really was that night and she promised not to "spill the beans".'

'It's nothing concrete but I agree, it does sound rum. Well, Dulcie needs to prove she's innocent, if she is.'

'How can she do that?' Louisa was willing to do anything. If Dulcie was in the clear, then so was she.

'If we could prove there was a relationship between Adrian Curtis and Dulcie that was a sympathetic one, it might help her case.'

'How could it be proved?'

'Letters, or some token of affection that passed between them. I don't know.' Guy suddenly looked exasperated. 'It's very frustrating because sometimes two people might be really very fond of one another and yet there is nothing to show for it.' He had raised his voice without meaning to do so, then turned away from her abruptly, pretending to study a doorway.

Louisa touched his sleeve and he turned back, an apologetic look on his face that matched hers. 'I'll go and see her,' she said. 'Dulcie will have to provide the key to prove she's not guilty.'

'But she hasn't yet,' said Guy. 'Is she really prepared to take the fall rather than admit that someone from the Forty did it?'

'It seems so,' said Louisa. 'But I'm not and I'm going to do what I can to save her. It could have been me, Guy.'

'What do you mean?' He was puzzled.

'If I hadn't been saved by you and the Mitfords, I could have been like her, driven to crime because there was nothing else.' She wasn't going to admit how close she had come to returning to that life again but she knew it. 'I owe it to everyone to solve this.'

CHAPTER FORTY

~~~~~

When Louisa returned to the flat, supper had not yet been cleared from the dining room. Quickly, she went to her room, which was really a storage room with a camp bed set up in it, took off her hat and coat, then returned to the kitchen. With any luck, the cook would have left something for her to eat. Gracie the maid who came in daily was much older and they had yet to manage a conversation beyond pleasantries. Usually Louisa would have welcomed the company but she was grateful now that she wouldn't be expected to make small talk. She found a plate in the lower oven of the range with some slices of warmed, rather dry ham and boiled carrots and potatoes. It would do.

She'd only managed a mouthful or two when Nancy came in. 'There you are!'

'Sorry,' said Louisa, trying to chew down the ham. 'Were you looking for me?'

'Only just now,' said Nancy, pulling up a chair. 'Don't stop eating, carry on.'

Louisa speared a few soft slices of carrot but felt self-conscious.

'Pam's been telling me about this child at Mrs Brewster's.'

223

Louisa nearly choked and took a drink of water. 'What?'

Nancy laughed. 'Don't look so serious, I'm perfectly safe. But do you really think the child is Adrian's?'

'I don't know. They share a likeness but I couldn't swear to it.'

'Who can? Will you ask Dulcie?'

'I had thought of it. I'm not sure what good it would do except that I'm sure she's innocent and perhaps this would prove that she had no intention of murdering the father of her child.'

'That's what I thought,' said Nancy. She looked gleeful, and so much more grown up than Louisa felt, in a black London coat and skirt with a silk shirt. 'So, I want to come to the prison with you.'

Thankfully Louisa had swallowed her food now and the danger of choking had passed. 'I don't know that that's a very good idea.'

'What on earth is wrong with it? Woman can come too. It'd do her good. She could do with being a bit more worldly.'

'Lord and Lady Redesdale would have an absolute fit.'

'They don't need to find out. Let's go in the morning, before we get the train back.'

'I'm not sure it's possible. You have to get permission to visit in advance.'

'Have you been to see her before?'

'Yes,' said Louisa, unsure where this was going but feeling certain she wouldn't like to find out.

'Then you'll be on the approved list and when it comes to me ...'

'What?'

'I can soft-soap a prison guard, you'll see.'

The following morning, after a sleepless night, Louisa and the two sisters left the flat, having told Iris Mitford that they were off to the Army and Navy stores for last-minute Christmas shopping. She had expressed surprise that so many presents were being bought by them this year but didn't stop them from leaving. As before, Louisa walked to South Kensington station and took the Piccadilly line all the way to Holloway Road station. With fourteen stops, it felt like a long journey and was not helped by Pamela, who kept her head stuck in the fashionable novel *Mrs Dalloway* by Virginia Woolf, yet almost never turned a page. Nancy chattered on but Louisa felt she hadn't the stomach for it this morning. What if they were turned away at the gates? It would all be to nothing and the risk would still be there that one of them would let something slip to their parents and she'd be out of a job immediately. Aristocratic families did not like their daughters visiting convicts, she was sure of that.

When they were finally walking towards the prison, Louisa felt the two of them suffer the same jolt of fear and surprise that she had experienced when the imposing building loomed into sight.

Pamela tugged at Nancy. 'Koko, I don't think we should do this.'

But saying something like that was to throw the gauntlet at Nancy's feet: it served only to stiffen her resolve and provide another opportunity to belittle her younger sister. 'Don't be such a scaredy cat. We need to find out the truth about all this and we're the ones to do it.'

At the gates, the three of them waited in the long line of visitors. Nancy watched every person with her green eyes but Pamela looked fearful, her head bent towards the ground, avoiding the people around them and the prison itself. When they reached the visitors' desk inside, Louisa gave her name and Dulcie's, and was approved with a nod. The prison officer looked at Nancy and Pamela, who shrank back as if she hoped her coat would swallow her. He jerked his chin. 'They with you?'

'Yes,' said Louisa, 'Miss Nancy Mitford and Miss Pamela Mitford.'

He looked down his list. 'Their names aren't down here. They can't come in.'

Pamela looked relieved and started to turn to leave, but Nancy pulled her back. 'Oh dear, officer,' she said. 'Uncle Winston will be disappointed.'

The officer paused writing. 'Huh?'

'Winston Churchill, the current chancellor of the exchequer?' said Nancy, blamelessness painted on her face. 'He's our dear uncle and he asked us to tell him how we found the prison conditions today. It's all part of being a cabinet minister, you know. Really understanding how everything is, from the grass roots up.'

The officer's nose twitched. 'Your uncle, you say?'

'Yes,' said Nancy, sounding almost like Queen Mary in her aristocratic hauteur. 'Our very dear uncle.'

He looked from side to side. 'Reckon it'll be all right this once.' He scratched their names into the logbook. ''S long as you put in a good word, eh?'

'Of course I will, Mr . . . ?'

'Marsh,' he said. 'Mr Marsh. Been here thirty-eight years, not long off retirement.'

'Congratulations, Mr Marsh,' said Nancy, her smile on him now as bright as headlamps. 'It's this way we go, is it?'

The three of them headed into the visitors' room, Nancy joshing Louisa with her elbow. 'Told you so, didn't I?'

'I don't approve,' said Louisa. 'Winston Churchill is not even your uncle.'

'Cousin by marriage. Close enough,' said Nancy. 'The point is – we're in.'

Pamela seemed to have relaxed now that they had got past the guard. 'It's ghastly in here,' she whispered to no one in particular. 'Awful smell of boiled cabbage.'

'It's not a hotel, is it?' said Nancy patronisingly, and Pamela went quiet. Louisa was more concerned about how Dulcie would react to seeing all three of them on the other side of the grating, given that she had had no warning. They sat in wooden chairs tightly pushed together and Louisa saw fear on Dulcie's face when she saw them but she didn't get up and leave.

'What's going on?' said Dulcie as she sat down. She looked thinner still, and waxen, like a nocturnal creature who never saw sunlight. Something lay behind her eyes that made her seem years older than the trio of young women who sat opposite her.

'They want to help, Dulcie,' Louisa said, as warmly as she could, though Dulcie was sitting as still and cold as ice. 'There's something I want to ask you, and please don't be shocked.'

Pamela, to Louisa's surprise, spoke up. 'We had better get on with this as we don't have much time. Miss Long, we went to see Mrs Brewster.'

Alarm registered on Dulcie's face.

'When we were there, Louisa met a small boy. Mrs Brewster told us that he is your son. Is that correct?'

'Yes,' said Dulcie, caught too unawares to deny it. The fact that the secret was out dissolved her to tears. 'How is he? I miss him. It's been so long since I've seen him.'

Louisa interjected now. 'He's fine. I took him some clothes. He seems quite happy with Mrs Brewster.'

'But I haven't sent any money. I can't. I've been afraid she'll get rid of him and I'll lose him.'

'She did mention the money,' said Louisa, as there was no point in pretending otherwise. 'Is there someone in your family who could help?'

'No one,' said Dulcie. 'I daren't let anyone know. If the For—' She stopped herself in time. 'No one can know where he is,' she said, looking Louisa directly in the eye. 'I mean it.'

'What about the Curtis family?' said Pamela.

Dulcie turned to her, her eyes red now. 'What about them?'

Pamela spoke evenly. 'Who is this boy's father?'

Dulcie looked at Louisa who gave her a smile of reassurance. 'Adrian Curtis,' said Dulcie at last, and gave a shaky sigh. 'He knew about Daniel – that's my boy's name. He even met him a few times but he couldn't have anything to do with him. Not really. He'd have been cut off from his family with no money.' She said the last words bitterly.

'The point is,' said Nancy, taking control, 'if you can prove that Adrian was your boy's father, then a jury might be less inclined to believe that you were the murderer. At the very least, you might be spared a sentence of execution.'

The word hung heavily between them all.

'But I can't,' said Dulcie, still upset but calmer now. She had had, after all, many lonely hours in her prison cell to think this over and resign herself to her fate. 'It's my word against theirs and who will believe me? Especially now.' She took a breath, and could be seen physically pulling herself together. For a few minutes they sat, muted, before a bell rang and chairs started to scrape. The thirty minutes were up.

'We've got to go,' said Louisa. 'I'm sorry, Dulcie.'

'Go and see my boy, would you? Tell him his mum loves him, give him a kiss.' Her voice broke.

'Of course,' said Louisa, convinced now that Dulcie could not be the murderer and more determined than ever to find out the truth. If it wasn't Dulcie then who could it be? The Forty? Or one of the guests at the party? After all, they were there that night, and any one of them might have had the opportunity to do it.

CHAPTER FORTY-ONE

The journey back to Iris's flat was quiet as Louisa, Pamela and Nancy each digested what they had seen and heard. Louisa knew she had taken them out of their world and though she felt a little guilty about this, there was a part of her that was pleased, too. Perhaps she herself would seem less of an alien to them and just someone who had simply been born into a different set of circumstances. She didn't want sympathy, pity or even to change who she was, she wanted them to understand.

Pamela was brisk on their return, for once taking charge over Nancy, telling her they needed to get a move on to get back home. She had been the most unsettled by the prison and was anxious to return to 'normal life'.

'What is normal anyway?' snapped Nancy.

'I'm not sure I know,' sighed Pamela, 'but I won't feel right again until I'm back in the saddle.'

Louisa was packing their suitcases as the two girls bickered when their aunt walked in. 'Hello, girls,' she said amiably. 'I've decided to come back to Asthall with you this afternoon. I've telephoned to your mother and let her know. London is too much for me in the run up to Christmas – I'd rather be lying on the sofa eating Mrs Stobie's cake.'

Louisa's ears pricked up at this. If Iris accompanied Pamela and Nancy on the train, she could stay behind. She wouldn't win any favours with Mrs Windsor or Lady Redesdale, let alone Nanny Blor, but that felt less pressing than what she needed to do for Dulcie.

When their aunt had left the room, Louisa admitted her plan to the sisters. Nancy merely raised an eyebrow but said nothing while Pamela said all this only made her wish they could get the very next train out.

When she had waved them off, a note from her to Mrs Windsor in Nancy's pocket – they had told a puzzled Iris that Louisa had a family emergency – Louisa felt an exhilarating rush of freedom. She decided to take a bus to Piccadilly and hoped that Guy was at Vine Street station before she made her next move. What she wanted to do was to go and see Mrs Brewster alone, to try and find out if there was anything in the boy's belongings that would prove a connection with Adrian Curtis, and maybe help the dressmaker find an alternative to the workhouse.

At the police station, a message was sent to Guy and he came out to the front where she was waiting on one of the wooden benches, hoping she didn't look like a criminal.

'Louisa,' he said, pleased to see her but concerned too. 'Is everything all right? Has something happened?'

She wasn't sure how to begin. 'Can you spare five minutes?'

Guy nodded, 'Yes, of course. Tell me what it is.'

'Dulcie has admitted that she had a child with Adrian Curtis.'

'Can she prove it?'

'Of course not. No one can.' Louisa was exasperated. 'But it all adds up in her favour, doesn't it? We're running out of options. It's almost Christmas and her trial is due to start in the New Year.'

Guy's quietness revealed neither agreement nor disagreement.

'I'm sure she's protecting someone but I don't know if it's someone from the Forty or someone else,' Louisa went on.

'Can you explain why?'

'She must have wanted to discuss something about their child with him, possibly blackmail. That would explain why she needed to meet him. I just can't understand why he would meet her again in the bell tower if they'd had an argument – one where he had hit her, remember.'

'I agree,' said Guy. 'That was always a puzzle to me, too.'

Sergeant Cluttock came out to the front, on his way somewhere, and gave Guy a quizzical look but didn't interrupt them.

'Even so, if Dulcie went to meet someone from the Forty, why would Mr Curtis be there too?'

'I still don't have an answer for that,' she admitted.

They sat in silence for a minute. 'What if the Forty knew about the child?' said Guy. 'What if they arranged for Adrian Curtis to be killed as revenge?'

'Revenge for what?'

'Fathering the child and then abandoning him, and Dulcie.'

'I don't think the Forty are cold-blooded like that. They're thieves, not killers.' Louisa knew she was in danger of defending them as her own but she'd seen them in the pub. They had been rowdy lawbreakers, certainly, but they hadn't struck her as bloodthirsty.

'If not them, then perhaps the Elephants.'

'Perhaps.' She felt reluctant to pin herself to any theory. Everything suddenly seemed so vague and theoretical, one set of words against another. But she had been to that prison, she'd seen Dulcie's white face. It was life and death, it wasn't a game of chess.

'Whatever the answer, Miss Long knows something she's not telling us,' said Guy. He knew this was serious, Louisa could be certain of that. 'Perhaps I could talk to her myself.'

Louisa felt alarmed at this. She didn't want Dulcie thinking that she had increased suspicion on her. 'But other things aren't quite matching up,' she said hesitantly. 'With the others who were at the party.'

Guy looked at her, shocked, and then laughed. 'Don't tell me one of Nancy's friends did it!'

'I don't think you can rule them out.' Louisa felt self-conscious now and started picking at stray fluff on her coat. 'One of them, Miss Phoebe, admitted to me that she faked her ankle sprain so that she could be alone with Mr Atlas. That means she doesn't have an alibi.'

Guy rubbed at his glasses and pushed them up his nose. 'I must say that's a rather worrying admission. But she was with Mr Atlas at the time of the murder, wasn't she? So it doesn't really make enough of a difference.'

'And another time I saw a knife in Miss Clara's evening bag.'

Guy blinked. 'They are in another world, aren't they? Did she say why she had a knife?'

'She hinted that men, possibly Sebastian Atlas, tried to make her do things but when we'd seen the knife she said they wouldn't be trying that again.'

'We?'

'Pamela and I were there.'

Guy nodded. 'And which one is Sebastian Atlas?'

'He's the tall, thin one with the very blond hair. I can't say I like him terribly much, though I couldn't tell you exactly why. He behaves oddly too. I saw him sneak out when everyone was at the theatre, and I was waiting in the foyer. He had a quick meeting with a man in the street and looked as if he was buying something.'

'It's an easy guess as to what he'd be buying.' Guy stood. 'I'm so sorry but I need to get back to work now. Can I walk you to the door?'

Louisa smiled gratefully. 'Of course.'

But as they walked, Guy whispered, 'The murder case isn't one I'm supposed to get involved with – it's not on my patch – but I'll try to find the reports from the inquest and take a look at who was at the party and what their alibis were. I do agree with you that if Dulcie is innocent, we need to prove it. If she was supposed to meet a man at the bell tower that night, then we need to find him, too.'

As Louisa stepped out into the street she wondered what it was she was feeling, this different, sunnier mood, despite the grey sky and sharp wind. Then she realised: she had somebody on her side. It felt good.

CHAPTER FORTY-TWO

~~~~~

Louisa turned into Mrs Brewster's road feeling almost giddy with happiness. Perhaps it was no more than being able to walk along with no small child beside her, no errand ordered by Mrs Windsor, no need to be somewhere other than where she wanted to be. Her work in service had been largely easy and comfortable, she knew that, and she was still grateful for the money and the security. Nothing she did was back-breaking or filthy and everyone treated her fairly, if peremptorily at times. But in London one was only too aware of the young women who went out to work for themselves in modern, exciting jobs, before going home to their own flats to change for a night out dancing or being taken for supper. Perhaps that would never be her world but it had come close enough for her to taste. She was fired by something else now – not fear, which had kept her moving for so long, but ambition. That was a grand and brave word for a girl like her, but yes! Ambition was what she had.

She pushed open the front door – it never seemed to be locked – and practically ran up the stairs to the flat, ringing on

Mrs Brewster's doorbell in three short staccato bursts. Mrs Brewster opened the door and looked at her in surprise.

'Hello,' said Louisa, 'can I come in?'

'*Si, si*. Come in but I am sorry, I was not expecting you . . .' Her voice trailed off and her hand waved to her workroom, which was not messy – the materials were neatly stacked – but it was clear she had been at work. There was a dress half done on the machine and odd snippets of material and thread on the floor. Daniel was on the floor with a set of building blocks, stacking them up high before gleefully knocking them down. When Louisa put her head into the room he turned and, seeing her, smiled and waved.

'I have been to see his mother,' said Louisa.

Mrs Brewster did not react outwardly to this but she went and picked Daniel up from the floor. 'Come,' she said. 'We will have tea.'

Louisa followed them both to the kitchen, where Mrs Brewster boiled a kettle and gave Daniel a crust of bread to chew on. When the seamstress opened the cupboard to pull out the box of tea Louisa saw that it was almost empty. It didn't quite add up, somehow, that she should have such a lot of sewing work from presumably well-heeled clients, if the likes of Miss Charlotte were commissioning her, yet had absolutely no money at all. Still, she had said something before about Mr Brewster and gambling debt. Perhaps she was having to cope with a nasty situation. And Louisa knew there was nothing so exhausting as being poor. She felt guilty about the money she had spent on her haircut when she could have given some to Mrs Brewster.

Louisa put Daniel on her lap and stroked his soft hair. She gave him a kiss on his forehead and smiled at him. 'That's from your ma,' she said but he did not respond, concentrating hard on the bread he had clamped in his fist.

The old woman was swirling hot water around in the teapot before emptying it and spooning out the leaves carefully, when she said with a sob, 'I don't want to give up the *bambino* but . . .' Tears sprang unbidden to her eyes and she wiped them away quickly.

'I know,' said Louisa. What more could she say? She was powerless.

There was a sudden ring at the doorbell, followed by three loud knocks. Mrs Brewster jumped and almost dropped the cups and saucers she was carrying to the table. 'Stay in here,' she warned and left quickly.

Louisa kept hold of Daniel but he whimpered when Mrs Brewster left the room and started to wriggle off her lap. 'Stay with me . . .' she was saying, when she heard raised voices in the hallway outside. Mrs Brewster was speaking in a shrill, rapid combination of Italian and English, even more so than usual, pleading that she had nothing to pay them with.

The other voices were male, with strong south London accents and a brusqueness that could be detected even on the other side of the door. Louisa couldn't be sure how many there were – two, three? Daniel had dropped his crust and his lower lip was quivering, his whimpering getting louder. 'Sshh,' said Louisa, but he started pulling on the door handle. Louisa was trying to listen to what was going on but the voices were muffled now. They must have gone into the workroom, though Mrs Brewster's incessant talk could only mean she wanted them to leave.

For half a minute Louisa turned her attention away from Daniel when she realised he was already out of the door bawling loudly. She froze, unsure whether she should try to grab him back, but it was too late.

'Who've we got here then?' she heard through the door, open just a few inches but enough to make the voices clear.

'He's just a boy,' said Mrs Brewster, her rising panic clear.

'Not yours though, is he? Unless medical science has started miracles,' laughed one man.

There was definitely a second younger man. 'Started baby farming, have yer?'

Daniel had stopped crying now. Either Mrs Brewster had picked him up or he was silenced by the atmosphere. Louisa had learned from the nursery that children were sensitive to the moods of adults, even if they couldn't understand the reasons.

''Ere,' said the first man. 'You earning money for looking after this one?'

Mrs Brewster didn't reply, or at least Louisa couldn't hear her say anything.

'Could be useful to us,' said the second. 'Tell you what, if the next time we come back you still ain't got that money you owe us, we'll take him instead. There's plenty as want a nice pretty boy like him. Fair enough, don't you think?'

Still, there was nothing to be heard in reply. Moments later, the door slammed shut and only then did Louisa step out into the hall. She went quickly to the workroom and saw Mrs Brewster clutching on to Daniel, no longer crying but not looking like the happy child he had been when she had arrived only half an hour earlier. On the table by the sewing machine was a large brown paper parcel.

'They will come back,' said Mrs Brewster, the dark rings under her eyes even more pronounced.

'Who were they?'

The dressmaker's shoulders hunched forward and she dipped her head, avoiding Louisa's eyes. 'The Elephants. Usually it is another who comes, who brings me the materials, but I owe them money. These are nasty men and they frighten me.'

'You mean the material you work with, it's supplied by these men?' Louisa knew what she was asking: did she knowingly receive stolen goods?

Mrs Brewster could hardly bear to admit it but she did. She looked up now, beseeching. 'I had to, I cannot afford to buy it from the shops. His mother, she introduce me to them. And it is good stuff, you know. What do I do? I must pay them.'

'We'll think of something,' said Louisa, 'I promise.' Truthfully, she knew she had no right to make such a pledge but she could not abandon that boy, not if he was in danger from the Elephants. Daniel, after all, had brought none of this upon himself but had been born into an unlucky situation. She knew how that felt, at least. The most important thing was to get him out of there, but where could she take him?

CHAPTER FORTY-THREE

Taking Daniel from Mrs Brewster's hadn't been a struggle in so many words but the old woman had been overcome at the moment of departure. The seamstress had given Louisa a rather pathetic cloth bag of Daniel's things – a few clothes, some toys – which also included a photograph of Dulcie, not in a frame but pressed between two pieces of plain card and bound with a ribbon. Of Adrian Curtis there was nothing.

There was deep sadness in Mrs Brewster's face as she turned towards the room Daniel was in. 'I shall miss him.'

'I know,' said Louisa. 'I'm sure Dulcie will be in touch to thank you for everything that you've done. You've been kind to look after him so well.'

To this, Mrs Brewster said no more. Daniel was playing with his blocks, paying no attention to the conversation above his head. Even when Louisa bent down beside him and touched his arm, he continued to concentrate on his task, carefully balancing a red wooden brick upon a yellow one. Mrs Brewster called over, '*Bambino*, listen to the lady.'

Only then did he turn around to Louisa and she saw herself reflected in the pools of his pale blue eyes.

'Daniel, I'm going to take you back to your family to look after you.'

He said nothing but turned back and picked up another brick.

'Come along now. I'll buy you some cake for tea, a chocolate one. Do you like chocolate cake, Daniel?' Louisa felt her voice faltering. If Daniel refused to come with her, she wasn't sure what she could do. In the end, she firmly picked the boy up, holding him under his arms and then tucking his legs around her waist. He squirmed and tossed out his arm, his starfish hand clamping open and shut, his eyes shut. A wail hovered on the edge of his trembling lips.

'Pass him a block, please,' she said, and Mrs Brewster handed him a red one, which Daniel took and clasped with both hands, tucking his head down into Louisa's neck and holding the precious piece of wood close to his chest as if he would never let it go.

Once out in the street, the enormity of what she had done hit her. There was now a boy of three who depended upon her utterly and if her plan went wrong she knew she had nothing else in place. All that mattered was saving Dulcie's life, and the boy had to be the key.

It was getting on for late evening now, so Louisa bought Daniel a bun from a nearby café – not enough for supper, but he ate it with relish while Louisa sat him on the floor of a telephone box. Dulcie's family name was 'Long', she knew that much, and if she was one of the Forty Thieves then her family must have lived in Lambeth, within half a mile of the Elephant and Castle. Louisa went through the phone directory and soon found three addresses for Longs in the right area. She wrote them down and then telephoned Vine

Street police station. She left a message for Guy, asking him to meet her, with Mary Moon, at Lambeth station at eleven o'clock that night. Hopefully that would give her enough time.

Given her long day and how heavy and tired Daniel was, Louisa decided to take a taxi from Earl's Court to Lambeth. This was all costing money she should be giving to her mother but she pushed the guilt to the back of her mind. She'd have to deal with that later.

The drive south of the river – which she'd had to persuade the taxi driver to do by paying him half the estimated fare upfront after he grumbled about driving over the bridge ('I won't get a fare for the way back') – took almost an hour. She sank back into the seat, Daniel fast asleep now, and watched as the street lights prettily lining the Embankment rushed past her view. On the other side of the bridge the night seemed blacker. The cab was soon driving down narrow streets with barely another car in sight. Twice they had to stop and ask a passer-by for directions.

She asked the taxi to wait while she knocked on the first door, leaving Daniel inside. But the woman who answered said the Longs had moved out a few months before and she didn't know where they'd gone. At the second address, nobody answered and the house looked empty. Louisa felt the nerves course through her, terrified now of what would happen if she didn't find Dulcie's sister.

The third house, 33 Johanna Street, was in darkness but for a light in an upstairs window, half-moons of yellow showing through the tops of the closed curtains. The taxi driver had taken pity on her now and turned his meter off. He sat, engine idling, by the side of the road, with Daniel stretched out on the back seat, a wisp of a snore puckering his lips. Louisa knocked on the door, shivering on the step, then stood there long enough to watch a man walk the length of the street on the other side. She knocked again and then heard someone coming down the stairs before, finally, the sound of bolts being drawn.

The door was opened by a short man in striped flannel pyjamas that Nanny Blor would have itched to wash and iron. 'What?' he said. It wasn't friendly.

'I'm a friend of Dulcie's,' said Louisa.

At this, the man stuck his head out. 'Who you with?'

'No one.'

'What's that taxi doing there then?' He seemed more nervous than aggressive, and Louisa could see the stubble on his chin was mostly grey.

'It's waiting for me. Please, there's nothing to be frightened of. I'm trying to find her sister, Marie.'

This startled the man. 'I don't know anything about Marie.'

He slammed the door shut and slid the bolts fiercely back into place.

Of course, he must have thought she was one of the Forty trying to track down Marie. How stupid she was! Louisa bent down to the letter box and shouted through it. 'I'm not one of them, I promise.'

There was no response. There was only one thing for it. 'I've got Daniel with me. Dulcie's boy. Please, you've got to help.'

The man clearly hadn't stepped away from the door. In a flash, he opened it again. 'You've got Dulcie's boy?'

'Yes,' said Louisa, cold and afraid now, deeply uncertain she'd done the right thing but not knowing what else to do. 'He's in the taxi.'

'Christ alive! Bring him in.'

Shortly afterwards, Louisa was in the kitchen, the taxi had been dismissed and Daniel was asleep on a settee in the front room, covered with a blanket. Marie had been woken up and come down to join Louisa and the man who she now knew to be Dulcie's father,

William. Louisa didn't have much time – Guy would be waiting for her at Lambeth station and she had to hope he'd hold on for her – but she'd explained to them how she'd come to know Dulcie, that she believed in her innocence and that she'd rescued Daniel from being sent to the workhouse.

'She'd never tell us where he was,' the father said. 'She was afraid that if Alice and that lot found him, they'd use him to get to her. But we was worried for the little fella.'

Marie nodded in agreement. 'It's better he's with us,' she said. 'We're family.'

'Do you know who the father was?'

Marie and William exchanged a glance. 'That Mr Curtis, wasn't it? Not that he'd have called himself the dad. Washed his hands of the poor kid soon as he could.'

'Look,' said Louisa, 'I want to help prove that Dulcie didn't do it – the murder, I mean.'

'She didn't,' said Marie. 'She's not like that. I know some of us can be rough but not Dulcie. She's been wanting out ever since I got started. It's my fault she ever . . .' She choked a sob and William rubbed his daughter's back.

'I think Dulcie knows who did it but can't tell the police,' volunteered Louisa.

'She knows?' Marie wiped her tears away with the back of her hand.

'I think so,' said Louisa. 'I think she was meeting someone that night, a man who went between her and the Forty. She could have arranged that he'd take the things she'd stolen and sell them on. I think whoever that was was the man who killed Adrian Curtis and she won't tell the police who it was because if the Forty find out she grassed him up, the punishment they give will be worse than any sentence a judge hands out.'

'If it was one of those Elephants, they're more than able,' said Marie grimly. 'But what would they have had against him?'

'Might they have known he was the father of Dulcie's boy?' asked Louisa. 'Could it be revenge for her having gone outside the gang? Or for him having nothing to do with Daniel?'

Marie nodded. 'I suppose so. Word gets about.'

William dropped his head in his hands.

'What I'm really trying to say is, I could tell the police,' said Louisa. 'I could say I saw him, it could come from me. Not Dulcie.'

The father looked at her, the pupils of his eyes so large they had turned his eyes black. 'Would you do that for her?'

'The Forty won't harm me, they can't,' said Louisa. 'They don't know who I am.'

'They will!' said Marie, alarmed, but she failed to hush her father who spoke at the same time, loudly and firmly. Louisa couldn't miss it.

'Billy Masters,' he said. 'That's who you want.'

CHAPTER FORTY-FOUR

⟨decorative flourish⟩

Earlier that same day, Guy and Mary had been at Vine Street station locked in a friendly battle.

'Please, Guy. Take me to the 43 again.' Mary Moon had had her hands clasped in prayer, eyes open as far as they would go, pleading.

Guy had laughed but he still hadn't understood. 'Why do you want to go so much?'

Mary had put her hands in the pockets of her jacket and pouted. 'I just do, and I can't go alone.'

'I don't know that it's a nice place for nice women.'

'Maybe not but if I'm to be a policewoman of any merit, I can't be shocked by anything.'

Guy had thought it over. He had wanted to return to the club because if there was a connection between Lord De Clifford, Dolly Meyrick and the Forty Thieves, the 43 was the most likely place to find it. It could help to have a girl by his side as it made him look more like a regular customer. On the other hand, he was wary of seeing that other police officer there. Guy was pretty sure George Goddard, the officer heading up the Vice Squad, wasn't at the 43 for work, and if he wasn't then observing a senior-ranking policeman at a nightclub seemed somehow indiscreet, like watching him in his own house. Guy might not approve of his drinking illegally and being surrounded by Merry Maids, but it wasn't any of his business either. Harry had warned Guy not to say anything to any of his colleagues in case word got around that he'd snitched. More and more, Guy was sure that there was some sort of underhand business going on but he got the feeling that he was the only one not inclined to shrug it off.

'Fine,' he had said at last, 'meet me at the Eros statue at half-past eight tonight and we'll go together.'

'Thank you, Guy!' Mary had jumped and looked as if she was going to kiss him in gratitude but stopped herself just in time. So Mary had an agenda of her own, Guy thought then, but he wasn't sure what it was.

At the appointed hour Guy was standing in Piccadilly Circus, enjoying the flashing lights of the advertisements and the excited hubbub of people as they walked around, planning their night out. He was feeling quietly smart in a suit he'd splashed out on recently. Even his brother Bertie had commented on the fashionable cut and good quality of the grey cashmere, though he'd had to dodge the inevitable questions on why – and for whom – he was all dressed up. Guy's brothers went drinking in the local pubs in Hammersmith; Soho nightclubs were rather out of their ken. Somehow he hadn't wanted to mention Mary, whether because he didn't want to jinx it, or because he wasn't sure what he felt about her, he couldn't say. And Louisa was on his mind again. Anyway, he reminded himself sharply, tonight was work.

Lost in thought, he hadn't noticed Mary standing in front of him, waving and laughing.

'You're such a four-eyes,' she giggled.

Guy did his best not to register surprise but though he had seen her in her own clothes when they were tailing the Forty, and though they had even been to the 43 together, it was clear that tonight she intended to have an effect. Her hair was a sharp bob with a perfect kiss curl shaped by each ear and she wore a silver cloche hat that had a wide-fishnet veil pulled over her face and tucked under her chin. The effect, with her dark red lips, was captivating. Though she had her coat buttoned up, he could see trails of silvery beads looping on the hem of her dress peeking out from beneath and shoes with a heel. Most of all she looked giddy with excitement, dispelling his confusion of feelings with the grin of a schoolgirl.

They walked to the club, or rather, Guy walked, Mary trotted along, clicking on her heels and bobbing up and down in a way that was quite disconcerting. He had grown used to her clomping in boots, which she complained were made of hard, uncomfortable leather. At work, her hair had to be pulled back tightly with not a strand out of place and no make-up was permitted. Though the men at the station teased and people frequently gawped at her in the street with her policewoman's hat and long skirt, Guy had grown used to her practical look on their shifts together. His tongue was tied now and he found himself caught between wanting to give her a good night out, as she was clearly in the mood for, and keeping the tone more suitable for a work assignment.

At the entry to the club, the hulking spectre they had come to know as 'German Albert' stood guard. He looked at Guy warily but opened the door. Inside, Dolly Meyrick was at the desk, collecting each guest's ten-shilling fee. After the mob had ransacked the club she was taking no chances. On seeing Guy, she gave a wide smile.

'Nice to see you back,' she said, 'and you've brought your sweetheart with you this time?' She accompanied this with a sideways glance in Mary's direction.

Guy involuntarily took a step away from Mary and started to protest but then saw Mary look rather offended. 'We're just coming in for a moment,' he said. 'My friend is in the band.'

'Let me fetch someone to find you a nice table, Sergeant Sullivan,' said Dolly, a woman who though young – she couldn't have been more than twenty – must have had the charisma and competence of her mother.

'No, really, I—' started Guy, but Mary pulled on his arm and he went quiet. He wasn't at all sure about accepting the hospitality of the club's owner. Surely he was breaking some sort of law? He would just have to make sure he didn't drink any of the alcohol. Or dance with any of the Merry Maids. He couldn't even look at them, in fact. Oh, damn. Why had he agreed to come along tonight?

Dolly clicked her fingers and a young woman came out of the shadows, wearing a red flapper's dress with a band around her head that had an elaborate black ostrich feather attached to it. When she stood by him, Guy had to move his head to prevent his nose from being tickled.

'Follow me,' she said after a quick word with Dolly.

Unable to do anything else, Guy and Mary walked behind her and down the steep steps to the basement below. It wasn't as crowded as before, though a good number of people were dancing to the band, and Guy saw Joe Katz crooning at the microphone. The flapper girl led them to a table with two chairs and swooped off, like a bird of prey, thought Guy grimly. He looked around but couldn't see Alice Diamond, although he had to admit that the combination of his eyesight and the dimly lit room meant he couldn't be certain. Mary had handed her coat in upstairs but kept her hat on and was sitting cross-legged on the chair, her legs jiggling, moving her head about.

'What are you trying to look at?' asked Guy.

Two spots of pink bloomed on Mary's cheeks. 'I was just looking at the band,' she said. 'Did you say Harry would be here tonight?'

Oh, thought Guy.

'Yes, he should be. He's at the back.' He resisted pointing out that Harry's small stature made him hard to see.

He knew he should have the manners to ask Mary to dance but was saved by the arrival of a waiter with a bottle of champagne and two glasses. 'On the 'ouse,' he said, and disappeared.

Mary looked at Guy, a glass halfway to her lips. 'Can we drink it, *please*?'

'We're within licensing hours,' said Guy. 'It's not for me to give you permission. I'm on duty myself.' Immediately he regretted saying it. Why was he so prim at times like this?

Mary was chastened and put the glass back down. She blinked hard a few times and looked straight ahead of her.

Abruptly, the music stopped. Joe announced a short break and the dancers spilled off the floor, weaving their way back to their tables or up the stairs to the bar on the first floor. It was then that Guy noticed a man with blond hair and thought he recognised him as one of those who had been in the circle of friends with Nancy and Pamela Mitford before. He had been seated but stood as two women who had been dancing came up to him at the table. They looked familiar, too – the dark-haired one, Guy was certain, was the sister of the man who had been killed at Asthall Manor. She had a guarded look about her but he supposed he could hardly blame her, given the circumstances. The other girl was very pretty, small and blonde, wearing a dress that made him think of fallen rose petals in the late summer. As he watched, Dolly Meyrick approached the table and sat on the knee of a man he hadn't noticed before, a younger-looking chap in a fashionable, well-cut suit. There was something about the atmosphere of their group that Guy found puzzling. Although they must have known each other well, there was an awkwardness in the way they stood about, as if they were not quite comfortable. The pretty blonde one was drinking with frequent, nervous sips, her blue eyes flashing, looking about as if hoping someone would come and take her away. Dolly and her suitor were the only two who seemed happily lost to the rest of the club, nuzzling each other and talking in close whispers. The very blond man had a bruised, grey look about his face and was batting off the one Guy thought was the dead man's sister – Charlotte Curtis, that was her name – who was pawing at his sleeve but in a lazy, ineffectual manner, like a sleepy cat.

'Hey, amigo, great to see you here!' Guy was jolted by a whack on the side of his head. Harry was standing over him, a teacup in one hand with liquid spilling in drops over the edge onto Guy's suit.

'Careful!' Guy said, rather too sharply.

'All right, keep your toupee on.' Harry chuckled and winked at Mary, who giggled back.

Guy looked at them both. 'You've met before, haven't you?'

Harry and Mary exchanged a private glance. 'You might say that,' said his friend, and Mary's cheeks went pink again. Guy had introduced them the last time he'd been in the 43 but he wondered now if they'd met up on their own since then.

'In that case, I'm going to leave you to it. Excuse me,' said Guy and before Harry could stop him, he was out of there, twenty minutes after he'd arrived, needing to get away from the crowds and the smoke, needing to breathe in the night air.

CHAPTER FORTY-FIVE

Guy pushed past German Albert and looked about him. The street, as usual, was busy with its out-of-hours trade. Despite having left the club in a hurry, he wasn't ready for the night to be over. The adrenalin was running through him, and he realised he should probably go back and make sure Mary got home safely at the very least. He was angry with himself for not spending more time trying to see if any of the Forty or their associates were there. But how to do a policeman's work when a policeman shouldn't be in there? He needed a moment away to think it through, so he went to a café over the road and ordered a hot chocolate. When the waitress raised an eyebrow, he said: 'I mean it, a hot chocolate. I don't want rum in it or anything like that.'

'Whatever you want,' she said, putting her notebook back in her apron pocket and sloping off. Guy found a table by the window and sat close to the glass, where he thought he could at least make himself useful observing the comings and goings of the 43. It wasn't yet nine-thirty and street trade was slow. It would pick up when the clubs started to kick their clientele out, probably around three o'clock in the morning. Guy knew the fashion was to go to two or three clubs before finding somewhere that would either serve a Chinese meal or ham and eggs in the early hours. It seemed a pretty louche way of life to him. The table next to him had another man sitting alone who had kept his hat on and the collar of his coat turned up. Probably another policeman, thought Guy. Or a man waiting for the working girls to start their shifts.

Guy drained his hot chocolate, enjoying the crunch of the sugar at the bottom of his cup. As he pulled out enough coins to pay for it, a quick glance outside hitched on two men standing in the shadows a few yards from the door of the 43. German Albert was facing in the other direction – was he on lookout? One of the men wore no hat and his gleaming blond hair was visible even in the dark – this had to be Sebastian Atlas – while the other was shorter, lighter on his feet somehow. There was some sort of exchange going on between them – Guy was certain Mr Atlas was handing over money in return for something. What Louisa had seen him do before was not a one-off then. Without stopping to think, Guy threw the coins on the table, grabbed his hat and ran outside and across the road, narrowly dodging a car that blared its horn at him. The two men looked up and both ran in opposite directions. Guy decided to leave Nancy's friend for the moment. Guy wanted the man who was selling.

The man ran down Gerrard Street, Guy not far behind, straining to keep him in sight. There were enough people on the pavements to slow the man down as he dodged in between them and Guy was catching up, but then the man ducked down a side street. Guy turned the corner and swore – he'd lost him.

There was a noise at the other end, an 'Oi! What do you think you're doing?' and Guy realised his culprit had run smack into a uniformed officer who was holding onto the struggling fellow. To run into one policeman was bad luck but two looked like carelessness.

'Keep a hold of him,' Guy shouted. 'I'm Sergeant Sullivan, with the Vine Street station.'

'Right you are,' came back and Guy ran towards them. By the time the three of them were together, the wanted man had handcuffs on behind his back.

'I ain't done nothing,' he said, and Guy could see now he was young, barely twenty-one, and a good foot shorter than him, with pockmarked skin and dull eyes. His breath was stale but his clothes were stylish; he wore his collar up and there was a flash of red silk lining. The better to blend in with his smarter clients presumably.

'I think you have,' said Guy. 'What were you selling back there?'

'Nothing.'

Guy searched through his pockets and pulled out a packet of cigarettes, a box of matches, a few coins. 'That's it, guv,' said the boy. 'Now let me go.'

Guy only sighed in reply and reached for the inside pocket of the coat, pulling out an enamelled cigarette case, inside which were several small packets made from folded white paper. 'What am I going to find in these?'

The man gave a look of surprise. 'I don't know. Someone must have put them there. Now I think of it, this isn't my coat. I must have picked up the wrong one.'

'Give over,' said Guy. 'You're coming with us.'

At the station Guy carried out the interview, alongside Sergeant Oliver, an officer on night duty. He'd had to dismiss the uniform who had helped him because he was attached to a different station. The paper packets contained white powder and were confirmed as cocaine when Sergeant Oliver dabbed a bit and put it on his tongue. After that, it was quick to charge him with possession and intent to supply, though the culprit, Samuel Jones, denied everything and protested his innocence throughout. Guy listed Jones's possessions, from cigarettes to a wad of pound notes, then noticed he was wearing a distinctive pair of cufflinks. 'What are those?' asked Guy.

'Lapis lazuli,' Jones said, proudly. 'Proper quality these are.'

'Where did you buy them?'

Jones flicked his eyes down. 'I didn't, someone give me them.'

'Who gave them to you?' Guy persisted.

'What's it to you?'

Guy wanted to impress Oliver, or rather, he wanted word to get around that he was someone who knew his stuff. He wasn't going to let this one go easily.

'Would you prefer that I make this more difficult for you than it needs to be?' he said, deliberately making his voice as hard as he could. 'We could wait a week for the magistrate and I'm sure you could enjoy the prison hospitality at your leisure until then ...'

'I can't tell you who and even if I could, I wouldn't,' said Jones. 'Someone posh. Someone grateful.' He smirked and Guy saw Sergeant Oliver smirk too.

'Outside the club tonight, who was that with you?'

Jones was silent.

'One of your regulars, was it?' Guy pointed to the cufflinks, the blue stones set in gold like sand around a piece of the deep blue sea. 'He gave you those, did he?'

Jones said nothing.

'I'll take that as a yes then, shall I?'

Sergeant Oliver smirked again but this time he was on Guy's side.

'You can take it however you want,' spat Jones.

'Take him off,' said Guy to the uniform. 'The magistrate'll deal with him in the morning.'

Jones shouted and started kicking out but the sergeant dragged him out of the interview room.

Guy made an official note of Jones's items and put everything into a large brown envelope. Except for the cufflinks. These he needed to show to someone else. He had a feeling they were going to help him. Only before he could do anything about it, Guy was handed a message. 'It's from a Miss Louisa Cannon,' said the young constable. 'She said it was urgent.'

The instruction was clear but its meaning was not. 'Meet me at Lambeth North underground station at 11 p.m. Bring Constable Moon.' He could only hope he'd make it in time. And why did she want Mary there? He'd have to find out.

CHAPTER FORTY-SIX

⌒

The Longs' house was only a few minutes' walk from Lambeth North station. Louisa hurried there, her coat wrapped tightly against the biting wind, and prayed that Guy was still waiting for her – she wasn't sure how late she was but from his expression she guessed it had been a while since eleven o'clock. Mary Moon was beside him, stamping her feet, which were shod prettily rather than in her usual uniform boots, her arms folded tightly across her chest with her hands tucked in. Louisa rushed up to them, taking them both by surprise as they'd been looking in the opposite direction at that moment.

'I'm so sorry,' she panted. 'I'll explain everything, but thank you for coming.'

'What's going on?' asked Guy.

As he spoke, Louisa realised that she had frightened him with her message and she was sorry for that. 'We need to catch a bus,' she said. 'We're going to Elephant and Castle. I'll tell you on the way.'

*

Sitting upstairs on the bus, Mary and Louisa beside each other and Guy behind, they each turned to face each other. There was only one other person there, a man smoking at the back, eyes half closed, his head leaning into his upturned collar, as if he was trying to pretend he was already in bed.

Louisa whispered urgently as she told them the story of Daniel, meeting Dulcie's father and sister and, finally, the name that had been mentioned to her: Billy Masters.

'I want to go to the Elephant and Castle and find out about him. If he did it, there will be rumours at the very least.'

'What? You can't go in and start asking questions about Billy Masters.' Mary was appalled at the idea.

'I'll tell them I want to join up. They've met me before, they know I'm loyal to Dulcie – I didn't tell the police that I knew about her connection to them. That's got to count for something.'

Guy shook his head. 'It's too dangerous, Louisa. I can't allow it. Not unless I come with you.'

Louisa was caught off guard when Mary interjected: 'No, you being there is what will make it dangerous. You're a man, you'll be too easily noticed.' She turned to Louisa. 'Let me come with you. Two is better than one. It's safer, if things turn.'

Guy opened his mouth as if to protest but quickly thought better of it. 'If you do that, I have to be nearby, in case anything happens.'

The journey was a short one and when they were a stop along from the big roundabout at the heart of Elephant and Castle, the three of them disembarked.

They had only walked a short way when Louisa stopped. 'Guy, I don't want you coming any further with us. It's too risky. We'll meet you back at the bus stop. You can wait there quite easily.'

Guy was reluctant but could see that these two women weren't going to budge an inch. Bloody hell.

'Fine,' he said. 'I'm not happy about it though.'

'We can handle ourselves,' said Mary and, taking Louisa by the arm, she walked the two of them off and away from Guy, who unhappily watched their receding backs.

As Louisa and Mary rounded the corner, they saw that the Elephant and Castle was open for business. Pubs may have had to stop serving at eleven o'clock but those with punters that didn't care too much for the law were only too pleased, it seemed, to carry on past the witching hour. Though the windows had been darkened by closed curtains, they saw three women only a little ahead of them pull the door open to enter, releasing a blast of noise and cigarette smoke into the cold night air.

'Quick,' said Mary. 'If we get close behind, we'll look like we're in their group.' They ran up and caught the door just before it shut. As they jumped inside, they were almost immediately pushed back against the door. It was the thickset woman Louisa had met when she came with Dulcie, the same one who had attended the court trial, and she didn't look any more attractive or pleased at their reunion.

'You,' she said, and Louisa could smell the gin on her breath as she leant into her, their noses almost touching. 'What are you doing here?'

'I'm a friend of Dulcie's,' gasped Louisa. 'Remember?'

Louisa realised with burning clarity that she had overestimated her sense of belonging with the Forty, or that they would recognise that she had not given Dulcie away during the inquest. To them, she was no more than an irritant, a buzzing insect. And she was trapped in their web.

'I know who you are,' said the woman, making even this statement sound like a threat. 'But who is this?' She jerked her chin at

Mary and narrowed her eyes. Mary shrank back a little, though Louisa was a little awed at her steely resolve. She hadn't run off as she might have expected.

'A friend,' said Louisa, her voice small. Two other women had appeared.

'What's going on, Bertha?' said one. She was wiry, with a well made-up face but without a trace of good humour in her demeanour.

'I've got it,' said Bertha, broadening out her shoulders. 'Don't worry.' She grabbed at the lapel of Mary's coat. 'Who are you?'

'Vera,' said Mary. Bertha looked at Louisa perhaps to see if there was a response to this but Louisa kept her face neutral.

'Can we talk somewhere?' said Louisa.

'We can talk here,' said Bertha, who hadn't let go of the coat. The two women behind her started to shift on their feet while a taller woman beside them took a cigarette out and lit it. Bertha had her cue. 'We've got all the time in the world,' she continued.

'We want to join the Forty,' said Louisa boldly.

Bertha looked at her, her currant-eyes open as wide as they could go. 'What do you think we are? Some sort of gentleman's club? You don't pay a fee and sign up.' She started laughing helplessly at her own joke.

'I know that,' said Louisa, 'but I want some of what you've got. Nice clothes and a bit of your own money. My mum was a laundress and it was a hard life. I want better.' This was a brave speech and Bertha momentarily looked as if she might be impressed.

'We think Dulcie's innocent,' said Mary suddenly and Louisa panicked. She knew this was a bad move.

The henchwomen were alerted and Bertha looked Mary up and down. 'You do, huh?'

Louisa and Mary were trapped. The pub doors, heavy on their hinges, were closed behind them and opened inwards. Bertha stood in front of them, her wide figure spread by her ham-like thighs set astride. Behind her were the two women at her shoulders, bristling with the anticipation of a decent brawl. Louisa could hear that the pub had gone quiet. Their exchange had not gone unnoticed. And this was not even the worst of it.

There was a shudder in the atmosphere. Heads turned and elbows nudged, drinks were nervously sipped. Louisa knew this signal. Something was about to kick off and she was right at the centre of it. Bertha had dropped Mary but there was no gap, nowhere for them to run and they couldn't turn and open the doors without getting grabbed backwards by their collars. She didn't dare even look at Mary, she could feel the fear coming off her in waves like those on Brighton beach in the winter. She didn't know what to do. She'd rushed here, blindly, certain that she was one of them, that somehow she'd make herself understood and they'd see she was on their side. But her time, such as it was, thieving with her uncle Stephen was long ago and even if there was some secret language amongst lowlifes – which there wasn't – she'd long forgotten how to speak it. Who had she been kidding? Her world was servants' quarters and nursery bedtimes, Nanny Blor's consternation over missing jigsaw pieces and knowing that Lord Redesdale's bark was worse than his bite.

Even more stupidly, she had brought Mary. What for? She'd wanted *to show her*, like some pugilistic idiot. She'd wanted Guy to see she was not just tough but clever, too, and for Mary to witness this and be made to feel inadequate by comparison. Vanity, that's all it was. She felt like a bloody idiot. An idiot in danger of serious attack.

As she was thinking this, stricken, Bertha suddenly stumbled and tottered to one side, her mouth opened to say something and then quickly shut. She'd thought better of it. Standing in front of them now was the tall woman Louisa had seen in there before, and in the 43, with her well-cut clothes and rings on every finger. The Queen herself. Alice Diamond.

CHAPTER FORTY-SEVEN

Fear clung to Louisa's skin and made her hairs stand on end. She could do nothing but watch as Alice crossed her arms, the diamonds glittering on her long fingers, with nails that were short but clean. Her dark eyes looked at them both before her, her mouth in a tight slit that you couldn't slip a stamp through. Bertha started to say something but Alice shut her up with a glare.

Mary was completely frozen to the spot. Not only could she neither move nor speak, if she had gone any paler she'd have been transparent.

Louisa tried to swallow but her mouth was completely dry. She tried to speak but no more than a croak came out. Alice roared with laughter and Bertha made a sound that was probably a giggle but was more resonant of a shotgun spraying pellets.

'You're quite the honoured guests, aren't you?' said Alice, and looked from side to side, waiting for her loyal subjects to titter politely at her joke. They duly did, of course.

'They've been sniffing around about Dulcie,' growled the woman who'd stamped on the cigarette.

Alice leaned forward slightly, her smile gone. 'I'd get your nose out of that nasty smell, if I was you.'

Louisa dared to speak up. In for a penny and all that. 'I don't think she did it. I think she's been set up by someone.'

Alice said nothing but clicked her fingers and someone handed her a cigarette, already lit.

'She's going to take the fall for a man. That's what I think.' Louisa was all too aware of Mary beside her, her elbows pressed into her sides as if she was trying to make herself as small as possible.

Alice picked a bit of tobacco out. 'Tell me more.'

'I don't know any more,' said Louisa. 'It's just that it doesn't add up. Dulcie's admitted to nicking the jewellery but said she's innocent of the murder. I think she was meeting someone that night but can't say who it was because they'll do for her when – if – she gets out of gaol.'

The silence in between roared in Louisa's ears. She pressed on. 'I think it might be someone you know. What if he's trying to set you all up? Trying to bring down the Forty.'

Bertha spat on the floor. 'No man can bring us down,' she said.

'What if it was Billy Masters?'

'Who gave you that name?' Bertha shouted.

Before Louisa could react, another woman came into view, curious perhaps at the scene going on by the door. Louisa only just registered her, her mind desperately wondering how to say she knew Billy's name, but Mary reared back as if she'd been struck. The woman came up and looked at her closely, then hit Bertha on the shoulder.

'It's the old bill.'

Alice spun round. 'Did I hear right?' she said

'Yeah, she's the one who nicked me at Debenham and Freebody.'

Louisa didn't dare even try to look sideways but she was afraid now that Mary would faint. Was there anything she could say to get Alice to understand that a terrible mistake had been made and she was only trying to help prove Dulcie's innocence?

No, there wasn't.

Out of the corner of her eye Louisa saw that some chairs had been pushed back and one woman had pushed her sleeves up, the better to reveal black and purple tattoos that twisted from wrist to elbow. She could hear the soft wheeze of the pump as the barmaid continued to pull pints, and the occasional click of a match striking. The pub had settled, like an audience waiting for the curtains to rise, comfortable in the knowledge that they had their tickets and the star performer had arrived.

Only, tonight the show was cancelled. Alice clapped her hands once, laughing when Louisa and Mary jumped. She turned to Bertha. 'I think this policewoman is nervous but she shouldn't be, should she?'

Bertha growled. She actually growled, like a dog straining at a leash.

'No,' said Alice, 'we're very nice. There's nothing here for the police to worry about.' She turned back to Louisa. 'I'd ask you to stay for a drink,' she continued, 'but I don't think you'll accept, will you?'

Neither of them responded, not knowing at all how to read this.

Her voice lowered. '*Now* would be a good time for you to go.'

Louisa slowly started to turn, looking over her shoulder the entire time but nobody else in the pub moved an inch as she opened the heavy door and Mary shot out. Louisa was about to run too, when Alice grabbed her by the arm and whispered into her ear. 'On the other hand, Dulcie Long ought to be nervous. Ours boys followed you. You and her son. All the way to that sister's house. Now there's two traitors in that family and I don't like that. I don't like that at all.'

She let go with a shove and Louisa ran out of the door and onto the street not knowing where she was going, so long as it was far away from the Elephant and Castle and all who drank there.

CHAPTER FORTY-EIGHT

~~~~~~

Somehow Louisa ran back the way they had come and hit the road where the bus stop was. Only when she was sure that nobody was behind her did she bend over, hands on her knees, and try to get her breath back. Her chest hurt and her eyes ached. After a few moments she stood up straight but immediately felt sick; unable to prevent it, she vomited over somebody's garden wall and prayed it had gone into a flower bed. Slowly, with trembling legs, she walked back to where they'd agreed to meet Guy, and saw him standing there, his arms around Mary, her head leaning against his chest. It wasn't what she wanted to see but she couldn't blame her. If she'd got to Guy first, she'd have done that too.

Louisa went nearer and when Mary saw her she broke away from Guy. She'd been crying. 'I'm so sorry, Louisa,' she said. 'I was useless but I was so frightened . . .' A fresh bout of tears overcame her.

Guy looked like a balloon that had lost all its air. 'I should have come with you.'

'No,' said Louisa, 'it would have made it worse. Only now I'm worried about Marie. We have to warn her.'

Mary blew her nose and started to recover herself. 'What do you mean?'

'Alice whispered something to me as we were leaving, about Dulcie betraying her. Someone followed me from Mrs Brewster's. And I said Billy Masters's name, which made one of them angry. Because of us, Alice thinks that Dulcie has talked to the police about him and the rest of them. And now they are going to want their revenge.'

'This means there *is* a connection between Dulcie and the Forty, and this man, Billy Masters. He's the key. Do you think he's the one that met her at Asthall Manor?' Guy, who had had a horrible half an hour waiting for Louisa and Mary to come back, wanted badly to redeem himself by solving this.

'There's a connection,' said Louisa, 'but we don't know any more than that, do we?'

'There's no hard evidence,' said Mary.

'No,' sighed Guy.

It was late now, and a chill had seeped into their bones. Louisa was overcome with tiredness and hunger but she hadn't arranged anywhere to sleep that night. She'd had a vague idea that she'd be able to get the last train back to Shipton but that would have departed some time ago.

'You can stay with me,' said Mary. 'My room's only small but I can make up some cushions with a blanket on the floor.'

So they said goodbye to Guy and caught two buses to Mary's room in a women-only block for nurses and the few female police officers working in London. Her quarters were cramped with barely space around the bed, sink and chest of drawers, though she kept it proudly neat with a jam jar in which she had stuck sprigs of holly and berries. Louisa hardly noticed the details as it was after one o'clock by the time they got there and even the marrow of her bones was crying with exhaustion. They crept about as quietly as possible – the walls were very thin, said Mary – though she insisted on making Louisa's bed comfortable and even offered to make her a hot chocolate on the camping gas stove she kept in her room. Only Louisa had fallen asleep with her boots still on before Mary had even finished the sentence.

CHAPTER FORTY-NINE

∼≈≈∽

When Louisa let herself in through the back door at Asthall the next morning, Mrs Stobie was halfway through her preparations for lunch. She raised an eyebrow at the bedraggled nursery maid.

'You're a sight for sore eyes,' she said sternly. 'Nanny Blor's not given you away but I think you'd better make it up to her quick.'

Louisa could barely nod to this, exhausted as she was from her restless sleep and early train ride without breakfast, topped by a long walk in the cold and drizzle back to the house. She trudged up the stairs to the nursery, hoping to slip into the bathroom for at least a reviving strip wash with a flannel and hot water before announcing her return. Tom, Diana, Nancy and Pamela should all be in the library, if not out walking. Debo, Unity and Decca might be in the schoolroom with colouring books and pencils. It had become Nanny Blor and Louisa's most regular form of entertainment in the Christmas holidays on days that were too miserable and damp to take them outside between breakfast and luncheon, though the afternoon walk was never missed, even if it was raining cats and dogs.

Louisa found the nursery quiet when she reached it and was able to slip into her room and change after a brief wash and splash of ice-cold water on her face. Nanny was in the corner of the schoolroom, occupying herself by sharpening the pencils with a pocketknife. Debo rushed over to Louisa when she came in and gave her a big squeeze around her knees, and Unity and Decca looked up to wave hello but quickly resumed their colouring. It was as if her being away had made no difference at all.

Yet back in London, her being away had made all the difference, hadn't it? She was terrified for Marie and Daniel. They needed to be warned that Alice Diamond knew Dulcie's boy was with them but how to tell them without revealing that she was the one who had been so stupid as to lead them there? Those men must have seen her leaving Mrs Brewster's. What made it even more awful was that the Forty also believed that Dulcie had given Louisa – and a policewoman – Billy Masters's name. He would be more important to them than Dulcie. If any of them saw either her or Mary, their lives would be in peril. At Asthall Manor she was safe but these thoughts would cycle endlessly in her mind giving her nightmares.

'I take it the emergency is over?' said Nanny.

Louisa nodded, doing her best to look nonchalant. 'It turned out not to be as bad as was first thought,' she said, hoping she hadn't given herself away. Nancy always said that Nanny was the only one who could make her feel shame for something naughty, and Louisa knew exactly how she felt. At least she had only missed a day and she would find a way to make it up. Louisa knew that Nanny Blor was used to having her around but she couldn't help feeling that now Debo was no longer a baby and the others were getting older, there was less and less need for her to be there. Of course, there was always tidying to be done and chores such as ironing the children's clothes and mending the nursery linens. But, truthfully, none of it was onerous and with the governess around most of the time, there was even less for her to do. Perhaps that was why she had allowed herself to be so distracted by everything going on in London.

Where the routine of the children's daily life had given her comfort before with the regular-as-clockwork timetable of meals, walks, laundry and baths, now it felt suffocating. Debo was a placid and easy child but Unity and Decca were withdrawing into a secret world of their own, talking in a language that nobody else could understand. Yet they were not at all alike, so while they were wrapped up in their own plans, spending hours in their shared room or in a corner of the library, their giggles would be suddenly interrupted by arguments and soon there would be shouting and the stamping of small feet.

Tom was home for the holidays but, at sixteen, he considered himself a young man and preferred to seek his father out, accompanying him on long walks and shoots, rather than be the source of entertainment for his sisters, who plied him with endless questions about school and the food he was allowed to eat there. Diana, fifteen years old and womanly in looks and behaviour, resented her confinement to the nursery and was frequently frustrated in her desire to accompany either Nancy or Pamela in whatever outing or task they embarked on. Alone, she would read in the library, a sulky expression on her face that had started to take on the perfectly carved outlines of a marble bust. In company, she had a tendency to prickliness, which exasperated her mother.

Yet, Louisa knew none of them were any worse than they had ever been and she was still very fond of all of them. She hoped her misgivings were no more than her mind always roaming elsewhere.

Even if she hadn't been afraid for Marie and Daniel, she didn't want to be outside London any more. Perhaps what Nancy had was catching: Louisa was beginning to feel oppressed by the beauty and wide-open spaces of the countryside and longed instead for the freedom that came with the tightly packed men and women on the dance floor of a seedy club in Gerrard Street.

CHAPTER FIFTY

❧

It was Ada who told Louisa the surprising news that Charlotte Curtis was due to arrive at the house later that day.

'She's coming in the run-up to Christmas apparently,' said Ada, as they cleared away the lunch plates from the nursery. 'Bit rum, if you ask me.'

Louisa was surprised that neither Nancy nor Pamela had mentioned it to her but she thought she had probably put their noses out of joint by staying behind in London.

Charlotte arrived at four o'clock, collected from the station by Nancy, with Hooper driving the car. There was a week until Christmas Day but with her mother recuperating in a nursing home in the south of France, Charlotte had asked if she might spend that week with the Mitfords at Asthall. Everyone thought the request odd, and it had been discussed in the kitchen by Mrs Stobie and Ada, as well as in the drawing room by Lord and Lady Redesdale. Why would she want to spend Christmas at the house where her brother had been killed? Louisa heard various theories suggested: that she wished to investigate further the circumstances of the murder; that she had been looked after in the days immediately afterwards by Lady Redesdale and wanted more of the same comfort for her grief; that she had nowhere else to go, not having stayed at the family homes of her other friends. Nancy thought it was simpler than that: Asthall Manor was reasonably close to Oxford and she would want to see Adrian's friends.

When she arrived it was certainly clear that Charlotte was still in deep mourning. Each layer of her clothes was richly and sumptuously textured, pigmented a black so intense they were almost purple. Louisa thought everything she wore was brand new, with every cuff, collar and hem bearing the crisp look of the not-yet laundered. Her hair fell in thick, chestnut waves to just below her chin and her eyes were made larger and sadder with kohl pencil, a daring style of make-up outside London. She moved slowly but with grace and waved delicately at her luggage in the hall as if it were a metaphysical burden someone else must carry. All the same, she did this with the sure confidence of a woman who had never been asked to lift anything heavier or less glorious than a diamond ring.

Lady Redesdale had arranged for everyone to gather in the library, where she felt the atmosphere would be less formal and more suitable to this young woman they hardly knew staying with them. She had frankly confided in Mrs Windsor – who told Mrs Stobie, who told Ada, who told Louisa – that she was concerned that the youngest children may feel their Christmas joys would be muted by Miss Curtis's presence but equally knew that she was glad of an opportunity to mitigate the guilt she felt at the death having happened at Asthall. If they could give her a happy time there perhaps Miss Curtis would remember things differently. Lord Redesdale was far more disturbed by the idea of a flapper spending so much time in his house and unduly influencing the more malleable minds of his daughters but it was always possible the servants had misinterpreted the distant shouting and repeated slamming of his study door.

At any rate, there they all were, gathered together in the library where the advent calendar leaned on the mantelpiece, the seventeenth window opened that morning by Decca to reveal a cheerful robin redbreast. Louisa brought down Debo, Unity and Decca from the nursery, each girl tidied up from their afternoon's blowy walk, with hair rebrushed and tied up in a velvet ribbon, in clean dresses with white socks and buckled shoes. Tom came in from his walk with Farve, along with Pamela who had been in the stables, while Diana had remained in the library all afternoon reading a book on Elizabeth I as she lay on the sofa. At least, that was what she told her mother. The governess had been dismissed until January and the children had been vocal in their belief that there was no need to do anything 'improving' until she returned.

Ada brought in a tray of hot buttered crumpets, which the children fell upon after Charlotte declined one, asking only for a cup of China tea with no milk and a sliver of lemon. Louisa stole furtive glances at her and was more certain than ever that she could see a likeness to Daniel in her; more than the dark curls of their hair, it was the sulky mouth and soft chin she shared with her brother. Even when happy, the Curtis bloodline would always look resentful in a minor fashion – one ice cube too many in their drink, say, or a hem that came undone halfway through a party.

The tea passed in a fairly desultory manner, with the children the only ones to offer lively chatter, asking Charlotte what present she most hoped for at Christmas and whether she liked robins or Jesus better ('on *Christmas cards*, Muv!' they exclaimed when their mother protested). Perhaps it was the flatness of this atmosphere that prompted Nancy to announce suddenly that she was planning a dinner party for the following night.

'What?' said Lady Redesdale but she had been wrong-footed. Nancy knew she would not want to tick her off in front of Charlotte.

'Sebastian and Ted are in Oxford, it would be easy for them to come down,' said Nancy with insouciance.

Charlotte's face visibly lit up at this news.

Nancy carried on, taking advantage of her mother's tongue-tied response. 'I spoke to Clara on the telephone this morning and she said she'd like to join us. Perhaps we could ask Phoebe, too.'

There was a guttural sound from Lady Redesdale's throat but Nancy cut her off. 'I've already spoken to Mrs Stobie and she said that so long as she can do us a simple supper of roast chicken then she's got enough food in. We'll set up the table in here and then you and Farve needn't be disturbed by us.'

Iris Mitford, who had been observing the scene with her usual quiet elegance, laughed at her niece's nonchalance, although not disapprovingly. Lady Redesdale's high forehead crinkled but she spoke in a resigned tone. 'I suppose if you're not going back to London before Christmas, it would be nice for you, Charlotte?'

'It would mean a lot to be able to see everybody,' said Charlotte, and Louisa saw from the flush on her neck that this was, indeed, the real reason she had wanted to come to Asthall Manor. Charlotte turned to Nancy. 'Perhaps not Dolly. I expect she's got to run the club in any case.'

Nancy laughed. 'Fine, not Dolly. Come with me, let's go and telephone the others.'

What, Louisa wondered, was Nancy's game?

She didn't have to wait long to find out.

CHAPTER FIFTY-ONE

Louisa was in the linen cupboard the following morning, having decided to rearrange the shelves for no reason other than that it gave her an excuse to stay in there for an hour or two. It was more of a small room than a cupboard, with three walls lined with deep shelves and a high window. The smell of freshly laundered cotton made her nostalgic for her mother and she had learned that the powerful emotion gave her a peculiar combination of comfort and heartache. When she needed her other senses overwhelmed, this would do the trick. At this point, Louisa was trying not to think about Dulcie because she had done little else in the small hours of the night, her thoughts whirling around like a dervish and producing not one single resolution. She could not write to warn Dulcie of Alice Diamond because all letters were read by a prison officer, nor could she find an excuse to get back down to London again so soon without risking her job. And anyway, even if she did warn Dulcie it wouldn't do any good: it would just leave the wretched girl fretting in a prison, unable to tell her family.

As Louisa was deciding whether the single bedsheets should go on a lower shelf so that they could be more easily reached by a helpful child, Pamela came in. Louisa knew that Pamela sometimes liked to hide in here too, usually to read a book when she was in retreat from her sisters. The linen cupboard guaranteed warmth with its hot water pipes running along the back wall, even when Lord Redesdale's strict instructions about the fires being lit meant the rest of the house was ice cold. No book was in Pamela's hand this time.

'Lou,' she said, 'I need your help.'

Louisa tried to look as neutral as possible before committing herself to a promise. A Mitford daughter might ask for help with reviving a dying mouse or rescuing a rabbit caught in one of the hated gamekeeper's snares as easily as other children wanted their shoelaces tied.

Pamela closed the door behind her and the two of them were almost pressed together. 'Nancy wants to do a seance,' she said.

'A what?' Louisa couldn't work out what Nancy would want to do this for.

'You know, when you try to talk to the dead.' She was whispering as if ghosts might be eavesdropping from behind the folded pillowcases.

'Yes, but why?'

'She thinks we could talk to Adrian, to find out what happened.'

'I thought you believed in ghosts.'

'I do!' Pamela was earnest.

'Then don't you think that's rather dangerous?' Louisa wasn't sure if she believed in ghosts but this seemed to be tempting something unnatural and she didn't like the idea of it. Nor would anybody else. Nanny Blor would be distraught if she discovered it.

Pamela's shoulders dropped. 'Yes, I do. But you know what Koko's like, when she gets the bit between her teeth.'

Louisa felt herself wavering. It was a long shot but if any of them had seen Dulcie with this Billy Masters or could recall something of him, it might be worthwhile. There was an opportunity here, with all of them gathered, to try and prise some information. If she struck lucky, she'd have something to tell Guy, something that could be of genuine use and he might tell his boss about what she had done.

Did she want to join the police? She ignored the thought.

'When does Nancy want to do it?'

'It has to be after Muv and Farve have gone to sleep. In the library, after supper.'

'I can't believe I'm asking this but what do you need?'

'Nothing really, a tablecloth and four candles. It'll be me, Nancy, Charlotte, Sebastian, Ted, Phoebe and Clara. Nancy asked Oliver, which is so embarrassing.'

Louisa didn't say anything but she understood. Poor Pamela, always being set up with him. It wasn't as if either of them ever showed much relish at the prospect. There had been one awful day in the summer when a tennis party had been set up, only for Pamela to find that everyone deliberately tiptoed away, leaving only her and Oliver in the court. She had heard them giggling on the other side of the hedge and had been mortified.

'Anyway, it turns out Oliver can't come. His mother isn't keen, I bet. So we'll need you there, too.'

'Are you sure?'

Pamela made an impatient click with her tongue. 'There has to be an even number of people for a seance and I can't exactly ask Tom or Diana. Diana's too young and Tom will give us away to Farve, they're thick as thieves now.'

This kind of remark caught at Louisa like a tiny splinter under her fingernail. 'In that case, when Mrs Windsor has retired for the night I'll come to the library with the candles. It'll most likely be around midnight. The witching hour.'

To this Pamela pulled a face of mock alarm as she pulled the door behind her.

CHAPTER FIFTY-TWO

❧

As Louisa had nothing to do with Nancy's supper party but had to stay in the nursery with Nanny Blor and the younger girls, she saw nothing of the others' arrivals, although she had been aware of a flurry of arrangements with a grumpy Hooper inveigled into various trips to the station to collect the guests who came at inconveniently different times. Despite Nancy's report that Mrs Stobie would cheerfully make them a simple supper, she grumbled like Mount Etna as she ordered Ada to peel the potatoes while she made an apple pie. Ada and Louisa, however, were both cheerful. Thanks to Lord Redesdale's unpredictable temperament, there weren't often guests in the house and it made for a welcome change in the daily routine. Ada's pregnancy was starting to show now and she told Louisa she rather thought she'd pack as much in as she could before she had to stop work. 'You'll have to come around and tell me all the gossip,' she teased, and Louisa had smiled though her heart had sunk. Was that to be her future?

At a quarter to midnight, when Louisa was sure that Diana had finally fallen asleep, she went downstairs. There had been a terrific battle earlier as Diana had wanted to join Nancy and her friends but Lord Redesdale had expressly forbidden her to do anything other than say hello to them on their arrival. Diana's powers of sulking were legendary but on this occasion her father would not be moved.

Louisa went to the kitchen and saw that Mrs Stobie had already gone to bed. There was no sign of Mrs Windsor and her sitting room was dark, so she must have finished her work. Quietly, Louisa went to the dining room and fetched four silver candlesticks and new candles, as well as a clean tablecloth from the side dresser. In her inability to do anything else – she was keenly feeling the frustration that she had no idea what Guy was doing about the threat to the Longs – at least she was busy.

When Louisa came into the library she could see that Ada had cleared away the supper things earlier. Pamela was up and stoking the fire, putting another log on. Sebastian and Ted were leaning on the chimneypiece, smoking and talking to each other. There were several empty wine bottles already on the side and Louisa saw that the port decanter was half empty. Charlotte was on the sofa, clad in what had become her customary inky black, smoking. She didn't stir at Louisa's entrance but Pamela looked frightened. She had started to shake her head at Louisa, as if warning her off, only she did it too late as Nancy, who had been sitting by Clara on the window seat, jumped up and clapped her hands.

'Oh goody! You're here,' she exclaimed.

Charlotte looked up sharply. 'What's going on?'

'Koko, I don't really think we should ...' It was clear that Pamela's nerves about ghosts had squashed her earlier acquiescence with the seance plan.

'Nonsense,' said Nancy briskly. Louisa was reminded of Nanny silencing the claim by Unity that Father Christmas was actually

Lord Redesdale. 'Everyone,' she went on smoothly, 'we're going to do a seance and try to talk to Adrian.'

'I don't think we bloody are.' Charlotte threw her cigarette in the fire. 'I don't believe in any of that. It's asking for trouble.'

'Don't you want to talk your brother?' said Pamela, courage plucked.

'You say that as if I were refusing to telephone him up. He's *dead*. I can't speak to him any more than I can take my head off and carry it.'

'Well, if it's not real there's no harm in trying, is there?' said Nancy. 'And if it *is* real then we might find something out.'

'What exactly might we find out?' Sebastian had stretched out along the length of the sofa, Charlotte's lap a cushion beneath his head.

Louisa stood there, ignored, the candlesticks getting heavier by the second.

'Who killed him, of course,' Pamela said boldly.

'We know who did that,' said Seb, still horizontal, eyes hooded. 'And she's about to be sentenced to death for it.'

'Louisa doesn't think Dulcie is guilty.' Nancy looked at her nursery maid as she said this, a direct challenge. Louisa felt herself go red and longed to put down the things in her arms.

Ted turned on his heels, his back to the fire, and looked at Louisa as if seeing her for the first time. 'You? What do *you* know?'

Louisa's tongue felt thick and heavy in her mouth, her lips so dry they had stuck together. She tried to speak but couldn't do it without difficulty. 'I think someone else met Mr Curtis at the bell tower, before Dulcie got there.'

'Why do you think that?' Ted's eyes had narrowed.

Louisa had never wished more strongly that she could vanish in a puff of smoke. 'It's only a theory,' she mumbled. Bloody Nancy.

Charlotte pulled another cigarette out of her silver case and Louisa saw her fingers were trembling. It took two matches before she managed to light it.

'Why haven't any of you said anything to me?' she muttered, as she struck the box.

'Why don't we ask Adrian?' said Nancy, and she stood to take the candlesticks from Louisa. 'Now is the perfect time.'

CHAPTER FIFTY-THREE

⁓

Louisa laid the white cloth on the long table that had been set up for their supper earlier, then placed the four candles on it. Pamela lit them and Nancy turned off the electric lights. At this Charlotte stood and announced that she was going to bed.

'No,' said Nancy firmly. 'Whatever you think of this, there's the possibility that we could discover the truth behind your brother's death. We have to try it.'

'We know the truth,' said Charlotte. 'Our maid pushed him off the church tower. In case you'd forgotten, she's in prison awaiting trial and nobody expects less than for her to be hanged for it.'

'What if someone else *was* there that night, in the church?' said Pamela.

'Don't be a child,' snapped Ted, and Pamela blinked back fury.

'You're only a year older than me, you know,' she said and he made a sort of conciliatory noise in response but said no more.

Clara and Phoebe both stood and went to sit at the table in unison. Phoebe looked defiant, her good looks hardened by the shadows of the room. Louisa sensed that a large country house such as Asthall was not her natural habitat. At a party she could be beautiful and vivacious; at a small supper she seemed exposed. There were traces of a London accent that hinted at a more interesting background than the usual Home Counties set.

Pamela stepped towards Charlotte and took her arm. 'Come and sit down. Of course nobody is suggesting anything of the sort but we want to help. Let's just try this.'

'How is the spirit going to talk to us?' asked Nancy. 'We don't have a Ouija board.'

'We can put a glass of water on the table,' said Pamela, 'and ask the spirit to make the water move in answer to our questions. Louisa, would you do that, please?' She sat down.

Clara called out, her voice deliberately light, trying to ease the situation. 'Come on, boys, join us. You're all getting hot under the collar but it's just for fun.'

Sebastian came over in smooth, easy strides. 'I don't care one way or the other,' he said, taking a seat beside Pamela. Charlotte looked at him then, as if he had betrayed her.

Louisa fetched a glass and then the eight of them were sitting with their knees under the table, in the near darkness, with only the glow from the fire and the candlelight to reveal their faces.

'We hold hands,' instructed Pamela, 'and then we ask Adrian if he is here. I'll do it as only one of us can be the medium and I'm the one who believes in this.'

Charlotte tutted but allowed her hands to be held by Pamela and Nancy, sitting on either side of her. Ted took Clara's in one hand, Nancy's in the other. Louisa sat on the other side of Phoebe, who was beside Pamela. On her other side was Sebastian.

'Adrian Curtis, are you there?'

Now that they were sitting there in the dark, the atmosphere was less strained. Nonetheless, Louisa was ill at ease holding Sebastian's dry hand on one side, Phoebe's tight grip on the other.

She was glad that despite Pamela and Lord Redesdale's fervent belief that Asthall Manor was haunted, she had never felt disturbed by any icy, mysterious presence. Nancy, too, had always declared herself impervious to any ghost. All the same, Louisa did have one idea for making this a useful exercise and she wasn't above a gentle nudge in the right direction if necessary.

There was complete silence and the glass of water remained as still as a stone.

'Adrian, if you're there, let us know by the water,' said Pamela once more.

Nancy rolled her eyes at this but Louisa saw that Charlotte was staring at the glass intently and she looked afraid.

Rain spattered on the window and somewhere there was the sound of wood creaking, for which there were a number of innocent explanations but it made one or two of them shudder. Everyone had their eyes on the middle of the table when they saw the water in it shake slightly. Nancy gave a start. 'What was that?'

'Ssh,' hushed Pamela. 'Adrian, if it's you, we want to ask you about . . .' She appeared to look for exactly the right phrase to use. 'About the last time we saw you.'

Again, the glass trembled. Louisa concentrated on making sure her feet were planted on the floor. Was it possible that one of them had knocking knees that were causing the tremors? Yes, it was entirely possible.

And yet, and yet . . .

Charlotte's eyes were completely fixed on the glass.

'We want to know the name of the last person you saw.'

Sebastian tried to pull his hands away but both Pamela and Phoebe drew him back.

'Aren't we supposed to ask a question we know the answer to first?' whispered Clara. 'You know, to establish communication?'

Ted barked a laugh. 'We're not actually doing this seriously, are we?'

Nancy rebuked him. 'We're here now. We might as well.'

Pamela tried again. 'We want to know the name of the last person you saw. I will call out letters of the alphabet. Spell the name out by making the water move.'

A tense quiet had stalked into the room.

'A.'

Nothing and nobody moved and it seemed that everyone's breath was held.

'B.'

At this, the glass trembled.

'B,' acknowledged Pamela calmly, before she went back the start of the alphabet and this time the glass was still from 'A' until the letter 'I'.

There was a shifting between them, a reconfiguring of fingers and hands, prompted by sweat or stiffness. Charlotte's breathing was growing shallower.

Once more, Pamela stepped through the alphabet until at 'L' the glass shook again.

Ted leapt up. 'This is ridiculous,' he shouted. 'I'm not doing this any more. Someone is doing this and whoever it is, I'll tell you one thing. It's not bloody Adrian.' He moved away from the table and Louisa saw the flare of the match on his face as he lit a cigarette.

Charlotte had burst into tears and, whether it was her or something else, there was a jolt to the table and the glass was knocked over, spilling water fast over the smooth tablecloth, which made her scream and cover her face with her hands.

'Stop this now,' she said. 'I insist. Stop it! *Stop it!*'

Clara got up and switched the lights on. 'I agree. Let's have a drink and do something else,' she said.

Louisa had risen slightly ahead of her and reverted to her maid's role, busily clearing away as if she hoped she could make them forget she had been sitting at the table. After all, it was the gentle pressure of her knees on the tabletop that had produced the desired effect.

What she really wanted to know, however, was why the letters 'B.I.L.' had made Ted tremble from head to foot.

CHAPTER FIFTY-FOUR

G uy knew that the answer wasn't to post a policeman on watch outside Marie Long's house. If seen, it could only worsen Alice Diamond's rage against the family. Nor would it be possible to put someone undercover nearby. No motor car could sit unobserved for even a day in a Lambeth street without raising suspicion. Besides, Cornish would never agree to it. There wasn't enough to go on, only a nebulous threat that the Forty might exact some kind of revenge on the Longs at some point. What they needed to know was when Alice would strike and where. And he needed to find Billy Masters.

There was another problem: the only people he knew who could identify Billy were Dulcie Long and her father but they would both have their reasons for keeping quiet.

Mary and Guy were in the station the following day, tired and fretful.

'We have to warn Dulcie's family,' said Mary.

'I don't see what good it could do except frighten them,' argued Guy. 'It's not as if they don't already know that they have angered the Forty.'

'But they've got the little boy with them now. Supposing he's in danger, too.'

Guy sighed. 'If we find Billy Masters then it's probable we've got the man who killed Adrian Curtis, or knows who killed him. They're part of the same network. That will mean Dulcie is free to go. She and her family can do what they like then.'

'It's no kind of freedom if the Forty think Dulcie gave Billy up to the police. Where would the Longs go? They can't all just up sticks and move house. It's not as easy as that, Guy.' Mary gave him a reproachful look. 'You know it's not.'

'Yes, I do know. But I also know that I'm a policeman and my job is to solve crimes. The most important thing is that we find Billy Masters.'

They both drained their cups. On this point they weren't going to agree but did it really matter? They had no leads. Where he might be was as much of a mystery as before. What's more, if he was on the run from a murder, he could be anywhere.

'There's only one answer,' said Guy. 'We're going to have to talk to Dulcie, maybe even interview her father and sister.'

'It will endanger them,' said Mary.

Guy was resolute. 'We have no choice.'

It took some persuading to get permission from DI Cornish to interview Dulcie Long at Holloway Prison as, officially, the incarcerated maid was being held as part of a murder investigation by the local constabulary in Oxfordshire. But given that Cornish was running his own criminal investigation into Alice Diamond and the Forty, of which Dulcie was a part, there was a strong case for his involvement.

'Always causes bad blood,' said Cornish. 'Provincials are as territorial over their cases as Jack Russells. You'd better bring back something worth having.'

'Yes, sir,' said Guy. 'We're getting closer, sir. I know it.' He hadn't told Cornish about Mary's encounter with Alice Diamond in the Elephant and Castle. How could he? They'd had no warrant, no protection. He'd had absolutely no right to send Mary in there. The more he thought about it, the more foolhardy he realised they had been. Supposing she and Louisa had been badly beaten? Instead, he'd told Cornish that he'd had a tip-off about Billy Masters as a fence from a source at the 43. That was enough. It didn't need to be about the murder investigation at all, so far as his superiors were concerned. Not, at least, until he had presented them with the prize evidence he was after, and he was surer than ever that he could do this. That would get him a promotion to the CID, which would mean proper pay. More than that. It would mean respect.

Permission gained, it needed only one telephone call and Guy was on his way to Holloway Prison, where Dulcie Long waited for him in an interview room. He felt a pang of guilt that he hadn't asked if Constable Moon could come with him but he wanted to do this alone.

The white sky highlighted the dark prison's stark reality of its purpose, unnerving Guy as he approached and serving as a grim reminder as to why he was on this side of the law. There were no signs of the coming Christmas in Holloway, only keys that rattled on the warden's belt as she led Guy through several long, grey corridors with doors that closed heavily behind them. In the interview room, Dulcie Long was waiting, handcuffed to a chair, looking slight and defeated. Guy nodded to the warden standing in the corner and sat down, pulling out his notebook.

'Thank you for seeing me, Miss Long,' said Guy.

Dulcie's mouth made a quick downturn. 'I don't think I had any choice.'

Guy coughed and decided not to press the point. 'I'm here to see you about your connections with the Forty.'

'What?' It was clear that Dulcie hadn't been expecting this. She tried immediately to cover up her shock. 'I don't have no connections with the Forty.'

'Miss Long. I'm a good friend of Louisa Cannon's. She's told me everything. It really isn't going to help you at this point to deny it.'

Panic showed then. Guy saw that this shared knowledge, intended to protect her, had left her feeling even more exposed.

Tears started to roll down Dulcie's face. 'My family . . . '

'We'll do what we can to protect them,' said Guy.

'How?'

This left him stuck for words, so he took the easy way out. 'That's confidential.'

'You ain't going to do nothing.' Fear had turned to fury. 'You're all bent. You don't care for *my kind*.' She spat at Guy and the warden stepped forward.

Guy put out his hand. 'Leave it.' The warden went back to the corner and Guy wiped the spittle off his glasses.

'Miss Long, I strongly suggest you co-operate with me. That will give your family the best chance of our protection.' He picked up his pencil and notebook again, as if starting afresh. 'We know about your son.'

'Has that bitch told you everything?' said Dulcie. She looked genuinely surprised now, as if it hadn't occurred to her that she could be so deeply betrayed.

'She has told me what she needed to in order for us to prevent you from being sentenced to death.'

'There's no point,' said Dulcie flatly. 'If you lot don't get me, *they* will.'

'Your son proves that Adrian Curtis and you had . . . an understanding,' said Guy. 'It might make a jury look on you more favourably.'

'It won't stop them thinking I'm guilty,' said Dulcie.

'Then you need to tell me about Billy Masters,' said Guy.

At this Dulcie's attention was held.

'His name has been given to us in connection with you. How do you know him?'

'I don't.' She stopped, watching Guy's reaction.

'I only need you to tell me how I can find him,' said Guy. 'You're in here, you're safe from the Forty, aren't you?'

At this Dulcie gave a hollow laugh. 'I ain't safe nowhere and I ain't telling you nothing. You need to leave me alone.'

'Miss Long,' said Guy, 'your boy Daniel is with your sister, Marie. She's looking after him now. If I'm going to keep them safe, you have to tell me what you know.'

'Not Daniel.' Dulcie's voice cracked. 'He can't be there. If anyone finds out that you've talked to me, then he's in danger. I mean it.' She started to gasp for breath as the panic took her body over. 'Please, don't let anything happen to my boy.'

'Tell me where to find Billy Masters and I won't.'

CHAPTER FIFTY-FIVE

D olly Meyrick sat on the sofa at the back of the 43 and regarded Guy with a steady gaze. 'The name might be familiar,' she said at last. 'But I couldn't tell you any more than that. As I told you before, while we have many loyal clients come through the doors, we don't know each of them personally. Besides, it's usually my mother who is here. I'm just looking after things until she returns from Paris.'

Guy had refused to fight with the soft cushions this time and stood opposite her, holding his policeman's helmet in his hands. 'I believe he may be one of the Elephant and Castle gang,' he said.

'We don't like those boys here.'

'But they have been here.'

Dolly shifted slightly and crossed her legs. 'Yes, but not by invitation.'

Guy decided to try another route. 'What about Alice Diamond and her girls? The Forty Thieves.'

'We'd hardly have all of them here at once.' Dolly laughed, as if Guy was being puerile. He swatted away the annoyance.

'But you *have* had Alice Diamond here.' It wasn't a question.

'Yes, we have. She behaves herself. We like to welcome every-body, if they keep to our rules.'

'And your rules are on the side of the law, Miss Meyrick?' Guy could be wry if needed.

Dolly wouldn't be drawn into this. 'Sergeant Sullivan, it's very nice to chat but I do need to get things ready for tonight. Is there something I can specifically help you with?'

'I need to know where to find a man called Billy Masters. If you can't tell me, perhaps you know a man who can?'

Dolly stood and smoothed out her skirt. 'Fine, let's talk to German Albert. Follow me.'

Downstairs, in the basement, there were various people at work setting up the club for later. The floor was being swept, the ash-trays cleaned, the lamps dusted. Without the dancers there or the music playing, a dazzling electric bulb hanging from the ceiling with no shade revealed the rather tired paint on the walls and scuff marks on the floor, a stale smell of cigarettes lingering in the air. German Albert was sitting in the corner reading a newspaper, drinking coffee out of an incongruously tiny cup. Not dressed in black tie or looming by the front door, he looked a rather more manageable size. Dolly interrupted him, introduced him to Guy and then left them to it.

German Albert regarded Guy suspiciously, saying nothing. Guy nearly began by apologising and then reminded himself that he was here as the law and had nothing to be afraid of. Not even a doorman that measured six foot six at fully drawn height.

'I'm trying to find someone called Billy Masters,' he said.

German Albert looked at him blankly.

'He's one of the Elephant and Castle gang but I believe he may operate alone,' Guy pressed. 'He knows a maid that used to work for another of your regular customers, Miss Charlotte Curtis.'

'I don't know their names.' True to his nickname, there was a strong German accent. 'Not my business.' He turned to pick up his newspaper again.

Guy was really feeling exasperated now. 'Sir, I'm not here to cause any trouble but it wouldn't be difficult for me to do so if I wished. I suggest that you help me here.'

The doorman looked up to the ceiling and seemed to think it over, then dropped his chin and looked at Guy with cool blue eyes. 'No. I don't know who he is. I cannot help you.'

Guy took a beat of his own. 'I arrested a man not long ago for selling drugs outside here. He came from inside the club, with one of your more regular clients. Samuel Jones.'

German Albert showed no response to this but kept a dead-eye stare at the wall. Guy continued as if they were chatting. 'We found several packets of cocaine on him. I wonder where he gets his supply from? We've been reading in the newspapers lately that Germany produces the most cocaine. There are rather more lax laws over there and it gets sent here through various channels.'

A corner of German Albert's mouth twitched involuntarily.

'I wonder,' carried on Guy, 'if we were to take a look through your rooms upstairs, whether we might find something to help us with our enquiries?'

'You have no warrant,' he said thickly.

'Oh, I wouldn't worry too much about that,' said Guy. 'I think I can drop by here any night and find that you have allowed one or two activities to go on after midnight that might not be looked on too kindly by any court.'

'What is it that you want?'

'Tell me where to find Billy Masters.'

'I don't know where you find him. Sometimes he comes here.'

'Is he coming here tonight?'

German Albert shrugged. 'Maybe.'

'Then I will come, and you can point him out to me.'

The mouth twitched again. 'If you like.'

'Thank you,' said Guy, 'you've been most helpful.'

At last, he was one step closer.

CHAPTER FIFTY-SIX

❧

The morning after the seance had been a subdued one. Naturally, Nancy declared to her mother that the dinner had been a great success. Pam told Louisa that they had stayed up for another hour, trying to regain something of a more carefree atmosphere, which hadn't quite been attained. The two of them were talking in the linen cupboard after breakfast, a place they had now become accustomed to meeting each other.

'Farve was awful this morning,' Pamela giggled. 'Called Seb an absolute sewer because he saw him preening in front of a looking glass.'

'If anyone can cope with Lord Redesdale, it's that one. How was Lord De Clifford this morning?'

'What do you mean?' Her face changed. 'Not you as well, Lou? I do wish everyone would stop trying to match me up with someone. He's engaged to Dolly Meyrick.'

'I'm not.' Louisa smiled. 'Sorry, it's only because he looked a bit shaken up last night.'

'He did, didn't he? He seemed fine this morning; quiet,

perhaps. We should never have done that last night. I feel terribly about it now.'

Louisa folded the last of the pillowcases in the pile. 'I'd better get back to the nursery. See if anybody needs me.' She gave a rueful smile. 'I don't expect they do.'

But when she got there, she saw a letter waiting for her, propped up against Nanny Blor's carriage clock. It was stamped Holloway Prison and when she opened it she found only a very short note:

Louisa
Get Daniel now.
Dulcie.

Shaking, Louisa put the note back in the envelope and then into her pocket. That Dulcie had genuine cause for concern was clear. Beyond that, she couldn't think straight. Hurrying, she ran down the stairs and into the hall, which was thankfully empty. Sneaking into the telephone cupboard, her voice quavered when she got through to Vine Street station and asked for Sergeant Sullivan.

He wasn't there.

Louisa left a message, telling him that she'd had a note from Dulcie warning her that she had to get Daniel.

'Is that it?' asked the officer at the end of the line.

'That's it,' said Louisa. What else could she say? But if she couldn't get Guy to Johanna Street quickly, she was going to have to go there herself. The question was how. She couldn't ask for another day off without Mrs Windsor sacking her for it. Louisa thought. Sebastian was returning to Oxford, and Ted was going with him. Charlotte was staying, of course. That left Clara; Louisa was going to have to get her help.

*

Louisa knocked on Clara's bedroom door. 'Come in,' came gaily from the other side.

'Oh, it's you,' said Clara when Louisa came in. 'What can I do for you?' She was bent over her suitcase, open on the bed, folding into it her pastel coloured dresses.

Louisa hesitated then reminded herself that Dulcie – and Daniel – had a lot more to lose than she did. Of all of them, she thought Clara was the most sympathetic; perhaps because she was American she seemed to see Louisa less as a servant and more as a person. And her desire to be an actress meant she enjoyed a little drama and intrigue.

'I do have a favour to ask.'

Clara looked at her, open but not yet quite willing to commit herself.

'I need to go to London but I can't ask Mrs Windsor – that's the housekeeper – for time off.'

'Why do you need to go to London?'

'I can't say why, Miss Clara. I promise you I would if I could but it is serious.'

'I don't see how I can help.' Clara closed her case and snapped the locks shut.

'I thought, perhaps, you could say to Lady Redesdale that you felt ill and you needed assistance to get home, in case you fainted or were sick on the train, and then I could volunteer to go with you.'

'Oh, I don't know . . . ' Clara trailed off but Louisa could see the idea had taken root.

'I thought of you, you see, because of your acting work.'

Clara smiled at the flattery. 'It's true. And I'm a proper actress, not like Phoebe. She used to be a dancer at the 43, did you know that?' She put her finger to her lips, *don't tell*. 'She thinks that's why Adrian turned her down when she made a pass. She was so angry! Of course, it wasn't that at all and she moved swiftly on to Seb—' Clara stopped suddenly, remembering who she was talking to. 'I'm sorry, forget all that.' Embarrassed now, she smoothed her hair and rubbed her lips together. 'Yes, let's do it. I'll help you.'

CHAPTER FIFTY-SEVEN

For hours, Louisa had gone over Dulcie's note in her mind, wondering what she had been told that had prompted her to send it. She'd hinted that the Forty had been able to get to her inside, so if they were planning something, they would be able to let her know about it. Would they do something if they knew a child was in the house though? Surely not. But Alice Diamond believed she had been betrayed and Louisa knew how those networks operated. Loyalty was thicker than blood.

Clara's acting skills hadn't let them down and Louisa had been rapidly given permission to accompany her on the train. What she hadn't quite explained to Mrs Windsor was that she wouldn't be returning on the next train back. No matter. The train journey had felt like a long one with Clara asking Louisa what the emergency was and Louisa having to deflect every question until the American was quite offended. From the station, having waved Clara off at the earliest opportunity, Louisa had tried again to get through to Guy to no avail.

Now, at last, she stood in Johanna Street and wondered if she'd made a fool of herself, rushing down there. There was nothing obviously untoward; the lamps threw their lights on a swept and tidy street. Nevertheless, she shivered as she stood outside number thirty-three, nerves and the cold evening making light work of her wool coat. She'd knocked and waited as the sounds of someone moving in the hallway came closer. William Long opened the front door, a napkin still tucked into his shirt collar, the bemused look on his stubbled face that one had when unexpectedly interrupted in a task. There was a tiny residue of mustard in the corner of his mouth.

'Louisa.' He sounded neither pleased nor annoyed at her appearance. 'Has something happened?'

She looked behind her, as if confirming that she had indeed come of her own free will and there was nobody there to urge her on, then turned back to him. He hadn't been sent a note by Dulcie, then. Why not? 'No, not really. I just ... I wondered how Daniel was getting on.'

William broke into a wide grin. 'Ahh, he's a good lad. Come on in, then. We've almost finished our tea but there might be a spare bit.'

Louisa half-heartedly started to say that they needn't bother but she could smell the sausages as she came in and her mouth watered. In the kitchen at the back of the house was a wide square table, around which sat Marie, with Daniel on her lap and a young man who was introduced as Eddy, Dulcie's brother. He paused only briefly in his eating to grunt hello, bent low over his plate, using his fork as a shovel. Louisa had become so used to the straight-backed table manners of the Mitfords, she'd forgotten that her father used to eat like this too, famished at the end of a working day.

Louisa didn't know what to think. After the hours of panic and worry she had had on the way here, she had arrived to a scene of domestic harmony. Had Dulcie been imagining things? Had she,

Louisa, misinterpreted the note? She felt for it again in her pocket, as if touching it might give her an answer. If William and Marie were unconcerned, she didn't think she should frighten them unnecessarily.

In the absence of any other clear plan, she decided to sit down and wait it out for the time being. Perhaps something would reveal itself. Daniel had been chewing on a bit of sausage that he held on to like a miniature Henry VIII but when he saw Louisa he held his arms open. Marie passed him over and Louisa saw relief flicker on her face. Her own stomach protruded roundly and now her hands were free, she rubbed it. 'He's getting too heavy for me,' she sighed.

Louisa held the boy easily but took a chair indicated by William and they sat together.

'How's he settling in?' she asked, needing conversation to distract her thoughts.

'Fine,' said Marie. 'Poor love, he's been moved about like a puppy sold at market but he's home now.' She stood and took away her brother's empty plate to the sink. 'Do you want some tea?' she said to Louisa. 'Won't take a minute. Frying pan's still hot.'

Louisa felt her stomach gurgle. 'If it's no trouble . . .'

Marie smiled. 'No, no trouble.'

William pulled the napkin out of his collar and pushed his chair back noisily. 'I'll leave you girls to talk. Eddy and I are going to sit next door.' He nodded at his son who got up wordlessly and followed his father out of the room.

'Have you heard from Dulcie?' asked Louisa, when the men had left.

Marie was prodding the sausages, already spitting in the fat. 'Not a word. I wrote her to let her know Daniel was with us and she wasn't to worry. You don't never know if they get their letters though. If she's lashed out or something, they punish you like *that* and we wouldn't know about it.'

'Lash out?' said Louisa, trying not to sound too alarmed.

'She's got a temper, has Dulcie. I've told her to watch it but she's got a mind of her own, that girl. Not much you can tell her. Here you go.' Marie put a plate down in front of Louisa, two browned sausages and two slices of buttered bread. 'Want a bit of sauce?'

'Thanks ever so,' said Louisa, surprising herself with a return to the vernacular of her pre-Mitford life. She put Daniel on the chair next to her; he had moved on to chewing a toy – of indeterminate shape thanks to its bitemarks. She ate quickly and with relish, enjoying the sting of mustard behind her nose when she put a bit too much on. Sated, she sat back and watched as Marie finished the washing up. There was a feeling of peace and warmth in the house, with almost no sound but for the water sloshing in the sink. Daniel started grizzling and Louisa put him on her lap, where he snuggled down into her.

'Shall I put him to bed for you?' asked Louisa. 'I'd like to do something to help.'

Marie dried her hands on a cloth hanging off a chair. 'I'll do it with you. Eddy and Dad'll want to come in and sneak themselves a bit of bread and butter. Tea's never enough for them.'

They went up the stairs and Marie showed Louisa her room, where Daniel slept with her, in a makeshift bed on the floor. It was small, with rather drab walls but Marie had added some feminine touches – a scarf draped over a mirror and a Christmas star hanging in the window. The overhead bulb had no shade and dazzled their eyes after the dim hall. There was no sign of a man's belongings in the room. Louisa felt at home somehow, there in Johanna Street, and Marie felt like one of her kind. That was her only explanation for asking an impertinent question. 'Where's your husband?'

Marie sat heavily on the bed and lay down. 'I don't know. I haven't seen him for a few months. We're not even proper married. I just say that because. You know.' She gestured to her stomach. 'I expect he'll come back when he's knows it's come out all right and is his. You can tell, can't you? They always look like the father when they come out.'

Louisa nodded. 'Yes, of course.' She looked around and saw a washbasin with some grey water in it. 'Shall I fetch some warm water? Wash his face?'

'You'll have go to downstairs,' said Marie, lying down. She looked ill suddenly. 'Sorry. I'm only five months gone but I get so tired. Dad says I'm not eating enough but it all makes my insides churn.'

'I won't be a moment,' said Louisa. She put Daniel on the bed and he lay beside his aunt, his big eyes closing as Marie's hand gently stroked his soft, dark curls. Louisa picked up the washbasin and was just balancing it on her hip to give herself a free hand to open the door when she heard a loud bang from outside that jolted her and spilled the cold water onto her dress. The last time that had happened had been the night of Adrian's murder.

It had sounded like a gunshot but she told herself not to be so idiotic, it must be a car backfiring. Only then she heard yells and shouts in the street outside and now she realised that what they had been waiting for had happened at last. The Forty had come.

CHAPTER FIFTY-EIGHT

⌇⌇⌇⌇⌇

G uy folded the note and put it in his pocket, maintaining a face of calm but the worry bloomed in his mind like gathering storm clouds. Mary was in a back office, tidying up files and getting ready to go home when Guy came in.

'I've had a message from Louisa,' he said. 'Seems as if she's been sent a note from Dulcie and all it says on it is "Get Daniel now."'

'What's she asking of you?'

'I don't know. What if my interviewing Dulcie has made her overreact, suddenly worrying about her son?'

Mary considered this. 'I think there has to be more to it than that. Dulcie would know it wouldn't be easy for Louisa to take Daniel. Why would the sister let him go? And where does Dulcie think Louisa could take him?'

'What are you saying? That she's been warned of some plan, by the Forty?'

'Or Billy Masters. Who's to say he hasn't got wind of our sniffing around?' said Mary.

Guy rubbed the back of his neck. 'But surely they wouldn't deliberately harm a small child?'

'No,' agreed Mary, 'they wouldn't. But either way, Dulcie knows that something has happened to him or is about to happen.'

'Could it be that warning Louisa was told the night you went to the Elephant and Castle? Alice Diamond is going to take her revenge on the family.'

'What would they do?' Alarm showed in Mary's eyes.

'I don't know!' shouted Guy, in fear and frustration. 'Sorry. But it could be anything, couldn't it?'

'Then we must go there.' Mary started to pack away the last of her things.

'It's dangerous,' said Guy. 'We don't know how many of them are planning to go there, let alone how. I certainly don't want you there.'

Mary grimaced but did not fight this point.

Guy's mind raced, stumbling over the hurdles, as he tried desperately to think what the best course of action was to respond to Dulcie's cry for help. He looked at the clock on the station wall: just gone six o'clock. His shift was almost over. But they couldn't go to Johanna Street alone, they would need reinforcements. Cornish was no longer in his office so he couldn't be asked. The night-shift inspector would likely say that if there was a serious cause for concern, Dulcie Long would have told the prison authorities to alert the police in Lambeth. And it wasn't in their parish, anyway. There simply wasn't enough to go on.

'What were your plans for tonight?' said Guy.

'I'm meeting Harry at the 43,' she said, a little shyly. 'But I can put him off, if you need me.'

'No,' said Guy, 'go there. You can keep an eye out for any of the Forty showing up. I was going to go later, in case Billy Masters turned up.'

'I can look for him.'

'I don't think Harry's bosses at the club would be too pleased if his sweetheart started pointing fingers. Just keep a lookout and you can tell me if anything suspicious happens.'

'I'm not his . . .' But she thought better of it and was quiet. 'I'll let you know.'

Guy hurried home. He needed to change into his civvies before he went to Johanna Street. Whatever he did, he couldn't show up in uniform. It would ignite even a tame event into a fireball if any of the Forty were there. Neither did he wish to be alone so he decided to take Socks with him. In spite of the fact that Guy had to spend most of his waking hours out of the house and it was his Dad who walked and fed the dog, Socks unquestionably belonged to him. As soon as Guy opened the door, a tangle of black and white fur would be leaping up at him, begging for a rub behind the ears before lying down on his back with an expectant look on his face that Guy could never resist. He was a soppy dog but his years with Louisa's uncle Stephen had taught him how to sit calmly at his master's side looking as if he might attack on a signal. That could be useful, too.

'You've missed supper,' called out his mother as Guy came through the door.

'Sorry, Mum,' said Guy, hastily untying his laces and hanging his jacket on the hook. 'I've got to go straight out.'

He poked his head around the front room door. His father was at the wooden table by the window, a newspaper spread out before him, a pencil in his hand. He liked to do the crossword every evening, now he was retired. 'Keeps the wheels turning,' he'd say at least once every night, tapping the side of his head with his forefinger. Bertie, the youngest brother and the only other one who hadn't yet married, was on a low stool opposite their mother.

She was winding a ball of wool and Bertie had a resigned look on his face, familiar to each son. Guy's mother looked up at him, a worried crease between her eyes.

'Anything I need to know?' she asked, mid-wind, her elbows resting on her knees.

'No,' said Guy. 'I won't be late. I'm taking Socks with me.' At this, the dog's ears pricked up and he leapt straight onto all four paws as if a switch had been pressed. Guy went up to his room to change his clothes and when he came back down the stairs, Socks was sitting patiently by the front door, waiting for him. Guy grabbed his coat and hat and closed the door gently behind them.

There was a cold wind that sliced through Guy as he hurried back along the street to the bus stop, grateful to see the warm lights of an approaching bus. Socks jumped on skilfully, with Guy swinging on by the corner pole, and they both stood looking out, refusing to sit down. The streets were busy, with men and women hurrying home, but there was a lightness to the atmosphere, the sense of Christmas coming soon – the smell of burning chestnuts in the air and the sound of a choir singing carols outside the church, a bucket rattling for coins. But Guy did not stop to enjoy any of this for he had Daniel on his mind, and he was afraid.

CHAPTER FIFTY-NINE

⁓

Marie sat up. 'What was that?'

'I don't know,' said Louisa but before she could say anything else she was silenced by the ever-louder yells in the street. Daniel was alert too, looking at his aunt as if searching for his cue – were these frightening noises, or some sort of game? Marie said nothing but held him close to her.

Louisa put the bowl of water back on the side and went to the window, not daring to open it and lean out but needing to know what was happening. Johanna Street was perfectly ordinary, with low terraced houses that were largely indistinct from one another, bar the windows and front doors in various states of tidiness, like a line of schoolboys. Louisa knew that the neighbours would all know each other by sight, if not by name, and the children would be playing or fighting together out on the scrubby road most afternoons, without too much fear of cars coming down. At night, the women would close their houses up and draw the curtains, send the children to bed and sit in their back rooms, keeping themselves to themselves. Some on the road would be up to no good and it was better to keep your ears and eyes shut if you didn't want the bother of the police. Ask no questions, tell no lies.

Not tonight.

Windows had flown open and curtains pulled back, revealing the watchful yellow eyes of the houses opposite. Louisa could see two or three men, silhouetted by the lights behind them, wondering perhaps whether to join in or whether to see them off. Or shout from behind the safety of their locked front doors. Louisa stood to the side of the window, holding the thin curtain, and looked down. The crowd that had gathered outside number thirty-three looked to be about thirty men and women, mostly men she thought, with the women at the back yelling lustily. Startled, Louisa realised that Bertha, Elsie and Alice Diamond were amongst them. They looked riled, possibly drunk, and were urging the men on, some of whom waved large, blunt sticks. A knife flashed and was just as quickly hidden again.

Louisa froze and tears came unbidden to her eyes. This was it for her, it was all over. And she had brought Daniel here, brought this frenzy of terror to the house in their wake. She turned to Marie, wild-eyed. 'Is there a key for your door?'

Marie had curled up completely around Daniel, stroking his head, whispering to him that everything would be all right.

No it bloody well wouldn't.

'Marie!' Louisa shouted, yet even so it was hard to make herself heard above the yells which were becoming louder and more urgent by the second. 'A key! Have you got one?'

Marie looked up, eyes red, and shook her head. No.

'Has any room up here got a lock on the door?'

No.

Louisa pushed the chest of drawers in front of the door and looked around for something else, anything, to add to its weight.

There was a suitcase, a side table, some books. She piled them all up there. At the very least, they might add to confusion, might trip up whoever came in. As she looked around trying to find something else heavy, there was a sudden roar from the crowd and the sound of breaking glass. Louisa rushed back to the window. A man had staggered backwards, holding his head, blood pouring through his fingers. Now there was a surge, the men and women moving forward as a single, terrible force and Louisa felt the house shake. They had smashed the front door down.

William and Eddy. They were downstairs; they would be first. She hoped they were strong, that they could fight. But they were outnumbered and the crowd was fierce, louder, nearer. Louisa could hear some of what they were saying now: 'Traitors' and 'Kill the old . . .'

There was no doubt left. She would be next.

CHAPTER SIXTY

～

G uy had crossed London from Hammersmith to Lambeth by bus and Tube, a map in his back pocket. On the train he had studied the map and memorised the route from Lambeth North station to Johanna Street. He'd remembered Louisa telling him the name of the road the Longs lived on but not the number of the house. If he got there and there was no sign of any trouble at least there was no harm done and he could lie low and keep watch for a few hours. If there was trouble then, he thought grimly, it would be all too clear which house it was happening in.

With Socks loyally at his side, never stopping so much as to sniff at something, the two walked fast down the side streets, keeping in the shadows. It was cold but the pace meant Guy felt warm and he pulled his scarf undone so that it flapped loosely as he strode. There was little noise and few cars around, the occasional man went past, hat pulled down low, smoking. Then as he came closer to his destination, Socks's ears pinned back and Guy's blood ran cold. He could hear loud yells – angry calls and jeering, though he couldn't yet make out the words. Carefully he walked at the edge of the pavement, out of reach of the pools of light thrown by the street lamps, and looked around the corner at the top of Johanna Street.

Unlike those he had just gone past, the houses here had their lights switched on, people standing at their windows, one or two in an open front door, watching the terrifying sight of thirty or so men and women gathered around number thirty-three. A few of them waved glass bottles – some had been thrown violently to the pavement and smashed – and some held long sticks, thick and heavy. He saw one woman standing beneath the light of a street lamp, her face twisted and ugly with the promise of violence before her. There were women standing at the back of the crowd, their hands in the air, urging the men to go in, to beat the bastards. Near the front he saw one woman, taller than the rest, her yells the lustiest and the most bloodthirsty. The sight was apocalyptic and frightening, like watching wolves gather and fight over a pathetic straggle of sheep. Whoever was in that house didn't stand a chance.

As fast as he could, Guy retraced his steps to where he remembered running past a telephone box. They were few and far between here and he'd been lucky to see it. Sweating, his hand slipping on the door handle, he hurled himself inside and picked up the handset, his other hand clicking the phone repeatedly, shouting for the operator. When she answered, she was calm and efficient and put him through to the nearest police station. Guy gave the address and explained the situation as briefly as he could but leaving no doubt as to the urgency. 'Send several men,' he said, 'in cars. As quickly as possible. Please!' He'd given his officer number, they'd know he was serious.

By the time Guy returned to top of Johanna Street, he could only pray he'd made the call in time. As he turned the corner, there was a smash of glass and Guy saw a window had been kicked in; on the floor above hands threw up a sash and a jar came flying out, hitting one of the men on the head. He cried out in pain and the crowd's shouts grew louder, like an engine roaring into life. Without warning, a hand appeared in the air from the middle of the mob, holding a gun, and fired a shot. There was the briefest of silences and a woman who had been standing on the front step of one of the houses opposite ran inside and slammed her door shut. Then the baying began again, the threats less words than the cries of animals. There was a sickening thud as the men kicked at the front door. Guy looked up and saw the one thing he had hoped more than anything not to see. Louisa, half-hidden by a curtain, peering out at the mob below. She was trapped and he was helpless.

CHAPTER SIXTY-ONE

⁓

The house they were in was not a large one. There were just two flights of stairs that led up from the hall on the ground floor, where the kitchen and the front room were. Louisa knew she, Marie and Daniel only had a few minutes while William and Eddy tried to hold back the men but it was certain they would be beaten. There was no telephone in the house and there was little point wasting time trying to signal to the people standing in the windows opposite. They wouldn't have telephones either and had probably decided that the inhabitants of 33 Johanna Street deserved what they were getting as none of them had come out to help disperse the mob.

For God's sake, had her message not yet reached Guy? Had no one in the street called the police?

Of course not. For the same reasons no one had ever called them on the Peabody Estate when Louisa was growing up. Even in the most serious circumstances, nobody ever wanted the boys in blue turning up. If there was retribution to be handed out, they'd rather do it themselves in a way that was quick and direct. No courts, no judges, no lingering.

Marie was sobbing now, though quietly, without hope of being heard or comforted. Daniel lay curled into her arms, completely silent but his eyes open.

Mere minutes had passed since that shot had sounded but Louisa felt as if she had relived her life since then, thinking of her mother, the Mitfords, even her uncle Stephen. What would they do when they heard what had happened to her?

There were muffled yells and cries coming from downstairs, with thumps that could be anything – a man being thrown to the floor, a head being smashed against a wall. There was nothing they could do but wait.

Outside, Guy froze. He could see the men piling into the house, the women staying outside but not letting up with their urging cries. Louisa had disappeared from the window and all at once, rage invaded Guy and sent him running down the street, almost flying, Socks racing beside him, ears back. He had almost reached the crowd – one or two women had turned to look at him and he caught the silver flash of a knife blade – when the sirens sounded. Everyone knew they had only seconds left. Most of the crowd had started to run off by the time the three police cars turned into the street, two at one end, one at the other. Men jumped out and began to give chase.

Guy pushed into the house, feeling a sharp pain on his cheek and kicks at his legs as he went past the women, but he barely noticed, not caring if he was attacked now. All he knew was that he had to get to Louisa and Daniel; he had to try. Inside it was dark but for a gaslight in the hallway, and all around were noises of chaos and fighting, shouts from men of anger and pain. He started up the stairs. On the first floor a man turned around as Guy approached and made a startled movement when he saw him. He tried to push past Guy to go back down the stairs but Guy blocked him and threw a punch that landed with a satisfying crack on his jaw. The man fell and stumbled down the steps, his feet catching on the rips of the shabby carpet.

'Get him,' commanded Guy, not looking back but ahead. There was only one closed door, behind which he knew he'd find Louisa, and he needed to be the first man there. Socks had heard his master and leapt at the escaping man, his teeth bared, a growl deep in his throat. By the time Guy was pushing at the door on the second floor, four policemen had come behind him and grabbed the man. Socks turned round and flew up the stairs past Guy, barking at the last closed door.

Marie looked up at Louisa and they held each other's gaze, their ears as alert as a cat's on a mouse hunt. They heard the distant sound of a police siren, but one that was coming closer.

Then the thump of boots coming up the stairs. Louisa sat on the floor, her back to the chest of drawers, her feet up on the side of the bed, using all her strength to press back against the door. Her eyes squeezed tight with the tension and it was all she could do to prevent herself from yelling out in fear and pain. There came heavy footsteps of one man or two, she couldn't be sure – it was hard to hear above the crowd, the ever-closer sirens, the fight in the room below. A dog began barking outside their door, alerting the man, or men, to the presence of humans and then Louisa felt the pressure of the door being pushed against her. With all her might she pushed back until she heard the man shout: 'Is Daniel in there? I'm not with them, let me in. Let me in, I say.' Still, Louisa couldn't be sure, couldn't trust the voice.

Outside there were shouts of 'Police' and then the cries started to die away as the mob scattered.

The pushing against the door stopped and Louisa heard the footsteps run in the hall, away from the door and then towards it at speed before there was a massive shove, one that dislodged Louisa's feet too. She leapt up, ready to rush at the door, when it opened inches more and she heard the voice calling for Daniel. She knew now who it was. The door was pushed open a tiny bit further and Socks darted in, barking, his claws scrabbling as he skittered on the rug.

Quickly, Louisa moved the chest away from the door, enough to let Guy in. As the sirens drew up outside she threw herself against his chest and let his strong arms wrap around her. Tears flowed down her face as he bent his head close and spoke softly into her ear. 'I'm here, the police are here. I'm sorry, so sorry. It's over now.'

CHAPTER SIXTY-TWO

⁓

'Let's get out of here,' said Guy, and he helped pull Marie off the bed, handing Daniel to her, who was whimpering quietly. 'Brave boy,' Guy whispered to him kindly. They could hear that already the noise had died down and there were only the pained shouts of William and Eddy, who had been badly injured. Policemen were all over the house and there were various calls about an ambulance, the need for bandages, a cry for water. On the first floor, the young man who had tried to get past Guy was pinned by two sergeants, and he yelled and kicked out hard. Finally he was brought to stand so that Guy, Marie and Louisa could get past him, but as they did, Daniel cried out, 'Billy!'

Everyone had turned to look at the boy, except for the restrained man who twisted his head away.

'Hang on a minute,' said Guy to the policemen. He walked up to the man who had gone completely quiet and was breathing hard, staring down at the floor.

'Look at me,' said Guy, adrenalin, fear and relief flooding his body like a medical cocktail to induce invincibility. '*Look* at me.'

The man lifted his head, though he kept his eyes averted, and

Guy saw the grey, rat-like features of the man he had arrested after he had seen him selling drugs outside the 43. 'Samuel Jones?' asked Guy, doubt having set in now.

Marie came up to the man too. 'That ain't no Samuel Jones,' she spat. 'That's Billy Masters.'

Down at Tower Bridge police station, there was jubilation when the officers realised that key members of the Forty Thieves and the Elephants had been caught and arrested. But in spite of the celebrations, Guy had been frustrated in his attempt to interview Billy Masters. At Johanna Street, while Billy was being bundled into the police car, Louisa had filled him in about what had happened at the seance and he was keen to know more.

'It's not your patch, is it?' one particularly supercilious DI had said, practically elbowing Guy out of the station. In the end, he had had to telephone DI Cornish who had been in the middle of a particularly delicious spotted dick with custard at his club. Eventually, it was agreed that Guy could talk to Billy as part of his own ongoing enquiries into the Forty, and DI Cornish acquiesced to share his leads and information on Alice Diamond's gang with the Tower Bridge police if it meant getting enough evidence together so that 'she can be locked up before we throw the key into the Thames'.

By the time Guy, a plaster on his throbbing cheek, was sitting opposite Billy Masters in an interview room it had already been a long night for them both. A uniformed officer stood in the corner, with Socks curled up by his feet. Billy had been found with a knife in his possession and identified by Eddy Long as one of his attackers: these charges were going to be pressed and taken to trial as quickly as possible. This was in no doubt. What Guy needed to find out now was if he was a murderer, too. DI Cornish sat in on the interview, his black bowtie undone and a cigar out on the table between them.

'We've met before, as you recall,' said Guy.

Billy, his wrists handcuffed behind the chair, stared back; only the tiniest movement of his shoulder proffered his agreement.

Guy had his notebook out in front of him and never had he been more grateful for his assiduity in recording details, in spite of the fact that Harry had teased him for being a swot. 'On the night in question, the fifteenth of December, you were witnessed making a sale of cocaine to a guest of the 43 nightclub and, on arrest, gave your name as Samuel Jones of 48 Maryland Street.'

Billy made no response to this. Cornish took up his cigar and tapped it on the table top before lighting it slowly, both hands unnecessarily cupped around the flame as if they were on a windy cliff and not in the airless back room of Tower Bridge police station. More style than substance.

Guy carried on. 'We can confirm now that your name is William, or Billy, Masters. Is that correct?'

'If you say so.'

Guy knew this was going to be difficult but Billy Masters didn't know how determined he was. This was Guy's moment and he wanted DI Cornish to witness it.

'The cocaine supply you relied upon for your sales to the guests of the 43, and elsewhere no doubt, came from Mr Albert Mueller. Is that correct?'

'I want my lawyer.'

'Look, sonny,' said Cornish, an effortless bad cop. 'You haven't got a lawyer. You'll get one when you need one. Right now, I suggest you answer these questions if you want a prison sentence and not a hanging. Got it?'

Billy said nothing but a twitch started up in his right eye.

'Mr Albert Mueller has already confessed that he supplied the illegal drugs to you, as well as identifying the potential customers that you might sell these goods to.' This was a lie on Guy's part but one that he felt was necessary. He needed Billy to feel more cornered than a chicken in a shed with a fox. Make that two foxes. 'I suggest you tell us the truth here, because I've got some harder questions coming up for you and you may find it beneficial if you have earned our trust first.'

'I ain't talking,' said Billy. He was nothing if not devil-may-care in the face of the law.

'Fine,' said Guy, flicking over the pages of his notebook. 'It may also be noted that I'm fairly confident that if I talk to Mrs Sofia Brewster of 92 Pendon Road, she will identify you as a supplier of stolen materials. Goods that appear to have been taken from Debenham and Freebody and Liberty's, to name but two. Shoplifted by various members of the Forty Thieves and passed on to you for a quick sale. Busy lad, aren't you?'

The twitch picked up its pace.

Cornish lit his cigar and started talking even as the smoke was still streaming from his mouth. 'The point is, we've got Alice Diamond and the rest of them are going to fall like dominoes. Her reign is over and for the likes of you, there's nowhere to go. If you talk we can make sure the judge looks on your sentencing with lenience. Or, we can force it out of you. Which do you prefer?'

Guy wished Cornish would leave this interview to him and keep the bullying tactics out of it but he couldn't begrudge the man. That the queen herself had been arrested tonight, on charges that would stick, was already a cause for celebration. And that Guy had been the one to call the police had earned him a slap on the back. This had been immediately tempered however by Cornish noting the call had been made from a telephone box en route, after Guy's tip-off from Louisa, and not as a direct result of any investigation.

'Do you or do you not admit to supplying Mrs Brewster with stolen goods, ones that had been passed to you by members of the Forty Thieves?' directed Guy.

Billy exhaled. 'I might've gone to Mrs Brewster's and helped her out with a bit of this and that.'

There was a pause while Guy weighed up whether or not to press on with the real matter in hand. But, really, what was he waiting for? Courage? Hadn't he proved he did have that after all?

CHAPTER SIXTY-THREE

❦

'Where were you on the night of Friday twentieth November?'
Billy looked up sharply at this. 'What?'

Guy repeated his question.

'I don't know. Soho or somewhere, if it was a Friday night.' But he didn't look as sure of himself as before.

'Do you know a Miss Dulcie Long?'

'Sort of,' Billy croaked.

'You see, we think you arranged to meet Miss Long in the bell tower of Asthall Manor, where she was due to hand you jewellery stolen from the house that night.'

Billy was struck silent but fear showed in his eyes as clearly as a torch light.

'Only, she wasn't to know that you had already made arrangements with some of the guests at the party that was happening that evening. Lord De Clifford, for one, engaged to Miss Dorothy Meyrick of the 43. Perhaps you were intending to supply the guests with some cocaine – as you usually did for Mr Sebastian Atlas and Mr Adrian Curtis—'

'No!' Billy shouted but couldn't move, his own arms pinning his body to the chair.

'You took these cufflinks, didn't you, in lieu of payment?' Guy pulled out from his jacket the lapis lazuli cufflinks he had taken off Billy that night; he'd carried them around with him since, like a talisman, hoping they would bring him luck or divine inspiration to solve the connection. Perhaps it had actually worked.

'Only, it wasn't enough and when Mr Curtis, whom you had arranged to meet in the bell tower, did not hand over the money you were expecting, you got into an argument and pushed him off.'

'No, no, I didn't.' Billy was afraid now, his face flushed. Guy saw now how young Billy was. For all his bravado before he looked barely old enough to shave.

'Or did he fall?' Cornish interrupted. Guy hid his annoyance but he didn't need Billy to be given a get-out clause like that.

'It didn't happen like that.'

'*Like that?* So how did it happen then? Enlighten us please, Mr Masters.' Guy felt in control now. From here it could only go smoothly. He'd got his man and soon Cornish would be promoting him to CID.

'Yes, I knew that lot would all be there at the party, and I had some idea of supplying them with a bit of cocaine. Nothing much, just a little extra on the side, you know how it is.'

Guy and Cornish stared at him. Their look told him they did not know how it is.

'Not that they knew I'd be there but Dulcie'd told me about the party. And yes, I'd already arranged to meet her. I'd been told by . . .' He stopped and grunted, as if forcing the words out of himself. 'Has Alice Diamond really been arrested?'

Guy and Cornish nodded in perfect symmetry.

'Right, well, Alice told me that Dulcie was doing a job for them, so we spoke on the telephone and sorted it to meet at the bell tower. The maids always get their rooms searched first, you see, when stuff goes missing.'

'Carry on,' said Guy.

After another pained grunt, Billy said: 'I was all set to meet her at two o'clock in the morning, so I'd driven down and left my car about a mile down the road and walked to the church. Only I'd misjudged how long it would take and got there a bit early. I went up into the church but before I got to the tower I could hear there was some sort of fight going on, between two men, and I didn't want no part of whatever was going on there. So I ducked down in between the pews and then a few minutes later it all went quiet and I put my head up a bit and I saw . . .'

'What did you see, Billy?' Guy could feel himself on the brink of something major here, as if a crowd was around them, ready to burst into thunderous applause.

'I saw a man running off.'

That was *it*? A man running off?

'You didn't see Dulcie Long?' asked Guy.

'No, I never saw her. I was early and I'd lent her a watch, to be sure she'd get there on time.'

'Then why haven't you said anything before? If she's one of the Forty, why haven't they found a way to help us prove her innocence?'

Billy swore under his breath. 'You lot know nothing, do yer? Because it suited them to have her out of the way. They told me she was threatening to get out and go straight, and that sort of thing makes them nervous. I was told to keep quiet.'

'This all seems very convenient,' said Cornish. 'You didn't do it but you saw "a man" running off.'

Billy yelled out as if in pain. 'It wasn't me! Look, you've got me

329

with Mrs Brewster and all the rest of it. And I do a bit of work for the Forty, and a bit of this and that at the clubs. But I'm not a killer, I'd never do that.'

'So who was it, who was the man?' Guy had to stop himself from turning over the table in frustration.

'I don't know. It was pitch black in that church, and he had some sort of cloak on, a hood or something. I just know it was a man and he was running fast.' Billy's breathing came and went in staccato bursts.

Cornish stood up and did up the buttons on his jacket. 'Right, I'm off. Sullivan, get this man arrested and charged for the various confessions here. You'd better let the local DI near Asthall Manor know about this, and I expect he'll take it from here. Might want to interview Mr Masters himself.' He nodded to the uniform in the corner. 'Night, all.'

It wasn't Dulcie Long and it wasn't Billy Masters.

Who killed Adrian Curtis?

Guy was going to have to go to Asthall Manor and find out.

CHAPTER SIXTY-FOUR

The Evening Standard, Thursday 24 December 1925

STREET DOOR SMASHED IN

HOUSE INVADED BY MEN AND WOMEN

REMARKABLE POLICE COURT STORY

A remarkable story of a raid on a house by over a score of people was told at Tower Bridge Police Court, London, yesterday, when Alice Diamond (23), Bertha Scully (22), Billy Masters (23) and Phillip Thomas (30) were charged on remand with being concerned together in maliciously wounding William Long and Edward Long, his son, at Johanna Street, Lambeth, on Monday night, December 21st, by cutting them on the head and arms with some sharp instrument. Scully and Masters were charged also with assaulting Sergeant Sullivan, and Scully with obstructing the police. All were now charged with causing malicious damage at 33, Johanna Street, to the value of £8 17s. 6. Maggie Hughes, aged 27, was also in the dock to answer the first and last charges.

Lord Redesdale folded the newspaper and put it down on the side table next to his armchair. 'Seems your friend Sullivan was quite the hero,' he said drily. The news that Louisa had had a part in this riot had been received coolly by her employers. She knew it had unsettled them to discover that she had kept close ties with Dulcie Long.

All of the Mitford children and their parents were gathered in the library for tea, and Louisa had brought in the newspaper, by way of breaking further news. It was Christmas Eve but the rush of parties was over, with Lady Redesdale content to refuse any further invitations for the week except for shoots. As far as she was concerned, this was when no work was done, except by the servants. The younger girls, Unity and Decca, had already started to take on the glazed look of overfed piglets, resistant to their father's insistence that they go outside and instead lying on the sofas reading until he swore they'd go blind with it. An enormous jigsaw puzzle lay on a long table at the back of the library, two-thirds completed, and Debo sat below the heavily decorated tree, picking up and shaking each wrapped present. Diana and her aunt, Iris, were deep in conversation, talking at length and seriously though Louisa suspected it was about nothing more earth shattering than the latest fashions and hairstyles. Diana made no secret of the fact that she was already preparing for her debutante season, a mere two and a half years away, in spite of her frequent moans that she would die of boredom long before that.

Nancy had been fretful and bored, tetchy with all her siblings except Tom, who always seemed to have a pass for grace and favour. Pamela was the only one who looked happy, having spent a long day out hunting. The fact that her hair permanently suffered from being squashed under a hat and that her thigh muscles burned only added to her sense of contentment. She had told Louisa that she had no desire to return to London, where the shine of the nightclubs had long worn off and she wanted only to ride until it was time to get out into the garden and sow vegetable seeds.

Nancy and Louisa had rehearsed the next part together; their hope was that the ambush would make it too difficult for Lord and Lady Redesdale to stop their plan.

'Beg pardon, m'lord,' began Louisa, 'but there's been a further development that I need to let you know of.'

Lord Redesdale looked at her sharply and his wife put down her book. 'Yes?' he said.

'You see, Sergeant Sullivan strongly suspected Billy Masters had committed the murder of Adrian Curtis but he denies this.'

'I should think he did, that awful maid did it,' said Lady Redesdale, as if she had been both judge and jury.

'We don't think she did,' interjected Nancy.

'We?' muttered her father, but he didn't stop her from continuing.

'Several things don't make sense for her to have done it. Why would she have arranged to meet him in the bell tower again, when they had already met, and had a row?'

'Because she wanted to get her revenge,' said Tom, who had been listening quietly from the sofa.

'Even so, why would he have gone to the bell tower to meet her?' carried on Nancy. 'He must have thought he was meeting someone else there.'

Louisa spoke up now. 'In the interview, Billy Masters confessed to a number of other crimes but denied the murder—'

'That's hardly a surprise, is it? These ruffians aren't going to admit to something like that,' scoffed Lord Redesdale.

Louisa politely ignored this. 'He said he had arranged to meet Dulcie Long, to take the stolen jewellery from her. But he'd got to the church earlier than arranged and heard a row in the bell tower.

Two male voices, and then a silence before one man ran off. He just saw him though it was pitch black and he was wearing a sort of hooded cloak.'

'What are you saying, Louisa?' Lady Redesdale's concern was etched in the deep lines at the sides of her mouth.

'Sergeant Sullivan would like to come here, your ladyship. He'd like to meet the persons who were here that night as part of his investigation into what happened.'

'But that local bobby, Monkton? What's his name?' Lord Redesdale was practically spluttering.

'DI Monroe,' said Louisa.

'That fellow. I mean, this is his patch. Surely if he thinks the maid did it, and she's in prison waiting for trial, what earthly good can it do to have Sullivan up here trampling all over everything?'

'That's just it, Farve,' said Nancy. She'd stood up now, agitated by her excitement. 'He's not really supposed to but it's clear Dulcie didn't do it and we think Sergeant Sullivan can solve it. But he can only do it if everyone's here. So that's why I've invited everyone back here for a New Year's Eve party.'

'What? And I suppose you've already talked to Mrs Windsor and Mrs Stobie about this?' Lady Redesdale's fury wasn't hard to miss. 'It means a lot of extra work for them.'

'No,' stammered Nancy, knowing she'd been caught out. 'They wouldn't agree without your knowing about it.'

'Quite bloody right too!' shouted Farve, slamming his hands down on the sides of the chair and making Unity and Decca sit up from their prone positions on the sofa like a pair of jack-in-the-boxes.

'The fact remains, Farve, that everyone is coming, including Sergeant Sullivan who will interview them.'

'Are you really saying that you think one of your friends committed this terrible act?' said Iris. 'That's rather a leap.'

'Of course not!' said Nancy, getting pinker with impatience. 'He just wants to ask everyone again about what they saw that night, in case something was missed.'

To everyone's astonishment, Pamela stood up and said, 'I wouldn't be so certain about that, Koko,' before she walked out.

'That's that, then,' piped up Diana, who had been completely silent, her body taut with tension as she listened to every thrilling word. 'We've got a murderer coming to stay.'

CHAPTER SIXTY-FIVE

～～～

Guy took the train from Paddington to Shipton on New Year's Eve with some trepidation. In spite of reassurances from both Louisa and Miss Nancy that he was welcome, he couldn't quite believe it. Louisa had told him that the eldest Mitford sister had been only too happy to have an excuse to have another party, though she did admit that Miss Pamela had been more reserved. His biggest concern, however, was not whether he would spoil the party but that the local detective inspector, who had overseen the murder case, would be far from delighted if he found out that Guy had been down to Asthall Manor to ask questions of witnesses. It might be deemed unethical at best, sackable at worst. For this reason, he hadn't felt he could include Mary Moon, although he felt guilty that he was leaving her behind when they had done so much work together. At the same time, he could be within touching distance of solving this and if he did, his career would be made. No more watering the plants in the station or directing the traffic at Piccadilly Circus.

Just to be safe, however, he had decided to travel down out of uniform and then he could claim to have been there as a friend of Louisa's and not as a policeman. Louisa told him she would book a room for him to stay in the village pub and, other than that, he could do no more to prepare himself.

The question was: who did he suspect?

Guy had managed to see the court records from the inquest, which included a statement by DI Monroe summing up the whereabouts of the guests at the time of the murder – as it had been estimated – and when the body had been discovered. He decided to pull out the notes he had made but had to do this with some difficulty. The carriage was busy and Guy was fairly squashed up against an end wall by a large lady in a vivid pink coat with matching hat. She had a handbag on her lap and every two minutes reached in for another mint, her elbows jabbing into Guy's side as she did so. Her sucking noises were no less intrusive either. When Guy wriggled to get his pencil out of his jacket pocket, close to his neighbour's plump hip, she looked at him and glared as if he was being a nuisance. Guy remembered why he preferred to walk everywhere.

He looked at his notes again, taken from police records and things Louisa had mentioned to him.

Clara Fischer

No alibi, in the dining room alone when DL's screams were heard.

Motive: she had 'history' with AC. Revenge? Keeps a knife in her bag (but she's an actress). Shares a secret with Lord DC about her whereabouts that night?

Billy says he saw a man running away, albeit in a cloak with a hood – she could have disguised herself?

Lord De Clifford

No alibi, in the boot room alone.

Motive: Was AC threatening to expose his fiancée's links with Billy? Potentially hired Billy to kill AC? Treasure hunt was initially his idea. A man with a cloak and hood was seen running away – his costume for the party that night was Dracula.

Phoebe Morgan

Original alibi – sprained ankle – since confessed to be false. Second alibi: she was in the drawing room with SA. Could she have slipped out when he left the room?

Motive: Revenge. She was rejected by AC. A former dancer at the 43, she could have known BM and hired him to do it?

Oliver Watney

No alibi, alone in the telephone room.

No motive. Ruled out.

Nancy Mitford

Alibi: In the morning room with Charlotte Curtis.

No motive. Ruled out.

Charlotte Curtis

Alibi: In the morning room with Nancy Mitford.

No motive. Distress visible at the time. Ruled out.

Sebastian Atlas

Alibi: In the drawing room with Phoebe Morgan. In statements, Charlotte Curtis saw him leave the room but he was seen a few minutes later by PM when he gave her the present, then returned to the drawing room.

Motive: None clear and was a close friend of AC's. Ruled out.

Pamela Mitford

No alibi, was alone in the smoking room.

No motive and character assessment rules her out.

Over and over again, Guy read his notes. By the time Hooper came to collect him from the station, when the afternoon light had begun to fade to its wintry dusk, Guy knew who his man was. And now he was going to get him.

CHAPTER SIXTY-SIX

Louisa was in the kitchen when Guy arrived, Debo at her feet as she fetched her a glass of milk. He knocked hesitantly on the door and when nobody called out, stepped inside, his London shoes clicking on the flagstone floor.

'You're here,' said Louisa, smiling and walking towards him. 'Hooper collected you with no trouble then?'

'I'm not sure I'd say that quite,' chuckled Guy. 'He muttered darkly about having to make several trips to the station this afternoon but I'm here in one piece, aren't I? No complaints from me.'

'Sit yourself down and I'll get you a cup of tea, kettle's just boiled. You've arrived at a good time. Mrs Stobie's with Mrs Windsor in her sitting room, planning the supper, and Ada's up in the nursery. I was just about to take Miss Deborah out for a walk around the garden.'

Guy set his overnight bag down and pulled up a chair. 'Hello, Miss Deborah,' he said to the little girl, who shyly put out her hand for him to shake.

'Hello,' she said. Then she turned to Louisa, 'Who's this man?'

Louisa laughed. 'He's a friend, Sergeant Sullivan.'

Debo said nothing to this but climbed up on to a chair beside him and began to drink her milk in tiny sips, like a cat.

Louisa put the cup and saucer on the table, with a jug. 'Have you had any news of Daniel, and Marie?' he asked.

'Just the one letter but they're fine. They're in Johanna Street still. She says they've never lived anywhere else and they're not going to be frightened off. Anyway, with Alice Diamond and the rest of them locked up, they've not got the worry any more. Daniel's settled with them. All we need to do now is get his mother back to him.'

'I know,' said Guy. 'I promise I don't think of much else.'

'Drink your tea and join me and Miss Deborah for our walk. It would be good to talk to you before they all get here, and you can see your room in the pub when I have to get back to the nursery.'

'That,' said Guy with a wide smile, 'would be perfect.'

It was cold outside but not raining at least, and with coats on they could keep out the chill easily enough for a half-hour amble around the garden. Guy couldn't help himself: as he watched them walk a little further ahead, Debo's hand tucked inside Louisa's, the thought of what might be pulled at his heart. Quickly, he caught up with them and they started to walk around the side of the house, but when they approached the gate in the wall that led to the churchyard, Guy and Louisa headed towards it in silent agreement.

'Go and count the angels for me, Miss Deborah,' said Louisa to her young charge, and the girl skipped off on a familiar route around the tombs and gravestones.

'So this is where it all happened,' said Guy.

'Yes, right here.' They were standing almost exactly where Adrian Curtis's body had fallen. Guy looked up at the bell tower and the glassless window through which he had been pushed. The sky was slate grey behind it, doing little to leaven the mood.

'I think it was Lord De Clifford,' said Guy. 'He has no alibi because he was alone at the time the murder must have happened. More importantly, you said the treasure hunt was his idea when they first discussed it in London. And he has the strongest ties to Billy Masters. They could have cooked it up between them.'

'You think Billy was an accessory then?'

'It's possible. But even if Billy wasn't a part of it, from what you described of Lord De Clifford's reaction at the seance, it's possible Adrian Curtis was threatening to expose Dolly Meyrick's connection with him. There's a connection, at the very least, and one that he finds frightening.'

'And Charlotte Curtis said that her brother was very against his engagement to Dolly Meyrick. That might have upset him.'

'How did they get Adrian Curtis to the bell tower though? That's the piece in the jigsaw I can't fit,' said Guy, still staring at the ledge. It was definitely high enough to kill a man that was pushed off it, even a robust one.

'Have you seen the items he had on his person when his body was recovered?'

'Yes, but there's nothing there. I copied the list from the inquest records,' said Guy.

Deborah was still on her trail of angels. She looked up and saw Louisa looking at her. 'Seven!' she called out happily.

'Well done!' Louisa called back. 'Keep going.'

Guy had his notebook out. 'There are the details of what he was wearing, a bit odd of course because he was in costume as a vicar. But in his pockets he had: a handkerchief, a box of matches, a silver cigarette case engraved with his initials and containing six cigarettes, a silver toothpick holder and a piece of paper with the typed words, "Come here to find the cross and pray I don't toll for thee." That's it.'

'Say that clue again,' said Louisa.

'Come here to find the cross and pray I don't toll for thee.'

'There's something wrong with that.'

'What do you mean?' said Guy, scrutinising his notebook again, as if the words could yield a deeper secret. 'It's obvious the answer is the bell tower.'

'That's my point,' said Louisa. 'All the clues had objects as their answers. Everyone had to contribute a clue for which the answer would be an object that would be commonly found. Because a number of them would be playing it, they'd all have to be able to find it and then take it back to Mr Atlas and Miss Morgan in the drawing room, before they could get the next one.'

'So there were eight players and they all had eight clues each?'

'Nine clues, because Phoebe Morgan was supposed to have been playing. They all played a different clue at any one time. Nancy explained it to me – it was so that you didn't have all the players looking for egg cups or whatever at the same time.'

'Egg cups?'

'What can I say?' said Louisa. 'Upper-class people do very strange things for their entertainment. I've learned that here, if not much else.'

Guy smiled at this. 'But you were saying about this clue.'

'With this clue, the answer is a place. It's not a thing to collect. What if only Adrian Curtis had that clue? What if he was

343

deliberately given a clue that no one else had, one that would send him to his death?'

At that moment, Deborah came running up to Louisa and clamped her arms around her legs and lifted her head up to her beloved nursery nurse. 'Nine angels, Lou-Lou! I found all the angels, there are *nine*. And guess what? I found one devil too.'

CHAPTER SIXTY-SEVEN

﹏﹏

At eight o'clock on New Year's Eve, Nancy stood in the library in front of the fire dressed in a long black gown of draped satin, with her purple-buttoned gloves and a borrowed necklace from Lady Redesdale of rubies and diamonds set in yellow gold spikes that fanned out around her slim white neck. Her hair had been waved and the bob recently cut so that it stopped just below her ears, showing her neat chin and narrow nose to great effect. Her eyebrows were expertly arched and her lips dark red. She looked, in short, like the chatelaine of a great house. Louisa knew that the surprise she was about to spring on her guests was, for her, the pinnacle of her social life: it would far outweigh any childish games or fancy-dress parties that the London crowd would doubtlessly be indulging in on this night. It was also the reason Nancy had requested that her guests wear white tie.

'Grown-up sophistication is the dress code,' she had said to Louisa sagely, while getting ready earlier, which had almost made Louisa giggle, but Nancy was twenty-one years old now and her country friends were starting to get married. Perhaps she thought she should be, too.

However, it was the hidden theme of the night that was, of course, why Louisa and Guy Sullivan were standing behind the door that led to an anteroom, as they waited for everyone to arrive. The long table had been set up at the end of the room by the bay windows, laid with a tablecloth and ready for the dinner that Mrs Stobie had begrudgingly agreed to cook, appeased by the news that Lord and Lady Redesdale would go out and not need anything themselves. They were due to dine with the Watneys but had told Nancy they would have a drink with her guests before they left for the evening. Pamela followed closely behind in the dress that Mrs Brewster had made for her; it had already been put to good use at two hunt balls – which Nancy had declined to attend – and though it would suffer eventually from overuse, on this night it looked fresh and pretty, hiding Pamela's unfashionably large bosom. The deep pink sash mirrored her plump lips and her eyes shone their brightest blue after a whole day spent outside on her horse. Diana had been allowed to come down for the drink, though she was to leave when the dinner began. Her flaxen hair was long and thick, her eyebrows still untamed but her figure had already developed into that of a lean young woman so that even in her short-sleeved yellow dress the poise and drama of the beauty that would soon be unleashed was highly visible. Nervous now, she perched on the edge of the sofa, her hands fidgeting with the tassels on the cushions.

Next into the room was Sebastian with Charlotte. A perfectly aligned pair in height and figure, they stood together like young birches in the wood, with Sebastian wearing a white jacket and trousers, Charlotte in silver. He looked reluctant but whether that was to do with being at Asthall Manor or alongside Charlotte, Louisa couldn't say. Despite the rumour of their engagement there had been little sign of affection between them. Phoebe and Clara

346

had been put in a room together, so naturally came down at the same time. Phoebe's dancer figure was beautifully showcased in a long silk dress of champagne gold; Clara was in her trademark chiffon, this time in sky blue with a silver plaited rope that hung loose around her hips. Lord De Clifford – Ted – was the last one down from his room, an elegant silhouette as usual, his evening dress the best tailored in the room, but his dark eyes bore the bruising of insomnia and his skin looked wan beneath his almost black hair, smoothed back and gleaming with brilliantine. Louisa wondered why he had agreed to come this evening, given that his fiancée, Dolly Meyrick, had pointedly not been invited. But when she saw him go straight to Charlotte as he entered the room, she wondered if that was part of the answer. Whether it was brotherly love, given the many summers they had spent together in childhood, or something more ardent, she sensed his protectiveness over her.

Louisa admonished herself: she must be wary of reading into things simply because she and Guy believed themselves to be on the brink of solving the murder. They very well might not be, after all.

As everyone had arrived, Mrs Windsor had given them a glass of champagne and they all stood on the rug in front of the fire, talking in low voices. There was an air of expectation, of waiting for the party to really start. Then there was a cold rush of air as the door opened and Oliver Watney came in. He cut an unprepossessing sight even in his evening clothes and round glasses, rather like Guy's. Apologising for his lateness he explained that the car was waiting outside, ready to take Lord and Lady Redesdale to dinner with his parents.

'That's our cue,' said Lord Redesdale with undisguised gratitude in his voice. These were not his people.

'Happy New Year, everyone,' said Lady Redesdale with bright

347

finality, but concern creased her brow. The shock of Adrian Curtis's death so close to the house was something she had not yet recovered from and neither she nor her husband enjoyed being at the centre of scurrilous gossip, whether in the village or further afield. 'One should only ever appear in the newspapers three times,' Lord Redesdale had said more than once. 'Birth, marriage and death.' Nancy always wrinkled her nose at this.

'Yes, happy New Year.' There was a short pause while Lord Redesdale put his glass down on a side table and straightened up. 'Behave yourselves. Nancy, don't do your usual thing of changing the clocks tonight, will you?'

Nancy looked at him, all wide-eyed innocence. 'I don't know what you mean, Farve.'

'Yes, you do. All this nonsense of putting them back by half an hour. It's not good for the clocks and then when you reset them you never do it properly. The one in the drawing room was out by three minutes for weeks after Pamela's dance.'

This reference, however slight, to the fated evening of Adrian's death sent a chill through the room. But Nancy spread her hands open wide. 'You don't need to worry, old thing. Off you both go now and have a lovely time. We'll see you for luncheon tomorrow.'

Behind the door, Louisa and Guy held each other's gaze with bated breath. Their moment in the spotlight had drawn near.

CHAPTER SIXTY-EIGHT

When Lord and Lady Redesdale had left the room with Diana, followed by Mrs Windsor, anxious as ever to ensure every detail of her employers' comfort, Pamela walked into Louisa and Guy's eyeline, indicating with a signal that they should step out now.

At the same time, Nancy exhorted her guests to find somewhere comfortable to sit. 'We have something planned,' she said grandly. 'A sort of play, if you like, only we will all be the actors in it and I think you already know your lines.'

'Oh, marvellous,' said Clara. 'Now you can all see what I can do, instead of teasing me about it.' She flashed a look in Ted's direction when she said this.

Guy coughed. 'Excuse me, Miss Mitford, but I don't think we should underestimate the seriousness of this.' All the guests turned to him then, bewilderment on their faces.

Unlike them, Guy was not dressed in white tie but in his best suit. Best for him, at any rate. Louisa was in her usual work dress, though her bobbed hair and pretty face made her a match for any high-society beauty. In Guy's eyes at least.

Nancy, not wishing to lose her position as ringmaster, waved an arm towards Guy, encouraging him to continue.

All eyes upon him but reassured by Louisa's presence at his side, Guy spoke again, with a little more volume than before. 'Good evening. I will try not to take up too much of your time.' He looked at the expectant faces before him and tried not to cough, despite what felt like a hair caught in his throat. Just then, Sebastian turned sideways to light his cigarette from a candle on the chimneypiece and as the flare lit Guy realised that he definitely *had* been the man buying the cocaine from Billy Masters outside the 43.

'You may not be aware but recently I was involved in the capture and arrest of some notorious London criminals—'

'Yes, I heard about this,' Clara interrupted, animated by the news. 'There was a riot and they caught this famous gang leader, Alice Diamond. A woman!'

Two spots of colour appeared in Guy's cheeks. 'That's the one,' he said. 'On the same night, I arrested a man called Billy Masters . . .' Ted reacted to this, as he had expected; only a twitch, covered up by a big gulp of his drink, but a reaction nonetheless. 'While he has been remanded on other charges, I discovered that he had been at the bell tower on the night of Mr Curtis's death.'

This time there was a reaction from everybody of varying kinds. Nancy looked merely satisfied to have shocked them all, whereas Pamela was worried as to how this would turn out. Charlotte looked upset and Clara began to comfort her, only to have her hand shrugged off. Phoebe smiled, as if unaware that this was a real crime that was being discussed here. Sebastian raised an eyebrow and threw his cigarette into the fire. Oliver Watney started coughing, as if his drink had gone down the wrong way. Ted had gone five shades paler and started stammering.

'What was he doing here? Do you know? What was he after?'

'That's just it, your lordship,' said Guy. Louisa had carefully explained earlier who was who. 'He has explained to us that he arranged to meet Miss Dulcie Long, to take possession of the jewels she had stolen. He often worked for the gang I mentioned just now, selling on their goods. But we have reason to believe that some of you in this room may know him, and in order to rule you out of the murder enquiry, we need to establish what connections there are, if any.'

Ted stood up, having gone in an instant from white to pink. 'This is absolutely outrageous! What are you suggesting? There *is* no more murder enquiry; there is a woman in prison awaiting trial and a sentence. The case has been closed. How dare you come here and accuse us!'

Nancy giggled, which only made Ted worse. He marched over to a small tray that had been put out by Mrs Windsor earlier with decanters of whisky and port and poured himself a large drink.

'We have strong reason to believe that Miss Long did not commit the murder,' said Guy.

'What reasons?' Charlotte said this, her dark eyes like deep wells of water.

'Billy Masters has told us that he never met Miss Long at the arranged hour because when he arrived at the church he heard an argument between Mr Curtis and another man; that he heard Mr Curtis fall and then saw the second man run away.'

'Could he identify this second man?' Sebastian had not sat back down again after lighting his last cigarette.

'No, sir,' said Guy. 'Not clearly. He was wearing a hood and cloak.'

'So you've chosen to believe the word of a convicted criminal that he arrived at the church and heard something, then saw a man he can't identify run away. Oh yes, officer, you've got one of us bang to rights.' Sebastian laughed and turned to Nancy. 'Honestly, darling, you're going to have to do better than this for our entertainment tonight. Is this really what we've turned down Loelia Ponsonby's party for?'

Nancy looked crestfallen and Charlotte gave Sebastian a glare but he ignored her.

Louisa gave Guy a tiny nudge at his back. Encouragement.

'We thought perhaps, if everyone was willing, we might stage a re-enactment of the evening—'

'No.' Charlotte said this firmly and loudly as she stood. 'Nancy, I don't know what you're playing at but this is too awful of you. As if I could bear to be a part of this charade. My brother died, in case you didn't notice.' She choked back a sob and went to the drinks tray where Ted put his arm around her, Sebastian watching every move. 'Pour me a large drink,' she muttered to Ted.

Guy was at a loss. He realised now he'd been seduced by the house somehow, that he had come to believe in his powers after the arrest of Billy Masters and thought he could do this. Of course, it was ridiculous. Expecting them to go through it all again. If one of them was guilty they would hardly confess, would they?

No, they would have to do it in a more traditional fashion: by process of elimination.

CHAPTER SIXTY-NINE

Much to Louisa's surprise, it was Pamela who spoke up first in the bewildered silence. 'Don't you all want this solved?' she asked the room.

'But it has been solved. Dulcie Long is in prison,' said Clara.

'Haven't you been listening? Billy Masters has admitted that there was no sign of Dulcie when Adrian was killed.'

'You English don't pull punches when it comes to stating the facts, do you?' Clara muttered. 'Where I come from we use gentler phrases like "passed away".'

'That's the whole point,' Nancy replied. 'There was nothing gentle about it. That's why it has to be resolved.' She turned to Guy. 'Is it possible that Billy Masters did it, and he's just throwing you off the scent?'

Guy shifted on his feet. Nancy made him feel as if he was in the dock and she a stern barrister. 'Of course, it's possible.'

'He's not exactly honest, is he? It could be no more than a clever bluff to admit guilt to the other things, in the hope that you would be distracted from the really major one.' Nancy was in her stride now and the others were hanging on to her words.

Nancy walked into the centre of the room to address everyone at once. 'We were all there and we are all innocent. I say we help Sergeant Sullivan go through the movements of that night. It might tell him more accurately where and when everybody was and then we can see for once and for all whether it was Billy Masters or Dulcie Long.'

'Or the two of them together,' said Ted.

'Or indeed that,' agreed Pamela.

There was a slam as Charlotte put down her cut-glass tumbler. 'You all do what you want to do. I am having no part of it.' She left the library and exited through the Cloisters, presumably back to the house and her room.

Clara went to follow her out but Nancy held her back. 'Leave her,' she said. 'She can't go anywhere. There are no trains and Hooper won't be driving her back to London. She might calm down and join us again later.'

Phoebe sidled up to Sebastian and put her long, white arm around his neck, tipping her pretty head onto his chest. 'Don't be sad, darling.'

'I'm not,' he said tersely and pushed her off. Phoebe shrugged and went to pour herself another glass of champagne but she blinked back tears as she did so.

'Your ankle is better then, Miss Phoebe?' said Louisa, definitely loud enough for everyone to hear.

Phoebe looked up, surprised. 'Um, yes,' she said. 'It was nothing, really.'

'Nothing because you hadn't sprained it at all?' Guy had interjected this time.

Nancy looked at him sharply. 'What's going on?'

He ignored her and carried on. 'You told Miss Cannon that you faked your ankle sprain, so that you might be left alone in the drawing room with Mr Atlas.' This wasn't a question.

354

Unable to evade this, Phoebe gave a bitter laugh. 'Yes, so what?'

'You're lucky Charlotte's left the room,' said Clara, earning her a vicious look from Phoebe.

'Which means that your alibi was not real,' said Guy, with confidence. 'You could have left the room at any point and met Mr Curtis, to go with him to the bell tower.'

Phoebe did not have any real friends in the room, thought Louisa. Nobody leapt to her defence. Sebastian smirked and lit another cigarette, watching her coolly.

'What sort of question is that?' Phoebe tipped her drink back and took a large swallow.

'It's not a question,' said Guy. 'You were alone in the drawing room at some point – we know Mr Atlas left to give Miss Pamela Mitford a birthday present. Could you have slipped out then?'

Phoebe neither agreed nor disagreed with this statement but took another gulp and looked around her. 'Aren't any of you going to say something?'

But nobody responded.

'Fine,' snapped Phoebe. 'I did leave the room shortly after Sebastian left.' She paused and seemed to think it through before carrying on. 'I went through the French windows and stepped outside. It was cold and I was only in my costume so I didn't want to stay out there for long. I just wanted a bit of time to myself because . . .'

'Because?' prompted Guy.

'I wanted a quick sniff, if you get my meaning. And I didn't want to share, so I didn't want anyone to see me. I couldn't tell that ghastly inspector man or he would have charged me.' She tried to look insouciant, and failed. 'I couldn't have stood it if my mother had found out.'

'A sniff?' asked Pamela, quietly.

'Cocaine,' said Nancy. 'Do you really know nothing?'

Pamela blushed but said no more.

'Not that I approve,' Nancy added with a raised eyebrow.

'I'm hardly the only one,' Phoebe retorted. Then she sat down on the sofa, near to the fire and cut off any further conversation by staring intently into the flames.

One down, thought Guy, five to go.

CHAPTER SEVENTY

M rs Windsor came into the room and if she was startled by the silence and the sight of Guy and Louisa standing before the guests as if delivering a speech, she was too professional to show it. 'Dinner will be served shortly,' she said, directing herself towards Nancy.

'Thank you, Mrs Windsor,' Nancy replied, as confident as any mistress. The housekeeper left and there was an expectant hush hanging in the air.

'Should we wait for Charlotte?' said Clara.

'No,' said Sebastian.

'You're a man of so many words,' Nancy said with a smile, but he didn't return it.

The lull was on the verge of becoming a self-conscious embarrassment when Guy spoke. Louisa felt a surge of pride at his calm, when she knew how he must feel to be standing before this room of glamorous young people, any one of whom a newspaper editor would have been thrilled to have photographed on the society page. She only hoped that none of what transpired that night would put them by the headlines.

'I apologise for this but I need to establish a few more facts,' said Guy. He pulled out his notebook and flicked through a few pages to find his place.

Oliver, who had been completely quiet until then, called out: 'I say, *is* this meant to be a game? Because it seems most awfully serious to me. I mean, I don't know what the rest of you are thinking but I think I'd prefer a round of rummy.' He gave an attempt at a smile – not something his face was built to do easily – and Pamela gave him a sympathetic look back.

'It isn't a game.'

'Oh, righto. I suppose you'd better carry on then,' said Oliver, waving a hand at Guy as if signalling to him to continue, before lapsing into a minor coughing fit. Pamela fetched him a glass of water and then sat back down again, her hands folded in her lap.

'Lord De Clifford, if I could check on your movements for that evening?'

'If you insist,' said Ted, seated now beside Clara. 'Although like the others, I am finding this rather tiresome. We've already spoken to the inspector.' He leaned back onto the sofa and spoke out into the air, as if sending his words out like arrows from a bow. 'I doubt you have any official right to do this. There will be a trial soon and we may any of us be called as witnesses. This whole conversation could be against the law.'

This was a weak spot, Louisa knew. She wondered, could Guy be charged with impersonating a policeman if he wasn't in uniform but asking questions of witnesses? Witnesses on a case that was not his investigation? Could this be classed as interfering with witnesses? The one thing they had on their side was the final piece of the jigsaw they had both found that meant they were certain they had their man. If they got him tonight, surely any judge would gloss over the means they used to get him?

Guy pressed on. 'I believe that at the moment Miss Long was heard screaming outside, you were alone in the boot room. Is that right?'

'I'm not answering these irrational questions.'

'The reason it's important, your lordship, is because there is compelling evidence to show that you had previously made the acquaintance of Billy Masters.'

At this, Ted sat up. 'What evidence?'

'Billy Masters has confirmed that he met you at the 43 nightclub on several occasions. The one owned by your fiancée's mother.'

'I'm not denying I go to the 43 but all sorts of rogues go there.' At this, Ted gave a half-hearted chuckle. 'That doesn't mean I know them. He knows who I am, of course – everyone does, because Dolly's been running the place for the last few months. He's told you he knows me to make it look like he's got some sort of influence, I suppose. Well, he bloody hasn't.'

'How do you know what sort of influence he has?' Guy was settling into his role as interviewer. The harder they threw their punches, the quicker he dodged the blows.

Ted put his head in his hands briefly. 'Oh God. Look, he's caused trouble for Dolly. Showing up, selling things, picking fights. He always seems to be in six places at once and none of them where he should be. I may have had to warn him off once or twice. That's why he's pointing the finger at me now. To get his own back.'

Guy nodded and absorbed this but then apparently ignored it. 'In which case, there was opportunity for you to hire Billy Masters to kill Mr Curtis.'

Ted laughed now, whether out of nervousness or relief, no one could tell. 'Why would I do that? Adrian was a good friend of mine. I practically grew up with him.'

'Yet he opposed your marriage to Miss Meyrick and had no

compunction about telling you so. It was your very closeness that meant he could hurt your chances of seeing it through. Perhaps you needed him out of the way. Or perhaps he threatened to expose the sordid workings of the 43, which would have made it impossible for you to marry your fiancée.' It was a long speech for Guy and he drew breath at the end, wishing he could pull out his handkerchief to wipe his brow.

Ted shook his head. 'You've gone off on completely the wrong track.'

Nancy intervened. 'Yes, Guy, I think this is going too far. You can't start making accusations against my guests. We had better end this here. Besides, Mrs Windsor will be here soon to start serving supper.' Everyone stirred at this, albeit a little stiffly, having been held in rapt attention for several minutes.

'No,' said Pamela, and Nancy looked up at her sharply. 'Sergeant Sullivan must do this. It's important that each and every one of us is without question proved to be in the clear.' She paused. 'If each of us *is* in the clear, that is.'

'Oh God, Woman. This isn't a game—'

'I know,' said Pamela. 'That's exactly why I'm insisting this is done properly.' She had stood her ground and won possession of it. 'Sergeant Sullivan, please. Continue.'

'Thank you, Miss Pamela. You were alone, Lord De Clifford, according to your statement. But here's the most difficult thing for me: Louisa was in the kitchen and she would have either seen you go into the boot room or heard you once you were there but she didn't. Don't you see? I want to rule you out but I can't.'

Everybody held their movements stone still.

'He wasn't alone,' said Clara. 'I was with him, in the dining room. We were ...'

Now she hesitated, waiting for a cue from the man who had come to sit beside her.

'You had better tell him, Clara. I'll face the music.'

'We were kissing. We couldn't say anything about it because of Dolly.' She blushed and pulled an apologetic face at Ted. 'I liked you once, you know.'

'I know,' said Ted, shamefaced. So, he *was* guilty – but not of murder.

CHAPTER SEVENTY-ONE

Pamela came over and whispered to Louisa. 'I think you had better give us a few minutes to calm down. Why don't you go off. I'll come and find you shortly.' Louisa nodded and she and Guy slipped out of the library through the passage that led to the kitchen.

'I had better see if Mrs Stobie needs a hand, if you can wait for me.' Louisa had been able to do her usual bedtime duties in the nursery earlier but she was not sitting easily in this strange space between being a servant and present at the dinner, where neither she nor Guy were exactly guests.

'Isn't Ada working tonight?' asked Guy.

'Goodness, are you showing off your policeman's memory? I'm impressed.'

Guy grinned.

'Yes, she is. She's pregnant now so working as much as she can before she has to stop. It'll be hard for her and Jonny when the baby comes, with only his wage coming in.' Louisa stopped herself short. 'But yes, you're right. They won't be needing my help. What do you want to do?'

'I'd like to take a look at the rooms where the party took place, to see for myself where everyone was and map out the evening as far as I can.'

Louisa cast a glance at the door to the kitchen, as if Mrs Windsor would overhear them. She wouldn't approve. 'All right but let's walk there quietly.'

In the hall the two fires had embers still glowing and there were lamps switched on, waiting for the return of the master and mistress of the house. But the rooms that led off it – the drawing room, morning room, dining room, smoking room and the telephone cupboard, which was not actually a cupboard but a very small room with a chair and side table crammed in it – were all in darkness. Louisa shivered in spite of her wool cardigan; the rooms in this house seemed to leak warmth as soon as nobody was in them. They went into the drawing room, Louisa switching on a single light so the yellow walls glowed like a faded sunset. Guy noticed the French windows, beside which Nancy's typewriter sat on the table, almost tucked out of sight behind the screen.

'That extra clue,' he said. 'It could have been typed up at some point during the treasure hunt, when everyone was coming and going. No one has mentioned it but perhaps Monroe never thought to ask.'

'I don't think he asked much,' said Louisa. 'He'd got his culprit; the only answers he was looking for were the ones that said he'd done a good job.'

'You know policemen too well. Anyone would think you'd been spending time with one.' They caught each other's eye in the half light. 'And those French windows. It would have been easy enough for Miss Morgan to slip out and back in again. What's out there?'

'Just the garden.'

'Is there another set of French windows leading to another part of the house?'

Louisa thought carefully. 'No, only the back door from the kitchen leads out.'

Guy put his hands in his pockets and gave the room a final once over. 'Everybody started in here and left to find the answer to the first clue. Do you know what that was?'

Louisa nodded. 'A whip. They might have looked in a number of places for one. The boot room, the stables, Lord Redesdale's study even. Miss Pamela would know he keeps one in there, not one he uses. Sentimental value.'

Outside, an owl hooted, soft and low. Guy reacted and Louisa remembered how it felt to be a city person out here in the country, with its mysterious sounds.

'When you went to the dining room and found Miss Pamela and Mr Curtis in there, they had both completed the first clue and been given their second, you think?'

'Yes,' said Louisa, glad the shadows hid the flush of shame she felt again at remembering her part in that night's events. 'Each clue had an object as its answer and I saw Mr Curtis put a fork in his pocket when he left the room.'

'The fork wasn't in his pocket when he was found later,' mused Guy, 'presumably because he'd handed it in to Mr Atlas and Miss Morgan, after he'd had the argument with Miss Long. Assuming he simply rejoined the game and came back in here to get his third clue.'

Again, Louisa showed that she agreed with this.

'It's at that point that he left and went to the bell tower, we think?'

'I can't say for certain,' said Louisa. 'After Pamela came to find me in the kitchen, immediately after she had overheard the row, I stayed there. I didn't know where Dulcie had got to but I couldn't

364

go looking for her. She didn't want anyone to see her eye and start asking questions, so she said she would stay out of the way.'

'But we know she was waiting to meet Billy Masters, if not Mr Curtis.' Guy went quiet and Louisa felt the chill working its way into her bones. She'd have liked to have gone to stand by the dying fire in the hall at least but didn't want to disturb Guy's thoughts.

'How long was it between Dulcie leaving and you hearing her screams?' he asked.

'I couldn't say exactly but I think it was about three-quarters of an hour.'

'The question is: where was everybody in that time?'

Then light flooded the room and they both looked up to see Pamela standing in the doorway. She had switched on another lamp and was watching them both with a curious expression on her face. Had she been listening?

'You have remembered about Nancy and the clocks, haven't you?' she said.

Now they knew what was to happen next.

CHAPTER SEVENTY-TWO

While Pamela went to fetch the others from the library, Louisa went around the ground floor switching the lights on. She could only cross her fingers that Lord and Lady Redesdale would not return until well after midnight and that Mrs Windsor, believing them all to be in the library, would be in her own sitting room with Mrs Stobie to see in the New Year with a glass of sherry. There had been no sight or sound of Charlotte since she had flounced out but it was possible she would return at any minute. They would just have to take the risk of upsetting her again. This mattered too much.

Nancy came in first, her eyes shining from the wine drunk over supper. 'Are we really going to do this?' she said.

Guy nodded. 'I'd like to, I think it's the only way for us to get to the truth.'

'I think the others will do it except for Sebastian, who can't be moved to do anything he doesn't want to do.'

'Fine, I'll play the part of Mr Atlas,' said Guy, which made Nancy hoot with laughter.

'Sorry,' she said, 'but it's not what one would call good casting.'

Guy decided to ignore this. 'Miss Cannon, perhaps you could be Miss Curtis, as she is still elsewhere?'

Louisa gave a nod and continued to busy herself in the drawing room, straightening out occasional objects. She didn't want to stop and think about what they were doing.

Clara, Phoebe, Ted, Oliver and Pamela all came in together, the earlier tension having dispelled a little, though Ted flashed a look of anger at Guy. He wasn't quite over having been brought so close to such a serious accusation earlier.

Everybody sat down on the sofas but the cold got to them fast. 'Are there any blankets in here?' said Clara. 'Honestly, these English houses. Do you not believe in comfort at home?'

'Farve doesn't,' laughed Nancy.

Sebastian came in last, smoking a cigarette. 'I fail to see what's so humorous,' he snarled at Nancy. She started to reply but he cut her off. 'I take no pleasure in remembering the death of my good friend.'

'Except for the money it means your fiancée will now inherit,' snapped Phoebe.

Sebastian regarded her placidly. 'We're not engaged.'

'I'm not sure Charlotte knows that.' Phoebe spoke with the tenor of someone who had been watching Miss Curtis more closely than might have been deemed comfortable for either of them.

'She does.' Sebastian sat in an armchair and crossed his legs. 'We broke up after Christmas.'

'Then why have you come tonight, you bastard?' Ted tried a jocular tone but didn't quite pull it off.

Sebastian made a small grimace. 'She's not in a good way. I thought I'd better keep an eye on her.'

Guy gave a cough. 'I'd like to start this, if I may. The only time in the evening where we know exactly what was happening when was at half past one. Because that's when the clocks were changed.'

'Back to one o'clock,' said Nancy.

'The old party-time trick,' noted Clara. 'I can't say it works seeing as we all know you do it.'

'Hooper doesn't,' said Nancy. 'I thought it would give Charlotte a bit longer when he came to collect her to take her back to the Watneys.'

'Did anyone see you do it?' asked Guy.

'I don't think so. Everyone was all over the house. I don't know who was where, when.'

'You changed the clocks in the hall and in here, is that right?'

'Yes,' said Nancy.

'Could you do it, as you did before, and perhaps you'll remember if you saw anyone.'

Nancy went out into the hall to change the clock and returned a minute or two later to the drawing room. 'I remember Seb and Phoebe were in here, and Charlotte, too. She'd just got her second clue and brought it back.'

'Miss Fischer and your lordship, do you think this was the time you were in the dining room?'

Clara put a hand to her face and looked at Ted. 'Yes, I think it probably was.'

'Were you in there for some time?'

'We'd both gone in there for our second clues. I think I was given the one Adrian had just had – with the fork as the answer – and Ted was looking for a napkin ring.'

'That was Miss Pamela's second clue, which she had completed,' pointed out Louisa.

'So that means that Mr Curtis must have been given his third clue by this time, and left the drawing room already,' said Guy. He chose not to mention what he believed that third clue to have been. 'In that case, I need Lord De Clifford and Miss Fischer to go to the dining room. Mr Watney, can you recall your clues?'

Oliver looked pale. 'Yes, I knew the answer to the first but hadn't yet found a whip. It took me some time.'

'Why?' said Pamela. 'You know where to find one, our house is not so different from yours.'

Oliver took a shuddering breath. 'The truth is, I had no desire to partake in this idiocy. I decided to retire to the telephone cupboard.'

Pamela looked at him sympathetically. 'Did you telephone anyone up?'

'No,' said Oliver. 'I read the telephone directory. I found it most calming.'

The more Guy knew of the upper classes, the more eccentric he found them. 'If you could return to the telephone cupboard, please sir.'

Reluctantly, Oliver took himself off.

Guy removed his glasses and rubbed his eyes. The strain of it was exhausting him and the early dinner that Mrs Stobie had given him seemed a very long time ago. He could have done with a glass of wine but none had been offered.

'Right, so it's half past one. Lord De Clifford and Miss Fischer are in the dining room, and they are in there for some time. Mr Watney is in the telephone cupboard, where he also remains. Mr Atlas and Miss Morgan are in here. And you come in, Miss Nancy, to change the clock back by half an hour. Did anyone see you do it?'

'The two of them were talking, Phoebe was on the sofa with her legs up and she was looking at Seb as he mixed some more drinks, so I'm not certain they noticed me.'

'Could you change the clock as you would have?'

Nancy picked the carriage clock off the mantelpiece and with her back to the room changed it in a trice before replacing it. It now said one o'clock. 'I thought I'd make it as real as possible,' she said.

'What happened then?'

'Seb gave me my next clue, and I headed off to Farve's study to work out the answer, which I thought had a matchbox as something to do with it.' She looked at everyone. 'Fine, I'll go in there now.'

'Wait.' Louisa stepped to the side to interrupt Nancy. 'You said Miss Charlotte was with you when you heard the screams.'

'Yes, I came back and picked up the next clue, which Phoebe gave me. Charlotte was in here too, so we both went to the morning room together. We'd decided to solve our clues together.'

'How did you get there?' asked Guy.

'Through there, of course,' said Nancy, pointing to an inner door that joined the two rooms.

'So you didn't go through the hall. And are you also saying that Sebastian wasn't in here when you returned the second time?'

'I think that was when he had come to meet me,' said Pamela. 'He found me in the smoking room and said that now it was officially my birthday, he wanted to give me a present.'

'Yes,' said Guy. 'This was in your statement. In the hall he took a box out from under a table there that he'd hidden earlier. It had a brooch in it and it was this that he gave you. You noticed the time then, didn't you?'

'Yes, it said it was quarter past one in the hall but I knew that Nancy would have changed the clocks, so really it was quarter to two.'

Sebastian stood up. 'Does anyone else want a drink? I'm not sure I can listen to more of this.'

Without waiting for an answer, he left the room.

*

'Sorry, Miss Pamela,' said Louisa. 'But you need to go into the hall. And Miss Nancy ...'

'Fine,' snapped Nancy, 'I'll go to the morning room.'

Phoebe was left alone with Louisa and Guy. She perched on the edge of the sofa, a lit cigarette in one hand, a nearly empty glass of wine in the other. Her pretty mouth was set in a thin line.

'Miss Phoebe,' began Guy, 'we need you to say what happened now, truthfully.'

'It wasn't much,' she said. 'You've heard most of it. After Nancy was in here and must have changed the clock – she was right, I didn't notice – Adrian came and was handed his next clue. He left quickly – he wasn't in a good temper, which isn't surprising given what we found out later about his row with Dulcie. Then Charlotte came in, I suppose to get her clue, too, though I wasn't concentrating much.'

'Was she in here for long?'

'A few minutes, I suppose. She said that it was after one and so Seb should give Pamela her present. They both left the room and I took the opportunity to step outside.'

'Did you have a coat with you?' Louisa, feeling the cold now quite badly, remembered that it had been a late November night and not much warmer.

'I had a wrap. I had to wander off a bit though, to find some-where I could ... you know, without being seen. I didn't want anyone to see me through a window.'

'How long were you out of the room?'

Phoebe took the last two drags of her cigarette and stubbed it out. 'I hadn't thought about this before but now that you say it, it is odd. Because I was gone for at least twenty minutes but when I came back into the room the drawing room clock showed that it was only a little after quarter past one. I don't know why I noticed but I did. As if I'd only been gone a few minutes. I expect I just put it down to Nancy's party time trick.'

'Had anyone been into the room while you were out?'

'How would I know?'

Louisa and Guy looked at each other. 'We need to call the others back,' said Louisa.

'And I need to call DI Monroe,' said Guy.

Phoebe looked up at them. 'What do you mean? What have I said?'

'We know now that Mr Atlas was gone from this room for at least half an hour, even though the times that you and Phoebe said you had seen him were only a few minutes apart. Someone helped him by changing this clock twice and there's only one person that could be.'

'What are you saying? It's not me.' Phoebe laughed. 'I mean it, seriously, it's not me. I didn't like Adrian but not enough to kill him.'

Guy looked at her, his blue eyes steady behind his glasses. 'I didn't mean you.'

CHAPTER SEVENTY-THREE

P hoebe, Louisa and Guy went out into the hall, going through the morning room first to collect Nancy. In the hall, Pamela was sitting on a hard wooden chair by the fire, on which she had thrown another log. Guy knocked on the door of the telephone cupboard and Oliver came out, looking sheepish. 'Is it over now? Or is it nearly time to sing "Auld Lang Syne"?' he asked.

'Not quite,' said Guy grimly. He went into the cupboard himself and closed the door behind him.

Louisa had gone to the dining room to summon Ted and Clara, who were pointedly sitting at either end of the long table when she went in. They looked cold and nervous.

'What's going on?' Ted asked, more than once, but Louisa couldn't think what to reply, so said nothing.

In the hall, they all gathered. Guy came out and said, 'I've called the station. They're going to try and find DI Monroe but they'll send a uniform down in any case.'

Nancy jumped at this. 'What the *hell* is going on?'

Still, neither Guy nor Louisa chose to enlighten her, or anybody.

'Where is Mr Atlas?' said Guy.

Everybody was at a loss. 'We don't know, do we? You had us all holed up in our rooms,' said Ted. Then his jaw suddenly dropped. 'My God man, that's exactly why, isn't it?'

A shiver of fear darted through each of them.

Pamela said, 'I'll check Charlotte's room.'

'I'll come with you,' said Louisa.

'No, don't. If it's me alone and Seb is with her, they won't suspect anything. If I'm not back down in five minutes, come up.'

Pamela left and the others stood there, listening to each of her steps landing on the wooden stairs, which were covered only by a worn-out wool runner. Nobody spoke, or hardly even to breathe. But no sooner, it seemed, than she had reached the top that she was on her way back down. 'She's not in her room.'

A noise came from outside, startling them. 'What was that?'

'An owl?' said Guy.

'No,' said Pamela. She went to the front door and stepped out briefly. When she came back in, she looked deathly pale but her voice was calm. 'I can hear two people shouting.'

Guy rushed out and pushed past her, apologising as he did so. Frost had already settled on the grass in front of the house and the bare branches of the trees were bending slightly in the biting wind. It was dark with not much moonlight, and Guy's eyes could see even less than usual. He listened hard and heard shouting. It was coming from the other side of the garden wall. Where the churchyard lay.

Louisa came out and went to Guy's side, holding onto his arm. She heard the voices, too. Without saying anything, the two of them ran together, Louisa holding his hand and leading the way.

As they drew nearer, the shouts became louder – a man's and a woman's. Behind them, too, were the distressed sounds of Nancy and her guests but much fainter. The wet of the grass silenced their fast footsteps and when they reached the church door the shouting had not abated.

Still silent but no longer holding hands, Guy and Louisa moved stealthily through the open door. The church was in almost complete darkness and their eyes had to adjust. The sound was coming from the other end and above. The bell tower.

CHAPTER SEVENTY-FOUR

———

Slowly, carefully, Louisa and Guy made their way down the aisle, holding on to the edges of the pews to feel their path. As they did so, a cloud moved out of the way of the moon and a thin shaft of light came through the stained glass windows as they reached the staircase that led to the bell tower. In seconds they were up and saw Charlotte standing in the glassless window, her back to the night air. She had been crying, that much was clear, her skin mottled, her eyes red. The soft curls of her dark hair had been blown about by the breeze and she trembled in her evening dress. Her shoeless feet balanced on the sill, her hands holding on to the stone edges of the narrow opening. Standing before her but not reaching out, was Sebastian. His hands were in his pockets, fury showed sharply on the planes of his face.

He had seen Guy come up into the tower, followed by Louisa and now his anger radiated from him, as if it could knock them back.

'You stupid bitch,' he said to Charlotte, who shook with sobs.

Louisa started to run forward but Guy pulled her back.

Seb looked at them both. In the half-light, he looked spectral and forbidding. 'Why don't you both crawl back to whatever pitiable place you came from? Look at the damage you've caused.'

'We didn't cause this damage,' said Guy. 'You did.'

'I don't know what the hell you're talking about.'

Charlotte had stopped her cries, and now stared at Guy, her eyes wide open, wild with fear.

'The only part I'm not clear on, is why you wanted your friend dead,' said Guy.

Sebastian took a step closer to Guy and Louisa felt herself shrink back as he did so. 'I don't know what you're implying but I think you had better tread very carefully.'

Charlotte was quiet now but her cheeks were wet from tears that were still running down.

Guy's shoulders had broadened and his feet were placed apart, keeping him firm. If Sebastian hit him, he wouldn't go down. 'Why did you do it, Mr Atlas? Was it revenge or jealousy?'

Seb laughed at this. 'Why would anyone be jealous of that bore? He was a snivelling junkie. He cared as little for me as I for him.'

Something had loosened in the atmosphere, breaking something between the four of them. Whether it was the cold, the night, the narrow walls of the bell tower or the realisation that the game was up, Louisa couldn't say. Perhaps it was all those things.

'I thought you were friends?' said Guy.

'We were useful to each other,' replied Seb.

Charlotte's knees buckled and she looked as if she might lose her balance. She cried out and Louisa ran to her, grabbing her by the waist and saving her from her brother's fate. They both fell to the floor, Charlotte gasping from the shock and the cold hardness of the flagstones beneath her. She pulled herself to her knees and wiped her face with the flats of her hands. 'I thought you loved me,' she sobbed.

'As if you would know what that was,' Seb spat. He took a silver case out of his pocket and put a cigarette between his lips, lighting it with a lighter that released a strong scent of petrol. In the brief flare of the flame his eyes were hard and black. 'Now that she's decided not to throw herself out of the window, I think I'd like to go back to the house.'

He started to walk out but Guy grabbed him by the arm and didn't let go. 'Not until you've done some more explaining,' he said.

'Let go of my arm.'

'You see,' said Guy, 'we understand that you stayed in the drawing room so that you could type another clue. One meant only for Adrian Curtis, which would send him here. The only clue that had a place for its answer, not an object.'

Seb exhaled cigarette smoke to the side and regarded Guy coolly. Guy had let go of his arm now but stood close to him, blocking his way to the exit. Charlotte had stopped crying and was listening too, her bare arms covered in goosepimples. Louisa kneeled on the floor beside her, her limbs aching from the anticipation of what would happen next.

'You knew, didn't you, that Dulcie Long would be coming to the bell tower to meet Billy Masters. Did he tell you that?'

Seb's eyes flickered at this and he threw his cigarette on to the floor, grinding it out with his shoe.

'You were seen buying something from Billy outside the Haymarket Theatre by Louisa, and I know you did some kind of a deal with him outside the 43 because I arrested him that night, after I saw you both.'

This caught Sebastian by surprise and Guy saw it register on his face before he could stop himself. 'So what if I buy from him?' he said. 'That doesn't mean anything.'

'I think you gave Billy the cufflinks that your friend, Mr Curtis, gave you as a present. As a thank you for letting you know that he would be here on the twentieth November, and in lieu of something extra to be given to you that night. Billy thought you were expecting a gift of cocaine, when what you really wanted was someone else to take the blame for the murder you were planning to commit.'

Sebastian scoffed. 'I've never heard such nonsense. I'm going down now.'

Charlotte stood up now, ashen-faced. Louisa knew that if she touched her she'd be as cold as ice.

Guy put his hands in his pockets and pulled out the lapis lazuli cufflinks he'd taken from Billy. This time he looked at Charlotte. 'I believe these belonged to your brother.'

Charlotte cried out and doubled over.

'The timing went wrong though, didn't it? Billy showed up early, and saw you running away. You had tried to disguise yourself as Lord De Clifford by wearing his cloak – helpfully left by the front door in the hall – but you didn't know that he and Clara Fischer were together in the dining room. Everyone was supposed to be playing alone, weren't they?'

Louisa saw Sebastian's eyes flicker now. He was getting less certain of himself, she was sure of it.

'Dulcie Long took the blame but you didn't care about that, did you, Miss Curtis? In fact, it was more convenient.' Guy spoke with confidence now.

'What are you talking about?' Charlotte's voice was tight.

'Dulcie's son with your brother, your nephew Daniel. Is he a threat to your inheritance? The one you were going to get when your brother was dead.'

'It's her word against mine,' said Charlotte. The steel had returned to her voice in spite of her disarrayed appearance. 'Who do you think will be believed?' Then as if she had let go of a rope she'd been clinging to, she breathed out and gave Sebastian a look of despair. 'Besides, what inheritance? My brother spent it all. And when *he* found out ...' She started to cry again but more quietly this time. 'He no longer wanted anything to do with me. He broke off the engagement.'

'I don't recall ever proposing,' Sebastian sneered. 'I'm hardly the type to go on one knee.'

'You promised,' sobbed Charlotte, but Sebastian turned away.

Outside, a car could be heard pulling up on the gravel beside Asthall Manor. The police had arrived. Then a clatter as the rest of the friends came up the stairs. As they edged into the bell tower, there was no mistaking the atmosphere they met. Along the back wall, Nancy, Ted, Clara, Pamela, Phoebe and Oliver lined up. They held their breath, afraid to speak.

'Shall I explain to everyone how you did it?' said Guy.

Sebastian shrugged.

'You knew that Nancy would change the clocks back thirty minutes at half past one.'

Louisa saw Nancy stiffen at this.

'What's more,' continued Guy, 'you knew that this was common knowledge. Any confusion over timings would be put down to this party trick. Your mistake was your attention to detail, if I may say so. You were the only guest who used the clock as his alibi.'

Pamela stepped forward slightly. 'Do you mean, when I said I saw Sebastian in the hall at quarter to two? That is, it said quarter past one on the clock but I knew it was out by half an hour.'

'Yes,' said Guy, 'but it was in fact two o'clock. Miss Charlotte had put the clock back a further fifteen minutes. So that when Phoebe saw Sebastian leave the drawing room shortly after one, Pamela saw him apparently minutes later. In fact, it was half an hour.'

'Spell it out,' said Pamela.

'Miss Charlotte bought Sebastian just enough time to come here to the bell tower and catch Adrian Curtis unawares. We know there was a brief struggle but he was drunk and by the time your former friend would have realised what you were trying to do, it was all over.'

Sebastian's face looked as though it were sculpted from rock but a cry broke from Charlotte. Guy turned to her. 'You planned it together.'

It wasn't a question but Charlotte answered with a barely perceptible nod. 'He said he'd marry me if there was money and we only needed to get Adrian . . . ' She stopped and looked at Sebastian but he would not turn towards her. 'We only needed to get Adrian out of the way and we'd have what we wanted. He'd always loathed my brother though he hid it well, so long as he could get what he wanted from him. I knew that. Only I hadn't realised that meant he hated me too.' She broke down finally into sobs that made her thin body twist like a dying snake.

They heard the heavy footsteps of the police coming up the stairs.

'Sebastian Atlas,' said Guy in front of eight witnesses, 'I'm arresting you on suspicion of the murder of Adrian Curtis and conspiracy to murder alongside Charlotte Curtis.'

CHAPTER SEVENTY-FIVE

❦

That night, little sleep was had by almost all of the household except for the youngest children, who slept peacefully
throughout. Tom, thankfully, had been away, staying with a friend
from school but Diana was almost speechless that she should –
once again – have missed a proper event in her own home.

Almost immediately after everyone had come down from the
bell tower, the police had taken Sebastian and Charlotte away for
questioning. After DI Monroe had – perhaps somewhat grudg-
ingly – commended Guy for his good work, he invited him down
to the station, too. There had been a lot of commotion and talk in
the house, the shock rippling out through the friends, and Lord
and Lady Redesdale when they returned.

Lord Redesdale was both furious and apparently unsurprised
that 'those sewers' should have committed the ultimate sin. 'I
expected no less of your so-called friends, Koko,' he had shouted
at his daughter. 'I don't want *any* of them here, ever again.' Lady
Redesdale took him up the stairs in a hurry, her pale face betraying
her own upset at such a calamity happening in her house.

Oliver Watney had scuttled off back home as fast as he could, leaving Pamela concerned that he had been shaken by events. Clara, Ted, Phoebe and Nancy had sat up in the library until Mrs Windsor found them still there when she rose at six o'clock in the morning and packed them off to bed.

When Louisa had woken early next morning, she dressed quickly and quietly and went out into the nursery, ready to prepare breakfast for the children. Nanny Blor was up already. Nanny had been woken by the police arriving but, afraid, had sat in her sitting room in the dark, waiting for Louisa or Pamela to return and tell her what had happened. When they had both come up the stairs, fizzing with the details of the evening, it was Nanny who had made them all hot chocolate, insisting they sat and drank it until they were soothed enough to go to bed.

'I do understand that this was a very unusual and awful thing to have happened,' said Pam, her cornflower-blue eyes blazing even after such a long night, 'but I feel rather like Farve. I don't think Nancy's friends are for me. I'd really rather stay home.' She blushed. 'Don't tell Nancy, she'll rag me.'

Louisa understood. Pamela, on the brink of adulthood, had to decide how she wanted to live her life. She had never had the caustic wit or social ambition of her elder sister and enjoyment of the country life she had been brought up in had come easily to her. She was a good rider and unabashed about the pleasure she took in food and learning to cook. Nanny Blor had patted Pam's knee and told her that she was sure to go on adventures of her own one day. But for now, yes, perhaps a spell at home was what was called for.

For Louisa, it was different. She felt she had come to the end of her country life. Quite apart from anything else, when Lady Redesdale learned the truth, as she inevitably would – that Louisa had shown Dulcie Long to an empty bedroom and then sent

Adrian Curtis there – she would surely question the wisdom of her employment with the family.

After breakfast, Louisa went down to the village. It was New Year's Day and everyone was up and getting ready for the hunt. Even Pamela, in spite of her late night, had got up at dawn and gone to the stables. Louisa hurried round to the pub where Guy was staying and sent someone up to knock on his door and bring him down.

'Louisa?' Guy appeared a minute later. He looked a touch grey around the edges, and his clothes were wrinkled, as if he'd slept in them. 'Sorry,' he said, gesturing to his creases. 'I didn't get back from the station till late. Mr Monroe needed me to help with the statements. They both confessed, it was as good a result as we could have hoped for.'

'And Dulcie?'

'She'll be out soon enough. The time she's done already will be enough for the theft.'

'You did well, Guy.' Louisa was happy for Dulcie. She would be reunited with Daniel. Perhaps she could even work as a seamstress with Mrs Brewster, get herself straightened out and away from the Elephants. Not that they would be bothering her now they knew the police were all over it.

'Thanks.' Guy grinned. 'I'd better be getting back to London, I suppose. Not sure how many trains will be running today.'

'We can find that out for you. I wanted to talk to you first, though. Shall we walk?'

Guy fetched his coat, hat and scarf and the two of them went out into the village. It was the kind of day that showed off in its fullest splendour everything that she had ever loved about Asthall. The early-morning frost hadn't yet melted on the grass, there were happy shouts of the village children as they came out to see the hunt gather and the Cotswold stone glowed warmly, as it always did, even in a blue winter's light.

'I'm going to hand in my notice,' she said.

Guy said nothing but raised his eyebrows.

'They won't want me there, anyway. Even though it was Sebastian and Charlotte that did it, and not Dulcie, I think they'll believe I bring too much trouble to the house.'

'Don't be too sure. You've been there a long time, you've worked hard.'

'I know. But I'm ready for a change. I want to go back to London.'

Guy stopped and looked at her. They had walked up a short hill and the quilt of fields hemmed with hedges spread out behind Louisa's silhouetted figure, the tip of her nose pink from the cold and her eyes squinting slightly against the sun.

'What will you do there?'

'I thought I might apply to train as a policewoman.' She burst out laughing when she saw Guy's shocked face. 'I'm not absolutely certain.'

'It's not that I'm saying you're crossing on to the other side quite . . .'

'Almost. You're right. It is but I thought – if you can't beat 'em, join 'em.'

That made Guy laugh, too. He put his arm around her shoulders and they looked out into the distance together, standing there quietly for a few moments until they both knew they couldn't put off the rest of their lives any longer.

POSTSCRIPT/
HISTORICAL NOTE

On 2 March 1926 Alice Diamond was charged at the Central Criminal Court for intent, burglary, riot damage and assault, receiving eighteen months' hard labour. Her cohorts Bertha Tappenden and Maggie Hughes were also arrested for the attack on the Britten family (on whom I based the Longs), which occurred on 20 December 1925. This marked the end of Alice's reign as 'Queen' of the Forty Thieves.

In March 1926, Lord De Clifford married Dorothy ('Dolly') Meyrick at a London registry office. As he was only nineteen years old and marrying without his mother's consent, he lied about his age and was later fined £50. They had two children but separated in 1936.

Pamela Mitford and Oliver Watney were briefly engaged in 1928 until his mother talked him out of it. Pamela conceded as she, too, had been having second thoughts.

*

Kate Meyrick, the owner of the '43' nightclub in Gerrard Street, had been released from prison in April 1925, after which she left for Paris until 1927. Her daughter, Dolly, ran the club in her absence. In early 1929 George Goddard, who had been running the Vice Squad from Savile Row police station, was jailed on corruption charges and Kate Meyrick was sentenced to fifteen months' hard labour for bribing him.

Please note that while parts of this book have been based on real people and historical events, all conversations have been completely imagined. The murder of Adrian Curtis is fictional.

A NOTE ON
HISTORICAL SOURCES

I read several books in the course of researching this novel but am especially grateful to:

Bad Girls: A History of Rebels and Renegades, Caitlin Davies (John Murray)

Dope Girls: The Birth of the British Drug Underground, Marek Kohn (Granta Books)

The Mitford Girls: The Biography of An Extraordinary Family, Mary S. Lovell (Abacus)

Alice Diamond and the Forty Thieves: Britain's First Female Crime Syndicate, Brian McDonald (Milo Books Ltd)

The Mitfords: Letters Between Six Sisters, edited by Charlotte Mosley (Harper Perennial)

Nights Out: Life in Cosmopolitan London, Judith R. Walkowitz (Yale University Press)

A Woman At Scotland Yard, Lilian Wyles (Faber and Faber)

ACKNOWLEDGEMENTS

For their inspiration, guidance and patience I would like to thank: Ed Wood at Sphere/Little, Brown, alongside Andy Hine, Kate Hibbert, Thalia Proctor and Stephanie Melrose. Also Caroline Michel at PFD, with Tessa David; Hope Dellon and Catherine Richards at St Martin's Press. For research and historical checks (but admitting any mistakes as my own): Sue Collins and Celestria Noel.

To Simon, Beatrix, Louis, George and Zola ... thank you.